DEAD BROKE,
COLORADO

DEAD BROKE, COLORADO

WILLIAM W. JOHNSTONE

AND J. A. JOHNSTONE

PINNACLE BOOKS
Kensington Publishing Corp.
kensingtonbooks.com

PINNACLE BOOKS are published by

Kensington Publishing Corp.
900 Third Avenue
New York, NY 10022

All Kensington titles, imprints, and distributed lines are available at special quantity discounts for bulk purchases for sales promotion, premiums, fund-raising, and educational or institutional use.

Special book excerpts or customized printings can also be created to fit specific needs. For details, write or phone the office of the Kensington Sales Manager: Kensington Publishing Corp., 900 Third Avenue, New York, NY 10022. Attn. Sales Department. Phone: 1-800-221-2647.

PINNACLE BOOKS, the Pinnacle logo, and the WWJ steer head logo Reg. U.S. Pat. & TM Off.

First Printing: April 2025
ISBN-13: 978-0-7860-5148-9
ISBN-13: 978-0-7860-5151-9 (eBook)

10 9 8 7 6 5 4 3 2 1

Printed in the United States of America

1885

PROLOGUE

Allane Auchinleck was drunk that morning.

But then, most wastrels on This Side Of The Slope would have pointed out that Allane Auchinleck was seldom sober any morning, any afternoon, any evening. Any day of the year. Since he had barely found enough gold in Colorado's towering Rocky Mountains to pay for good rye, he brewed his own whiskey. It wasn't fit to drink, other miners would agree, but it was whiskey. So they drank whatever Allane Auchinleck was willing to sell or, rarely, share.

Auchinleck charged a dollar a cup—Leadville prices, the other miners would protest, but they paid.

After all, it was whiskey.

And in these towering mountains, whiskey—like anything else a man could buy or steal in Denver, Durango, Silverton, or Colorado Springs—was hard to find.

Besides, Auchinleck usually was so far in his cups that he couldn't tell the difference between a nickel and a Morgan dollar. For most miners, one cup usually did the job. Actually, two sips fried the brains of many unaccustomed to a Scotsman's idea of what went into good liquor. Two cups, a few men had learned, could prove fatal. Auchinleck held the record, four cups in four hours—and was still alive to tell the story.

Although, it should be pointed out that those who had witnessed that historic drunken evening would swear on a stack of Bibles—not that a Good Book could be found this high up—that Auchinleck's hair, from topknot to the tip of his long beard, wasn't as white, but had been much thicker, before he passed out, not to awaken for three days. That had been back in '79.

But then, Auchinleck was accustomed to forty rod, and it was his recipe, his liquor, his cast-iron stomach, and his soul, the latter of which he said he had sold to the devil, then got back when Lucifer himself needed a shot of the Scotsman's brew.

On this particular glorious August evening, with the first snow falling at eleven thousand feet, Auchinleck was drinking with Sluagdach. Most of the miners had already started packing their mules and moving to lower, warmer—and much healthier—elevations. Some would head south to thaw out and blow whatever they had accumulated in their pokes. Many would drift east to Denver, where the heartiest would find jobs swamping saloons or moving horse apples out of livery stables. Others would just call it quits as a miner and find an easier way to make a living.

But not Allane Auchinleck. "Mining is my life," he told Sluagdach, and topped off his cup with more of his swill.

"Aye," Sluagdach said. "And a mighty poor life it has been, Nugget."

Nugget had become Auchinleck's handle. There are

some who say the Scotsman earned that moniker because of his determination, and not for his lack of profitable results. More than likely, the moniker had stuck to the miner like stains of tobacco juice because Nugget was a whole lot easier to remember or say than Auchinleck.

That was the year Sluagdach came in as Auchinleck's partner. It made sense, at the time (though Sluagdach was a touch more than just fairly inebriated) when such a partnership had been suggested in a tent near the headwaters of the Arkansas River.

They both came to America from Scotland, Auchinleck had pointed out. They could enter this deal as equals. Nugget still had his mule; Sluagdach had had to eat his. Sluagdach had a new pickax, while Nugget had been the first to discover that Finnian Kuznetsov, that half-Irish, half-Russian, had run into a she-bear with two cubs and had not been able to raise his Sharps carbine in time. The she-bear won that fight, and the cubs enjoyed a fine breakfast, but Nugget had given the Russian Irishman a burial and taken the shovel and pack, and a poke of silver, and Kuznetsov's boots and mink hat. Although he did not let his partner know, Nugget had also found the dead miner's mule (lucky critter, having fled while the she-bear and cubs enjoyed a breakfast of Kuznetsov), which is how come Nugget brought a mule into the partnership, his own having been stolen by some thief, or having wandered off to parts unknown while its master slept off a drunk.

"I said," Sluagdach said, raising his voice after getting no response from his drunkard partner, "that a mighty poor life it . . ." But the whiskey robbed his memory, as Nugget's whiskey often did.

"Who can be poor when he lives in this wild, fabulous country?" Nugget said, whose tolerance for his special malt had not fogged his memory or limited vocabulary. "Look at these mountains. Feel this snow. God's country this is."

"God," Sluagdach said, "is welcome to it."

That's when Nugget, against his better judgment, reached into the ripped-apart coat that he had also taken from the dearly departed dead miner and pulled out the poke. By the time he realized what he was doing, the poke had flown out of Nugget's hand and landed at Sluagdach's feet.

The muleless miner stared at the leather pouch, reached between his legs—he did not recall sitting down, but that Scotsman's liquor had a way of making men forget lots of things—and heard the grinding of rocks inside. It took him a few minutes for his eyes to focus and his brain to recall how to work the strings to open the little rawhide bag, and then he saw a few chunks fall into the grass, damp with snow that hadn't started to stick.

No matter how drunk a miner got, he was never too far gone not to recognize good ore.

"Silver," he whispered, and looked across the campsite at his partner.

"That's how Leadville got started," Nugget heard himself saying.

"Where was his camp?"

After a heavy sigh, Nugget shook his head.

"Best I could tell," he explained, "he was on his way down the slope when 'em cubs et him."

"To file a claim." Sluagdach sounded sober all of a sudden.

Nugget felt his head bob in agreement.

One of the nuggets came to Sluagdach's right eye. Then it was lowered to his mouth, and his tongue tasted it, then it went inside his mouth where his gold upper molar and his rotted lower molar tested it. After removing the bit of ore, he stared at his partner.

"This'll assay anywhere from twenty-two to twenty-five ounces per ton."

No miner on This Side Of The Slope and hardly any professional metallurgist from Arizona to Colorado would doubt anything Sluagdach said. No one knew how he did it. But he had never been more than an ounce off his predictions. Sluagdach had never made a fortune as a miner, but his good eye, teeth, and tongue knew what they saw, bit, and tasted.

Unable to think of anything to say, Nugget killed the bit of whiskey remaining in his cup, then belched.

"Where exactly did that ol' feller got et?" Sluagdach asked. His voice had an eerie quietness to it.

Nugget's head jerked in a vague northeasterly direction. Which he could blame on his drunkenness if Sluagdach remembered anything in the morning.

Finnian Kuznetsov had met his grisly end in a grizzly sow and her cubs about four miles southwest.

"Think this snow'll last?" Sluagdach asked.

"Nah." It was way too early, even at this altitude, and, well, twenty-two to twenty-five ounces per ton had to be worth the risk.

* * *

They set out early the next morning, finding the hole where Nugget had rolled Finnian Kuznetsov's remains and covered them with pine needles and some rocks, which had been removed by some critter that had scattered bones and such all over the area. Then they backtracked over rough country, and around twelve thousand feet, they found Sluagdach's camp.

Two months later, they had discovered . . .

"Not a thing," Sluagdach announced, although he used practically every foul word that a good Scot knew to describe that particular thing.

By then, at that altitude, winter was coming in right quick-like, and their supplies were all but out. This morning's breakfast had been piñon nuts and Nugget's whiskey. Sleet had pelted them that morning; Sluagdach had slipped on an icy patch and almost broken his back, while Nugget's mule grew more cantankerous every minute.

"We'll have to come back next spring," Sluagdach said.

With a sad nod, Nugget went to his keg of whiskey, rocked the oak a bit, and decided there was just enough for a final night of celebration—or mourning—for the two of them.

It was a drunk to remember. Sluagdach broke Nugget's record. "Shattered it" would have been a more accurate description. Five cups. Five! While Nugget had to stop drinking—*his own whiskey*—after three.

It wasn't because he couldn't handle his wretched brew. It was because he now saw everything. He saw that Sluagdach would dissolve the partnership. Sluagdach would come back to these beasts of mountains and find the Russian mick's discovery. Sluagdach would go down in history. Allane "Nugget" Auchinleck would be forgotten.

Auchinleck. What a name. What a lie. He remembered way back when he was but a lad, living near the Firth of Clyde in the county of Ayrshire on Scotland's west coast and his grandfather, a fine man who had given Nugget his first taste of single malt when he was but four years old, had told him what the name "Auchinleck" meant.

"A piece of field with flat stones," the old man had said.

It had sounded glorious to a four-year-old pup of a boy, but now he scoffed at it all. *A piece of field with flat stones.* Oh, the stones were here all right, massive boulders of granite that held riches in them but would never let those riches go. And flat?

He laughed and tossed his empty cup toward the fire.

There was nothing flat on This Side Of The Slope.

That's when Allane Auchinleck decided it was time to kill himself.

He announced his intentions to Sluagdach, who laughed, agreeing that it was a fine, fine idea.

Sluagdach even laughed when Nugget withdrew a stick of dynamite in a box of dwindling supplies. *Laughing? That swine of a Russian mick.* No, no. Nugget had to correct his thinking. Sluagdach was a Scot. The Russian mick was Finnian Kuznetsov, dead and et by a Colorado she-grizzly's cubs.

"I'll speak lovingly of you at your funeral," Sluagdach said, and he cackled even harder when Nugget began to cap and fuse the explosive.

It wasn't until Nugget lit the fuse by holding the stick over the fire that Sluagdach acted soberly.

For a man who should, if the Lord was indeed merciful, be dead already, or at least passed out, Sluagdach moved like a man who really wanted not to be blown to bits.

He came charging like that she-bear must have charged the old Russian mick, and the next thing Nugget recalled was his ears ringing and the entire ground shaking. Somehow, Sluagdach had knocked the dynamite away, and it must have rolled down the hill toward that massive rock of immovable stone.

Nugget could not recall the explosion, but his ears were ringing, and he felt stones and bits of wood and more stones raining down upon him. They would cover him in his grave. Peace of earth. God rest this merry gentleman.

"You ignorant, crazy, drunken fool."

That was not, Nugget figured out eventually, the voice of St. Peter. He sat up, brushing off the dust, the grime, the mud, the sand, and looked into the eyes of his equally intoxicated fellow miner. His partner.

He didn't think anyone would call him sober, but he realized just how drunk he was—and how close to death, real death, he had come.

"Oh . . ." however, was about all Nugget could muster at that moment.

"Oh." His partner wiped his bloody nose, then crawled out of the rubble and staggered toward the smoking ruins of part of the camp they had made.

"Mule!" Nugget remembered.

The brays gave him some relief, and as smoke and dust settled, he saw the animal through rocks and forests about three hundred yards away. It appeared that the tether had hooked like an anchor between some rocks and halted the beast's run for its life. Otherwise, the mule might be in Leadville by now.

Maybe even Omaha.

He started for the animal, but Sluagdach told him to stop. "Come up here!" his pard demanded.

Well, Nugget couldn't deny the man who had stopped him from killing himself. He climbed up the ridge, where he looked down into the smokiness.

He could smell the rotten-egg stench of blown powder. And he could see what one stick of dynamite could do. It had created a chasm.

And unveiled a cave.

"Get us a light," Sluagdach said.

Somehow, the campfire still burned, and Nugget found a stick that would serve as a torch, so they walked, slipped, skidded, and slid down into the depression and toward the cave.

"Bear," Nugget remembered.

"If a silvertip was in there, it would be out by now," Sluagdach argued.

They stopped at the entrance, and Nugget held the torch into the opening.

The flame from the torch bounced off the left side of the cave. Slowly the two men staggered to that wall, and Nugget held the torch closer.

"The mother lode," Sluagdach said.

He didn't have to smell and taste the vein of silver to

know that. What's more, when they moved fifty yards deeper into the cavern, the torch revealed something else. At first, Nugget thought it was an Egyptian mummy. He had seen an illustration in one of those newspapers he could not read.

But this wasn't a mummy. He held the torch higher, praying that it would not go out. At least there was no wind here to blow it out.

"It's . . ." Nugget could not find the words.

"The biggest . . . chunk . . . of silver . . . I ever . . . did . . . see."

I am dead, Nugget thought. *Or I'm dreaming*.

His partner stuck his dirty pointer finger in his mouth, getting it good and wet, then touched the gleaming mummy that was a statue of precious metal.

The biggest nugget Allane Auchinleck had ever seen. The biggest one anybody had ever seen.

Maybe he was dead after all.

Sluagdach brought his pointer finger, sloppy with his slobber, and rubbed it on the giant nugget. It was shaped like a diamond. A diamond made of pure silver.

Sluagdach then put his finger back in his mouth.

His eyes widened.

"It . . . I . . . I . . . aye . . . aye . . . It . . ."

That's when the wind, or something—maybe Sluagdach's giant gasps at air—blew out the torch.

And Sluagdach collapsed in front of the silver diamond.

Nugget never knew how he did it, but he found his pard's shoulders and dragged him out into the fading light of the camp. The old man stared up. But his right hand gripped the coat above his breast, and the eyes did not blink.

"Your ticker," Nugget whispered.

Yes. The sight of that strike . . . it had been too much for a man, even a man who had downed five cups of that lethal brew.

That meant . . .

Nugget rose. "No partner." He ran back to the campfire, found a piece of timber, part of the suicidal destruction he had reaped, and stuck it in the coals till the end ignited. The wood must have been part pitch, because it blazed with a fury, and Nugget raced back down, past his dead pard, and into the cave, where he held the blazing torch again.

It was no dream. No drunken hallucination. It was . . . real . . . silver . . . the strike of a lifetime.

He ran back, ready to mark his claim and get his name onto a document that made this . . .

"All mine."

When he stepped outside, it was dark. He walked slowly, using the timber as his light, and stopped in front of the body of his poor, dead pard.

"I won't forget you," he whispered to the unseeing corpse. And in a moment of generosity, he proclaimed:

"You're dead, and I was broke, but Colorado will remember us forever, because I'm naming this mine and the town that'll grow up around it 'Dead Broke.' That's it." He felt relieved.

"Dead Broke, Colorado." He nodded. The flame seemed to reflect in the dead man's eyes, and maybe it was because of the light, but he thought Sluagdach nodded in agreement.

"Dead Broke, Colorado," he said again. "Because who would want to work and live in a place called Sluagdach Auchinleck?"

1886

CHAPTER 1

From *The New York Daily Comet*

"The town of Dead Broke, Colorado, high in the fabled Rocky Mountains, was burying two miners, a lady of the night, a gambler, and a city policeman when I exited the stagecoach on a crisp autumn day."

That's what I wrote in my tablet as soon as I learned from Slick Gene, the constable of this vibrant—and, as you readers likely have deduced, violent—town after stepping out of my conveyance, which the citizens in this remote town call a city.

Slick Gene went on to explain that the two miners got into a fight over who would buy the first drink for the lady of the night, the gambler decided to bet on the miner with the pearl-handled derringer, and the city policeman stepped inside, either to drink the special mixture of gunpowder, egg shells, one plug of chewing tobacco, and grain alcohol that was aged ten days in an oaken bucket and then sifted through a straw hat, or to collect his payment from the owner of the establishment, who happened to also be the betting gambler.

What happened next won't be positively known until

we find the dearly departed in the afterlife—as the only persons inside the establishment at the time of the, perhaps, misunderstanding, were the gambler, one John Smith, owner of the appropriately named Smith's Place; the raven-haired sporting woman, known as "Raven"; Sweet's mine employee Sean "Irish" O'Rourke; Granite Mine Company employee Mac "Scott" O'Connor; and city policeman John Jones.

Slick Gene says that John Smith was shot four times, stabbed twice, and that his head was bashed in by a heavy spittoon. Raven was shot twice and stabbed four times. Irish was shot five times, and Scot the same; Jones was beheaded with an ax.

"This will be some funeral, and your gravedigger will be quite busy," I comment.

"Well . . ." Slick Gene offers me a cigar, which I accept, and he takes another for himself and lights both fine smokes. "It ain't the record. Seven got kilt last year, but that wasn't contained to one bucket of blood, as it spilt out onto the street and ended in Chin Lee's Bath House."

He stops to remove his hat as Raven's coffin passes, Slick Gene being a gentleman.

"As far as the gravedigger"—his hat is returned to his curly black hair—"Jenkins the undertaker owns the lot where we plant 'em, and he has graves dug six at a time. So they's ready. Kids like to play hide-and-seek all the time there."

He sees the perplexed look on my face.

"Orphans," he explains. "And come fall, we'll have about twenty graves dug. Can't dig graves after the hard freezes come. And hard freezes come early this high up on This Side Of The Slope."

The last coffin passes.

Well, it is not a coffin. The only coffin was Raven's. Wood is not scarce, though many trees have fallen to be turned into cabins and homes and businesses and privies, but most bodies are wrapped in bedrolls or sheets or the heavy winter coats of the deceased. Newer residents who have found rich veins of silver are now building frame homes, and bricks and stones are being freighted in from Greeley, Denver, Pueblo, and Colorado Springs. The mayor of Dead Broke paid for the lady's coffin, which was brought in from Denver. It was originally bought for a mine owner who died of natural causes, but the delivery was delayed.

"We had us a hot spell," the lawman says. "Rare for us. And Mr. Albany started to ripen up, so we just used the best quilt he had. Mr. Albany was a generous fellow. Just ask any of those on his payroll. So we figgered he would have donated his casket to that handsome woman. He sure did like the ladies."

A boy beats a drum as he follows the last of the dead and a handful of mourners.

Slick Gene and I smoke our cigars for a moment, then the lawman says, "You'll be wanting to see the mayor."

It is not a question. "That would be most helpful."

"I figgered," Slick Gene says. "That gal from Denver wanted to talk to him. So did the scribes from *Harper's*, *Frank Leslie's*, San Francisco, Tombstone, Colorado Springs, Boston, London, Paris, Omaha, Cheyenne, San Francisco—no, I already said San

Francisco—Salt Lake City, Denver—but that Denver inkslinger was a man, not the woman who come first—New Orleans, and Kansas City. Well, Nugget ain't shy. He likes to talk. I'll take you over to his place."

Nugget is the duly elected mayor, and the miner whose strike led to this bustling, if somewhat rowdy, city two miles above sea level.

His name is Allane Auchinleck, but in this rapidly expanding boomtown, he is called Mayor "Nugget." The nickname comes from one of the geological wonders of our Western territories and, indeed, the world.

Roughly one year ago, Nugget found one of the richest silver veins—in a cave that was unearthed by a stray stick of dynamite. The mayor gladly allows me inside his home, a three-story masterpiece of wood, where his den houses the great miracle of silver—a nugget, shaped like a diamond, that weighs 1,776 pounds. On occasion, Nugget says, he used to chip some off when he was short on cash, but now that his mine is working shifts around the clock and his company has expanded into three other mines that aren't as productive as Dead Broke No. 1 but certainly bring envious looks from less fortunate operators, his credit is good across Dead Broke, Colorado, and, indeed, our entire United States.

"If I ever wanted to see England or Germany or Africa, I guess my credit would be good in them places, too," he says. Then grins. "And if it wasn't no good, I'd just buy the country for myself."

The gem is one of the wonders of the world. Four guards, each armed with four pistols, a shotgun, and a Winchester repeating rifle, are on duty every minute of every day. Six men have been killed trying to steal this fortune, three killed outright, and three more hanged after a speedy (three minutes is indeed speedy) trial on the front porch of the wonderful home of Mayor Nugget.

Dead Broke, dear readers, is far from broke.

As I sip fine bourbon on the covered and screened porch of Mayor Nugget's home, the peals of hammers, the whines of saws, the snorts of oxen, the squeaking of heavy wheels of wagons, the songs of workers, and the curses of mule skinners come from all directions. Dead Broke constantly grows. More and more people arrive, some to seek their fortune in the rugged mountains, others to take their fortunes from men and women who live and work here.

My first sight of a bloody and ghastly shootout is far from all one finds in this magnificent city. Although I stopped counting the number of saloons at 43 and the number of brothels and cribs after 69, I have found three theaters—*Othello* was being staged on my first evening by a troupe from London at the Camelot, while a reading of Milton was scheduled at the Paramount and a burlesque attracted a standing-room-only crowd at the Dead Broke Entertainment Hall. One can find the usual beef houses and cafés with checkered curtains, but there are six Chinese restaurants, three places serving spicy chow from south of the border, a French bistro, four German names, and Jake's Italian Q-Zeen. There are four doctors, two dentists, nine undertakers, three cobblers, sixteen livery stables. The population is 9,889, Mayor Nugget tells me.

One of the guards beside the Diamond Nugget clears his throat.

"Them five that got kilt yesterday," he points out.

Our fine, bearded, rail-thin mayor laughs, and he faces me. "How many folks was on that stagecoach you rode in on?"

"Twelve inside," I say, "three in the boot, six up top. Plus me."

Nugget looks back at the guard who had spoken.

"Take away five, that's ninety-eight eighty-four. Plus twenty-one . . . Hey, Nugget, we've topped ten thousand. Not even counting the inkslinger, since he'll be going back East."

"That's cause for a celebration," Nugget says, and he takes me to the Paramount for a performance—and no one cares to hear my argument that Dead Broke is still ninety-five living residents short of ten thousand.

But aged bourbon and a wonderful ballet make me forget about such picayune thoughts. The air is fresh when we depart the theater, the skies so close one can almost touch the stars, and even at ten in the evening, Dead Broke is alive and well. Banjos and tinny pianos play all across this city.

Slick Gene is killed the next day. Shot in the back.

"Dagnabbit!" Mayor Nugget roars. "Now we're below ten thousand. That's it. I'm bringin' real law to this city! I'm sendin' fer Syd Jones."

"Syd Jones!" I cry out.

Syd Jones, the lawman who tamed Denver. Who tamed Laramie. Who cleaned up Tucson and Dodge City. Who shot it out with the Jones Gang in Prescott, Arizona Territory, and buried all four of them. The hero of fifty-nine dime novels—of which I penned four of the liveliest and best-selling, and highly recommend

Slick Syd; or, The Silver Star's Chase After the Dirtiest Scoundrel in Arizona Territory—and the man who could light a match in a woman's mouth from forty-four paces with a single shot, blindfolded, and fired over his left shoulder without peeping.

"That's right . . . we're bringin' law and order to Dead Broke, so folks will stop writing that 'Dead' is what Dead Broke is all about."

Yes, Dear Readers, Dead Broke is changing. Dead Broke is losing its roughshod, violent ways. Syd Jones will tame this town. And as the silver keeps coming in by the ton and ton and tons more, Dead Broke is far from Dead. Dead Broke is rich, vibrant, and soon to be safe for all sexes, all ages, all citizens of our glorious United States.

Dead Broke will live forever.

1893

CHAPTER 2

The third riot in four days began Monday morning. It would have started on Sunday—keeping the streak going for a third consecutive day—if Crosscut Saloon owner Sara Cardiff had not revealed her peacekeeping abilities by tapping three beer kegs and one case of real bourbon and declaring all drinks were all free for the boys of the E F & G Mining Company.

The "Effigy" was the latest silver mine to close, but even Bryn Bunner, who had lost his job and organized the first riot that Friday, could not persuade anyone to break windows, burn down a building, run anyone wearing sleeve garters or a cravat out of town on a rail, or shoot out the streetlights when there was free booze to get drunk.

Bunner sat across the street, watching the boys get well into their cups, frowning over the fact that he had a hatchet with nothing to chop up. He was so upset, he didn't hear Sara's footsteps or smell that fancy French perfume till she sat down next to him on the boardwalk in front of Percy Stahl's groggery. Percy wouldn't open his saloon till dusk these days, and he closed it up at seven—if not earlier. Longtime residents of Dead Broke could recall when Percy's never closed.

The sweet mix of sassafras and barley eventually worked its way through that thick black mustache and beard, causing Bunner to blink and slowly turn his eyes to find Sara's translucent blue eyes. With a pure smile, she lifted a stein of lager.

Wearing a blue dress, Sara was two inches over five feet, her yellow hair pinned up in a bun. She almost always wore blue. Maybe because it matched her eyes. Maybe because she was superstitious. Most people figured she was superstitious, since she was a gambling lady and ran a fine saloon where the dealers and the gal spinning the roulette wheel didn't even cheat. They didn't have to, she had told drunken losers who wanted to shoot up her place, because she hired only the best. Then she would buy the losers a round or two, maybe even let them dance with her, treat them to coffee and wish them better luck when they tried their luck next time.

Bunner stared at the beer, sighed, and shook his head. She cocked hers and gave him that Cardiff look.

He took the beer and drank it down in a handful of gulps, wiped the foam off his mustache and beard with the sleeve of his flannel shirt, and set the stein on the boards between Sara and himself.

"Here's to the Effigy," he said, and let out a labored sigh. "God rest her merry soul."

"I'm sorry," she said.

He snorted. "What for? You still got a place to work."

She shook her head. "Not for long, the way things are

going." She reached over and patted the massive, scarred, hairy hand closest to her. "Why don't you come over and have a snort?"

His big head shook.

"It's on the house."

"I don't take charity." He pouted.

"You're something else," she said, sighing.

"You're one to talk. We might have gotten some attention if you'd let us go about our protest."

Her eyes never lost their softness and sympathy, and her voice was level and assured.

"'Protest,' Bryn? Is that what you call it?" Her hand slipped off his. "On Friday, you wrecked the office after Mr. Schäfer and Mr. Von Bauer shut down the S V and B."

"Well, they's the ones who fired all of us."

"They didn't fire you, Bryn. They lost their jobs, too."

"They was owners."

"Who lost more than you did. Or those other poor miners."

"Them two Germans is rich enough."

She shook her head. "Because they saved their money instead of spending it on beer and roulette."

"Boyle's wheels are crooked."

That she wouldn't deny. But she gave him her grandma's look. "Boyle runs one gambling hall. There were, what, forty or more here? You never once came to my place."

He frowned, and mumbled something.

"How's that?" she asked.

"Nothin'," he said.

She knew she sounded just like her mother. "It didn't sound like nothing."

"You're too . . . nice . . . to see me . . . drinkin' . . . or gamblin'."

"You're drinking now," she told him.

"Well." He sighed. "Times have changed."

She breathed in a lungful of mountain air, held it for a while, and let it out like a lover's sigh.

Times have changed. They sure had.

She stared across the street. The only activity going on was outside of her place. Her two next-door neighbors had closed up their businesses, Björk's Guns: Repairs, Sales & Ammunition, and Archambeau's—well, just Archambeau's, where some of Sara's girls had side jobs, but, well, folks had to make a living somehow.

She remembered when she was making money hand over fist and fist over hand and back again. When Dead Broke was bringing in more money than anyplace in these United States and her territories. People earned money from working the mines or made more money than they ever dreamed of serving those miners, or those who depended on the miners.

Dead Broke was anything but dead. There had always been a lot of death in this city. Mines caved in. Fires could be even worse. Dead Broke had burned down twice, but had also risen out of the ashes new and improved. More buildings were brick or stone by now, and there was a mighty good fire department with two steam pump engines and a newfangled electric one. Well, before the Saturday strike, anyway. Bryn Bunner's boys wrecked the electric one, and then burned down Cottam's mercantile.

"How old are you, Bryn?" she asked him after a church bell finished chiming.

"Twenty-three," he answered.

She nodded. "Then you're probably too young to remember the Panic of '73."

"The what?"

"The Panic of '73."

"Was that after Custer got wiped out?"

She sighed. "No. That came three years later. The Panic was what they call a depression."

"Like a hole in the ground?"

"Like a bad feeling. A feeling of dread. Of hopelessness."

"Like I'm feelin' now."

She gave his hand another pat. "Something like that. But it's really a collapse in national finances. I'm not old enough to remember a lot of the '73 Panic myself. It had something to do with a railroad. People were losing jobs, businesses were closing all over the world, and it really hit our United States that fall, maybe late summer. It had something to do with railroads. And this company run by a fellow named Cooke. Well, he had to declare bankruptcy—that means he didn't have enough money to pay his bills—"

"That's why I never go on tick."

She nodded.

"Well, people, banks, the government, everything just sort of collapsed. Businesses closed. My pa lost his job. Couldn't find work except for handouts and maybe a day job mucking out a stable or something, for more than a year. Mama left him. Never saw her again. It was a rough time. I remember that. And this country of ours, it really struggled. But it ended. Took a long time. Years. Four, five, six years."

"You mean I'm gonna be out of work for six years?"

Sighing heavily, Sara wished she had brought out a bottle to drink herself.

She remembered other things happening during those bleak years. Workers walking out. Throwing stones at trains. Her grandfather on her mother's side writing about losing his job in Michigan when the lumber business completely fell apart. And since she and her pa and kid brother were living in Pennsylvania, she had gotten an up-close look at the 1877 railroad strike. Coal cars being overturned, a bridge being burned, and some soldier firing a shot, and other soldiers following his action. Her father wouldn't let Sara or her brother go out to play for two weeks. That's how scared he had been.

"What I mean," she said, "is that this won't last forever."

"How long will it last?"

She shrugged. "I wish I knew."

He picked up the stein and brought it to his mouth, his Adam's apple moving as though there was still some beer left. She thought about offering him another, or leaving to fetch one herself, but decided that if he at least pretended he was drinking a cold lager, maybe that would cool him down.

"All I know is mining, lady," he said when he finally lowered the stein.

Sara gave him her best smile. "That's better than knowing nothing except running a saloon and gambling hall."

"Maybe you can teach me how to deal?"

"I don't think you'd like that kind of job, Bryn."

"Reckon not."

"Want another beer?"

He shook his head.

"Whiskey?"

"I don't drink no liquor, just beer, ma'am."

"That's good. That's really good."

He stood, offered his hand, and pulled her to her feet.

"Reckon I'll go home," he told her.

"That's a good idea. Home's a good place to be. Go back and see your wife. She's probably worried about you."

She knew he was married. He had that look.

But his jaw set, and he stiffened for one brief moment.

"I don't reckon so, ma'am. Matilda did what your ma done. But I can't blame her none. A man's supposed to keep his wife in comfort. Can't do that when there ain't no work to be had in the silver mines no more." He pulled down the cap, turned, and walked back toward the one-room houses where most of the married miners lived.

Sara went back into the din of unemployed miners and saw that reprobate of a mayor, Nugget, drinking her free beer and whiskey.

"Thought there'd be another mess," he told her, and wiped foam from his mustache and beard. Then he pointed a crooked finger at two pistols stuck inside his waistband. "Thought I might have to protect my city, li'l lady."

"Maybe today will pass peacefully," she said with a sigh.

"Mebbe so. Yesterday was worser than that first one."

Saturday's unrest had indeed been bad.

Four businesses had been burned, three horses shot, two men killed, four wounded. One girl but ten years old had taken a vicious cut across her left cheek from flying glass that Doc Aimé Cartier said took nineteen stitches. Sara treated that fine doctor to three shots of brandy.

The way Dead Broke was going, she was buying lots of folks drinks these days. She had given Marshal Syd Jones a whole bottle after all those Saturday riots. He said he needed it to treat a knife wound, and she had seen the bloody rag wrapped around his lower right arm.

That got her to thinking about Dead Broke's lawman. She hadn't seen him. When she had passed toward his office way down on Tenth Street on her way to open up her place, the shades were pulled down and the door closed. He usually kept the door and windows open. Said he liked the smell of the Rocky Mountain air.

"Have you seen Syd today?" Sara asked.

The mayor belched, grunted, and spit. "Ain't nobody seen that yeller cur dog. Run off last night." The mayor pointed toward the stagecoach office adjacent to the Two-Mile Hotel. "Harry said Jonesy come in and bought a ticket, had his grip and his guns. One-way. For Denver City."

"Syd . . . left . . . ?" Sara couldn't believe what she was hearing. But then, the mayor, the man who had made Dead Broke what it was, wasn't always the most truthful with his statements.

"Left?" Nugget belched a foul-smelling burp. "He didn't leave, missy. He run like the yeller dog he is. Run. Just up and quit. Left his badge in the middle of the floor." He returned to the liquor keg and refilled his cup.

While Nugget was drinking, Sara said: "Syd. We can't . . . well . . . with all that's going on now with the silver collapse—"

"I don't wanna think about that silver stuff," Nugget said. "I got a silver diamond in my house, biggest one ever found, and I ain't sure it's worth a plug nickel right now. I don't know how I'm gonna afford to pay for 'em guards to keep nobody from a-stealin' it. And then what would I do?"

He stared at the cloudy skies. Clouds. Storm clouds, Sara realized. She was used to those beautiful blue skies. But this was fitting.

"Sluagdach!" Nugget bellowed. "Don't you laugh at me, you ol' reprobate. Don't you go mockin' yer ol' pard. You jes stop that infernal coyote yippin'. Yer still dead, pardner, but I ain't broke!"

He killed Sara's liquor.

"Yet," he whispered.

"Nugget," she said, then decided to flatter him. "Mister Mayor?"

That got his attention. Might have even sobered him up just a bit.

"Yes'm?"

"We can't go without a marshal in this town . . . I mean . . . this city. With tempers where they are. This town . . . this mountain . . . we're sitting on a volcano that's about to erupt. It has already spit out some lava and flames."

"What is lava, anyway?" Nugget asked.

She ignored his question. "You're the mayor, and a good one." How she managed to say that without laughing or crying was beyond her, but she kept pushing herself forward.

"We need a lawman. You need to appoint someone."

Actually, for some reason, she was thinking about Bryn Bunner. He was wild and reckless right now, but she just had a feeling that if he were sworn in . . . well . . . he was the type of man who kept his word, and certainly wouldn't break any oath. And he was big and strong enough to handle ten rioters.

"Don't I know it!" Nugget shouted. "I'm mayor. That's why I done called for an emergency meetin' in my office first thing in the mornin'. I ain't lettin' my town, my city, my silver mine, my world go down without no fight, li'l lady."

"A council meeting?" she asked. Sara wanted to be sure she had heard right, that this wasn't just her good liquor talking over his stupid, drunken brain.

"Town council. That's right. Just after breakfast."

"Your breakfast or . . . ?"

"Eight thirty in the a.m.," he said.

She eyed him coldly.

"You got word to all on the town council?"

"Yer darn-tootin'. I'm mayor. Ever'body on that council comes to my beak and call."

"Beck," she corrected.

"No. Jim Beck got kilt after callin' Boyle's faro dealer a cheat at the Lucky Dice . . . when was that?"

She didn't remember any Jim Beck. And so many people got killed at Boyle's gambling hall that names all ran together. Besides, she was madder than a hornet . . . and his highness.

"Listen to me, you ignorant reprobate. You summoned all the town council *but me*! Was *anyone* going to tell *me* about this assembly?"

He blinked stupidly at her.

Then he guffawed. "Why, shucks, that's right. We did appoint you. After yer husband got hisself accidentally kilt in that stagecoach wreck. Since folks said it looked like the state was gonna let you petticoats vote in the November election and we might as well beat the gun and put you on now. Nobody pays much mind in Denver to what we do nohow."

She held her wrath, and pain, at his bringing up Luke's death.

"I'll see you tomorrow," she told the mayor.

Sara didn't see him Monday morning, though, because she got word before she left her house that the assembly meeting had been postponed till Tuesday.

These days, she rarely saw her small house. The way things were in Dead Broke, Sara—and many other business owners—lived where they worked for one reason: To protect their businesses from being ransacked and/or burned to the ground.

The meeting was postponed because of Monday's riot. Which came after Jansen's bank was found empty, after some angry miners pulled down the locked iron gate in front of the front doors, used some dynamite to blow open the doors, then rushed inside to find the vault open and empty, and learned that Gyp Jansen had skedaddled during the night with every single penny.

The bank was burned down, taking the millinery next door, the four-seat privies behind the bank, and Lindale's bookstore with it. She would mourn the loss of the two businesses, but not Jansen's bank, as she kept her money in a Denver institution. Constance Turner had such wonderful hats. Her own designs. The latest fashions from London, Paris, New York, Cheyenne. And those books. Lindale carried everything any lover of words needed, from the Bible to Chaucer to Thoreau— how she loved just holding *Walden* in her hands.

Sunday had been a day of rest. That's what she heard some people say. Resting up to burn and loot again.

In fact, she and her two best—and biggest— bartender/bouncers sat in front of her Crosscut Saloon holding a shotgun (Harv Dumont), a Winchester repeater (Deke Burnett), and a four-shot derringer (herself) to make sure no one raided her stock of whiskey, wine, and beer, or burned the building down, just like the way the offices of the just-closed Joyful Mines headquarters and the company president's two-story home went up in flames and smoke.

But Sara was there, with her four-shot derringer in her purse, at the town council office above Dante Lupino's pawnshop the first thing Tuesday morning. She even had the coffee brewing before anyone else came in.

S.D. Sullivan arrived shortly afterward. He had been smart enough to bring a bottle of rye, in case anyone wanted to sweeten his—or her—coffee.

CHAPTER 3

"This town is deader than dirt."

Mayor Nugget stared as hard as he could at Dead Broke councilman S.D. Sullivan, who owned a mine that hadn't closed.

"That . . ." Nugget wished he had some of his personal liquor here, but since Dead Broke had turned civilized, he was forced to drink bottled rye, and sometimes even nasty wine or weak beer. He closed his eyes and shook his head, and when his eyes opened and were eventually able to focus, he saw his assembly just staring at him. All of them. Except Conner Boyle, whose left eye was nothing but glass. He never stared at anyone directly.

"That . . ." Nugget didn't know what to say. He felt like crying. Not only did he feel like it—he realized he was crying, feeling the tears drip down his dirty cheeks and into his rough beard.

Sometimes he wished he had never become some wealthy Midas. Whatever a Midas was. He didn't think it was like a Judas. Whatever a Judas was.

"I . . . just . . . don't know . . ." He hardly managed to choke out the words. Then he slammed his fist onto his desk, but quickly recovered to grab his tumbler of Miss Sara's good whiskey before it toppled onto the floor.

"Why?" he asked, sobbing. "Why is this . . . this . . . happenin' to me?"

"It's not just happening to you," Dylan Pugh said. "And it's not just happening to Dead Broke. It's happening . . . well . . . all over."

Dylan Pugh was a miner. He usually worked as a foreman, and he got appointed so that the miners themselves—and not just owners like S.D. Sullivan— would have a voice in the city government. Pugh's employer wasn't one of the big corporations or major producers, though, and it, for some reason, like Sullivan's, hadn't shut down operations. Yet.

"Yeah . . ." Nugget wiped his nose. "But . . . why?"

"It's quite simple," Pugh explained, "and we all knew this was coming after Grover Cleveland won election as president. So—"

Percy Stahl interrupted by pounding his right fist on the tabletop, and then pointed one of those bratwursts he called fingers at Nugget's nose. "Did you vote for Cleveland, sir?"

Nugget sighed. "I voted fer . . . what was his name? . . . Hickok? Did Wild Bill run—"

"Hancock," S.D. Sullivan whispered, and started massaging both temples with his first two fingers on each hand.

That gave Pugh time to finish his history lesson.

"Grover Cleveland prefers gold over silver."

"Who doesn't?" Boyle said with a snort.

"And Congress has been talking about repealing the

Sherman Silver Purchase Act for some time now," Pugh continued. "The Panic of 1873 was bad enough, but banks ran into trouble for many years—'84, and as recently as three years ago. But those weren't nationwide. New York suffered. Some of the nearby states did. A few banks got into trouble, investments went south, banks folded. One president, if I remember correctly, fled to Canada with millions of dollars of his depositors' money."

"A man after my own heart," Boyle said as he withdrew a cigar from his pocket.

"Like that four-flushing Gyp Jansen!" Sullivan pounded his right fist on the table.

Sara sighed. "Banks have been failing across the country," she said, and no one—not even Conner Boyle—interrupted the lady. "Gold reserves in the treasury started dropping. People started pulling out their notes from banks and buying gold. Cheaper gold. An investment."

The painter, Laurent Dubois, chuckled and raised his hand.

"So he's to blame for my town becomin' a mess!" Nugget bellowed.

"No one is to blame," Sara and Pugh said, their voices as one.

"Mayor," Sara said, and nodded at Dubois. "Laurent—"

"The big banks started selling what they could," Pugh said. "Banks between New York and San Francisco just couldn't stay afloat."

"But silver . . . my silver diamond. My . . . Hope Diamond of Silver?" Which is what two dime novels and several newspaper accounts had called Nugget's wonder.

"Some of us," Dubois said, lowering his hand and taking the floor for himself, "have seen this coming since spring."

Nugget spit, but missed the brass cuspidor. "Well, why didn't some of you tell me what you was seein'?"

Sara sighed. "Listen, gentlemen. We know that silver prices and gold prices are falling. We know that people are leaving. And you can't blame them. When there's no work, people have to go where they can find work. We live in a veritable Garden of Eden."

"Oh, Lordy," Nugget whined. "I had a veritable disease once. I sure don't wanna have that ag'in." He buried his head in his hands and sobbed for a minute.

That caused Sara to pour herself a shot of whiskey and shake her head.

"You'll be fine." Doc Cartier finally spoke.

"The question," Pugh said, "is not what has caused this panic, this depression, this exodus. The question is, how do we save our town?"

Nugget's head jerked up. "My town."

"Your town . . ." Pugh sighed.

The silence lasted only a moment, but the next noise came from the street. It was a noise common during Dead Broke's early years, before civilization and Syd Jones brought some semblance of law and order to the boom town.

Everyone hurried to the window.

"That's Caleb Holden!" Percy Stahl screamed.

"Yes," Sara heard herself whisper. "It is."

The gunman, a dealer for Conner Boyle's Lucky

Dice Gambling Hall, stood over the bodies of three dead men—miners, by the looks of them.

"I ought to go see if I can help any of those boys," the doctor said softly.

"No need," Boyle said. "Caleb Holden is a professional."

Boyle smiled at Sara's glaring face. "Look at it this way, missy. They didn't suffer."

Doc Cartier sighed, but turned, then stopped when he saw three other men checking the bodies, then covering their faces with the hats that had fallen into the muddy street. By then, Jenkins the undertaker was running up with his measuring tape.

"That would've been something to have seen down on the street," Percy Stahl shrieked with glee.

"I've seen enough of those," Sara whispered, and realized she was pouring herself another shot. And she never drank in the morning.

Nugget found his hammer, which he used as a gavel, and pounded the table.

"All right, so we knows we gots ourselves a . . . pandemic?"

"Panic. Financial depression. A downturn of the economy," the painter explained.

"And folks are leaving."

Doc Cartier glanced at the window and sighed. "Sooner or later."

"So what Dead Broke needs is to find a way to bring folks back to our town!"

They eyed Dubois—all of them, even Sara Cardiff, despite feeling a disturbance in her stomach and morning-whiskey-induced lightheadedness.

"Well," Pugh said, shaking his head, "most folks want jobs."

The painter snapped his fingers. "Miss Cardiff has the right idea. We live in a paradise. Never have I seen a more beautiful part in the world—and I have seen the Alps, Wyoming's Yellowstone, Rome . . ."

Boyle laughed. "You think people will come here to live . . . without jobs?"

"There are always jobs, sir," Dubois argued.

"There's also winter," the doctor pointed out.

"We've managed through the worst, the coldest of those hard winters," Pugh said.

"But," Sara heard herself saying, "how do we lure . . . ?" She didn't care much for that word. It sounded like something Boyle would say. "How do we bring them here with the mines closing, or at least getting rid of employees?"

No one said anything for two minutes. Then Percy Stahl yelled: "Bring in mail-order brides for the remaining townsmen!"

At first, she thought Stahl was joking, but then the mayor banged his hammer on the table and voiced a loud "amen" to that idea, Pugh nodded his head rapidly, and even the good doctor shrugged and said, "Why not?"

"All right," Boyle said, "if we're done—"

But the council was far from finished.

"Well, I'm not proposing fraud or anything like that—I mean, we don't want the state legislature looking into us, and certainly not the United States marshal . . . so . . ." Dylan Pugh's resolve started to wander down to lower elevations.

"Nothing said in this room leaves this room," the mayor proclaimed, and hammered his approval on the banged-up table.

"Salt some mines," he said.

"Not with silver, I hope," the doctor said with a laugh, thinking Pugh was joking.

"Diamonds, maybe," Sullivan suggested.

"Diamonds!" Boyle laughed. "In Colorado?"

"If Arkansas can have diamonds," Sullivan argued, "then surely the great sovereign state of Colorado can have 'em, too."

"Diamonds," the mayor said, his tail wagging like a happy dog. "Like my Diamond Nugget of Silver." The hammer banged again. "Approved!"

"Don't we . . . aren't we . . . isn't a vote called for?" Doc Cartier asked.

"Approved." Nugget's hammer sent a few splinters flying off the table.

"We need to do something about the violence erupting in our fair city." The good doctor finally walked away from the window. "Before anyone will want to come up here."

"Then have the mine owners stop closing down and firing those who keep this city going." Pugh looked angry. Sara thought she had seen friendlier faces on coiled rattlesnakes. Not in Dead Broke, of course. Rattlesnakes didn't care for this altitude.

Sullivan, being a mine owner, rightfully looked scared.

Boyle gave one of his dismissive sniggers.

Pugh reached into his pants pocket and pulled out a worn-out, folded-up newspaper, and began spreading it out over the tabletop—or what was left of it after Nugget's incessant hammering of his makeshift gavel.

"Well, we do have one problem. The Denver press. Actually, all the newspapers in Colorado—especially our competition, like Silverton and Leadville. They have been hammering us for years as a lawless town. A Sodom. A Gomorrah. A Tombstone." He tapped a head-line that Sara could not make out.

"An ice castle."

Blinking, Sara looked at the painter. Laurent Dubois seemed like he was dreaming. Or somewhere far, far away from Dead Broke. Altitude—this far up in the mountains—could cause lots of delusions.

"A lice castle?" Nugget let loose with a stream of profanity. "Us miners can't do much about vermin. And I take a bath in whiskey every Saturday. When it's warm enough."

"No . . ." The painter shook his head. "A castle . . . a city . . . a sculpture—my dream as an artist." He stopped, let a polite grin crease his face. "It has been my dream . . . not to paint buildings and signs and two-story homes, inside and outside. But a sculpture. A sculpture of our town. Our history. Made of ice."

The ice, Sara knew, never really completely melted at this elevation. And this being August, September would start cooling off. Snow could fall at night al-ready. She had seen sculptures of ice during the winter. Snowmen and snow animals.

"That," she heard herself saying, "might . . . might work."

"A bucolic scene. Children playing. Horses. Deer. Elk."

"And a she-griz!" Nugget's hammer landed again. "For the memory of ol' Sluagdach!"

"Who?" Pugh asked.

"Never you mind who. Painter. You're gonna carve us the greatest ice sculpture ever knowed in these parts."

Dubois looked like a child who had gotten everything he wanted for his birthday.

"The town of Dead Broke is gonna pay your rent for this ice sculpture. It'll bring in folks from Greeley and Denver. Even 'em misers down in Leadville will come to see your arc."

"Art," Dubois said.

The wife, or concubine, or maybe mother of one of the dead men killed by Boyle's gambling gunman wailed in inconsolable grief on the street below, reminding Sara Cardiff of what had happened minutes earlier.

"Ice sculptures and mail-order brides aren't going to save this town, gentlemen," she told them. "If you want folks to come a mile higher than Denver . . ." She waited until every mother's son of this town assembly looked her in the eye. "You first might ought to stop folks from killing each other."

"Miss Cardiff," Percy Stahl said, "this ain't near as bad as it was back in '86."

"It's bad enough!"

Boyle laughed. "That's what we get for allowing some female who thinks she can run a saloon and gambling hall onto our council of learned men of the world. I don't know why we even listen to a petticoat banter on and on about—"

Nugget's hammer silenced him.

"This is my town, buster," he said, and waved the business end of the tool at the crooked gambling hall operator. "And Miz Sara be a member of our council of assembly . . . of . . . congressional . . . senators." He nodded at the one woman. "I wanted to bring in some deputies before, but you always said our budget didn't allow for us spendin' no more money. But right now we ain't got no law."

"You can have a top hand in five minutes," Boyle said. "My man Holden is better with a gun than anyone in our Western states and territories."

"He ain't no Wild Bill Hiccup!" Nugget roared.

"Wild Bill has been dead pushing twenty years, old man!" the gambler hollered.

"Let's keep our tempers in check," the good doctor whispered.

"Boyle," Nugget said, "this is my town . . . there wouldn't be no Dead Broke if not fer me. And I'm worried sick—been worried sick since eighteen and eighty-five. Worried that someone is gonna shoot me, and steal my Hope Diamond of Silver."

Stahl chuckled. "You should have sold it before the whole economy went down the two-holer out back."

The hammer silenced the guffaws and sighs. "We needs to bring in a good lawdog!" Nugget roared.

"Why not bring back Syd Jones?" Sara heard herself suggesting. "If you'd paid him enough . . ."

But S.D. Sullivan panned that idea, his ears reddening. "If Jones were worth a nickel, he wouldn't have run out of town."

"When this town needed him most," Boyle said, adding to that argument.

Sara's mouth opened, but she realized this was a losing fight. At least these men were talking about hiring a lawman. That was the first step to bringing some sort of peace to Dead Broke. And besides . . . she could not deny the fact that Marshal Syd Jones, hero of several of those five-penny paper works of tripe read by schoolboys across the continent—and read to Dead Broke's mayor by chippies who could read, and sometimes a quiet little schoolkid named Joey Clarke—had fled town.

Or maybe Syd Jones had more sense than Sara and everyone else left in Dead Broke, Colorado.

A quietness filled the room.

"I still say Caleb Holden is a good gunhand. He knows the law."

Of course he does, Sara wanted to say. *Caleb Holden has broken every law in the state of Colorado.*

"Get me Drift Carver!" the mayor screamed.

Drift Carver? Everyone else seemed perplexed. Drift Carver was nothing more than the mayor's errand boy. The old-timer Nugget sent for when he needed something, usually whiskey, sometimes coffee, or to the bookstore—before Miss Lindale left—to get one of those cheap novels to read to him.

"You want us to pin a star on Drift Carver?" Doc Cartier asked.

"A drunken cripple could whup that little boy," Sullivan said with a contemptuous laugh.

"No. We don't want Drift to be our town . . . our city . . . marshal. But I'm a-gonna send him to Durango. We're gonna make Mick MacMicking Dead Broke's new town marshal."

CHAPTER 4

Mick MacMicking.

That name left the entire room silent.

Nugget even kept his fart quiet.

"Is . . ." Pugh looked across the table at Doc Cartier. "Is Mick MacMicking still in Durango?"

The doctor shrugged. But S.D. Sullivan said, "There was an item in one of the Denver papers that came up on last week's stage."

"I read that," Stahl said. "Said Durango had turned too peaceable for his liking. But he was still there. But he probably vamoosed."

The other councilmen began swapping stories that had heard, read—or, in Percy Stahl's case—actually witnessed (unless Stahl was lying) personally.

"Who's had more dime novels written about himself?" Dylan Pugh said. "Mick MacMicking or Syd Jones?"

"Be close," Laurent Dubois whispered. "Real close. But if he isn't in Durango—"

"Somebody there'll know where he lit out to," the mayor interjected.

Sara let out a long sigh. "Why don't you telegraph—"

"On 'count I don't trust 'em things," Nugget said. "And if you send a person with a pers'nal invite, it sounds a lot better than a bunch of scribbles on some piece of yeller paper."

Sara appeared shocked by the truth of the mayor's opinion.

"Didn't MacMicking start out as Jones's deputy?" Sullivan asked.

"In Tombstone," the doctor said.

"Or was it Dodge City?" Stahl asked.

Conner Boyle cursed, and did not even apologize to Sara Cardiff. "MacMicking is no better than Syd Jones. They both are creations of lousy writers. Those stories are all fabrications. They dream up adventures . . . the writers of those cheap dreadfuls dream up these stories. If you want to see a real gunman, come watch my man Holden light matches with a Colt from fifty paces. I'll tell you one thing. This is—"

This time, when Nugget's hammer splintered the tabletop, the noise left everyone's ears ringing. It was like someone had fired a .50-caliber Sharps rifle in the room.

"Boyle . . ." Nugget aimed the handle of the hammer at the cardsharper's chest. It almost looked like the mining kingpin was holding a .45 Colt at Boyle's chest. And Boyle's face appeared to show that he thought he was staring down a revolver's barrel, too.

"You keep forgettin', buster, that this is my town. I'm mayor. There ain't no town—you ain't got no gambling parlor here—if not for me. Me and my Hope Diamond of Silver. Folks keep votin' me in. And it's my job to do what's best for Dead Broke. And that's what I'm a-gonna do."

Sara wondered how many seconds, perhaps even minutes, passed before Doc Cartier broke the silence.

"So . . . I take it . . . the mayor's motion . . . is that Drift Carver goes to Durango to recruit Mick Mac-Micking as Dead Broke's next town marshal."

"Dern-tootin'." Nugget still held the hammer like a .45.

"It carries." Sullivan, acting as secretary, looked over at Conner Boyle. "Unanimously?"

Boyle smiled, but his eyes showed no humor, nor any sign of defeat.

"Of course. What's best for Dead Broke."

"Mick," they heard Sara whisper. "Mick MacMicking."

"Stupid name," Stahl said.

Sara closed her eyes. "Duncan," she said softly, but Sullivan was laughing at Stahl, and no one heard her.

"I wouldn't say that when Drift comes back with him," Sullivan said.

"If MacMicking comes here," the doctor said.

"He'll come," Sara said. "He'll come."

"Why would he?" the artist asked.

Pugh shrugged. "Maybe because Durango isn't in any better shape than we are."

"And Durango," Sullivan said, "is likely too quiet for a gunfighter of MacMicking's renown."

"He'll come," Sara said again, her tone almost hopeful.

"And I welcome him," Conner Boyle said suddenly, excitedly. "Yes, indeed. I welcome the law of the West to our city."

Dubois nodded. "We have made some progress. I think this was a good meeting."

The men all agreed. Sara just stared out the window.

"Do we . . . should we . . ." Nugget found the nearest bottle and had a long pull. "We still want to bring in them petticoats, don't we—'em mail-order brides, I mean?"

"Why not?" Sullivan said.

"And I can make my ice sculptures," the artist whispered.

"That's a wonderful idea," Sara said, encouraging the council.

"Will I be one of your sculptures?" Nugget asked.

Laurent Dubois grinned. "You will make a fine one, Mayor. You will be the first sculpture our visitors will see. Welcoming them. Welcoming the thousands who will come to Dead Broke this September."

"I gets to model fer ya?" Nugget asked.

"No." Dubois smiled as he shook his head. "I do it from here," he said, tapping his heart, and he looked at Sara. "From here," he said again in almost a whisper.

"Sure hope it's cold enough then," Sullivan said.

"It's always cold enough here," Pugh said.

"Ain't that the truth!" the doctor agreed.

"Meetin's over!" This time, Nugget used the whiskey bottle as a gavel.

Hands were shaken, and Sara and the others left for their businesses. But Conner Boyle poured himself a glass of whiskey and waited till Nugget turned at the door.

"Ain't you a-comin', pard?" Nugget asked.

"I am, Mayor. And this was a most electrifying

meeting. You are a fine leader. I would not be surprised to see you in the governor's mansion in Denver or . . . eventually . . . our nation's glorious capital as president of these United States."

"I just wanna see myself in Chasm Park."

That was the name of the area where his mansion, his mine, and his Hope Diamond of Silver remained.

"Well," the mayor said. "I need to go fetch young Drift . . . and tell him what's expected of him."

He turned, but stopped when the gambler called his name.

"Before you go, Mayor," Boyle said. When Nugget looked back at him, Boyle gave him the best smile a gambler could muster.

"Shoot, pardner," the mayor said.

First, Conner Boyle poured the mayor a full tumbler of whiskey.

And followed that with another.

Then, smiling, he said, "You read all those stories about the fast gunfighters in our Western territories, don't you?"

"Sorta. I have 'em read to me. Better that way. Saves my eyesight. Especially when some of them readers, the ones who sometimes play in them shows at the opry house . . . you know, *Hamlet*, and that one about Falstaff. I like that one. He likes good whiskey."

"Yes."

"They make 'em folks that ain't nothin' but words come alive. Gets it even more excitin'. A boy in town reads lots of 'em stories to me."

"Indeed."

Nugget waited.

Boyle said, "Those stories are set in places like Tombstone . . . the wild cattle towns of Kansas in the seventies. Deadwood in the Black Hills."

"Yep. Some in even Denver City durin' 'em Pikes Peak rush days of yore."

"Lore," Boyle corrected.

"Your. Uh-huh. Like I said."

"Well." Boyle put his arm around the thin man's shoulder and pulled him close. "What would you say if I told you how we can put Dead Broke, Colorado, into one of those works of literature?"

The old miner grinned underneath his thick, rugged beard. "You mean to tell me that you wanna write one of 'em storybooks?"

Boyle's smile looked as though it hurt.

"Not exactly."

Nugget waited.

"Have you read about Ben Usher?"

"Shucks, yeah," Nugget said. "He's one nasty feller. I bet I've read about him gettin' beat up. He gets beat up good. Or outsmarted. Sent to Yuma or some jail. One of these days he's gonna get kilt. Makes me wanna just cheer . . . whoever it was that beat him up. That feller . . . he's got more lives than thirty-seven cats."

This explaining might take Boyle the rest of the morning and into the afternoon, so he motioned to the nearest chairs.

It was, Boyle thought, a brilliant plan. Simple. Wonderful.

The first part was to bring in Ben Usher. Ben Usher was a hired gunman. He had been involved in five of the bloodiest gunfights in Dodge City, Tombstone,

Deadwood, Miles City, and Fort Worth. Mothers used to warn their children: "Don't stay out too late—Ben Usher has been seen in town." "Do your chores or I'll sic Ben Usher on you." "Eat your supper if you don't want me to tell Ben Usher what a bad boy you've been."

"Why'd we want a no-good murderin' killer come to Dead Broke?" Nugget asked. "He might want to take my Hope Diamond of Silver."

"No. He'll be here because he can't stand Mick Mac-Micking."

"I don't know why nobody would not take a likin' to that hero."

"Envy. Fast guns always want to prove they are faster."

Nugget seemed to accept that.

"It's simple," Boyle said. And it was.

If the Denver and Cheyenne papers—and even the illustrated newspapers back East, maybe even the *New York Tribune*, and papers in Chicago, Omaha, Kansas City, San Francisco—got wind that Ben Usher and Mick MacMicking were both in Dead Broke, they would come by foot, stagecoach, or horseback as fast as they could.

"The newspapermen would put Dead Broke on the map of the world," Boyle said. "This'd make us not just better known than Denver or San Francisco. We'd be as big as London, Rome, Paris."

Mick MacMicking having to face his archenemy, Ben Usher. Two men who despise each other.

"Marshal MacMickin' don't despise nobody," Nugget complained. "He don't often even kill more than a hundred or so in his books—and most of 'em is injuns out to lift his hair. And he always says, 'I hated to do it, but it had to get done.' Nigh ever' time he says that. Or somethin' like that. Unless Drift's readin' it to me wrong. Or Little Joey. But I think Little Joey reads real good."

Conner Boyle started to think that this explanation might take him all night. If not a week.

"You'll be the mayor of Gunfight City."

Nugget's head shook. "I'm mayor of Dead Broke, Colorado. Never even heard of Gunfight City."

This might take till the turn of the century.

"Listen. Ben Usher meets Mick MacMicking in the streets of Dead Broke. Newspapers write about it. Other newspapers pick up those stories. People flock to this town to see where Mick . . . I mean . . . Ben Usher . . . died with his boots on. People keep coming. Some of them stay. And Dead Broke, Colorado, is saved from ruin."

Nugget wet his lips. He said: "Hmmm . . ."

"But here's how we get more people coming to our town," Boyle said, and refilled Nugget's glass with the last of the whiskey in this bottle. "We don't just bring in Ben Usher." He let Nugget think about that before realizing that the less Nugget thought, the quicker this plan would be approved.

"Telluride Tom," Boyle whispered. "Dean Hill."

Nugget's head bobbed. "I recollect 'em names, too. In fact, that Hill feller . . . Drift read me something in our newspaper about him in some fracas in Creede."

"I read that same story." Boyle nodded in agreement.

"Well, we bring those two hired assassins to Dead Broke, too. Do you see?"

"See what?" The sun was starting to shine through the window.

"Telluride Tom and Dean Hill shoot it out. Maybe we bring in some others. A few gunfights to whet the appetites of those inkslinging boys of the press. That's just a highlight . . . like the juggling act or the dance or the pianist before the play begins out at the Dead Broke Theatre."

"Uh-huh."

"They write their stories. More people come to see a real gunfighting town. And then it's the grand finale of them all. A MacMicking–Usher duel on Silver Street. Right here in Dead Broke. You'll be the mayor of the most famous gunfighting frontier town in history."

"Will 'em newspapermen write me into their stories, too?"

"Of course."

"Even if I don't get into no shootout with Mick MacMickin' or Ben Usher?"

"You don't have to even see them."

"Well, I wouldn't mind seein' 'em. Well, maybe not Usher. Not with him knowin' I was seein' him. But Mick MacMickin'. Now, him I'd gladly meet."

"Well, if your boy Carver can bring him back, you'll pin the star on him. But you can't let him know that Ben Usher is coming to town."

"Cuz it's a surprise."

"That's right."

"And you think it'll do . . ."

"It'll do wonders for this great city's economy, Mayor."

"Well, it sure sounds different."

"That's another reason it will put us on the map."

"But . . . but that don't mean we can't still bring in 'em mail-order brides, do it?"

"You can have all the brides you can stand, Mayor. And all the ice sculptures that Frenchman can carve."

"Well, then, that sure sounds like an interstin' plan. As long as 'em brides—"

"As long as"—Boyle put a firm hand on Nugget's shoulder—"you don't tell anyone about what we have got up our sleeve."

Nugget looked at his cuffs, then nodded.

"I'd like to take my nap now," the mayor said.

"Of course." He patted Nugget's back as the man came out of the chair and headed to the door.

"Why did you even have to tell that fool what you were planning?" Caleb Holden asked his boss in Boyle's upstairs office at the Lucky Dice.

"Because our mayor will be paying the expenses of Ben Usher, Telluride Tom, and Dean Hill."

Holden thought that over before he nodded and killed a shot of whiskey.

"All right." He pulled out one of his revolvers, pulled the hammer to half cock, and rotated the cylinder over his left forearm. "I'd like a crack at them three good ol' boys. I'd turn 'em into good ol' dead boys."

"You might get that chance," Boyle said. "What

other top guns could we bring up here? In case we need some more hired killers."

Holden shrugged. "Ben Gunderson."

"He's a back-shooter!" Boyle exclaimed.

"So am I!" Holden countered. "Whenever I think the gunman might be able to put me six foot under, anyway."

"I thought Gunderson was in Yuma."

Holden grinned. "He was. Till he shot hisself out of that stinkin' desert hole and made his way into Mexico."

"Well, Mexico's a far piece from here."

"But Silverton's not far at all, and there's a redhead he admires in Silverton." Holden's smile widened. "He won't have so far to travel if what I hear is true."

"Ben Gunderson is in Silverton!" Boyle roared, then quickly dropped his voice to a whisper. "Who else can we get to Dead Broke in a hurry?"

"Boss, you don't want too many top guns in the same town. That can get . . . unfriendly."

"Who else?"

Holden sighed. "Faro Scott."

"Never heard of him."

"You would if you was ever in Missouri."

Boyle nodded. "Who else?"

"There's a guy from Texas. Mora's his name. I'll have to think on that one. He's a young'un. But faster than greased lightning. At least, that's what the word goin' 'round is. But he's also right deadly with a ten-gauge."

"If you remember his name, where he lives, or how to get word to him, let me know."

"All right."

"Anyone else?"

"None comes to mind right off the top of my head."

Boyle inhaled, let the breath out, and patted his coat pocket for a cigar.

"What about Killin' Ben Mitchum?" he asked.

"By thunder, boss, you're talkin' craziness now. You'll have every mad-dog killer in town. Killin' Ben Mitchum, he don't care who he kills, as long as he gets to kill someone. I bet he has to put new grips on his six-shooters every year because they gots so many notches on them."

"Last I read about Mitchum, he was in Arizona Territory," Boyle said.

Holden nodded. "Tucson. I think."

"If you get just half of them gunmen, it'll cost you a fortune."

Boyle had found his match. He bit off an end of the cigar, spit it out, then struck the match and lighted his cheroot.

"I'll bring in as many gunfighting killers as I can. No matter what it costs." He stuck the cigar in his mouth, sucked in a mouthful of smoke, and removed the cheroot to exhale.

"Any price is worth it to see Mick MacMicking dead."

CHAPTER 5

There were times when Duncan MacMicking regretted that he had handed over his city marshal's badge. Like this morning, when Alessandro De Luca had taken Duncan's dime in the tonsorial parlor, saying, "*Grazie mille*," instead of his usual, "No, no, no, *Signore* Poliziotto. It is *il mio onore*." The jolly fat man simply slipped the coin into his pocket and went back to the chef of Henry Strater's hotel to remove the hot towel from the man's face. De Luca didn't even offer to help Duncan out of that fancy chair.

Usually, though, that little pang of conscience disappeared after a few minutes. This time it happened three blocks up Main Street, in front of Wilson's Grog Shop, when Duncan saw the crowd of a half dozen men, four schoolboys, and even Reverend Fitzsimmons's oldest daughter playing hooky from school, two chippies and one-legged Frau Armbrüster crowding the boardwalk to watch the fight.

Duncan crossed the street to the crowd and tried to push his way through. There was a time when folks would have parted like the Red Sea, but even when he said, "Excuse me," to Frau Armbrüster, she just glanced at him, spit juice into the snuff can that she held in her gnarled left hand, and said, "I got here first, buster!"

Two behemoth miners stood on either side of the old hag, and the mean old biddy was tough enough, so Duncan backed away and headed toward the two ladies of the night. At least they were slim and shorter, and Duncan could see over their heads.

Kent Allison was a good ten years younger than Duncan, and probably fifteen pounds heavier. On paper, he looked like a really good lawman. He could read. That always came in handy. He could shout really loud. He could do math, if not in his head, at least on paper, and eight times out of ten, he got the ciphering right, or at least no more than three or four cents off. He also could match Duncan in target shooting with a Colt revolver or a Winchester long gun.

"Tin plates," Duncan had told him after that part of the interview, "don't shoot back. Remember that."

"I know," the youngster said. "I had to shoot two bad hombres in Laredo."

"Read about that in a newspaper," Duncan said. "You wounded both of them. Good shooting."

"Thank you, Marshal."

"Wounded men, son," he said softly, serious, but still in a friendly voice, "can shoot, stab, stomp, and strangle. Then they're still wounded, and you're just dead. Keep that in mind."

But these young whippersnappers, they just didn't listen to wise counsel.

Allison had countered with: "My goal is to become the first lawman in Durango not to kill someone."

"Durango!" Duncan had said, only half in jest. "You'd be the first lawman in the state of Colorado."

So here was young Allison, facing a miner twice the new marshal's size, and the marshal's Smith & Wesson remained holstered. The chippies were the only ones, it appeared, to be pulling for Kent Allison. But Duncan was used to that. Miners wanted miners to win, even if they worked for competing companies. Saloon tenders didn't care much for lawmen because star-packers, especially those in Durango the past dozen years, tended to frown upon loaded dice, rigged roulette wheels, and marked cards. And some of these men fondly remembered those days that were far from halcyon in places like Dodge City and Tombstone—even Denver during the Pikes Peak rush. Durango and even Silverton had gone through their own turbulent years.

Duncan brushed his newly waxed mustache. He let the fingers of his left hand feel the smoothness of his cheeks. Alessandro De Luca was an artist with either razor or scissors and comb. And that tonic he favored—his own special blend, handed down by generations and applied to men of all sizes and all bank accounts, dating all the way back to Abilene, St. Louis, Cincinnati, New York City, and Polignano a Mare. His Prince Albert still smelled like it had at Greenbaum's Finest Tailor & Funeral Director on Second Avenue. Plus he had started his day with a visit to the Mineral Bath House. It would be a shame to . . .

The two young ladies of the tenderloin gasped at the loud crack of a miner's fist slamming into a young lawman's jaw. Even Frau Armbrüster shouted, "Fall down, son," but the lack of teeth and the mouthful of snuff made her instructions hard to hear over the cheers of the miners on the boardwalk.

"Ain't you gonna do somethin', Marshal?"

Duncan stared into pretty eyes. Green. Just like his. Her face wasn't so good-looking, but women of her profession lived a rough existence. Still, her voice and those eyes reminded him of a wonderful woman he had known years ago. But he was . . . retired.

"Well, miss, it just so happens that I'm not the city marshal anymore, and—"

There was that awful crack again, and a gasp from the civilized minority in the gathering.

"Let him fall!" Mr. Murphy, who worked at the flour mill down the street, bellowed.

"He's had enough, Dabrowski," someone else echoed.

Duncan felt his features hardening. He had a clear view of Main Street, and saw Broz Dabrowski, that rough Polish miner whose thick head had dented, the story went, the barrel of Duncan's .45-caliber Schofield revolver three or four times. Dabrowski was holding Kent Allison upright with that ham-sized left fist of his and rearing back with his right hand to smash the kid's nose, which was already flatter than a hotcake.

The dime novelists would write something like: *Then, Mick MacMicking felt nothing but cold. His handsome face turned to ice, whilst his eyes, never blinking, focused with the hypnotic glaze of a diamond-back rattlesnake's. He stepped onto the street, not to face Death, but to deliver it.*

Actually, Duncan felt hot. The back of his neck would be redder than the rare beefsteaks he favored. But he mentally pushed that anger aside for a moment.

"Miss," he told Miss Green Eyes, "hold this for me, if you'd be so kind." And he held out his flat-brimmed black Stetson, which she took as if she were holding King Arthur's helmet. He removed the Prince Albert, and asked the prostitute's companion if she would keep the coat from getting dirty. Or bloody. Though blood wouldn't be so easy to spot on the black wool or flat collar of fine velvet.

When he stepped off the boardwalk into the dusty street, he heard Frau Armbrüster again. This time she was warning the big Pole.

"Watch it, Dab! A dude's coming up behind ya."

Broz Dabrowski released his grip on Allison's shirt-front and grinned viciously as Duncan strode toward him. The bully took five steps away from the young marshal, whose shirt had been ripped to shreds and covered with blood; whose face resembled an engineer's after a train wreck; whose hands hung limp at his side; and who tilted one way, then the other—yet, somehow, remained upright.

That's when Duncan decided that Durango was going to be in capable hands. That young lad was all right. Tough. Determined. And maybe he would learn a few things down the road. He certainly had learned something today—if his brain had not been scrambled from the battering of those giant fists.

"Good see you again," Broz Dabrowski said. "Long time I wait."

Duncan said nothing. He just walked.

The bullheaded bully's expression changed. He even took a cautious step back, then stiffened, straightened, and started to raise his fists.

"You stop." His right hand paused unclenched, and pointed a big finger—big even despite missing the top two joints after a mining accident.

Duncan kept his steady pace.

"I . . ." The man stiffened, then dropped into a stance that reminded Duncan of a bull about to charge.

That's when Duncan stopped on a dime. His eyes widened, he even let out a short gasp, and he brought his right hand up, cupping it at the side of his mouth, and yelled, "Don't do it, Kent! Don't do it!"

Broz Dabrowski whirled around, rearing back his right fist to pound the new marshal, only to see the young lawman exactly where he had been before the miner had turned to face Mick MacMicking. Leaning with the breeze, hardly conscious, barely among the living, just standing, moving to the left, then right, dripping blood on the street.

"Ack!" Realizing he had been duped, the brute spun back around to face his new challenger. "You son of—"

Duncan's right smashed the top and bottom lips and drove Dabrowski back five steps; he would have run into Kent Allison, but the young man happened to be swaying to his left. After using his right leg to stop from going backward another foot, the bully spit out blood and part of a bottom tooth, which cut his tongue. Then he drew back his left, but had to stop and block the right haymaker Duncan was swinging.

That proved to be another mistake.

Duncan's throw was a feint. The left caught Dabrowski's ear, and that one sent him staggering past the swaying marshal like the two men were performing some ballet at Durango's opera house.

"I will—" the miner started, but ended with a gasping, "*Oomph.*"

Duncan's right pounded the big stomach, and as Dabrowski doubled over, he met a hard left knee that was coming up. That straightened the miner in time to take a quick one-two-three-four series of jabs, then an uppercut, followed by another hard, swerving right that put Dabrowski on his knees. The bully was panting, his head bent, blood and saliva spilling onto the dust. The eyes were unfocused. The crowd stared in silent awe. Except for Frau Armbrüster.

She hooked the snuff out of her mouth, tossed it onto Main Street, and limped away, cursing and complaining loudly in her native language.

Duncan looked at his knuckles as he stepped back until he hovered over Dabrowski. He wanted to suck on that raw flesh. Hitting that hard rock of a hard rock miner was like, well, hitting hard rocks. His left pinky was jammed. A tooth had cut into Duncan's right thumb, and he had to fight the urge to shake the pain out of the digit or at least suck the blood a bit. Instead he waited till Kent Allison swayed back and came to a slow, awkward stop behind the wheezing, kneeling miner.

"He's all yours, Marshal," Duncan told Allison.

The naive kid rocked a few more times, and finally stopped. Those eyes focused on Duncan, perhaps seeing him for the first time.

"You whupped Broz good, Marshal," Duncan said. "Might as well put him in the dirt where he belongs."

Allison's eyes moved down and watched the back of Dabrowski's head. He looked up again at Duncan, who just nodded. Then his right hand pushed back the tail of his coat and found the Smith & Wesson in the holster. When the revolver started to slide out of the leather, Duncan took a quick step forward and whispered:

"No, no, no, not that way, Marshal." Duncan smiled. "Remember what you told me. You're going to be the first peace officer in Durango not to kill anybody."

The double-action .38 was out of the holster, but Allison's finger wasn't inside the trigger guard. He stared at the silver-plated revolver for a second, then the eyes came up again.

"Get a couple of fellows to take him to jail." Duncan nodded. "That's what I'd do."

He wasn't certain that the green kid understood at first. But after a long half minute, Kent Allison's head moved up and down. His split lips moved, but no words came out, just more blood that fell onto the dirt. Then he shifted the revolver and brought the hard rubber grips onto the top of the miner's head.

Down went the miner, face in the dirt.

Down also went Kent Allison, but Duncan moved fast and caught the man, taking the silver-plated .38 from the marshal's hand and holding the kid up with his free hand, eventually managing to get both arms around Allison from the back.

"I . . . licked . . . him . . ." A garbled laugh followed Allison's weak sigh.

"Whupped him good, son," Duncan said. The kid laughed louder, and then his head dropped forward.

Two volunteers with the Durango Fire Department

stepped out of the throng and hurried to Duncan. "Best get him to see Doc Adams," Duncan told them as they relieved him of his weight. He spun the double-action revolver around, the handle held out, the barrel pointed down, and the larger of the two men took it and shoved it into his waistband.

As they carried the unconscious lawman away, Duncan looked at the crowd, which was thinning out in a hurry. The chippies had already gone. Most people were fleeing like they would run from a spring flood. But two men Duncan knew weren't fast enough.

"Welsh, Sloan. Not so fast."

Sloan stopped and cursed. Welsh halted three steps later, turning around and pleading his case: "Oh, Marshal . . . don't—"

"But I know that you two know exactly what needs to be done, boys." Shucks, he had arrested those two handymen five or six times over the years. They weren't bad fellows. Far from it. Sloan was about as fine a farrier as could be found in southern Colorado, and Welsh tied the finest flies, which no trout in the Animas River could resist. They just weren't very good at holding their liquor.

But they were sober right now.

He motioned them toward him. "I bet you even know where the key to the jail cells is without even having to think about it."

Sloan swore. Welsh whined. But they walked toward the unconscious miner and the former Durango city marshal.

"That's right."

"This ain't your job no more, Marshal," Welsh said.

"You're not going to argue with me, are you, Jeremy?" Duncan said.

"No, sir," Welsh said.

"Happy to help," Sloan said. He might have even been halfway serious.

"Take him to the city jail. Put him in a cell. Preferably an empty one." They sighed, but went to work. While they argued over who got the torso and who got the legs, Duncan scanned the crowd, but didn't see anyone he needed.

The two drafted volunteers were lifting Drabrowski off Main Street.

"Don't forget to lock the cell door," he said. "Then you need to go find Doctor . . . Shevlin." That got their attention. Patsy Shevlin was the newest addition to Durango's resident medicinal masterminds. He could have asked the two men to fetch Doc Adams after he had tended to Kent Allison, but one reason Duncan had lasted so long as Durango's top city peace officer was because he spread things around. Different undertakers for different corpses. Different men when it came to posses. And different bystanders to haul men to jail or to doctors' offices.

Being a lawman wasn't always about law and order.

As Broz Drabrowski was carried off toward the boardwalk, Duncan took time to suck his thumb, then spit out blood that was quickly clotting and wiped his lips. He had made it to the boardwalk on the other side of the street when someone called his name.

That voice he didn't recognize, and he turned slowly, putting on a smile while casually moving his right hand to his waist, hooking a thumb over the gun belt, close enough to the holster.

He smiled again when he recognized the face.

"Drift Carver." The two men shook hands. "You're a long way from home, son. How are things in Alma?"

"Oh, Mick, I ain't been in Alma in a raccoon's age. Been in Dead Broke."

"Well, that's fine. Just fine. You're still a long ways from home. What brings you this far south?" He looked at his shirtsleeves, then reached up with his right hand and combed his hair with his fingers.

"That's what I come to talk to you about. I got sent here on city business."

"How's Syd Jones?"

"Can we talk someplace . . . quiet? I been ridin' a long time."

"Be my pleasure." He nodded. "There's a quiet saloon on Twelfth Street. But first, we need to visit this brothel in that alley."

Drift Carver howled with delight. "Now yer talkin'!"

Duncan grinned. "Hate to disappoint you, pard. I just have to fetch my hat and Prince Albert back."

He turned to lead the way, stopped, and spun around. "Let me clarify a few things about that hat and coat."

CHAPTER 6

Greedy G's Saloon was a small frame affair, drafty in the winter, sweating hot in the summer, and tucked between an apothecary and Lou's Barbershop. The apothecary got most of the business, as Lou spent most of his time drinking whiskey. Rumor in Durango had it that Gary Gleason got free haircuts.

But Lou wasn't drinking when Duncan and Drift Carver stepped through the batwing doors, letting those bang behind them as Duncan picked up an overturned chair and settled into it at the table closest to the doorway. A man wanted a breeze in this stuffy whiskey mill. Duncan nodded at the chair opposite, and Drift Carver settled into it, removing his hat and resting it on the tabletop.

"What do you want?" Duncan said. "It's on me."

"Beer for starters," Carver said.

"Beer," Duncan called out to Gary Gleason, who was bartending. "And the usual for me."

Three miners kept drinking whiskey at the bar, and Gleason topped off their shot glasses before finding a stein and filled it with foamy draft, then stopped by the potbellied stove—which didn't cool things down in the twenty-by-twelve joint—and filled a mug with black tar that some people might call coffee.

The beer was more suds than pilsner, but the coffee was just the way Duncan liked it: bitter, black, potent, and bad enough to make him appreciate what he brewed for himself.

Once Gleason had returned to his perch behind the bar, Duncan sipped from the pewter cup and nodded at the beer.

"It won't get any cooler," he told Carver, who picked up the heavy pewter and took a long pull, then wiped foam off his face.

"I've had better beer," he said, "but I ain't complainin'."

"You think the beer's lousy, you should take a swig of this hot tar."

Carver drank again.

"It's quiet, though," Duncan said. "This saloon, I mean. And for all his faults, Gary Gleason doesn't gossip, whatever he might hear."

When Carver nodded toward the miners, Duncan didn't even have to look. He just smiled. "They're refugees from Poland. Don't even speak English except for 'yes,' 'no,' and 'howdy.'"

Carver killed his beer.

"Want another?"

"Not right now."

Duncan took another sip of the bitter brew.

"All right. What about Syd Jones?"

First, Carver sighed. Then he sighed again. Finally he shook his head and said, "He started hittin' the hooch ag'in, Mick."

That made Duncan feel ten years younger. He breathed out a long sigh, and almost smiled. "Drift, I thought you were going to tell me he was dead."

Carver's head shook. "No, no, it ain't that. Well, he wasn't dead when I left fer Durango. But things got bad in Dead Broke."

"Things are bad all over. Especially in this state. Economy's in the privy. Businesses are closing left and right. Reminds me of when I was a young'un back in '73. But I don't see why a little panic, depression, collapse or whatever you want to call it would have a lawman hit the hooch. Before I turned in my star here, I told the city council, the mayor, and that new kid we hired to replace me that things are a whole lot easier keeping the lid on during these times than they are when everybody's booming and making a killing."

Carver stared, and Duncan waited as the miner wiped his mouth with the palm of his left hand, stared at the barflies and the bartender, and let out another heavy sigh, until he met Duncan's eyes.

"I think Syd lost his nerve."

Their eyes held till Duncan looked at his coffee. He thought about drinking some, but didn't want anything right now. Well, nothing short of a long pull of rye whiskey. A lawman, especially one who had been at it for as long as Mick MacMicking, heard stories of lawmen, some of them quite famous, old and young, who couldn't take the pressure. Badges made good targets, and while most of the population of a mining and ranching town like Durango—or even those blazing, rowdy Kansas cow towns—even the towns with wicked reputations like Dodge City, Tombstone, Abilene, and

Deadwood, if anyone had ever taken time to conduct a survey, folks would have been shocked to know that, overall, the general population supported lawmen, order, justice. It just took one or two hardcases or moral-lacking scoundrels, or some cowhand or miner who had way too much liquor to think reasonably, to give a town a reputation.

Or for a lawman to start questioning his sanity.

He thought back. How long ago? Ten years, maybe eleven. It had been in one of those cow towns in Kansas, though Duncan had worked in so many, he couldn't recall which one. The saloon, he remembered, was called the Alamo. But every end of trail in Kansas had a saloon called the Alamo. And one called the Lone Star. And another the Texas House.

The cowboy's name was, of course, Tex.

CHAPTER 7

Tex had buffaloed the bartender with the barrel of his Colt, sending the bald man tumbling down the bar, as Tex's pards kept shoving him till he reached the end of the bar, tripped over a spittoon, and hit the side wall, then slid down and toppled over, his bleeding, bald head landing in the spit, cigarette butts, chewed-to-pieces wads of chewing tobacco, and whatever else landed in a cuspidor at a rawhide place like the Alamo.

The plate-glass window became a target, and Tex put a hole through that one in the center, then he tried to put out one of the candles in the chandelier, but that bullet missed the wax, hit the wrought iron, and ricocheted into the right leg of the drummer from St. Louis.

Tex was yelling, "I'm the roughest, toughest, bestest man to ever come up the trail, and I'm ready to shoot anybody who says I ain't," when Duncan walked through the doors.

"Careful, Mick," whispered the nearest saloon girl, who had been unloading a tray of glasses and bottles of rye to some trail hands who were pale and wide-eyed as they stared at Tex. "He just turned loco and maybe caved in Logan's head."

Logan must have been the bartender who lay unconscious—Duncan could see the ripples in the liquid mix of foulness on the floor, and which had to be caused by Logan's breathing.

"Now, what do we have here?" Tex laughed, snatched a bottle from the nearest cowhand, and took a long pull as he took a few steps toward the bar, then staggered a bit to his left until he stood even with Mick, separated only by twenty-five feet and several cowboys from other outfits.

"Is he one of yours?" Duncan asked the closest cowhand.

"No, suh, ain't never laid eyes on that hombre before," the man whispered.

"He come in alone," the girl said.

"He didn't check his hogleg," said another waddy.

As if Duncan couldn't see that for himself.

"He calls hisself Tex," the girl whispered.

"Well," Tex yelled, "if this ain't my lucky day. I get good and drunk, and now I see a tin star that I get to put a hole right through."

Chair legs began scraping on the rough planking as men took their whiskeys, their poker chips and money, their hats, and themselves away from the tables closest to Tex or Duncan and moved slowly to the far wall. Those at the bar saw the door that led to the stockroom and into the alley and they filed through that.

The remaining bartender gathered the most expensive bottles of hooch from the backbar and then slowly sank to the floor behind the long bar.

"I'm gonna kill you, you Kansas Yankee lawdog," Tex said.

"All right," Duncan said. Tex's revolver was cocked, but the barrel was pointed at the floor—at least at that particular moment.

"Shoot'm, Tex, shoot'm dead," some drunk yelled from the farthest corner of the smoky saloon.

One of the girls, who was kneeling beside a shivering cowhand still in his teens with a new set of duds and clean hat, started reciting a prayer.

"You ready to die?" Tex asked Duncan.

Duncan did not answer. He started walking.

"Criminy," some Texan whispered.

"What . . . what you doin'?" Tex stuttered.

Duncan did not answer. He did not blink. He did not take his eyes off Tex. Most importantly, he did not let his right hand move far from the butt of his holstered pistol. Duncan could have been walking through a hay meadow . . . or along Front Street . . . or down the aisle of a church . . . on a boardwalk . . . on a stroll through the park.

He was alone. At least that's how he felt. Alone. And with no one in the Alamo Saloon except Tex, who tilted his head, blinked, and said, "What you doin', hombre?"

His boots sounded like booming thunder or stamping hooves against the planks, though he felt as though he were walking on soft, green grass—not the dried, weathered stuff that grew in Kansas, but the thick carpets of green he could remember from the South.

Tex blinked. His mouth opened. His left hand, the one that did not hold the long-barreled Colt, came up, and the index finger extended and trembled as he pointed, muttering, "You . . . you . . . you . . . bes . . .

besssst. You . . . you . . ." Then all out in a sudden explosion:

"You-better-stop-you-crazy-lawdog-else-I'll-shoot-you-down-like-a . . . !"

The left arm fell, and Tex started to bring the right hand up, but he forgot to thumb back the hammer.

It wouldn't have mattered anyway. The Colt was still pointing toward the floor, and a bullet would have missed Duncan by three feet had Tex been able to squeeze off a shot.

Instead, an instant later came the thud of a pistol barrel across a Texan's skull, the rattling of an unfired revolver as it clattered against the overturned spittoon, and the heavy crashing of a drunken cowboy onto the floor.

It was over.

Tex wouldn't wake up until the liquor, and probably his breakfast and noon meal, were out of his stomach and in the slop bucket in the jail cell.

Quickly, Duncan picked up Tex's revolver and turned around to the stunned faces of those in the Alamo. He checked first to make sure Tex didn't have any friends ready to fight, or to finish what Tex tried, but failed, to start. What he saw was looks of relief, shock, amazement.

He holstered his revolver and started shucking the cartridges from Tex's Colt.

"You," he said, pointing at the closest waddy, a man who looked sturdy and strong enough. "And you." He found another cowboy at another table. "Stand up. The both of you."

The men obeyed without hesitation.

Pointing the unloaded pistol at the unconscious form of Tex, Duncan said, "You're being hired, no pay, to take this drunk to the jail. You'll walk ahead of me. It's not that far. I'll tell you where to turn."

No one dared argue.

As the men moved toward Tex, Duncan looked at the bartender.

"Fetch a doctor for your fellow barkeep. Then have the doc send me a report." He turned to look at the unconscious, but still breathing, whiskey-pourer. "If he wants to press charges when he wakes up, let me know. We'll find the judge and get it done. If your boss wants to sue him for damages, he better see the judge, too."

By then the cowhands had lifted Tex off the floor. They forgot his hat, but Duncan slid the emptied revolver into his waistband, stooped, and picked up the dusty, battered old thing. Standing, he started back down the path he had taken to face down the blowhard.

He held one of the batwing doors open as the two conscripted cowhands carried Tex out of the Alamo and into the street.

The doors were banging as Duncan stepped off the boardwalk, noticing the crowd on both sides of the street. The newspaper would have another story about drunken Texas brutes, and the town council would be demanding that this town would never see peace until the cattle trade moved elsewhere.

Which was the way things went in trail towns.

Businesses wanted the money, but they soon got tired of what came with it. Busted heads. Businesses shot to pieces. And when peace came, deputies would be relieved of their duties. Marshals, too, fairly often, as the town decided a civilized police force worked much better than gunmen with badges.

"They spelled your name right," Syd Jones said.

He was sitting behind his desk, boots propped up on the corner atop a lawbook and the state constitution, holding the newspaper in his hands. He let the paper fold over and looked up at Duncan, who stood next to the potbellied stove as he topped off his cup of coffee, then filled another banged-up chunk of speckled enamel for his boss.

"They get anything else right?"

Chuckling, Duncan brought the two cups toward his boss's desk. After Jones folded the paper and tossed it onto the pile of dodgers and documents and circulars, dragged his boots off the desk, and straightened in the chair as he accepted the steaming brew of black, bad coffee.

"More or less," Duncan answered. "Some of them ten-dollar words, though, I don't know what they mean."

"You might want to learn them." Jones nodded to a big book atop a filing cabinet. "That there *Webster's* is a good place to learn 'em."

Duncan shot a quick look at the dictionary, then settled into the chair opposite his boss.

They drank their coffee in silence for a few minutes before Jones set his cup on a pad and tugged on the ends of his thick mustache.

"You just walked toward that cowpoke, pistol-whupped

'em, didn't even clear leather till he started to bring up his hogleg?"

The answer came as a shrug.

"Were you scairt?"

Duncan shook his head. "I didn't feel a thing. Almost like I was in the opry house, watching some playactor pretend to be someone else, doing something nobody in his right mind would do."

"I don't know how them thespians do that my own-self," Jones said, and drank more coffee.

"That wasn't what I meant," Duncan said, straightening in his chair. "It was—"

"I know what it was, kid. Something took a hold of you. You didn't think. You reacted."

He thought about those words for a full minute. Sipped more coffee. Goodness, it was wretched. Then he ran the words through his head again and looked at the town marshal.

"I guess that's about the way it was. What should I have done?"

Jones chuckled, dragged his boots off the desk, and slid his chair closer. "Nothin', I reckon," he said, setting his cup aside and straightening the papers before him. "It worked out for you." His eyes rose and hardened. "This time."

They studied one another for a long moment.

Then the marshal pulled out a paper and read it in silence. "One day, it might not work out quite the way you planned."

"I don't know that I planned anything," Duncan told him.

"I know. Like I said, you didn't think. You just did.

And that'll help you for a while. Next trail herds that get here, they'll have heard all about that whippersnapper of a deputy who don't know the meaning of fear. Cowhands gossip more than widder women or my aunt Mary Lou. But you just got to remember that now you have a reputation. And the things that come for him with a reputation can be dangersome. My advice to you is to know when to live up to your reputation. And when *not* to."

Duncan drew in a deep breath, holding it and letting those words bounce around inside his brain. He exhaled and leaned closer to his boss, his mentor.

"Can you teach me that?" he asked.

The iron face of the lawman before him moved slowly back and forth sideways.

"That ain't somethin' I can do. That can't be taught. That's somethin' you'll have to learn for yourself."

Disappointed, Duncan nodded.

"One of these days, though," Jones said after he shot down the rest of the terrible coffee and started going through the papers he had been ignoring for about a month of Sundays. "One of these days you will start to think. You'll start thinkin' that this kind of job ain't worth dyin' for. You'll start thinkin' 'bout that gal who's sweet on you. You'll start doubtin', start worryin', start debatin'. That's when you'll know it's time to hang up your badge and find a job that won't get you shot dead in the night, or buried and forgotten in some patch of nothin'. If you're lucky, you'll live to a ripe ol' age tellin' lies about the time you walked ten, twelve paces and cold-cocked a blowhard Texas waddy in a saloon in a trail town and got wrote up like you was Wild Bill Hickok and the second comin' of ol' Kit Carson."

Duncan waited, but the lawman kept going through those papers, so he stood, picked up Jones's empty cup, and took it back toward the stove along with his own.

"Or you'll just get killed and planted," Jones said to Duncan's back.

Turning, Duncan waited.

"Sometimes, the best thing that can happen to a lawman is when his grit is gone. Just ups and vanishes. Heard of an opry singer who was hittin' them C notes like there wasn't nothin' to it. Then couldn't find a key or hit the right note and got laughed right out of the theater. Some folks found that a sad story, and maybe it was. But for a lawman, somethin' like that can be a blessin'. On account that then . . . that lawman . . . well, he can just get back to livin'."

CHAPTER 8

Mother of mercy, Duncan thought. Ten or eleven years? No, that had to be closer to twenty. This was 1893, after all. Duncan had been seventeen when he first pinned on a deputy's badge back in '73. That was after two years of herding cattle himself, usually riding drag, till he got sick of eating dust twelve hours or more in the saddle each day, hardly getting a wink of sleep, and earning calluses on his blisters on his backside. He would turn thirty-seven in October—if he lived that long.

After a few years in Kansas, he had made a name for himself, first as Syd Jones's deputy, and then as a marshal, city and later federal—sometimes both—moving from trail towns to boom towns. Those terrible writers started cranking out dreadfully written, and hugely inaccurate, stories about Mick MacMicking. At first he had been amused, but that grew old. And no one had ever called him Mick MacMicking till the five-penny dreadfuls started coming out at prolific rates. Most folks these days didn't even know his first name was Duncan.

He remembered hearing some schoolkids yell in

Prescott, Arizona Territory, one time: "Mick MacMicking. See if you can say that three times real fast."

They sure had a point. Which is why he preferred being called Duncan. His parents had given him that name, and that was good enough for him. But at least he had yet to be given a handle like Wild or Bloody or Bad or Tall. Eventually, he grew to accept Mick.

Most, if not all, of the men he had arrested, and six or seven women, had cursed him with profanity he had not heard until he had pinned on a badge. And he had thought he could cuss like the best of the cowboys he had trailed with as a teenager.

He drank more coffee in Greedy G's as two more men came inside—businessmen from a block over—nodding their friendly, wordless greetings to the former lawman as they resumed their conversation and headed to the bar.

"What makes you think Syd lost his nerve?" Duncan asked Drift Carver.

"He got drunk. Run out of Dead Broke."

"Syd was ran out of town?" Duncan leaned forward as he questioned Carver.

"Nah. He just skedaddled. Though the way things have been goin', I reckon there was a halfway decent chance Nugget—Mayor Nugget, I mean—and the council would have asked him for his star sooner or later."

Duncan couldn't say he was surprised. Lots of lawmen he had known found solace in whiskey. Lots of cowboys, miners, ranchers—even ranch owners and mine owners—drank themselves into a drunken stupor, once a week, once a night.

"Anybody know where he ran off to?" Duncan asked. He wasn't interested in taking any job as a lawman, but he had been thinking about trying his hand as a professional gambler, until he decided to find a good place, a quiet town, a peaceful patch of the Western states or territories, and retire and watch the West and the world pass by. He could find Syd Jones, though, pick him up out of the trash or gutter, and maybe talk him into retiring with him. Syd had lived in log huts, soddies, even in jail cells when he was a lawman. Surely he could live with Duncan MacMicking.

They'd hunt and fish, swap lies, grow corn and potatoes, find a woman every now and then.

What a great thing, he thought. Retirement had some amazing possibilities. And nobody shot at you.

"Weren't like he left a note," Carver answered. "I heard Denver. But I didn't see him, or hear tell of him, when I caught the stagecoach south to Trinidad. Afore I took another one here."

Denver. There were plenty of alleys, shanties, and saloons in that city. It might take a month to find Syd Jones—if he were still there. But it was a start. Though Duncan figured he would just retire here in Durango. It was a beautiful place to live. Mountains. Streams. Trout jumping. Wonderful falls. Yeah, the snow could bury a person on a horse on some winters, but Durango had turned quieter—despite today's disturbance.

Maybe he could find his mentor and haul Syd Jones down here.

"The council wants to hire you as Dead Broke's lawman," Drift said. "They'll pay you your price—

as long as you remember that silver ain't what it used to be."

Duncan was drinking coffee when Carver spoke. Smiling, Duncan set the cup back on the table.

"Are they planning to pay the new marshal in silver?"

"No." Carver picked up that Duncan was joking with him. "Cash money."

"People are still making money in Dead Broke?"

The slim man shrugged. "Some businesses are doing all right." He turned to study the bar. "Better than this place."

"Gary Gleason does fine," Duncan pointed out. "The sun hasn't set, you know."

"Well." Carver leaned forward, no longer drinking, but putting his elbows on the table and his head in his hands. "What do you think, old pal? Come back home to the garden spot of the high Rockies."

Duncan sighed. The man had taken a long ride for nothing. They could have saved money and a lot of jostling in stagecoaches by just sending a telegram south from that faraway mining camp.

"Why would I leave Durango for a silver-mining town when silver prices keep dropping?" Duncan said honestly.

He let those words sink through Drift Carver's thick skull and into his brain.

"Thanks for the offer—and when you get back to that high country, you tell those council folks that I really appreciate the thought, the gesture, the offer." Sighing, he shook his head. "But keeping the peace doesn't pay like it used to, and the cards have been good lately."

He hated seeing that long face on Drift Carver. He

frowned when the old gent sighed heavily. He wished he could have found some words of comfort when Carver started shaking his head, and he half expected the messenger to break down in tears.

The saloon doors rattled again as another man, fanning himself with his bowler hat, came inside, and called out to Gleason as he hurried to the bar. He hadn't even noticed Drift Carver or Duncan.

Duncan followed the man with his eyes and found Gleason grabbing a bottle from the backbar. The thirsty merchant didn't interest Duncan, but he was considering asking Gary to bring Drift another beer, or maybe some whiskey that wouldn't burn a hole in a man's stomach.

Carver was muttering something as Duncan was about to wave Gleason over. Instead, he whirled around in his chair and locked his eyes on his old friend.

"What did you say?" He realized his voice sounded like he was questioning a prisoner in the Durango marshal's office.

"Huh?" Carver appeared to have been awakened from a deep sleep.

"What did you just say?"

"I didn't . . . I mean . . . I wasn't . . . I was just thinkin' out loud."

He leaned forward. "You said something, thinking out loud or mumbling or just spitting nonsense. But what did you say?"

Carver sighed. "I said, 'But Miz Sara C said you'd come.'"

He hadn't dreamed it. He had not misheard. *Ears,*

Syd Jones used to tell him. *Think with your ears. See with your ears. Hearing, in this job, is just as important as seeing. Sometimes, ofttimes, more important. You can't always see, in pitch black, during new moons, in dark alleys, in saloons with hardly any light. But you can always hear.*

"Sara C?" Duncan asked.

"Uh-huh." Now Carver was turning to the bar, and might have asked Gary Gleason for the cheapest whiskey he had.

"C," Duncan said, making sure he didn't rush his words, or mumble, or stutter. "C as in 'Cardiff'?"

"Uh-huh."

"Maybe thirty years old now. But not an old thirty?"

Drift Carver seemed confused. Duncan thought he might have to buy a whiskey for Carver to continue. Suddenly, a whiskey sounded really good to Duncan.

"I . . ." Carver swallowed. "I ain't no good about no gal's age. Ain't like checkin' a hoss's teeth."

"Not tall. But . . . ummmm . . . well proportioned. Golden hair. Blue eyes. Bluer than the summer sky in the Rockies."

"I ain't . . ." Carver swallowed like a criminal caught in a trap. "Her eyes I ain't never paid much attention to, neither." He leaned forward. "Your eyes is green." Moving back, Carver swallowed and his face paled. "Oh, now I remember."

"Remember what?" That came out so forcefully that Gleason and the fellows at the bar turned around to stare, but only briefly, then resumed their drinking and talking, because most people in Durango knew that you didn't want to get on Mick MacMicking's bad side.

Carver paled. He must have known he had let that proverbial cat out of the bag. "She told me not to mention her name."

"You didn't," Duncan said, forcing a calmness to his questioning and trying to get his heart rate down to something reasonable. "But just to make sure. Again: Yellow hair, blue eyes, five-foot-two. Likes to wear blue dresses. Looks like she's still in her twenties. Packs a four-shot derringer. Can deal, when she has to, from the bottom, but you can't catch her at it. And has a scar. Well . . . if you've seen that scar, I'll have to shoot you dead right here."

Carver looked as though he couldn't tell if Duncan was joking. And when Duncan thought about it later, he wasn't sure, either.

He waited. He wanted to reach over and beat everything Carver knew about Sara Cardiff and Dead Broke, Colorado, out of him. So he slid his hands under his thighs.

"That's her," Carver whispered after an undeterminable eternity. "Don't know nothin' about no scar."

Duncan let out a heavy sigh. "If you did, it would ruin my faith in women gamblers."

"Well," Carver said. "I reckon I ought to get a ticket on the stagecoach back to Dead Broke. Sorry to upset you, Mick . . . Marshal MacMickin' . . . maybe I'll see you around sometime and—"

"Stagecoaches take too long. I own three good horses. We'll use them. One doesn't mind a packsaddle.

We can make it to Dead Broke faster than a stagecoach can. I know the back trails."

"You mean . . . ?" Carver's eyes widened.

"Dead Broke has itself a marshal." Duncan was already standing and halfway out of Gleason's saloon before he finished that sentence.

CHAPTER 9

Sara Cardiff sat at the poker table of her Crosscut Saloon, playing five-card stud with dealer Logan Ladron. It was quiet that afternoon. It had been quiet for about a week now. The Penasco Mine had shut down two days earlier, Bunson's Hardware Store had closed, and, by Sara's guess, just from watching loaded wagons head past her business toward the road that led down the mountain, eight, maybe nine, more families had given up on Dead Broke and were going to Denver, or back where they came from, or some new spot where they might start over.

Hearing a horse whinny, she turned from Ladron and looked through the open doorway. That was someone riding into town, and she didn't recognize him or the dun horse he rode, but he had his black hat pulled down low.

"Your bet," Ladron said.

She looked down at her cards, took a peek at what she had just dealt herself, and checked her hole card just to be sure of what she had. That's how lazy she was getting. When she was playing cards for real, she never checked the hole card after her first look.

Stifling a yawn, she said, "Five thousand."

Logan looked at Sara's ace of spades and seven of hearts showing and then checked his hole card—which he never did, either, professional gambler that he was. Shaking his head, he said, "I guess my pair of kings have to call your five, and raise you ten."

He had a king showing, but not two. She smiled at him, and he grinned back and topped off his cup of coffee.

"Want some?" he asked.

"Nah. Call," Sara said, and dealt Logan a meaningless, from appearances, five, and herself a seven of clubs.

"Pair of sevens checks."

"Can't back down now, can I?" Logan said. "Ten thousand."

"I'll just call your ten this time," she said. "I'm feeling generous."

"Appreciate that. I haven't been bringing in a whole lot of cash to the coffers these past few months."

"Like anyone has." The last cards dealt didn't improve anyone's hand.

"Sevens still bet," Logan said.

"Ten thousand dollars again," she said with no enthusiasm.

"Well . . . I'm feeling generous, too," Logan said, "so I'll just call you."

She turned over a third seven.

"Three sevens." Logan laughed. "I'm glad I was generous, seeing I just have a pair of kings." He showed his king of diamonds.

"Now that's some game of poker!" a voice drawled from the batwing doors, and Sara and Logan watched as the man in the black hat pushed his way inside the all-but-empty saloon and strode toward them, his silver spurs chiming as he crossed the tiled floor and stopped at the poker table.

His clear eyes squinted at the felt cloth on the table, then his face looked across at Logan.

"Hate to disappoint you, stranger," Logan said, "but we were just playing for fun."

The stranger's eyes locked on Sara.

"You have heard about the panic going on," she said.

"Reckon everybody has," he said. "And I came here from Silverton, where it's just about the same, only not so high up."

Silverton wasn't too much lower than Dead Broke, and had started out as a gold town before silver took over. But this man was no miner. He wasn't a mine owner, either.

The gray frock coat had been pushed back to reveal the pearl handle of a nickel-plated revolver that hung low on his right hip. The tails of that coat hid the second revolver, on his left hip, but the bulge was obvious, as was the silver buckle on that belt.

He was a tall man, probably an inch or two over six feet, with polished black boots, black woolen pants with gray stripes, and a black vest over a blue shirt. The string tie had been loosened, and he had about two weeks of brown beard stubble over his face. Considering the rugged country separating Silverton and Dead Broke, two weeks would be a right reasonable amount of time to travel by horseback to this fading town.

But people didn't come to Dead Broke these days. They got out of it as quickly as they could.

"Can I treat you to a whiskey, stranger?" Sara asked. "Beer if you'd prefer. Coffee—Logan here brews real good coffee—if it's too early in the day, or our pilsner or our rye."

The man's cold eyes locked on her with a look Sara had seen far too many times. "And what else? That you don't give away for free."

Out of the corner of her eyes, she saw Logan's face tighten, but before he could say something, she laughed.

"A drink is all I'm offering, stranger."

He smiled. "That's too bad." He nodded toward the bar. "I reckon a whiskey would cut the dust."

Since no one was at the bar, Logan pushed back his chair. "Anything in particular?"

"Whiskey's whiskey. As long as it ain't Mex liquor. If I never see or smell tequila or mescal again in this world, it'll be too soon."

Logan walked to the bar, and the stranger rounded the table and took the dealer's seat. "He won't mind," he said, and nodded at the batwing doors. "And I don't like my back to windows or doorways. Like to see who's coming and who's going."

"It's mostly going these days," Sara said.

She was looking at Logan when her face hardened, and she turned back to the stranger.

"You can take your hand off my thigh," she said evenly, "or I can cut it off."

The pressure left, and the man laughed and brought both hands to the table, then lowered his right one so that it rested near the gun with the easiest access.

Logan returned with a glass filled with an amber liquid that almost made Sara's eyes widen. She made her face into a facade, though she wanted to kiss Logan on the mouth. He had brought the special liquor they always served Mayor Nugget—Nugget's own brew—whenever he visited the Crosscut.

But the stranger killed the shot in one swallow, making no face, not even coughing, and licking the moisture off his lips with his tongue.

"Ahhhhh," he said, and turned the empty shot glass over—not a drip slipping out—and set it down on the green felt.

"Well, I guess I shouldn't keep the man waiting. Where's the boss?"

Sara's head tilted. She stared curiously at this man.

"The boss?" Logan asked.

"Your boss," he said. "He sent for me."

"I'm the boss," Sara told him. "I run this place. I own this place."

The man frowned, and stared at the shot glass as though he wanted another. But Sara wasn't giving him anything else on the house. One shot. And that was all he would ever get free here.

"You're the boss?" For once, his eyes showed that there might be a living, breathing human being here.

"Sole proprietor."

His left hand felt the stubble on his face. "I was told to come to the best gambling parlor in Dead Broke." He turned toward Logan. "I don't reckon you sent for me."

"Nope." Ladron tilted his head toward Sara. "Like she said, she runs this place. Owns it. Clear title. And she pays me."

"I'll be . . ." He sighed.

"Didn't the man who sent for you tell you his name?" Sara asked.

The stranger's chuckle came out dry and sarcastic. "Well, I don't go around bandyin' names to strangers."

But, Sara thought, *you sure talk a lot. Too much.*

"The Lucky Dice," Logan said, and Sara caught the recognition in the stranger's eyes before he could return to that facade of his.

"How's that?" He turned back to Logan, but now he had revealed his hand. He spoke too fast, and there was a flicker of nervousness in his countenance. If he were playing poker, Sara figured, he'd be out of money in ten hands. Professional gamblers would take him for all he was worth. She didn't know his business, but those two guns he wore bespoke that he was a man of violence. He sure wasn't a professional gambler.

"It's another place in town." Logan hooked his thumb. "The Lucky Dice Gambling Hall. Take a right turn at the corner, and it's on the next corner. You can't miss it. Two dice are painted on the facade. Snake eyes. Which is fitting." He smiled. "You'd at least get an honest chance here."

He laughed. "Well," he said, patting the pearl handle of the revolver, "I only play sure hands. My own."

"What's the name of the man who owns that place?" Sara asked.

Logan stared at her in disbelief, but quickly realized her play. "Oh," he said, and snapped his finger. "I've got it right . . . It's . . . He's on the town council, right?"

"That sounds right," Sara said. "Is it Casper?"

"Yeah. No. No. His name is Conner. Conner Boyle."

"That's right." She smiled. "Does that name ring a bell, mister?"

He shook his head too fast. "Nah. That name's easy enough to remember."

"Well, his place and mine are about the only large establishments for drinks and cards still going strong, but there are a few smaller places. Mines might be closing, and people leaving, but the gambling and drinking establishments are still making some money."

The man grinned again. "Ain't that always the way of things, lady? Men sure like to drink. Sure like to gamble. Ofttimes, that turns out to help a man of my talents." He winked, sighed, and nodded at Logan Ladron and Sara Cardiff. "And I reckon I ought to find a hotel. Wash up. Is there a good barber in town? I could use a real good shave."

"I think we have two barbers left," Logan said, and pointed the other direction. "Lewallen's the closest. His son can knock the trail dust off that coat, too. And the Hostetler House is a good place, clean rooms, affordable. Two doors down from Lewallen's."

"You been mighty helpful," the man said, and winked lecherously at Sara. "Even if she wasn't as helpful as I'd hoped she might be. But we'll see. She might come around."

"Staying in town long?" Sara asked but did not look up.

"Maybe so. Depends."

They watched him as he walked through the doors and moved toward the horse he had tied to the hitch rail. Neither spoke, not even when Ignacio Tererro opened the door and said dinner was ready if they were hungry.

"I will throw it to the cats and dogs if you two do not come!" he bellowed.

"Give us a minute, Ignacio," Sara said.

Once the horse and rider passed the batwing doors, Logan turned to Sara.

She nodded. "I guess he doesn't need a haircut and shave after all," she said.

"And he might not be giving Henry Hostetler some business, and Lord knows he could use some—like all of us these days."

"Come eat, or it goes to dogs and cats!"

They stood and walked away from the poker table.

"He could have meant Percy Stahl," Sara suggested, but she was just throwing that name out there.

"Percy couldn't afford a hired gun," Logan said.

Sara stopped short, and Logan had to turn around.

"I thought he might be a gunfighter, but not one for hire," she said.

"Cats and dogs, they eat my food!" the cook bellowed.

"And they'll eat you alive if you open your mouth again," Sara barked, still looking at her best dealer.

Logan Ladron sucked in a long breath, which he held a moment before letting out the air.

"Boyle's the only person in town, other than some mine owners, who can afford that killer," Logan said. "And mine owners have no reason to spend money on gunmen. Not with the price of silver today."

"You know him?"

His head shook. "Not by sight, but from what he said—he was sick of Mexican liquor and he had been in Silverton before coming here—I'd bet that imaginary thirty-five thousand dollars I just lost to you that that hombre is Ben Gunderson."

"I've heard that name, but I thought . . ."

Logan was shaking his head. "He's so bad, the Pinkertons won't even look for him. Killed who knows how many men in those range wars in Arizona Territory, then escaped the few lawmen who were bold enough, or dumb enough, to go after him by riding into Mexico. I'd heard he had come up north, though, for some lady of the tenderloin he fancied. I didn't think it was true. Till now."

They started walking before Ignacio lived up to the threat he had made in the alley to dump out the dinner his cook had prepared.

"That doesn't make a lick of sense," Sara told Logan. "Conner Boyle already has Caleb Holden to back any play that piece of filth makes. There might have been a time when Dead Broke was wild and anything went, but not now. No one needs two top guns in this town."

"And there's not many men in Dead Broke these days who are worth killing," Logan said. "Now, don't hold me to what I said. I just think that's Ben Gunderson. The description fits. The way he wears his guns. And the fact that he didn't ride to get shaved and spruced up and to find a room first."

"I still don't like it," Sara said.

Ignacio opened the door for them, and the aroma of his cooking almost made them forget about gunfighters and hired killers.

"There could be a bright side to having Gunderson in Dead Broke," Logan said, waving his arm to let Sara enter the special dining and break room for dealers, bartenders, and saloon girls.

"Such as?" Sara asked as she walked through the door.

"Ben Gunderson and Caleb Holden could shoot each other dead."

She couldn't believe that she laughed at Logan's joke.

CHAPTER 10

Little Joey read:

"'The wind had been blowing dust across the flat plains of the desert town all morning, but stopped, as though time itself was put on hold, when Ben Usher stepped out of the Acme Saloon, his serpentine nature causing him to—'"

"What was that word you jus' read?" Mayor Nugget set aside the jar from which he had been sipping and leaned forward in his chair at the table, peering at the twelve-year-old who sat cross-legged on the carpet. How anyone could sit like that bewildered Nugget. The kid would have a future as one of those—what were they called—consort-shun-ists? He had seen one in the last carnival that came through Dead Broke, back when Dead Broke was richer than most of Colorado. Like their bodies didn't have a bone in 'em.

"What word?" Joey looked irritated, when he had no right to be. Nugget had promised him, as he always did, to pay the boy a dime for reading one of those cheap novels with the fun picture drawings on the cover, and some inside, as well.

"The one you jus' read."

Sighing, Joey looked at the page. "Serpentine?" he asked.

Nugget's head bobbed repeatedly. "That's the one. What's it mean?"

The boy shrugged. "I dunno. The serpent in the Garden of Evil was a snake. I guess it means he was like a snake. A snaky nature?"

Raising the jar to his mouth, Nugget took a healthy swallow, smacked his lips, and wiped his mustache and beard with the sleeve of his free hand. "Snakes. Yeah. That sounds like Ben Usher. Yeah. Snaky nature. He's always been cold-blooded in all 'em storybooks ya reads to me. Snakes. I don't like snakes."

"Who does?" the kid asked, and picked up one of the cheap candies Nugget had used to bribe him.

"That's why I like livin' this high up in these mountains. Hardly ever run across no snakes."

"There are no snakes in Ireland, either," Joey said. "Thanks to Saint Patrick. Dead Broke ain't . . . *isn't* . . . nearly as pretty as Ireland. Did Saint Patrick drive the snakes out of here, too?"

"No. Nobody drove nothin' out of here."

"Well, folks sure are leaving in a hurry now."

"Quit that talk. Serpentine. Snaky nature. All right. I can picture that no-count scoundrel now."

"You don't have to picture it. Here's a picture of him right on the cover." Using his index finger to save his place—because he surely would have hated to have to start reading this over again, and Nugget sure would have made him—he showed the cover of the novel. "That's him holdin' the lady with a knife to her throat, and her petrified, and that's—"

"I know who that is. The clerk at the mercantile tol' me all 'bout it. And you've read me enough 'bout Mick MacMickin'."

"Can I read about him now? I need to get home and do my chores and studying. That schoolmaster . . . he ain't quit—hasn't quit—Dead Broke yet, confound him."

"All right." Nugget set the glass on the edge of his desk. "Keep readin'. It's gettin' good now. You read good."

Shaking his head and whispering something that, to Nugget, did not sound right coming out of a twelve-year-old's mouth, Little Joey Clarke picked up the story, reading the part he had read earlier as fast as he could, then slowing down and losing much of his enthusiasm because a dime didn't buy as much as it once did for a good yarn.

"'. . . his serpentine nature causing him to look down the streets of dust and buildings of whitewashed 'dobe blocks. The sun was to his left, sinking slowly but brightly, and he knew which way to turn. He would have the advantage now, with the sun shining behind him—but first, he had to raise the ante in the most dastardly fashion.

"'Looking across the room, his evil eyes found the beautiful progeny, and, settling his right hand, the glove on it as black as his vest and hat, his heart and soul, on the pearl-handled grips—'"

"Usher had ivory grips in the last book you read me," Nugget informed him.

"Well, he changed six-shooters," the boy snapped. "He had green eyes in that one, too, and they're blue now."

"A pard of mine once told me that he was born with blue eyes, but they changed to hazel right quick."

"Can I finish this story? My ma will tan my hide and then my pa will whup me even harder."

"Go on. Go on. It's gettin' gooder now."

"'. . . pearl-handled grips of his instrument of death.'"

"I bet Mick MacMicking ain't afeared of Ben Usher."

"'He called to the sweet damsel, the lovely virginal beauty he had forced into this evil den of liquor and heartless souls: "Ma'am, now you shall come here, unless you want me to murder your grandmother, and you know I will, for my back is against the wall and I have nowhere to go except the fiery pits," and what could that poor lass do but obey this blackhearted devil, and rise, moving slowly but steadily to the entrance of this evil place.

"'Usher's smile was a sickening aberration'—don't ask me what that means, because I ain't never seen it before and ain't certain I pronounced it right nohow—'as the virginal lass stopped just a few feet before the soulless lieutenant of Lucifer himself.

"'Now the instrument of death left his holster, and the glove of gleaming black leather pulled the hammer to full, deadly cock, yet he did not point the long barrel with its history of murder and blood-spurting butchery at this gift to the Western territories by the God that gave us Martha Washington, Dorothea Madison, Pocahontas and Giuseppina Morlacchi, though none of the angels looking down from the majestic clouds had any doubt that the red-handed, soulless man before her would hesitate to put a bullet in her heart at the slightest resistance.

"'He smiled evilly, and told her, "You will walk in front of me. If you stop before I tell you to stop, if you run, if you trip, you will be killed instantly. We shall go to the stable and to gather the fastest horses to be had, and I will escape Mick MacMicking once more." There was no response, no reply, no protest. There was no need. Ben Usher had spoken, and he had to be obeyed, for justice could be fickle in this lawless, undiscovered country.

"'The door opened. The agonizingly slow march began. All the young girl thought of was, "If I am to be murdered on this day, at least it is a beautiful day, and a beautiful place, to die, and I shall go to my Maker with a conscience as clear as the Arizona Territory sky." Spurs sang out, out of tune and off-key, and she walked. The livery stable looked like a Roman cathedral or a coliseum in Athens, though it was but a squalid sand-colored structure, so common in this parched country. The walk took an eternity, and the young lass grew faint, seeing no movement anywhere in the town. It was as though the entire population had vanished. Her heart pounded, and she feared that her hero might have forsaken her. And then—'"

The door to the office opened.

"Nugget!" Conner Boyle's booming voice drowned out the noise of the door as it struck the wall and bounced back, shuddering.

He walked in, and a tall stranger stopped in the doorway behind him.

Joey Clarke sighed, mostly in relief, when the councilman and owner of this gambling hall came inside, because whenever Conner Boyle barged into the office, it meant that Joey would be sent packing. He wouldn't have to read to the mayor—not that he minded reading. He didn't want all his chums to know, but he liked books, almost as much as he enjoyed playing mumblety-peg with the boys. But if his schoolmates and buddies found out that he really liked to read storybooks, well, he would have to fight them just to regain their trust. But it was a nice day. And he bet his schoolmates were playing soldiers over at the sluice ditch against their parents' orders never to play near that channel.

"Gosh, Conner," Nugget said, "things is gettin' excitin'. Mick MacMickin' is 'bout to face down Ben Usher. I can feel it in my bones."

"Ben Usher. Mick MacMicking." The stranger came inside, laughing, and stuck a cigar in his mouth, pulled a matchstick from the inside pocket of his gray flock coat, and struck it against the buckle on one of the two gun belts he wore. He fired up the cigar and tossed the match onto the floor instead of into the trash can or brass cuspidor.

Nugget frowned at the stranger, but said nothing. The six-shooters the man carried prevented Dead Broke's mayor from saying anything to this man.

The stranger blew a plume of smoke toward the ceiling. "Wanna know why Mick MacMicking has never run across me in one of those five-penny stupid books?"

"Well," Nugget said, putting his hands on his hips, "just who in tarnation is you?"

"You can call me by the name my pap give me. Gunderson. Ben T. Gunderson."

Joey's eyes widened. Nugget stepped back.

"Ben Gunderson from Yuma way?"

The man shrugged. "Ben Gunderson from wherever he wants to be. And right now I be here."

"Get out of here, kid," Conner Boyle told the youngster. "Go play. Go study. Go read. Just go somewhere."

Joey started, but decided he would have a good story to tell his pals if he defied that hardcase Boyle and a top gun like Ben Gunderson—not that they would believe him, although Quinn Byrne might. That boy would believe anything.

"You want me to go, Mister Mayor?" he said, staring up at the stunned Nugget.

"Boy, I can throw you out the window," Boyle said.

Nugget blinked, and seemed to notice Joey for the first time. "Run along, Joey. It'll be fine." He reached down and took the book from the boy's hands, and dogeared the page. "We'll finish this tomorrow after yer schoolin'. I'll read it to you all the way to the finish. It's a crackerjack of an endin'. You'll be . . . amazed."

Amazed if you could read your own name, Joey thought, but he liked Nugget. And Nugget liked Joey's reading. And it paid good wages. Ten cents a day. Just to read something that wasn't in a schoolbook or on a chalkboard.

"All right." He grabbed his bag of schoolbooks and walked toward the door, but the door shut in front of him, slamming hard, and Joey jumped back to look up at the man who called himself Ben Gunderson.

The gunman pushed the tails of his gray coat back, revealing the two revolvers, his hands on both grips, and his knees bent as he sank till he could look Joey into the eyes. Joey had never seen eyes like Ben Gunderson's.

It was like something he had read in one of those

novels he kept reading to Nugget. The eyes were cold, unfeeling, dead. Joey had been born in Dead Broke, where it was too high for snakes. In all his life, he had never seen a rattlesnake. But now he knew what those writers meant when they described a mad-dog gunfighter's eyes. Joey felt his heart pounding, and his mouth went drier than that Arizona desert the writer of the dreadful he had been reading to Nugget described.

"You never saw me, boy. I ain't here." The man's voice was a deadly whisper. "If anyone finds out I'm here. If I hear any mention of my name while I'm in this town. If I even think someone knows I'm here, meeting with these fine, upstanding gentlemen, I will find you. You can't hide from Ben T. Gunderson. Fifteen men have tried, and they're all six feet under. Keep that in mind, boy. Because you'll be number sixteen. Do you understand what I'm tellin' you?"

Joey thought he made his head nod up and down.

But the killer just smiled. It was the most frightening smile Joey had ever seen.

"Say it," he hissed, sounding like the hissing those rattlesnakes made when he was reading to Mayor Nugget.

"I hear you."

The man nodded, then held out his right hand. "Let's shake on it."

He thought this was where he would die, but he stuck out his right hand, saw it shaking like that puppy dog he had seen a few days ago after Arby Scott yelled and screamed at it and shook a stick over its head.

"Mighty fine, boy," Ben Gunderson said, and he

shook the hand hard, but not too hard, then straightened and nodded down at the boy.

"Go play. Or read till you're blind."

Joey was out of the room in an instant.

When the door closed, Gunderson laughed coldly and took another long pull on the cigar, then walked to the mayor. He extended his right hand, keeping his left on the butt of one of his revolvers, and said, "Pleasure to meet you, Mr. Nugget."

Nugget's shake was solid, which surprised the gunfighter. He thought it would be soft like young Joey's. And the man's face was weathered, the eyes rheumy, and maybe a little crazy—no, a lot crazy—but not afraid.

"The reason Mick MacMickin' doesn't run into me in any of them storybooks you're so fond of is simple. MacMickin' . . . or Ben Usher . . . they'd be dead if they met up with me."

He dropped his right hand, and before Nugget could blink twice, the barrel was halving his beard, and the hammer was being cocked.

Nugget froze, and Gunderson laughed.

"If you gentlemen don't mind," Conner Boyle said, "we have some business to discuss."

"My business," Gunderson said, "is death."

But the thumb slowly lowered the hammer, and the revolver came down slowly, expertly, and slid into the holster.

Nugget looked past the gunman, who walked to the window and peered outside, still smoking his cigar.

"I forget, Boyle," he said, staring at the town councilman. "Why'd we send for this hardcase? No offense, Mr. Gunderson, I been a hardcase all my life. But why does we need him? Is he gonna replace Syd Jones as our marshal? I ain't sure how some of our councilmen and especially our council lady is gonna think about that."

Boyle sighed heavily.

"Pour me a brandy if you would, Mr. Mayor," he said. "And I'll explain it to you one more time."

CHAPTER 11

Everybody who had lived in southern Colorado for more than a year knew that it was a five-and-a-half-day ride from Durango to Watson's Station. Duncan MacMicking and Drift Carver made it in a little more than four.

"Remind me not to go on no more rides with you," Carver said as he stiffly, painfully eased his bruised and chaffed backside out of the saddle.

Duncan was already loosening the cinch to his saddle, and, with that done, he took the reins to the sorrel packhorse, leading it and the buckskin on a slow walk over the bridge that crossed an arroyo and about a hundred yards to the adobe railroad station.

"You ain't gonna let 'em hosses drink, is you?" Carver practically shouted as he pulled the roan he had ridden behind him.

"Yes." The horses plunged their noses close to the water and started drinking.

"They'll get colic!"

Duncan scooped up a handful and splashed his sweaty, dirty face, then lifted the canteen from his saddle horn and drank himself.

Wiping his mouth after swallowing, he stared at Carver. "Don't you drink water when you're thirsty?"

"Well . . . I ain't—"

"Any different than a horse," Duncan cut him off. "Let him drink. They've cooled off enough by now." He nodded at the paint horse Carver had ridden. "About half a bucket for starters." He stroked the neck of his buckskin. "You did fine, Sweet Sara. You did fine. Now you'll have a nice long rest in a stock car all the way to Denver."

After the horses drank, Duncan and Carver led them to the shady spot on the side of the station, removing the saddles and setting those and the blankets in the sun, but out of the dust, to dry. Then they walked inside the building.

"G'day to ye," said a cheerful man with a walrus mustache as he lowered the newspaper he was reading. "What might I do for ye?"

"When's the next train to Denver?"

The man pointed a long finger at the far wall, and Duncan looked as he withdrew his watch from the pocket on his britches. "Is it on time?" he asked.

"Last I heard. This line prides itself on being on time."

Duncan reached for his wallet as he walked back to the counter. "Two passengers. Three horses."

"Would the horses like a Pullman sleeper?" The man laughed and slapped his thigh, so Duncan felt obligated to at least show him a grin.

He paid with gold coins, took his change in bills and some change, and asked if there was a place to eat.

"Closest chuck is Walsenberg." He nodded at a pail

atop a shelf behind him. "That's why my missus fixes me something every day I work. I'd offer you some— my missus cooks mighty fine corn bread and ham—but I reckon I was hungry this day."

"That's all right," Duncan said, hearing Carver grumble something unintelligible. "We'll grab something on the train or eat when we reach Denver."

Carver spit into a bucket that served as a spittoon and said, "I knowed I shouldn't never've agreed to fetch you back to Dead Broke. If you ain't ridin' a body to death, you're slowly starvin' him till the wind just blows him to Brazil."

"Not much to do at Watson's Station," the clerk said. He must not have heard Drift Carver, who walked to what looked to be a fancy church pew—even had curved sides and a solid back—and settled into it, stretching his legs across the seat, not even removing his spurs. The wood was already carved with initials and someone's tic-tac-toe game and rowels from too many travelers to count.

The clerk handed Duncan the newspaper. "A passenger southbound left this. It's from Denver. Just two days old."

"I don't want to—"

Chuckling, the clerk slid the newspaper closer. "I done read that dern thing three times already. Don't reckon I missed nothing that I'll regret not learning about. Like I say, ain't much to do here at Watson's Station."

The newspaper wasn't one of the big ones in Denver, and Duncan wasn't in the mood to read anyway, so he started to politely decline the clerk's offer when the man said, "And did I hear your pard correct in saying you're going to Dead Broke?"

"You got ears, old man," Carver sang out.

Duncan frowned. He had long lost the habit of letting people know where he was coming from and where he was heading. It was a rule most gunfighters had, and it worked well for lawmen, too.

But the clerk seemed a friendly enough person. Like he had said, there wasn't much to do in a place like Watson's Station—and a railroad man here didn't have much chance to talk to anyone, but . . . His boot smashed a centipede that crawled from under a brass rail that ran along the side of the counter.

"A shame about what's going on in Dead Broke," the man said.

Shrugging, Duncan said, "Well, it's happening all over the West. Leadville. Silverton. And not just silver mines, from what I've been reading lately."

"You're so right, stranger, you are so right. But Dead Broke—well—page three. It's a shame. It's just a shame. I thought that town had gotten over its wild and rowdy ways."

Duncan took the paper, thanked the man again, and walked to the bench facing the one Drift Carver had stretched out on. Yawning, the old-timer crossed his legs again. The telegraph keys started chiming, and the stationmaster grabbed his notebook and pulled a pencil off the top of his right ear and hurried back to the chair in front of the apparatus.

Sitting down, Duncan opened the four-page broadsheet to the third page. Advertisements covered half the page, and the headlines were small. Some of them were hard to read, because Duncan must have been the fortieth person to have read the paper. One advertisement had been torn out, but the small headline in the middle of the page next to an advertisement for a pharmacist's "Drugs, Patent Medicines, Perfumes, Soaps, Toilet Articles & Other Items of Relief from THE SHERMAN LAW."

MORE DEATH IN DEAD BROKE

Mr. Horace W. Gilpin, prominent owner of the Gilpin & Greene Coal Company of Fort Collins, writes of another shooting in the high country of Dead Broke, where the Dead are beginning to outnumber the Broke—and that is saying a lot in these sad times.

According to Mr. Gilpin, and his story seems to be confirmed by reporting from other newspapers that have reached our office, Mr. Geo. Randall Fanning, former guard for the now defunct Rohling & Binford Mining Company, was gunned down in Percy Stahl's saloon three nights ago after a dispute over a card that Fanning said was palmed.

The offended man, Gunter Benson, suggested to Mr. Fanning that he withdraw the insult, but witnesses said that instead of a withdrawal, Mr. Fanning suggested that the Mr. Benson leave town while he was still among the living. More insults came forthwith, and Fanning, witnesses said, though Mr. Gilpin said he could not say who, drew first as the violence erupted in a flash.

Mr. Fanning's Remington revolver had not

fully escaped the leather holster—and, in fact, when the first bullet hit the poor man in the center of his chest, the .44 slipped back into the leather as Mr. Fanning straightened, turned slightly to his right, and muttered the prophetic statement, "I am killed."

Then he collapsed onto the floor, having breathed out his last with his dying words.

A coroner's inquest ruled that Mr. Fanning died with minimal suffering, and that the shooting had been a clear case of self-defense.

A lesson to all readers that the wages of sin is death. And gambling is a sin.

"Does the name Gunter Benson mean anything to you, Drift?" Duncan asked, after relaying the news to Carver.

"Nope." Carver recrossed his legs. "But I knowed Randy Fannin' well enough. Did you?"

"Can't say I recollect him."

"Good hand with a sawed-off scatter-gun," Carver said. "But not what I'd call greased lightnin' when it come to a short gun. By jacks, I reckon I could outdraw him. But that's a shame. He was a good enough sort." He sighed. "I don't recollect a shootin'—not even a knifin'—in Percy's grog shop in, gosh, four years. Could even be five."

He turned toward Duncan, but Duncan did not even see him.

"What's got into you?" The wiry old man's bones creaked as he swung his legs off the bench and, with a mix of groans and curses, sat up. "You didn't even know Randy Fannin'—least you don't remember him a-tall."

"Gunter Benson," Duncan said.

"And I don't recollect that name."

"It's a handle Ben Gunderson went by a time or two."

Life, or at least curiosity, returned to Drift Carver's eyes. "You ain't foolin'?"

"You ever known me to be fooling?"

Rubbing the back of his hand through his hair, Drift started fingering one of the holes in the brim of his hat. "Ben Gunderson was a long way south of Colorado the last I heard tell of him." He spit at, but was wide left of, the cuspidor and wiped his lips. "Nah. Must be some other Gunter Benson."

"Or the editor, or the writer of the letter, could have made it up," Duncan offered.

"Right. I doubt if a Denver paper would care about some ol' guard of a silver mine got kilt in Dead Broke no more than it'd give a fig if some gent got kilt in San Francisco or Montana Ter'tory. Or it could be just the way it got writ up. Feller named Gunter Benson got into an argument with poor ol' Randy and sent him to his maker. Ain't the first time somethin' like that's happened—in Dead Broke or any town in the West."

"Maybe so," Duncan said, but his eyes returned to the newspaper, and he kept reading page three over and over again—but not the advertisements or the other boring news.

"Ben Gunderson ain't got no business in Dead Broke, Mick," Carver said after a long while. "Nobody's got no business in Dead Broke. So don't go frettin' over this. Probably nothin' but a harebrained editor's idea to get more people to read his rag."

But it was, Duncan knew, the way Ben Gunderson liked to work. And for a man with Gunderson's reputation, and with the speed at which he could draw, cock, and fire a revolver, or just by the look of his hard, deadly eyes, he could intimidate a grand jury, a coroner, and more than a few lawmen. He didn't have to use his real name. He was that quick, that cold, that deadly, and without any conscience.

"You ain't got no business in Dead Broke, neither," Carver said. "It was even bogglin' my mind—what mind I got left—tryin' to figger out how come Nugget and the council sent me to fetch you . . . till I recollected you was more than a mite curious about Miss Sara Cardiff. But even a gal as good-lookin' as the beauty is . . . I still don't know how come—"

"Do you ever shut up?" Duncan said, finally folding the paper and setting it beside him on the bench.

The old scout chuckled.

"Well, now, if I was as young and handsome and famous as you is, I might find myself fancyin' Miz Sara my ownself. But I sure hope you won't ride to Dead Broke from Denver as hard as we rode from Durango to this here train station. It's a lot harder climbin' up to that miserable ol' burg than it is gallopin' from Durango to here. You might have forgetted just how high that town is. And the roads ain't never been good any time of the year. Blocked by mountains of snow in the winter, washed out with the spring melt, and you'll recollect

122   *William W. Johnstone and J.A. Johnstone*

that there ain't no fall and not much of a summer that high, neither."

"Seriously—do you ever shut up?" Duncan groaned.

"Nope. I snore when I sleep."

"I learned that already."

The old man laughed, and soon was snoring.

The northbound to Denver was on time. No passengers got off, and the conductor stared when he saw Duncan and Carver leading the horses to the stock car, getting them loaded, then carrying their saddles and tack to the passenger coach.

The conductor looked at the stationmaster/telegrapher, who chuckled and nodded. "You ain't dreaming, Timmons. I hate to see them go. They's real good listeners."

The coach was far from crowded. One man sat in the last seat, his black head pulled down, and the silver band around the Boss of the Plains caught Duncan's attention. He heard Carver's gripes as he passed empty seats before picking one a few seats in front of the black-hatted hombre, settling his stuff on the seat opposite him, and sitting with his back toward the north.

"My saddle ain't one of 'em fancy ones 'em Englanders use, pard," Drift Carver grumbled. "Had to haul this all the way from the 'dobe station to the stock car to here and all the way down, and when we reach Denver, I'll have to take it all the way back ag'in."

"A little sweat's good for you," Duncan said, without looking away from the black hat.

"Not when you're older than Methuselah." He looked for a spittoon, found nothing, and spit on the floor.

"How long will it take us to get to Denver?" he asked.

But Duncan did not hear. He didn't hear Drift Carver's profanity, or even his snores once the train jerked forward and creakily started north, picking up speed quickly, since there was not much to slow down for at Watson's Station.

Duncan hardly even noticed the conductor as he came by to perforate the train tickets, which he did without comment. Or maybe he had tried to engage Duncan in conversation. It wasn't like Duncan was listening to him. He just focused on the hat.

Before they reached Greenhorn Station, the train rocked a bit, and a long arm with a black glove caught the hat from tumbling off. The man straightened, looked out the window, and then looked forward, his eyes stopping when he saw Duncan.

Stubble covered his face, and the yellow mustache drooped down to his chin. He sat up, pulled the hat tightly over his matted hair, and quickly let his right hand drop out of sight. His left hand then came up and pushed the brim up just a tad.

He smiled, a quick, taut grin that was neither friendly nor menacing. Just a greeting.

Duncan raised his left hand underneath the brim of his hat, and gave a slight wave. He did not smile. Then a boy came by hawking peanuts, and Duncan paid him a nickel, and started eating. The man did not fall back asleep.

But then a man with Dean Hill's reputation as a hired gun wasn't about to go to sleep when Mick MacMicking was on the same train.

He wondered where that man-killer was going. For

the time being, it really wasn't Duncan's business, but the thought kept bouncing through his brain all the way to Denver.

Arizona Territory could still be wild and lawless. Montana was a bit of the same, just like Wyoming. And civilization had never really taken root in Texas, and plenty of outlaws were running wild in the Oklahoma country. But Colorado had tamed itself.

So what would bring Ben Gunderson out of hiding, and be enticing enough for Dean Hill to leave El Paso?

CHAPTER 12

After spending a restful night and enjoying a warm bath in her house on the northeast part of town, Sara dreaded going back to her saloon that morning. Most likely, it would be another week or two before she would get back to her house.

Luckily, she had a comfortable rocking chair and an oversized sofa in her office above her saloon, so she could stretch out whenever she wanted. In fact, she had been sleeping on it the past week or so, with a Greener shotgun in close reach and her four-shot derringer under the pillow.

The riots had become fewer these days, since there was less to burn in Dead Broke, but where anarchy ruled, one never could feel completely safe. She wondered why the Army had not been sent for. From what she had read about riots and upheaval, it was common for the governor to request military help when citizens started acting like animals instead of human beings.

She left the Greener with Logan Ladron and pushed her way through the batwing doors, keeping her right hand in the pocket of the jacket she wore, finding the cold feel of her derringer comforting.

Stopping at the window at Lupino's pawnshop, she saw some nice China porcelain that would make a wonderful birthday present for her mother over in Wilmington, North Carolina, but even though Dante would likely cut her a deal, she knew—in these days— she shouldn't splurge but horde her money. Besides, her mother had too much stuff in her house already. Her mother always said, "Just write me a letter. I don't need no more stuff."

But that vase sure was beautiful.

With a sigh, she moved past the window to the corner of the building, climbed the stairs, opened the door, and entered the meeting room of the Dead Broke City Council.

City? Dead Broke was quickly turning into a town. A ghost town.

She started to close the door, but a voice called out below, "Wait for us."

Recognizing the voice, Sara had the urge to close the door and lock it. But that wouldn't do any good. So she held the door open and waited as the boots clomped up the stairs—they sure were taking their good, sweet time—and watched that coldhearted gunman, who was calling himself Gunter Benson when everyone else in town was saying he was Ben Gunderson, just not to his face or whenever he was close enough to hear even a whisper.

Gunderson walked in without a leer or a smile, the tails of his gray coat pushed back to reveal both of the revolvers. Sara wondered which gun he had used to murder George Randall Fanning, who had always been a pleasant man when he drank or played cards at the

Crosscut. Murder. It was murder, no matter the ruling in the inquest.

Conner Boyle grinned at her but said nothing as he walked into the room. Then Sara closed the door.

"I reckon we gots ourselves a harem," Nugget said, pounding the table with a hammer.

"Quorum," Percy Stahl corrected, but Sara doubted if anyone heard or cared.

"Shut that door, missy," Nugget said, and Sara obliged him and found the seat farthest from Boyle and his hired killer. "I'm callin' this here emergency meetin' of the council to order." The hammer's head got stuck in the table this time, and S.D. Sullivan had to help Nugget pull it out from the wood.

"What's the emergency?" Dylan Pugh asked.

"Well, we ain't got no town lawdog," Nugget said.

Conner Boyle cleared his throat. "No word from our good Mr. Carver."

Percy Stahl cleared his throat. "Well, it's only been a week or so."

"A week in a war can set an army—or a city—back years," Boyle said. "And we are a city in a war."

Sara came right back at him. "We are a town in trouble, and the trouble is something that we did not start. And nor is Dead Broke alone. All of our towns and cities are in trouble. It's the economy. This town, if it is to survive, has to learn how to survive without silver mines."

The hammer pounded again, and this time Sara was relieved that Nugget was demolishing furniture that did not belong to her or the town council.

"And we done got some good i-de-errs," Nugget said

happily. "Percy's bringin' in a bunch of mail-order brides. Ain't that right, Percy?"

Color, what little of it there was, drained from Percy Stahl's face. "I am?" he squeaked.

Now Nugget held the hammer like a gun, waving it under the saloonkeeper's face. "Somebody better have writ down what you said in our last meetin'. You said you'd bring in brides for the remainin' townsmen."

"Just the bachelors, I hope," Dylan Pugh said, chuckling.

"I suggested it—"

"And we approved it," Nugget said. "Like we approved diamond mines and . . ."

"My ice castle," Laurent Dubois sang out.

"His ice castle." Nugget tore off another chuck of wood with the hammer. "It's cloudin' up today. Might get us a couple inches of white stuff. But, Percy, you best get 'em mail-order brides ready to get married."

Percy Stahl looked like he wished he had never been born.

"In the meantime," Conner Boyle said, "there is the matter of keeping the peace in this town. And I have just the candidate."

"You mean killer." The words escaped Sara's mouth before she realized she had vocalized her opinion. But she did not back down. Not even when Ben Gunderson— or whatever name he wanted to use on this particular day—started to rise, putting his gloved hands on the butts of those two holstered revolvers.

"That dead man put a hand on his gun first, missy," the killer said in a cold whisper. "Just like those miners at the inquest said he did."

"With his coat buttoned," Sara said. She even smiled as cold as she could at the crooked gambler and that man-killing friend.

"You weren't there," Gunderson whispered.

"I know. And you were there. Which is why Randy Fanning's wife is now a widow."

"Hey," Nugget said. "That's right. Percy. Maybe you can ask the widow Fannin' if she wants to be a mail-order bride. Shucks, wouldn't cost no postage, neither."

Boyle cleared his throat. "We need to get to the business at hand, my good friends, and we need a new marshal."

"I move," Sara heard herself saying, "that since we have heard no word from Drift Carver, and that he has not been given enough time to travel to Durango and back, that we table any talks of hiring a marshal—as we still have two deputies on the payroll."

"Second," S.D. Sullivan said, which surprised Sara.

"Call for discussion?" Sara said.

"Ain't I supposed to say that?" Nugget said.

"We just wanted to save your voice," Percy Stahl whispered.

All right, Sara thought. *Sullivan and Stahl are on my side. But that will not be enough to stop Boyle from getting his man-killer appointed marshal.*

Dylan Pugh and Doc Cartier did not look comfortable. They might abstain. Pugh had been in Stahl's saloon when the shooting—the *murder*—of George Fanning had happened, and Doc Cartier had examined the corpse. They both had seen just how fast Gunderson was, and how accurate he could shoot.

Another councilman spoke, though, and Sara started to breathe a bit easier.

"It would be embarrassing," Laurent Dubois said softly, "if a man of Marshal Mick MacMicking's reputation journeyed all this way—Durango is not an easy ride from our home—expecting to become marshal of our fine city, only to be told that he had made the ride for nothing."

"Then he should have gotten here quicker," the gunfighter seethed.

"Or sent a telegram," Conner Boyle pointed out.

That got Nugget to laughing so hard he almost fell out of his chair. "Telegram. Now that's funny, Conner. That's the only permanent-like job we have these days. That's the two Brady boys who ride their mules up and down this mountain, fixing the wires that get blowed down, knocked down, or just plumb fall down. Black b'ar took it down yesterday. And when Bill Brady come along, the b'ar almost et Bill Brady. He was treed for four hours, he said, before his brother found him and scared the b'ar back into the woods."

Conner Boyle fumed in silence.

"Newspapers from Cheyenne to Santa Fe would reprint those stories," Pugh said. "Dead Broke would be the laughingstock of the West."

"And," Doc Cartier added, "the next dime novel about Mick MacMicking might carry that story across the nation."

Democracy, Sara thought, could be a wonderful thing.

"I don't reckon it would do us much harm to give Drift a few more days," Nugget said, sighing. "I knows ol' Drift. Don't want his feelin's to gets hurt none. He might even get sore iffen he had to made that ride to Durango and back for nothin'. We can wait a spell."

"And what happens if Drift Carver comes back and tells us that the great Mick MacMicking told him to go drown himself?" Boyle asked.

"I come here by invite," Gunderson said in an icy voice. "I don't wait on nobody. You know I can keep the peace."

Sara had to stop herself from coughing.

"I proved that when I saved this town from getting shot up by that cur dog I killed in Stahl's saloon."

Stahl sank lower in his chair.

The compromise was coming. Sara knew that before the artist Dubois, always trying to keep the peace, made the suggestion.

"Maybe we can appoint Mr. Benson, Mr. Gunter Benson, as special deputy—"

"Chief deputy," Boyle interjected.

"Chief deputy," Dubois agreed.

The nods were slow, but they came. Sara, at the last minute, realized she should add something before this came to a vote.

"But just until we have a new town marshal," she said. She smiled her Southern smile at Boyle and Gunderson. She could do that to people she loathed. She could do that to an animal like Ben Gunderson. That's why she had been so successful playing poker.

"After all, the marshal, as all of Dead Broke's marshals have done, hires the deputies that he wants."

The hammer crashed down again.

"That sounds like a mighty fine plan. Motion carries. We wait a spell. Somebody needs to find a badge for our new deputy. And now we need to get down to more important matters. Percy, tell me what you got in the way of mail-order brides right now."

"How did the council meeting go?" Logan Ladron asked.

Sara was leaning against the bar, holding a glass of Tennessee sour mash in her hand, though she had been standing there for twenty minutes—if the clock was right—and had yet to even wet her lips.

"As well as it could have gone," she whispered.

"I have a hard time believing that." The Crosscut's best dealer put a boot on the brass railing and leaned against the bar, calling out to the bartender, "Same as the lady's, Deke."

He waited till Deke Burnett brought him a glass, then Logan tapped his against her full one and downed about half the whiskey. "I'm not calling you a liar, ma'am," Logan said with a smile, "but I have a hard time believing that the council meeting went 'as well as it could have gone.'"

Sara slid the glass closer to her, but did not lift it from the mahogany. "How's that?"

"Because Ben Gunderson isn't dropping through the gallows." He took another long swallow.

She smiled, even let out a soft laugh.

"In fact, I just saw him walking down Silver Avenue with a shiny tin star pinned to the lapel of his fancy coat."

"It's a deputy's badge," she said, and sighed heavily. "That's the best I could do."

"How long would it take a man on a good horse to get here from Durango?" she asked.

"It would depend on the route," the handsome gambler said. "And it would depend more on the weather. Durango isn't as high as we are, but that's still some rough territory. High mountains. And the roads, where there are roads, are far from easy."

"Duncan would take the train," she said.

"Duncan?"

Now Sara almost drank the whiskey. "That's his first name. Duncan MacMicking."

"I see."

She looked into the gambler's eyes. Yes, she figured, he did see. He saw quite clearly. Looking down at the glass, she pushed it away.

"If he's coming," the dealer said, "he'll be here directly. But there's no train to Dead Broke. And, let's face it, Drift Carver isn't the rider he used to be. The pony express shut down a mighty long time ago."

"I know." Now she drank, just a taste. She did know how to order good whiskey. This was smooth. It wouldn't eat a hole through your stomach and disintegrate your intestines. "He might not come."

"Drift?" he asked.

"Duncan." Now she killed the rest of the glass, which burned its way down her throat.

"He'll come," Logan said quietly, and sipped more of his whiskey.

"Not if Drift mentioned my name," she said, and wished she had another drink. She glanced down the bar, started to wave at the bartender, but stopped herself. "I told him not to."

She realized that Logan Ladron was staring down at her, studying her, sizing her up—even reevaluating her. Sara licked the rest of the whiskey off her tongue, breathed in deeply, and pushed the glass away. One drink was enough. Probably too many.

"I'm just guessing, Miss Cardiff," Logan said, turning formal, "that this is something you don't wish to talk about . . . especially in a place like the Crosscut Saloon."

"I think I've said too much."

"Not to me." He finished his whiskey. "I'm a gambler. A dealer in one of the finest, and most honest, gambling saloons where I've had the pleasure to earn my cut. I don't hear a thing, and I repeat absolutely nothing. I'm more honest than a priest."

She laughed softly. Logan had a way of calming her down. Now he nodded toward his empty poker table, and she left the bar and followed him. He pulled out a chair, and she sat, then watched as he sat next to her—not across from her, not where a fresh deck of cards and stacked chips waited for him to ply his trade, should anyone enter the Crosscut for an honest game of chance—perhaps the only honest game to be found in Dead Broke. Percy Stahl's place might have been a close second, but that was because Stahl's dealers weren't very good at cheating.

"Have you figured out why a man like Ben Gunderson would come to Dead Broke?" he whispered.

She shook her head. "He came because of Conner Boyle. I know that much. Conner wanted to make that man-killer town marshal. And he still might get that job." She felt like crying. "I wish Syd Jones never left town."

"Maybe it's a good thing Syd did vamoose." She stared hard at him, but softened as he explained. "He was drinking too much. You know that better than I do. He had also slowed down. Still brave as the best soldier, still honest. But he's like all of us. We slow down when we get older."

"He could have taken Ben Gunderson any day of the week." Sara heard the words she had said, but realized it was the whiskey talking. Logan was right.

But he said, "Maybe he could have taken Gunderson. Maybe not. But do you think he could have outdrawn Telluride Tom?"

She almost laughed. "What does Telluride Tom have to do . . . ?" The question died. She drew in a deep breath.

"Is that gunman here, too?"

"In the flesh. Rode in an hour ago. He was checking in at my hotel when I was walking over here. And, re-member, I worked in Creede before I left to work for you. I saw Tom many a time. We even shook hands when he was signing the register. No, don't fret. We're not buddies, but we played some poker in Creede."

He lowered his voice to a whisper.

"Dead Broke has been a lot of things over the years, has drawn its share of swindlers and bad men . . . but we've never been known for attracting gunfighters—and it wasn't just because we had Syd Jones as our lawman."

"What's bringing them in now?" Sara whispered.

Logan shook his head.

"Everybody's leaving this town. But gunmen are flocking to it. It doesn't make a lick of sense."

CHAPTER 13

The train reached Denver late at night, and it took a while before railroad hands opened the stock car.

"I ain't much for hotel sleepin'," Drift Carver said above the hissing locomotives, the numbing noise of heavy wheels on iron rails, the curses of workers, and the cacophony of noise in a city the size of Denver even at nine forty-five at night. "Maybe we can camp somewhere off the road west."

Duncan MacMicking threw his saddle on the back of his horse. "We're not leaving Denver just yet," he said.

"Well, I reckon I could eat. Ain't had nothin' more'n peanuts all day."

"We'll eat later." Duncan worked the latigo, got the saddle tight.

Carver didn't say another word, just focused on getting his saddle and bridle on, then took the lead rope to the extra horse and pulled himself into the saddle. Duncan walked his horse away from the tracks before cinching the saddle on once more, then mounted. He rode away from the bustling railroad station and stopped at a busy intersection, where Carver pulled up beside him.

"You ain't got no idea where he is," Carver said over the pounding of boots on boardwalks and dirt, from late-night drinkers, the squeaking of wheels of freight wagons, and, behind them, the screeching of locomotives. "You don't even know certain-sure that Syd Jones is still in Denver. He coulda hopped a freight east or west, north or south."

"If Syd's here," Duncan said, "we'll find him."

"This ain't Durango, Mick, and it ain't Dead Broke," Carver said. "They's more than a hundred thousand people livin' here these days, you dern fool. It'd take us a month of Sundays times forty to find Syd—and that's if Syd wants hisself to be found. You's needed in Dead Broke, son. You's—"

Duncan's stare silenced the old-timer.

Some miners, singing a song in some language that sounded like it came from Eastern Europe, crossed the street, which stopped the traffic long enough for Duncan to turn right, and Carver followed, pulling the sorrel behind him. For the first two blocks, there wasn't room for the two men to ride side by side, but the traffic became more manageable as they moved farther away from the railroad, and when Duncan turned left, they found themselves away from the gas streetlamps and in a part of Denver where, as the saying went, "anything goes."

Duncan pointed to his left, and Carver understood. He eased his horse closer to that side of the street and kept his horse at a slow walk, looking through the windows in the buildings that had windows, and through the open doorways. Duncan did the same on the right side of the street.

Sometimes, they would rein up, dismount—keeping a tight grip on the reins and, in Carver's case, the lead rope to the packhorse—step on the boardwalk, or what passed for a boardwalk, and look inside a saloon. Some saloons they didn't bother investigating. Too high-toned, even in this part of town. Duncan barely glanced at the houses of ill repute, though Carver sighed when he passed a fetching woman who looked like she would be enjoyable company.

"He could be in jail," Carver said after they finished their third block.

"Possibility," Duncan agreed. "We'll be at the city jail in a couple of blocks. We'll check then."

"They moved to a bigger jail," Carver said, pointing northeast. "It's over thataway."

Duncan looked in that direction. "Well, we'll get there at some point."

"And the law could have run him out of town. Folks complained too much, so the law got better at enforcing the vagrancy laws."

"Sign of progress, I guess." Looking left, then right, Duncan decided to try the right side first.

"We could split up," Carver said, keeping his horse from following its master. "Cover more ground."

"Then we'd spend an eternity trying to find each other. Come along."

Around eleven o'clock, they stopped at a café, where business was slow. Duncan hobbled his horse and let him drink, while Carver grunted as he secured his horse and the packhorse.

"I'm glad your belly is human," Carver said, and followed Duncan through the open doorway.

They sat at a table, and when the Mexican waitress came by, Duncan ordered coffee and hotcakes.

"Our hotcakes are what we are known for," she told him.

Duncan smiled. "I saw that on your sign out front."

"I hope you will be satisfied," she said, and looked at Carver.

"The same. Coffee to drink unless you happen to have some good whis—"

"Coffee's all you need."

Carver mumbled something unintelligible and the waitress smiled and ambled back toward the door that led to the kitchen.

"You ain't human," the old scout said when the waitress had disappeared.

"I need you sober," Duncan said. "Till we find Syd."

"Like I said, you ain't human. I might never taste another drop of whiskey 'fore I croak, and it'll be yer fault." The waitress returned with two steaming mugs of coffee and set them before the two tired travelers, gave them both a smile, and politely asked if they needed anything else before she brought their late supper, early breakfast, or whatever they wanted to call it.

Carver just stared grumpily at the coffee mug as Duncan thanked the waitress but said they would just wait for their food.

The meal lived up to its reputation. The hotcakes were huge, with mountains of butter melting atop them and excellent maple syrup. That, for the moment, silenced Drift Carver's complaints. The coffee was mighty fine, too.

"Your chef is a fine cook," Duncan said when the waitress returned to top off their coffees.

Wiping his mouth with his sleeve, Carver somehow managed to swallow the load in his mouth and nodded his compliments. "Yes'm," he said, pushing his cup closer to the steaming pot. "Yes'm. Don't know if I ever et nothin' this good."

She laughed. "You're just tired and hungry."

"I reckon that's true on both 'counts, ma'am, but it's still some mighty good eatin'."

"I'll be sure to tell my husband," she said, and turned back to Duncan. "Would you gentlemen care for anything else? We have pecan pie for dessert." Her smile widened. "That's my cooking. Raymond does what he does best, which is frying, charring, and broiling, but when it comes to sweets, he leaves all of that to me."

Duncan started, "Well, thank you but . . ." When he saw Carver's face, he grinned a bit and said, "I guess my partner has room for some pie."

"You ain't the devil's right hand after all," Carver mumbled when the woman left.

She returned quickly with a thick slice of pie and slid it in front of the old-timer.

"Anything else?" she asked.

"No, ma—" Carver began, but Duncan interrupted him.

"There is something you might be able to help us with, ma'am," he said.

Carver's only movement once he looked across the table was his jaws working on the pie.

"We're looking for a friend."

The woman's face tightened.

"Honest." Duncan gave her his best smile. "And the friend we're looking for loves pancakes better than anything."

Carver swallowed. "This side of whisk—" Stopping himself, he wiped his mouth with his sleeve again, and went back to eating.

"He's an old man. Bit of a paunch now." Duncan's grin widened. "Like most of us these days. In his sixties, hair silver. Big mustache." He looked across the table. "That's still the case, isn't it, Drift?"

A nod was all that came from the old scout as he cut a spoonful of pie and shoveled it into his mouth.

"I haven't seen him in a . . ." Duncan sighed. "A year and a half, I guess. Not quite six feet tall. Carries himself well, but he has been partial to ardent spirits."

"That describes a lot of people on this side of Denver," the woman said, her tone not cold, but far from the friendliness she had displayed earlier.

But that was something Duncan had expected.

"He's a good man," he said. "One of the best I've known. And he helped me find my path when I was heading for the devil's doorway. I feel . . . I *am* . . . obligated to do for him what he did for me some years back."

"If I could help you, mister, I would," she said, but did not walk away.

"He eats more pancakes than my pard here does. But at least he tastes what's in his mouth before it falls into his stomach."

"What's his name?" she asked.

"He'd be too prideful to give his real name," Duncan whispered. "But you'd remember him, even when he's almost at rock bottom. He'd work for a meal. Especially for your pancakes. He'd give you honest work. He'd eat his pancakes. He'd thank you, kindly. He'd tip his hat—if he still had his hat—and he'd carry himself out of this place—"

"Straight to the nearest keg of whiskey," Carver said, picked up his plate, and licked it, to the woman's astonishment, then set it on the table and, once more, wiped his mouth with his sleeve.

"Does your missing friend know what a napkin's for?" the woman said, still staring at Carver.

Duncan grinned. "He did the last time I saw him. And I don't think that's something he'd forget—no matter how much John Barleycorn he consumed."

She sighed. "There's a man who has been here three-four times. I'm guessing that's the man you're describing. Could be." She shrugged. "I can't say for sure."

Duncan breathed easier. "When's the last time he was here?"

She shrugged. "Two days ago, I think. Yeah, it was just two days ago." She sighed. "He was a mess. Worst I've seen him, but we fed him. I'm kinda like that. Mothering some folks, though he's old enough to be my grandpa. But he ate all that I could feed him, and then he insisted on working off his pay, but he did more work than I'd charge for all that he ate."

"How often does he usually come back?" Duncan inquired.

She sighed and shook her head sadly. "Whenever he has to eat. That'd be my guess."

"I don't guess you'd have any notion where he'd be staying," Duncan said softly.

"If he ain't vamoosed for Fort Collins or . . ." Carver couldn't stop his belch. "Parts unknown."

Her head shook. "I can't say for certain, but there was a stink to him."

There was a stink to Drift Carver, too, Duncan thought, and after riding horseback from Durango to Watson's Station, and washing up in horse troughs, there was a stink to Duncan right now.

"Fish," she said emphatically.

Duncan met her stare.

"Fish guts."

Carver burped, but remembered enough manners to beg his pardon.

"Walsh Kleghorn gets fish all the time," she said. "There's a good place on Lawrence Street, too. Papers in this city is always bragging about the fresh fish. Fresh trout. Lord, how I love fresh fish—but it just don't set well in my stomach, and my husband—that's my cook, I think I might have tol' y'all that, but maybe I didn't. Anyway, he never cared for fish, but he come from Kansas, so he growed up eating nothin' good."

Duncan waited patiently. Over the years he had learned that a good lawman didn't interrupt a person talking, because you didn't want to stop the flow, and you never knew what a man or a woman might say. Besides, his mother would slap him hard if he interrupted one of his elders, and, my word, how many times he had to listen to his aunt Rachel talk her head off about absolutely nothing. She had bored him so much, he'd had to dig his fingernails in his palms to keep from falling asleep.

"But that's not where I'd look if I were you," she said

at last. "I'd go down to Glasson's on Larimer Street. He gets his fish that don't sell from Frates. Yes, sir, I'd say that old fellow you's looking for reminds me of Frates's fish. Not day-old fish. Maybe week-old fish. Not trout. But fish that somehow gets into the irrigation ditches."

She punctuated her last word with a sharp nod of her head, and stared hard at Duncan, then Carver.

"You've been very helpful." Duncan pulled some coins out of his vest pocket, and stacked them on the table near his cup. "Very helpful. My partner and I thank you for the information—but mostly for the excellent supper. I haven't tasted anything that good in some time."

"It's now Thursday," she said. "The fish comes in usually on Thursdays. Which means that ol' man'll likely be workin' either at Frates's market or Glasson's eatery. Jus' follow your nose down Larimer to the stink of old fish. If he's still in Denver, I expect you'll find that feller you want there."

Duncan laid another coin on the table, then pushed his chair back. He didn't have to look at Carver, who slurped down the last of the coffee and found his hat.

"Y'all come back," she called to them as they walked out the door.

CHAPTER 14

After tending the horses and then making a trip to the privy, it took another ten minutes or so to get to Larimer, which swarmed with pedestrians, hacks, barkers, drunks and policemen. Duncan wondered if anyone in Denver ever slept.

The odor of fish reached them above the smell of tobacco smoke and horse apples about the same time Carver pointed to the sign on the left side of the street.

Fred Frates Fish, Poltry & Eggs

Spelling, apparently, was not the merchant's best quality. And from the foul odor, the woman at the restaurant had not been exaggerating.

The hitch rails were full, so Duncan dismounted and handed the reins to Carver. "I'll check this out," Duncan said.

"Fine with me." The old scout took the reins, then kicked his horse toward the nearest alley, just to keep some city copper from yelling at him to quit blocking the traffic.

Frates wasn't in, but a thick-necked, bald-headed

man in a stinking apron stained with blood and guts listened to Duncan's query, then wiped his hands on the messy apron and said, "I sell fish, mister, not information."

With a smile, Duncan pushed back the tail of his coat, revealing the holstered revolver.

The man lowered his hands and stepped back. "There's a law in this city, mack, that says you can't go 'round with no firearm. We're civilized here."

From what Duncan had seen, "civilized" was not the word he would use to describe this city.

"Now you get your gun and your carcass or I'll call the law, Mister Gunfighter."

Duncan's hands moved like lightning, wrapping around the filthy apron and jerking the man to him.

A heavyset woman, maybe in her forties or fifties, with her hair in a bun, gasped and dropped her pocketbook a few feet away, then stood frozen like a statue.

"You're talking to the law, mister," Duncan said, hearing the crowd inside the wretched little place fall into a hushed quiet. "And the name's not Gunfighter. It's MacMicking. Mick MacMicking."

He had never liked that handle. The alliteration sounded silly to him. That's why his friends knew to call him Duncan, and those who weren't his pals called him Mister . . . or Sheriff/Marshal/Constable/Chief/Deputy—whatever it said on the badge. Of course, right now he had no title, but that name, as much as he never cared for it, carried a lot of weight anywhere in the Western states and territories.

The man's face paled underneath the beads of sweat. Duncan shoved him against a tub of fish on ice, or what had been ice, but now had melted into stinking water.

"That old guzzler already got paid off. I sent him to Glasson's place." He nodded. "Block and a half down."

"I appreciate your cooperative nature." Once Duncan released his grip, the man staggered back, and almost sank to the disgusting floor.

Duncan let the tail of his coat cover his pistol, then he bent down and retrieved the terrified woman's pocketbook from the muck and grime covering the floor. He untied his bandanna, and cleaned the leather as best as he could, let the rag fall to the floor, and held it out toward the woman.

"Sorry to have frightened you, ma'am, but some people just don't respect the law."

"Th-th-th-thank . . . y-you," she managed to say, and took her pocketbook with trembling hands.

Touching the brim of his hat and giving her a gentle smile, he let his features turn to ice again. The men and women gave him a wide berth as he passed them, stepping outside and breathing in air that was far from fresh, but a relief to his nostrils when he moved away from the rotting stink of Frates's squalid market.

When he reached the alley where Carver waited with the horse, he nodded down the boardwalk. "I'm going to check Glasson's." He could see it from here, on the other side of the street.

"Want me to come?"

Duncan's head shook. "Better not." The congestion of the street made Duncan uncomfortable, and he could see the nervousness of the three horses. He had forgotten just how large Denver had grown. "I'll be back— with Syd if I'm lucky. Stay here, out of the way."

He drew in a long breath, and slowly let it out, before

pulling his hat down tighter on his head and stepping into the street. He let one carriage pass, then a hack, and stepped quickly before a couple of drunken riders closed in, dodged a weaving fat man whose breath could have left a weaker person drunker than a skunk, nodded at a prostitute but did not answer her calls, and found the relative safety of the boardwalk.

There was a loud fight going on at the first squalid saloon he passed, and he held his breath when he walked by the opium den. He was sweating. He remembered when that dime novelist had invited him to New York City, and, being young and impressionable, he had accepted. The novelist wanted to introduce him to a publisher and a playwright. After all, Buffalo Bill Cody and others had taken to theatrical stages back in the 1870s—before Colonel Cody established his Wild West exhibitions and earned himself a veritable fortune—which, knowing Cody, he had blown ten times over.

New York was even bigger than Denver. It had been sprawling, filled with more people than he could imagine. But it wasn't as bad as Denver. Mainly because, he began to realize, New York was populated by Europeans and Easterners. Underneath all that heat and all that humanity and more languages than Duncan could ever imagine, there was a sense of law and order. A feeling of civilization.

Denver was in the West, and the West would always be wild, unruly, untamed.

He saw the sign at Glasson's, located between two more saloons, and he opened the door and stepped in.

The aroma of fish frying reached him, sickened

him, and he removed his hat and looked at the tables. The café was quiet. Two miners sat forking food into their bearded faces.

A waitress stepped out of the kitchen and smiled.

"Anywhere you want to sit, mister . . . as long as it ain't taken already." She giggled at her humor.

Duncan nodded, but walked toward her, and watched her lips turn downward into a frown.

"I'm looking for the older man who brings your fish." He raised his hand to Syd Jones's height. "Frates said he sent him over here earlier."

Frates wasn't the louse he had threatened, but it was a name that the woman would likely recognize.

She did, and she smiled. "You mean Mr. Syd." Her bobbing head made Duncan's heartbeat increase. "He's a sweet ol' man, mister. I jus' love him to death. He's right good at gettin' all 'em nasty scales off 'em stinkin' fish. And he don't want nothin' but a few nickels or dimes for his work. Ask me, he's worth a lot more than Mr. Glasson pays him."

"Is he still here?" he asked, unable to hide the pleading.

She sighed, and Duncan's heart slowed.

"No. I'm sorry. He didn't even want nothin' to eat. Usually I'll bring him a plate. He don't eat like he should. Can I fix you a plate of fried fish or somethin' else?" Her tone seemed to suggest that the "somethin' else" would be her recommendation.

"No, thank you," he heard himself say. If he never smelled fish, cooked or raw, in another fifty years, he would consider himself blessed. "Any idea where I might find him?"

"Hey!" one of the miners bellowed. "Our coffee cups

are empty. And we need something to wash this lousy grub you serve to our bellies."

That heavy breath came out again, and her head shook sadly. "I don't even think he has a home, mister," she said, ignoring the belligerent miner. "Maybe he sleeps in the railyard. Lots of bums do, but he never struck me as no bum. Maybe he goes to a livery. Lots of them stablemen will let folks sleep there for a nickel or a dime, or if they'll muck some stall or somethin'. But I don't know." She must have read the disappointment in Duncan's face. "Well, the first place he'd stop would be . . ."

"Hey, gal, is you de'f or just hardheaded?" the miner yelled.

The man sitting across from him laughed.

"Knowing him," she said with another sigh, and hooked a thumb toward the saloon to her right, toward where he had left Carver and the horses, "that's where I'd look first. But for what he got from my boss and Mr. Frates, I don't reckon he'd still be there."

Chair legs scraped on the wooden floor, and Duncan looked away from the woman to see the loudmouthed miner stand, putting his hands on both hips.

"We are thirsty."

"Joe," the miner's partner said in a quieter voice, "sit down."

"I ain't afeared of that tinhorn. And when I want my coffee, I want it now."

"I'll be with you," the waitress said, "in a minute." She gave Duncan a pleading look. "I don't know where he'd be."

She turned toward the heavy steps that Duncan already

heard. "Let me get my coffeepot," she said hurriedly. "I'm comin' right over, mister."

The man was already there, and he grabbed her roughly by her left arm and jerked her toward him.

"When I say come give me somethin', you come a-runnin' . . . so now I gotta beat some sense into you so you won't forget the next time I come in here."

Duncan turned. The miner's partner was shaking his head and staring at his plate.

"You're not coming in here again, mister." The words came out of Duncan's mouth like frost on a winter day.

The big man released his grip and stared at Duncan, first as though he had misheard, and then smiling at the prospect of a fight.

"You've worn out your welcome," Duncan said. "And there's one thing I will not abide, and that is the mistreatment of a lady."

"A lady," the big man roared, and laughed. "There ain't no ladies on this part of town, buster. And I do whatever I please, and right now what pleases me is stompin' you till there ain't nothing left of you but spittle."

The man lunged for him, but Duncan easily side-stepped the giant and watched him stop himself at a table, which he overturned, taking a chair with it. Cursing savagely, the big man pushed himself away, barely keeping his balance, and swung a haymaker as he spun around, hitting nothing but air and spinning past Duncan. When the miner stopped and turned back, Duncan had the Schofield in his hand, but he twisted it around and brought the butt down hard on the top of the giant's head.

Yelling in agony, the miner dropped to his knees. Both hands came to the top of his head, and blood oozed between his fingers. His eyes rose, and he tried to do the same, but when the cold barrel rested on the bridge of his nose, he stopped and stared, his eyes crossed, and sweat beads popped between the river of blood that came down between his eyes and over his nose.

"Apologize to the lady," Duncan whispered.

The man started to bawl like an infant.

His partner laughed, and Duncan managed to get a glimpse of him as he dragged the ruffian's plate toward him and started spooning what the bleeding miner had left into his mouth.

"You done it again, pard," the man said as he chewed. "I coulda told you not to mess with that hombre." He dragged the man's cup toward him. "Shucks, you got a quarter cup of coffee left, but I don't reckon you're thirsty or hungry no more." He slurped the liquid, chuckling at his pard's misfortune.

"The lady," Duncan whispered, "is waiting for that apology."

"I . . ." The man snorted up some snot, swallowed, and turned his head in the general direction of the waitress. "Beggin' yer pardon, ma'am." His face kept turning paler. "I didn't . . . mean . . . nothin' . . . and . . . I be . . . real . . . sorry."

"Thank you," she said, but she was staring at Duncan.

Holstering the revolver, he nodded, then reached into

the inside pocket of his coat and pulled out a few paper notes, which he gave the waitress.

"That's for their meals," he said, nodding at the miner still at the table. "And for your kindness and all your help."

Outside on the boardwalk, he straightened his hat and let out a heavy sigh.

Drift Carver was right. It could take an eternity to find Syd Jones. The street was just as busy as before, but the boardwalk traffic had lessened. He thought about the saloon on the other side of Glasson's, but didn't think it was worth entering.

Then Syd Jones's voice came back loud and clear in his mind.

Leave no stone unturned, kid. Because you don't know what you'll find till you look.

He moved down the boardwalk, put his hands atop the batwing doors, and looked inside. Four men at the bar, too fat or too skinny and all of them too sober to be Syd Jones. Then he moved to the first saloon, looking inside again. It was busier, but far from crowded. He thought about stepping inside and having himself a snort. Duncan could use a shot of rye right about now, but that would be a waste of time and money.

Backing away, he moved down to the next crossing and looked across Larimer Street at the alley.

Then he swore.

Drift Carver wasn't in the alley where Duncan had left him. Nor were the three horses.

First he turned around, staring at the hitch rails, thinking maybe a Denver policeman had sent Carver and the horses out of the alley. He stepped onto the street, looking on his left side, then on his right, stepping out of the way of a passing hackney and just missing getting himself trampled by a rider on a buckskin horse.

He looked at the horses tethered on that side of the street and found no signs of the old scout or the three horses.

Swearing, Duncan spun around. "Carver!" he bellowed. "Drift Carver!"

People looked at him as though he was just another drunk in Denver or another crazy man.

Gathering his composure, he stepped back toward Glasson's, reaching the safety of the boardwalk.

Now, he thought, *I could really use a bracer.*

Then came a commotion about two blocks up Larimer Street.

CHAPTER 15

Syd Jones remembered it all so clearly.

Clementine. That tough little copper camp in New Mexico Territory, high in the mountains just four hops and ten jumps from Arizona country. That saloon where Grit Tankersley had entered. At least, that was the outlaw's horse. Well, not Tankersley's horse, but the buckskin stallion he had taken from Dick Mitchell, after he had practically blown Dick's head off with Dick's sawed-off Parker shotgun. That was after he had put Dick on the dirt with a .44 slug in the leg.

Dick Mitchell had been trying to stop Tankersley from stealing his best horse. Then, according to Mrs. Mitchell and her five-year-old boy, Tankersley had walked toward the man, letting the stallion trail him as he kept one hand on the reins and his right one on the big Dragoon Colt, cocked. He eyed the woman and boy, but they weren't any trouble. The woman was bawling and praying, and the kid was white as the clouds overhead and not even as threatening as those fluffy white clouds.

Holstering the Colt, he picked up the dropped scatter-gun, blew sand and dried glass out away from the hammers, and pulled both of them back with menacing clicks. Then he looked across the ranch yard and nodded at the wife and son.

"Your man says he's sorry to have to leave you all of a sudden, but that's the way things happen in this lawless country." He brought the stock to his shoulder, aimed, laughed, and pulled both barrels.

The woman fainted. The boy screamed.

Tankersley pitched the smoking shotgun onto what was left of the dead rancher. He had picked the right horse. The buckskin hadn't even flinched at the thundering report of the twelve gauge. Swinging into the saddle, he laughed as he rode away.

That's how the boy remembered it. And the mother, the wife, the widow remembered it that way, too—up to the point when she fell into unconsciousness.

Yeah, the stallion wore the Mitchell brand all right.

Jones stepped onto the boardwalk and put his left hand on the top of one of the batwing doors. The tinny noise of an out-of-tune organ could hardly be heard over the profanity and laughter, the noise of glass on wood, of liquor and beer splashing into shot glasses and mugs, the spinning of a roulette wheel. But there he was. Jones could make him out clearly. Tankersley standing with the shotgun in his left hand, barrel pointed at the sawdust on the floor. Bold as brass. Drinking whiskey between a man in a white porkpie hat and a redheaded gal wearing a flimsy outfit and shoes that didn't match.

Sucking in a deep breath that was more tobacco smoke than oxygen, Syd Jones pushed himself through the door and took about ten paces forward before he stopped, confused and . . . unarmed.

That's when he knew that he desperately needed a drink. His throat was raw. His hands started shaking. There was no Tankersley standing at the bar. Tankersley was dead. Syd Jones had shot him down a dozen years ago, though he still felt the .41-caliber slug rolling around across the left thigh bone. The drunken sot of a doctor hadn't been able to get the bullet out. Folks thought Syd would die of blood poisoning, but as he soon started pointing out, alcohol could cure most anything.

A hard hand pushed him from behind and he felt himself stumbling forward toward a card game. If it hadn't been for the fat blonde with a painted face, he would have crashed into the table. He almost took her with him, but she was a big woman and happened to turn around to see him stumbling wildly. She stepped forward and caught him.

"Watch out, sugar," she said, then stepped around him and cursed the mule skinner who was making his way to the bar. The big, rough man just gave her a wave of annoyance.

"He was blocking the way, and I'm in a hurry to get good and drunk."

She cursed him some more, but the man probably didn't hear a word.

"How about buyin' me a drink." The big woman smiled up at Syd. The sentence did not sound like a question. It was more like an order. But then the woman's face changed, and she drew in a deep breath and exhaled.

"No," she said. "I don't reckon you got enough coins on you to buy me that fine wine Harry stocks on his backbar. Ain't I right, sugar?"

Syd Jones felt his fingers dipping into the deep pockets of his filthy britches. He had six bits. He remembered getting paid, a whole dollar, but he had already spent two bits at his first stop. What had happened to the rest of his money? He turned around so fast the woman took a step back in surprise, and Jones looked for the mule skinner who must have picked his pocket. But he couldn't remember now what that rough-hewn character looked like.

Maybe . . .

He looked again at the woman. No, she hadn't stolen his change. She gave him a pitying look.

"Listen, old-timer," she said, and pointed toward the bar. "Harold doesn't give nobody no free drinks. He's such a skinflint, he don't even put peanuts or crackers on the bar. The beer's mostly stale and the liquor will burn away your ulcers and whatever it is that lines your stomach. So don't go over and try to ask for a free drink, and don't try to steal nobody's glass when he ain't looking, because all it will get you is a busted head and you'll get tossed headfirst into the street. And the streets is always busy around here. You don't want to get trampled by some surrey or freight wagon. Go somewhere else, buster."

He hardly heard a word she said.

She shook her head, looked at her drink, killed what was left, and set it on the table. Then another man came over, grabbed her fat arm, and led her away.

Syd Jones stared at the glass, wetting his lips, feeling

the beginning of the shakes. Another person pushed him aside, and then something crashed near the bar. He didn't look for a long while, for he was busy trying to remember where he might have put the six bits he had left, or had he already spent it? He just couldn't seem to clear his head.

Then he realized that everyone in the bar had turned mute. More than a few were moving out of the saloon, through the doorway, onto the boardwalk. Even the fat woman and the man with her hurried out.

Syd Jones turned around and saw another man in the center of the bar, holding a double-barreled shotgun.

"I'm gonna blow your head clean off, hoss," the man said. The barrels were resting underneath the chin of the man the fat woman had identified as Harold.

Harold's face was white as fresh snow.

There was about three feet of clear space on either side of the man holding the shotgun and the frightened beer-pourer.

That's when Syd Jones remembered Tankersley.

"Pardon me," he whispered, touching the shoulder of a man who had risen from his chair and was putting his right hand on the butt of a Smith & Wesson in his coat pocket. The man gasped and turned, releasing his grip on the pocket revolver.

It was such a puny thing, Jones didn't know if it was worth taking, but he reached for the .32 and the man made no attempt to keep the weapon. "I'm borrowing this from you," Jones heard himself say, and he quietly thumbed back the hammer and walked toward the fellow with the shotgun against the bartender's throat.

"Tankersley!" he called out.

The people behind him began rushing out of the saloon. The bartender's eyes widened and his face turned even paler.

The three feet of space surrounding the man holding the shotgun grew substantially wider.

"Don't . . . mis-ter . . ." The bartender's voice squeaked in fear of what might happen next.

The man with the shotgun turned around suddenly, and the barman dropped behind the bar.

By that point, people were diving to the floor, covering their heads with their arms, or curling up into balls.

The man brought the shotgun to his shoulder, just like Tankersley had done all those years ago.

"If that finger twitches, you're a dead man," Jones said, and he kept walking.

The man's jaw lowered. His eyes revealed confusion.

Syd Jones kept walking, his left hand free, the right still holding the Smith & Wesson, but the barrel remained pointing at the sawdust on the floor. He had to step over two shivering figures, but he never stopped looking right into the bearded man's eyes.

Then he was right before him, and Jones's left hand flashed upward, grasped the shotgun and jerked it toward the ceiling. A finger touched one of the triggers, and the gun roared, spitting out flame, smoke, and deer shot that blew a hole through the ceiling. Jones felt the heat from the blast and smelled the acrid odor of gun smoke. The man fell against the bar, and Jones jerked the shotgun from his hand while bringing the pocket revolver up and swinging it across. The cylinder struck the big man hard on the head, above the ear, and he crumpled to the floor, knocking over a spittoon, the dark contents pooling around his head.

Jones spun around. Tankersley might have friends here. But no one moved.

Tankersley, he then remembered, was dead. Had been dead for years.

He looked at the unconscious drunk. This wasn't New Mexico Territory. The shotgun wasn't a Parker. Syd Jones wasn't a lawman. Not anymore. He opened the breech of the shotgun and pulled out the unfired shell, dropped it into his pocket, and laid the hot twelve-gauge on the bar.

"Get up," he said with authority, and waited for the bartender—the skinflint who ran this joint—to stand shakily behind the bar.

The man's face was pale as a bedsheet—a clean bedsheet in a fine hotel. He looked around and must have seen people staring at the floor, so he inched closer and peered over the bar. He probably couldn't see much more than the drunken idiot's legs and boots, but he wet his lips and wiped the sweat and fear off his face, having more success getting rid of the sweat, and his lips quivered before he could whisper.

"Is he dead?"

"No." Jones laid the Smith & Wesson on the bar.

Now the batwing doors began squeaking as men began to venture inside. In the mirror behind the back-bar, Jones did not see the fat woman. And the adventurers who returned to this pigsty were far outnumbered by the ones who had no intention of coming back inside—tonight, and probably never again.

"Y-y-y-you . . ." the bartender stuttered. "Y-you . . .

You . . . I-I-I-I . . . j-ust . . . c-can't . . . th-thank . . . You . . . You s-s-saved . . .my . . . my . . .my . . ."

"Forget it." Jones remembered the shotgun shell, fished it out. What had he been thinking? He had no twelve-gauge. He set the unfired shell on the bar, too. "It's what I get . . ."

Paid. *Paid?* He wasn't a lawman anymore. Syd Jones wasn't shooting down Tankersley in some mining camp that no longer existed. He didn't even know why he had come inside this miserable saloon.

But that reason quickly returned when the bartender reached underneath the bar and came up with a bottle of brandy. The frightened man didn't even find a snifter, but pulled out the cork with his teeth and spit it onto the bar, where it bounced twice, then rolled toward the edge. He drank greedily, coughed, wiped his mouth and mustache with his sleeve, and looked again at Jones.

"I can't thank you enough, mister." The bartender lowered the brandy, and looked off to Syd Jones's right. The whiskey had cured his stuttering. "Someone go fetch a copper." Again he moved closer to the bar and peered over.

"You sure he ain't dead?"

"He's breathing," Jones answered without looking. Now his eyes locked on the bottle of brandy.

"Oh." The man finally noticed. "Here." He held the bottle out. "Let me get you a glass."

Jones felt the warmth of the bottle. His heartbeat quickened. Funny. He had been calm as a newborn when he was walking right toward that twelve-gauge, and now he thought he might start shaking so hard he would drop the bottle, watch the glass break and send that precious brandy through the cracks in the floor before he even took a sip of what he really needed. The very reason he had entered this rawhide place.

This time, however, he didn't have to beg or empty spittoons to get a snort. More than a snort. That brandy bottle had hardly been touched.

Syd Jones had never cared for the taste of brandy, but he didn't care. All he needed now was an alley or a stable or a hog wallow. He ought to get out of this run-down saloon.

Someone offered to buy Jones a drink, but that was just for show. Jones had a bottle of brandy, maybe three-quarters full, so he wasn't likely to accept an offer of watered-down liquor or stale porter. He just wanted to get out of here, but now folks were coming up to him, patting his back, trying to shake his hand, touching him like he was the man who had shot down Tankersley.

The place wasn't as crammed as it had been, but it felt like he was in the Alamo Saloon after four trail herds had paid off their crews.

"Good job, mister." . . . "You got a belly full of gumption, old-timer." . . . "I'd be honored to buy you a drink, sir." . . . "I haven't seen anything like that since Walt Cole shot it out with Dexter Linwood in Deadwood in '77." . . . "Can I shake your hand, mister?" . . . "Wild Bill Hickok and ol' Wes Hardin don't gots nothin' on you, old man." . . . "I'd be honored to shake your hand, old hoss." . . . "Ned Buntline couldn't have wrote up what you done, sir, and I'll be tellin' my grandkids what I saw here, sir. You're darn-tootin', I will." . . . "You got more courage in your little finger than Custer and all his boys had at the Little Bighorn."

Like old times. The good days. Back when Syd Jones was a name that demanded, and got, respect.

It felt like it took him an hour to reach the boardwalk, and it took him a good fifteen minutes to walk down that before he turned into a dark alley. By then he heard the policemen blowing whistles. It sure had taken them long enough to get to that saloon.

He came out on the other side, saw a livery, and figured that would be as good a place as any. He had a bottle of liquor, and a stall would be a good place to get roostered. And Tankersley was dead.

CHAPTER 16

He kept looking for Drift Carver—and his horses—peering down alleys, and checking the hitch rails. The saloons on both sides of the street began emptying, and hordes lined the boardwalks, staring at some saloon that looked like it had been built with rotted wood by drunks who knew nothing about carpentry. But Duncan had seen plenty of places like that in his years wearing a badge.

"Carver!" he yelled, cupping his hands over his mouth. He fought down the urge to ram his fist through a wall.

He crossed the street, glanced down an alley, heard police officers coming to investigate whatever had happened in that poor excuse for a saloon. Turning around, he stared down Larimer, hoping to find Drift Carver. Oh, the street was crowded, but no Carver, no horses.

"Did you see that old man?" a cowboy told a chippy as they walked past Duncan.

The chippy said, "He was older than my grandpa."

"I know," said the cowhand. "And he walked right into the barrels of that scatter-gun." "He had nerves of iron," said the girl. "Nerves of iron."

"Yep," said the cowhand. "If I got that much courage when I'm that old . . ."

Turning his head, Duncan stared at the miserable saloon. Then he made a beeline for it, weaving in and around pedestrians, clearing his throat, then barking orders until he was at the flimsy doors. Drift Carver and the horses would have to wait.

A uniformed officer put out his hand, but Duncan looked him in the eye.

"I'm Mick MacMicking," he said, and the arm lowered. The policeman turned and nodded at another uniform. "That's Sergeant O'Ryan talking to the bartender, sir."

"Thank you." Duncan nodded and walked into the filthy place.

The sergeant stopped talking to the sweating man with the mustache.

"Mister," the copper began.

"Mick MacMicking," Duncan told him.

This policeman was skeptical. "Anybody can say that."

Duncan laughed. "I don't know why anyone would. Sometimes I wish I were just plain old John Smith."

The cop thought about that while he sized up Duncan, finally chuckled, and looked back at the bartender. "You sure you've never seen the man before?"

"Like I said, Sergeant. He was a total stranger. But bold as brass. He just walked up to the drunk holding the double barrel on me, grabbed the shotgun—never seen a man move like that. It was faster than a rattlesnake strike. And the troublemaker had both barrels on that old cuss, but the next thing I knew, that fool was on the floor, knocked out till a week from Sunday, and the man was standing right before me."

"How old?" Duncan asked.

The man studied him. The sergeant remained patient.

"White hair. Old enough."

"My height?"

The man shrugged. "Maybe an inch taller."

"Mustache?"

"Yeah. And a fair amount of stubble on his face. If I hadn't seen what he done with my own eyes, I'd think he would have to have been a man twenty or thirty years younger."

"Where'd he go?"

The bartender shrugged. "Just walked out the door." He nodded up the street. "I think he went thataway, but I couldn't tell you for certain."

After slipping his notebook into his coat pocket, the sergeant turned to face Duncan. "You after this hombre?"

"I'm looking for a man who fits that description," Duncan said.

"He wanted down Durango way?"

"Not by the law. As far as I know."

"That's right. Didn't you retire?"

Duncan gave his best smile. "I thought I did. But something came up."

The cop chuckled. "That's what I keep telling my missus. One of these days, though . . ."

Another Denver policeman stepped into the light, shaking his head. "No sign of the man, Sergeant," he said. "Streets are like Chicago tonight. Someone thought he ducked down the alley. O'Halloran and Schultz looked up and down, but no sign of him." He glanced at Duncan and the bartender, then looked back at his superior officer.

"Want us to keep looking, Sergeant?"

The man shook his head, and pocketed his notebook. "No need. As far as I can tell, he isn't wanted for anything. Though I'd like to shake his hand. Old man had nerve, if what everyone says he did really happened." The sergeant turned to Duncan. "You want to find him, he's all yours. We'll be busy trying to keep other bartenders or patrons of these establishments from getting their heads blowed off."

He held out his hand. "It's a pleasure to meet you, Marshal MacMicking. Wish I could help."

Shaking the sergeant's hand, Duncan said, "You've got a lot more work to do than I have. I wish you a safe night."

All the officers laughed without much humor. "Haven't had one of those since they made me sergeant and took me off the desk."

Duncan grinned. "If you wake up the next morning, it has been a safe night."

"Ain't that the truth."

He left the saloon, turned right, stopped at the alley, looking again for any sign of Carver or the horses. Seeing none, he stepped into the alley and kept looking for Syd Jones.

The next street was just as crowded, and twice as rowdy. Duncan put himself into the mind-set of a drunk, or a drunk who wanted to get roostered.

He stood on a corner, close to a bullet-riddled wooden column supporting an awning over an opium den and a packed hitch rail. The pickpockets and thieves would be busy, and anyone with a bottle of brandy would be the man of the year in this street of debauchery. So Syd would seek some privacy.

Unless the urge to get drunk got the better of him—which was often the case.

He felt the touch of the rear pocket on his britches, and he spun around toward the horses. The Schofield was in his hand, and it smashed the upper arm of the thin little thief, sending him howling and crashing to the boardwalk. People stopped in their tracks. Those who had already passed him darted across the alley path and to the next boardwalk. Those heading toward him stopped and backed up.

The little man pulled a stiletto from his boot top and started to stand, only to have his chin meet Duncan's right boot. The punk's head struck the wooden frame of the opium den, and he cried out in pain. Before the thief could react, Duncan stood over him, the left boot crushing the hand that held the sharp pig-sticker. Duncan lowered his revolver toward the cringing man's nose.

Duncan's foot pressed harder. The man screamed.

"I'm going to let my boot up just a bit," Duncan said tightly. "That'll give you a choice. You can let go of the knife, or I bring my boot down and break all the bones in your fingers. I'm bigger than you are, so that won't take much effort on my part." He tried his best evil smile. "Or if I think you're trying something sneaky, like having your accomplice stick me in the back, this .45 has a hair trigger, and I'll just blow your head off."

He heard the beating of someone's boots on the street. That, he figured, was the pickpocket's right arm, running before the coppers arrived or his partner got his brains blown out.

The foot came up, the fingers relaxed as much as possible, and Duncan let the hand slide away, then he kicked the stiletto across the boardwalk, where it dropped in the alleyway's dirt.

Backing up, Duncan felt his back pocket.

"All you would have gotten was a handkerchief and a letter," he said, keeping the revolver aimed at the man's chest now. "Get up. But make it slow and steady."

"I think . . . my fingers . . . is all busted already," the man sniveled.

"Nah. I've broken many fingers. Yours are just bruised. Once the blood circulates, you'll feel better. But you won't be trying to pick anyone's pockets for a day or two." He waved the barrel of the pistol. "Up."

The man struggled to his feet, found his hat near a trash bin, and had to try three times before he could get a good hold on the brim and bring the bowler up toward his head.

"If you move one way or the other, I'll put a bullet in one of your knees," Duncan said, and stepped back till he was between the post and the hitch rail. Without taking his eye off the pickpocket, he told the crowd standing by the entrance to the opium den: "Go on about your business, folks. Don't stop. Don't look. Just walk on by."

Maybe ten or twelve did just that. Lots of others had already started fighting their way to the other side of the street, and those who were on the boardwalk on the other side of the alley had turned around and went to find any place where there wasn't a revolver in plain view.

When the last of the pedestrians had disappeared, the pickpocket stood trembling, holding his injured hand in the good one. Duncan's head shook. All the boy had to do was duck behind the fast-moving crowd, turn down the alley, and vamoose. But it was like Syd Jones always told him:

Criminals are stupid. That's why they're criminals.

A glance down the street showed no policemen. Duncan figured Larimer got all the peace officers at this time of night. Lowering the revolver till it pointed at the dirt, but keeping the hammer cocked, Duncan said to the thief. "I'm looking for a man, old-timer, mustache, stubble, dressed like a bum, carrying a bottle of brandy. Seen anyone like that?"

"No." That was barely a whisper, but the head shook.

"How about three horses, a buckskin and a roan, both saddled, and a sorrel with a packsaddle?"

"I don't pay no attention to horses."

"You wouldn't rob a packsaddle?"

The head shook.

"Might be safer than picking a lawman's pocket."

The man stared, swallowed, and brought his injured hand closer to his body. His lips moved, but he made no noise.

Duncan let more people pass, and they moved quickly once they saw his gun. Still no Denver police officers made an appearance.

"One more question, and if you answer it and I think

you're telling me the truth, I'll let you go. If I think you're lying, I'll take you to the first copper I find."

He gave that just a few seconds to sink into the brain, if the punk possessed one.

"If you wanted to get drunk in private, and didn't have a room, where would you go? Nearby."

The boy's head tilted. His eyes focused on Duncan, trying to read the lawman. He raked his teeth over his bottom lip, then wet it with his tongue and nodded across the street.

"Holbrook's livery," he said. "Through the alley. Then down two blocks—no, three—at the corner. It ain't much to look at on account it ain't much. But it's a tad quieter thataway, and Holbrook's got four more days before the law will let him out of jail."

The hammer clicked and lowered and disappeared.

The punk vanished just as fast, perhaps because a police officer finally appeared and was making his way down the boardwalk. Duncan let his revolver slip into the pocket, and he turned around and crossed the street and went into the alley, moving through it as fast as he could, turning right, then crossing that street to the other side of the boardwalk. He stopped and leaned against the wall to a closed grocery store, then waited a few minutes to make sure no one had followed him through the alley.

Satisfied, he walked to the next boardwalk and moved slowly now.

This was a hundred times quieter and less busy than Larimer. Over the first block he passed just one person, who looked like a miner and was focused on making sure he had not lost a tooth. The other side of the street showed no pedestrians. Most of the businesses were closed, and the one shop open, on the other side of the street, was a café with few patrons. His stomach, but mostly his eyes, told him that he could use a good cup of coffee right about now, but he kept focusing on finding that livery stable.

That was all that mattered.

Until he reached the next block.

Then he saw three horses tethered to a rail in front of a place called Hanson's Haberdashery. It was closed, and the nearest streetlamp was out, but there was enough light for Duncan to see the packsaddle on the sorrel, and the buckskin must have caught his scent, because its head jerked up and the horse whinnied.

Duncan made a beeline across the street. Well, he had found the horses. Hearing the snores, he stepped onto the boardwalk, which was in much better condition than the others he had walked on this night—or early morning—and moved to the bench and a water barrel.

Drift Carver's head rested on his hat against the water barrel, and his legs were pulled up. He stopped snoring and mumbled something that Duncan couldn't make out. Sighing, he kicked the old scout's nearest boot.

"I told you not—" Carver's legs kicked out, and he rolled to his left, pounding against the wooden wall, then cursed and turned his head. The eyes focused slowly and he blinked sleep out of them.

"Is that you, Mick?"

Leaning down, Duncan held out his hand. Carver eventually saw that, and reached for it, allowing himself to be pulled up. He fought back a yawn, shook the sleep out of his head, and nodded.

"Must have fell asleep." He yawned.

"Yeah." Duncan checked his anger. "What the devil are you doing over here? And why in—"

"Hold your temper, hoss," the scout said. "You was gone and I caught sight of Syd Jones."

Duncan's heart must have started racing like a thoroughbred. "Where? When?"

The old-timer turned and pointed. "Livery yonder."

He saw it now, but couldn't make out the name carved into a plank above the entrance to the corral. That had to be Holbrook's. That pickpocket had been right. Maybe. Duncan knew better than getting his hopes up.

"You could have come looking for me," he told the old scout.

"You know better than that," Carver shot back. "Larimer was swarming so much we'd miss one another. It'd take a month of Sundays, and I figured if that was Syd—and I'm just about certain-sure it was—I ought to stay here and wait for you to find me. Make sure Syd didn't vamoose."

"And you fell asleep," Duncan pointed out. "A sentry asleep—"

"Is rested for whatever comes next." His hands started patting his pockets for a chaw of tobacco. "I didn't make myself comfortable till I figured Syd had drunk half that bottle. I don't reckon he's goin' nowheres now. What time be it?"

Fishing out his watch, Duncan stared, shook his

head, and returned the key-winder. "Right about four forty," he said.

"Sun'll be breakin' right soon." Carver laughed. "At least I got some shut-eye. You'll be worthless."

"I can sleep in the saddle once we hit the road west." Duncan looked again across and up the street at the livery. "Bring the horses over. I'll fetch Syd."

And he started walking.

CHAPTER 17

"Well, hoss." Drift Carver turned up the flame of the lantern hanging from a nail on a post. "Now you seen it for yourself."

He knelt, picked up the bottle in the dirty stall, and shook it. "Good thing it was good brandy." He sniffed the opening. "Man drink a full bottle of what most saloons in this wicked city serves and they'd be buryin' him in some boot hill." He ran a finger into the bottle, brought it out, and licked the finger with his tongue. Sighing, he pitched the bottle into a mound of hay.

Syd Jones lay snoring, curled up in a fetal position. He had retched most of what he had drank, and had rolled around in his vomit. Bone-thin, he was, and in clothes that hadn't been washed in some time. The stink was overpowering, and the stalls of this stable had not been mucked probably since the owner wound up in jail.

"We can load him on the packhorse," Carver said. "Skedaddle out of Denver before he comes to."

Duncan knew Carver was waiting for him to say something. To say anything. But Duncan just stared down at the pathetic figure of a man he had looked up to. A man he still looked up to, even as he stared down at the old lawman, the drunk, in a miserable livery in Colorado's biggest city. A hero of dime novels—but more than that, Syd Jones had been a real hero.

"Mick." Carver's voice was hushed now. When Duncan made himself look into the old scout's eyes, he saw only sympathy there. "They need you in Dead Broke, son. They're depending on you." He glanced at the sleeping drunk. "He ain't gonna do you no good in Dead Broke. He might get you killed. You'd be worrying over him so much, you'd be inclined to take risks, to let down your guard."

There was a lot of truth to what the scout said.

"Or we can throw him up front of the packsaddle, let the sorrel carry him till he wakes up," Drift said. "Then he can walk the two miles up that mountain. That'll work the brandy out of him, certain-sure."

"Dawn will be breaking soon," Duncan said, and made a vague motion toward the place he had seen earlier. "Head over to that café that was opening up down the street. See if you can get a bucket filled with coffee and bring it back here. Black."

The scout started shaking his head, and mumbled a few things underneath his breath, then spit into the hay and sighed. "You want some breakfast with that coffee?"

"No. I don't think Syd could keep it in his stomach."

"Ain't likely to keep the coffee down, either. That's one thing I'm certain-sure 'bout."

Duncan found a couple of dollar coins and handed them to the scout.

"Dead Broke needs you," Carver tried again.

"I reckon," Duncan whispered, "right now Syd needs me more."

The old-timer grunted something unintelligible, then shoved the money in his pocket, pulled his hat down tight, and walked toward the open door of the livery.

Duncan waited till Carver had reached the street. Then he knelt, grabbed Jones's long arms, and dragged him to a cleaner stall. Finding the handkerchief in his pants pocket, he walked to the trough, thoroughly soaked the white cloth, and brought it back to the stall, where he knelt and began working on cleaning his mentor's face and hands as best he could.

The clothes were hopeless.

Maybe, Duncan found himself thinking, so was Syd Jones.

The last miners from the I&W Mining Corporation filed out of Crosscut Saloon as dawn began to break in Dead Broke. They left winners. Sara Cardiff had seen to that. The four Germans would have enough money to get them, especially the two married men with children, to some new territory. The one called Herrman had mentioned trying Moffat City, up northwest, where he heard a coal mine was looking for help. Friedrich said he was taking his wife and four children back East; his wife kept telling him they never should have left Pittsburgh anyway. The other two—Sara had already forgotten their names—were probably bound for Denver, where they would blow what Sara had let them win. But she couldn't stop folks from doing that. If she could, she would have been out of the gambling business a long, long time ago.

She had let the other employees leave earlier, dealing the last few hands alone. One of the young Germans kept trying to put his arm around her shoulder and pull her close to him—a German miner's idea of seduction, she figured—but he had consumed about half a keg of beer, so outfoxing him came mighty easy, and the alcohol slowed him down considerably so that eventually, he just stared at his cards, folded his hands, and didn't notice when what went into his stein wasn't beer but lukewarm tea.

Sitting at the poker table for minutes after the last miner left, she yawned, and finally made herself get up. Logan Ladron could restack the chips when he came in later today—if he came in at all. He might be following those I&W behemoths down the trail to points west, north, east, south, up, down. He would if he knew what was good for him.

Sara figured she should leave, too, but she wasn't ready to quit just yet.

She did take the deck of cards with her, toss it in the trash bin behind the bar, and walked to the stove where the coffeepot still sat. It still felt warm, so she filled a cup and drank it black. Then she found a basket and carried it to the poker table, where she tossed the empty glasses and steins inside, and brought it back behind the bar, where she poured another cup of lukewarm brew, well-aged but not what anyone would call good.

Sipping it, she was wondering what had become of Drift Carver, and why he wasn't back from Durango yet. No. She stared at the coffee, imagining it as a mystic's cup of tea and that she was reading the leaves to figure out just what the devil had planned for Dead Broke and Sara Cardiff.

Then the door pounded open and in walked Mayor Allane "Nugget" Auchinleck.

"Honey chil', we needs to get down to business." He strode over to her, putting his hands on what passed for hips on his rail-thin body.

"I'd rather go to sleep," she said.

Nugget pretended he was deaf.

"The way I figger it, ol' Drift got hisself ambushed by Sioux injuns on his way to Durango."

"Sioux," Sara said flatly, lowering the cup to the bar.

"Maybe he was comin' back, but that ambush could have been on his way there. It don't say in the copy of the Trinidad paper that fine young gal at Perdition's read to me."

"Paper." She couldn't bring her hand up in time to cover her yawn.

Nugget reached behind him, pulled out a crumpled sheet of newsprint, and spread it out on the bar, trying to smooth out the creases and push the ripped part together. He pointed.

"Right there," he said, tapping his finger, then stopping and leaning forward. "No, that ain't it."

The paper, as Nugget was looking at it, was upside down.

She wasn't certain her eyes would focus after spending nine and three-quarter hours dealing poker, but she found something.

"'Sue's Ambush'?" she read, making it a question instead of the headline's exclamation point.

"That's it." Nugget's small head bobbed rapidly.

She leaned closer, sighed, and shook her head. "A woman named Sue," she said, condensing the story, "jumped on a traveling salesman and kicked him relentlessly on the streets of Trinidad while bystanders laughed until a local constable came and dragged the salesman to safety."

Nugget sniffed, scratched his nose, and leaned down to where Sara's finger had marked the place she was reading.

"That what that them words spell out?" he asked.

"Not verbatim."

"Ver what? Was it writ in German?"

She took another sip of coffee. "Yes," she said, deciding that it was too early in the morning to talk to Nugget, whose breath reeked of forty-rod whiskey.

"You read German?" Nugget was impressed.

"Mayor," she said. "The Sioux haven't done anything but weep for their dead after Wounded Knee. The Indian wars are long over, and by the way I remember things, that tribe never made it this far south. They are still up in the Dakotas. How much have you been drinking?"

"That don't matter none." Still, Nugget slowly turned the paper around, finishing the tear so that the lower quarter of the page separated. He bent down and looked at the words, his lips moving as though he were reading, then shrugged, folded the remaining part of the paper, and shoved it back into his rear pocket.

"What matters is that we've got to get law and order back in this town."

She sighed. He hadn't brought that up in a couple of days, so Sara had hoped he had forgotten about it.

"You have Conner Boyle's gunhand doing just that on a temporary basis, don't you? Your pal Ben Gunderson. Remember?"

He stared at her with no comprehension.

"I mean Gunter Benson."

That made his eyes dance. "Oh, him. Well, Conner— I mean, the assembly, the council . . . no I mean . . . Me. Me. I'm mayor. The way I figure it, we can't tarry no longer. We need a permanent lawman."

She laughed without humor, and tossed the dregs from her cup into the basin. "Mayor," she said, "the way people keep flocking out of town, pretty soon your temporary—or permanent—lawman, Mr. Benson, won't have anyone to shoot in Dead Broke. But himself." Her head bobbed. "You know, I'd pay good money to see that. Might even pay for his burial, too."

Nugget's head shook. "I don't know what the devil you's talkin' 'bout, sister, but—"

The doors banged open again, and to her surprise, Sara watched Little Joey Clarke race into the saloon, calling out her name, then sliding to a stop, his face paling, as he spotted Nugget.

"Joey," Sara said, moving out from behind the bar and past Nugget. "What are you doing up at this hour? School doesn't start till . . ."

"I didn't know . . ." He bit his bottom lip, swallowed, and nodded. "Howdy, Mayor Nugget."

Nugget forgot all about important civic duties and murderers to make marshals.

"Joey. You got any new five-penny books you can read me?"

"Um. No . . . well, maybe. I think Hammerhead said he had one for me at his lumber mill . . . iffen I wanted it."

"You wants it, don't you?" Nugget cried out with excitement.

"I . . . I . . ." His eyes shot to Sara. "Reckon."

Sara found a way out. "Well, Joey, why don't I walk you to the mill and you can fetch that book and read it to our mayor later today." She turned to Nugget, giving him her most charming smile, and telling the mayor: "That's a grand idea."

Nugget's head bobbed. He probably had forgotten now why he came barging into the saloon.

"Let's go," she told Joey, and put her hand on his shoulder and led him toward the doors.

"You want me to lock up?" Nugget called out.

"Don't bother," she said. "There's not much to steal here anyway. And most of Dead Broke's thieves have gone to more prosperous environs."

When she turned down the block, she looked down at Joey and asked, "What's the matter?"

"I ain't . . . I'm not . . . I'm not rightly sure, but . . ."

"But?" She gave his shoulder a soft squeeze. "You can tell me, Joey. You know I never tell anyone's secret."

"It ain't a secret."

"Isn't."

"It isn't a secret. Just a . . . a . . . a . . . a . . . sus—" He wet his lips. "Suspicion."

Sara nodded. They crossed the empty street. The lumber mill was about four hundred yards away. She figured he would let it all out before they got that far. As usual, she was right.

"We—Alfie and me—was going fishin' this mornin' and there was a fella campin' at the bend, but he didn't have no fire or nothin' so we didn't know he was there. And, well, we sort of surprised each other. And Alfie dropped his pole, and I just raised both of my arms as high as I could 'cause the fellow had jumped up and had a big shotgun—looked more like a cannon—aimed at us."

"My goodness." She squeezed his shoulder. "That's frightful."

"Uh-huh. Alfie said he just about wet his pants."

"But he didn't shoot you."

Joey's head shook. "No." He looked up at her and smiled. "No, he lowered that big gun when he seed that we was just kids. Then he walked over to us and asked if we knowed where the Lucky Dice was. Alfie said he didn't, but he was lying. Everybody in town knows where Mr. Boyle's place is. And I said, sure, and told the stranger, and he thanked me, but told me not to tell nobody he seed me, and made Alfie say the same. Said he was Mr. Boyle's older brother, and was surprising him."

"I didn't know Conner had an older brother," Sara said, but she thought holding a shotgun on two kids was something Conner Boyle or his brother would likely do.

"He ain't his brother, Miss Sara," the frightened youngster said.

She stopped, and looked down, waiting till he looked up.

"Least, not unless he stole that shotgun he had pointed at us. I ain't never seen no shotgun with barrels that big."

Nor would Conner Boyle's brother, Sara thought, have any aversion to stealing a shotgun. But she asked, "How can a shotgun tell you if he's Mr. Boyle's brother or not?"

"It had silver engravin' on it. On the stock, I mean. So did the handle of the two pretty six-shooters he had holstered."

She waited.

"The engravin' on the butts of the pistols just spelled out three letters—D and B and M. But the writin' on the butt of the shotgun was D.B. and then M-o-r-a. D.B. Mora. Ever heard of him, Miss Sara?"

"I can't say I have," she said. She smiled, and nodded toward the lumber mill. "Lots of people carry shotguns, and lots of men wear revolvers. The West can still be wild, Joey. You know that. And you and Alfie just had a fright. I'm sure everything is fine. Now let's get that penny dreadful so you can keep the mayor happy."

Joey nodded, and they resumed their walk.

She didn't know any D.B. Mora. But she figured Logan Ladron might know the name.

CHAPTER 18

"What's that?"

Duncan made himself smile as he held the cup of steaming coffee in front of Syd Jones, who sat on his hands to stop the shakes, though whatever one wanted to call what he had on his feet kept moving sideways and his trembling wasn't from the cold. Denver was only a mile high, and the rising sun on this morning was warm.

"It's about as close to coffee as we have," Duncan said.

Syd Jones made no move to take the cup. His Adam's apple bobbed, and he turned his head left, then right, and finally stared at his moving feet.

"I don't want coffee," he said softly.

"It'll do you good," Duncan said.

The old head shook in protest, and he let out another sigh before looking up.

"What the devil are you doing in Denver, Mick?"

That's a plus, Duncan thought. *Syd knows who I am.*

"On my way to Dead Broke," he said. "You remember Dead Broke, don't you?"

The remnants of boots stopped moving, but Duncan noticed the old man sat harder on his hands. His teeth clattered for a moment, then Jones turned and coughed, spit out phlegm and didn't wipe his mouth.

"Dead Broke," he whispered.

"Yeah." Duncan tested the coffee, which wasn't bad seeing how the café, and not Drift Carver, had made it. "They lost their lawman. A good lawman, from what I heard. Asked me to come keep a lid on things."

"Hopeless." He crossed his ankles.

Moving forward, Duncan set the tin cup within easy reach for the wretched figure before he backed up a few spaces and dropped into a crouch, rocking on his heels now, staring at the man who had taught him everything a lawman, especially a green peace officer, needed to know to stay healthy and employed.

"You once told me there was no such thing as hopeless," Duncan said. "Remember?"

The head shook firmly. "I was wrong about lots of things."

"What happened in Dead Broke, Syd?"

The trembling stopped, and the left hand came out of hiding and inched its way toward the coffee cup. He touched it, then jerked his hand away from the heat. His eyes came up again and met Duncan's.

"You got . . . s-some . . . something to . . . to . . . sweeten this, Mick?"

Duncan shook his head. "No sugar."

"Tha-that ain't . . ." He couldn't finish.

The sigh came from exasperation and that sickening feeling in Duncan's belly. "Syd . . . what the devil happened?"

The Adam's apple moved again, and the old head shook. The hand touched the coffee cup, but this time stayed there, and after a long while, Syd Jones dragged the cup closer to him. He needed both hands to lift it toward his mouth, spilling a healthy dose as he brought it up, then drank some, though enough went down the corners of his lips, wetting the chin whiskers and staining the stains on his filthy shirt.

At least some of the coffee got to his stomach. That was a start.

"There ain't . . . n-nothin' to . . ." He set the cup in the dirt. "Nothin' for you in Dead Broke. Nothin' for . . . no . . . nobody."

"I don't know about that, Syd," Duncan said. "Oh, sure, towns are hurting—and not just silver camps. The Panic hit lots of places all over these United States and territories. Leadville probably shipped out more silver than Dead Broke, but you've been there long enough to know that town offers a lot more than just mines."

"The place is bedlam, Mick. And . . . well . . . I got old."

Syd Jones sure looked old. All of a sudden Duncan felt ancient.

"We cleaned up many towns, Syd." Duncan spoke softly. "I figure Dead Broke, pretty as it is, and as good of a town as you made it, deserves better. So Drift Carver came down to Durango and said the town council wanted me to help them get back on track. I took the offer."

"That was a fool thing to do. That city don't want law and order. At least, the muckety-mucks on the town council—well, not all of them, but certainly Conner Boyle . . ."

"Conner Boyle." Duncan smiled, and for the first time that morning, Syd Jones's eyes looked sober and alert. "Guess I didn't realize that sharper had settled in Dead Broke."

The onetime lawman's head nodded. "Got there a few months before the crash hit us like a ton of ore. I take it your paths crossed a time or two."

Nodding, Duncan kept the explanation brief. "He set up shop in Durango, or tried to, a couple of years ago. You know me, Syd, I never begrudged an honest man who made a living gambling. But I despise a cheat."

Duncan felt a bit of relief when Syd raised the cup and drank some more coffee. His right hand didn't shake as much now, and no liquid stained the beard stubble this time. He set the cup down.

"More coffee?" Duncan asked.

"Nah. My belly . . . it ain't exactly wantin' much of anything to stay down right yet."

He closed his mouth tightly and stiffened, but somehow managed to keep the coffee and anything else in his gut from coming up. Eventually, he looked back at Duncan.

"I take it . . . ." Again, somehow Syd Jones managed to keep whatever wanted to come up down. That man might not look like he did ten or twenty years ago, but he still was one tough man. ". . . Take it . . . that . . . Boyle didn't last too long in your town."

Duncan shrugged. "It was a pretty good fight."

Now a grin briefly made an appearance in that tired, unshaven, dirty, old face. "Wisht I coulda seen it."

The laugh was genuine. "Well, there's a chance you

can have a good seat for the second round." He leaned forward. "Come with me to Dead Broke, Syd. I can use some help."

The eyes closed, the chin touched his dirty shirt, and Syd Jones's head shook slowly, like the pendulum on a clock running out of time.

"Ain't no good no more, Duncan. Whiskey and age, nerves and too many swollen knuckles. You don't need me. Don't want you to get killed, lookin' out for this old man. Besides, it's just Conner Boyle and his gunhand who you gots to watch out for. The others . . . they're just angry miners, mad at the world, angry 'bout losin' their jobs. Can't blame folks like that."

Duncan took in a lungful of Denver air, which wasn't as clean as what he had been breathing in Durango— and not as thin as he remembered breathing in the higher elevations, especially way up in Dead Broke. He exhaled.

"Wish you'd change your mind, Syd."

The old man again bored his eyes into Duncan. "Nah."

"Who's Boyle's gunhand?" Duncan asked.

"Caleb Holden."

He ran the name through his memories. "I guess I've heard it, but I can't place him."

"You know the type. Young and fast and wanting to be remembered with the likes of Wild Bill."

Now Jones laughed, and shook his head. "You never was that loco, even when you didn't know nothin' 'bout being a lawdog or keepin' the peace. Why on earth do all these whippersnappers want to be remembered and be just like gunfighters who didn't live to see their fortieth birthdays?"

Duncan shrugged. "Fame's everlasting."

"But you can't enjoy fame when you're six feet under."

Nodding, Duncan wished he could stay right here, talking to his mentor, watching him return in just a few small moments like the rock-solid man of iron Duncan remembered from the Kansas ends of trail and assorted rough and rowdy camps on the Western frontier. He could see that in this poor old man slowly sweating out the booze he had been living on for some time now. If Duncan could sit here for a few weeks, maybe a month, he might have Syd Jones back on his feet.

But . . .

"You don't need the money, son," Jones whispered. "And you've gotten yourself writ up 'bout as much as Kit Carson and Jesse James—maybe even those two Bills, the Buffalo and the dead Wild one."

He tried to stand, but his legs weren't cooperating at the moment.

"And if Drift Carver came down to fetch you, you already knew that I had run out of Dead Broke. Got to be another reason you'd do something as foolish as what you signed up for."

Duncan tried to shrug.

"You never had gold fever. Maybe you'd want Nugget's big rock, that diamond of silver, and I reckon it would fetch a good price even with silver not worth a fig right now. And there ain't hardly a woman in Dead Broke who's worth—"

He stopped, turned, and those cold eyes did not blink as he looked hard and long at his one-time deputy.

Duncan put on his best poker face.

They stayed like that for almost two minutes, neither blinking, neither speaking. Finally, Syd Jones looked away and shook his head. "Nah, the women who ain't charging for a dance or something else, they got too much sense to give a scoundrel like you a second chance." He held out his hands, and, with great reluctance, Duncan walked over and pulled the old-timer to his feet.

"I 'precciate the offer, son, but I don't want to see you killed, and I sure don't want to get you killed. You take care of Caleb Holden and Conner Boyle, and you'll be fine." He turned again, spit into the dust, and, after wiping his mouth, straightened.

"Bryn Bunner," he said. "I reckon you'll have to whip him, too."

"Gunman?" Duncan asked.

"Nah. Miner. Big cuss. You know the type. Always angry . . . maybe with good reason . . . seein' how those miners work like dogs, makin' the owners and super-intendents and vice presidents and presidents and secretaries and treasurers and the investors a fortune. He don't trust no one, and he sure don't like tin stars."

"Did you have to whup him?"

The head nodded once. "But I cheated. I pounded the stock of a Parker twelve-gauge over the back of his head when he weren't looking."

Duncan laughed. "I'll remember that," he said, and shook the old man's hand. Then sadly, he watched Syd Jones walk to the road and head back toward the noisy, bustling town of Denver. His head bent low, making sure he put his feet down the right way, he moved unsteadily down the well-trod path, away from Duncan MacMicking.

He was still looking down the trail when Drift Carver came out of hiding, spitting tobacco juice and muttering every cussword he could think of under his breath. When he stood beside Duncan, his mumbling turned to bellowing.

"I knowed you didn't have it in you. You young whippersnappers just don't know how to handle a drunk or a fellow who ain't quite as fast as he once used to be. You can't show him no mercy, can't talk to him like he'll listen. What you shoulda done was conked him on the head with the butt of a pistol." He motioned toward the horses. "Then we coulda throwed him on that packhorse and lugged him all the way to Dead Broke."

Duncan didn't look away from the road.

After a few more minutes of wailing and preaching and swearing and stomping his feet, Carver let out a sigh and sucked in fresh air. After releasing that, he swore again. "That's what I woulda done."

"That won't work on a man like Syd Jones," Duncan said.

"That ain't all to it, sonny. I knows that. But I got the cure for a drunk. Week-old goat milk with a rotten egg from a mountain bluebird. Stir it up with a chunk of juniper, then you hold that old drunk's nose and don't let him breathe till he's swallowed his last drop." He smacked his lips. "That'll cure'm or kill'm, and that hombre"—he hooked his thumb toward Syd—"it ain't gonna kill'm. Not as much as he's been drinkin'."

"Syd Jones has to make up his own mind." Duncan walked toward the horses. Drift Carver started to shout some more, but instead muttered a soft curse and followed the lawman to the animals.

"He's already made up his mind, sonny. He's made up his mind to drink hisself to death. Lost nerve. That'll do it to many a man."

He lifted the stirrup to tighten the cinch.

"Well, I reckon it's for the best." Carver moved to check the packsaddle on the sorrel, then went to work on the saddle cinch on his roan.

"I'm not giving up on Syd yet," Duncan said, trying to convince himself of what he had just told the old scout.

"Yeah, I hears ya. Make up his own mind." He muttered a few curses and insults about men and women and horses and dogs younger than he was.

"Like when he made up his mind to go into that saloon where five of the Creighton boys were whooping it up." Duncan looked up over his saddle at Carver. "You remember that, don't you? You were there. I wasn't."

The scout sniffled, spit out his well-chewed tobacco, and pitched it as far as he could in the wind that started to pick up.

"I was there," he whispered. "And, yeah, I didn't go in with Syd because I didn't want to get shot all to pieces. Maybe I ought to head to Denver with that ol' hoss and get roostered till I ain't worth spit."

"I'm not sure I would have gone into that saloon, either, Drift," Duncan said. "Not with just a shotgun and a revolver."

He shook his head.

"He come out without a scratch on him. Those Creightons, I recollect the coroner saying, didn't have one ca'tridge in their six-shooters that wasn't fired already, and nary a one of 'em cut Syd's flesh. His shirt and pants and hat looked like they'd been visited by a swarm of moths, but he wasn't even scratched. And all five of 'em bad men was deader than dirt."

"That's the Syd Jones I remember. That's the Syd Jones who needs to remember that himself." Duncan pulled himself into the saddle and waited for his companion to prepare to ride to Dead Broke.

When Carver had a hold of the packhorse's head rope and a steady left hand on the reins, he pushed his roan up close to the lawman.

"I don't think you'll ever see that Syd Jones, son, ag'in, 'ceptin' in 'em dime novels Nugget has read to him."

Duncan's reply was to kick his horse into a walk and hit the trail to Dead Broke.

CHAPTER 19

They saw the black smoke long before they reached the high mountain town, too much to be coming out of a smokestack, but, as Drift Carver pointed out, too little to be the entire town of Dead Broke.

"You and I have both seen many a small fire wipe out a big town," Duncan said. He considered pushing the horse into a faster walk, but this was the steepest part of the trip, and all of the horses were already winded after coming through the narrows. This high up, even Duncan felt like a consumptive, sucking in what passed for oxygen.

"We gots us a crackerjack fire department," the old scout pointed out. "Even after Bryn Bunner got his hard rocks to wreck the electric pump engine."

It wasn't the fire that made Duncan want to get to the town faster. The image of Sara Cardiff kept appearing before him.

The air had a slight chill, but the sun was closer at ten thousand feet, and Duncan had forgotten just how beautiful the country was up here. It wasn't as colorful as the country around Durango, but it felt cleaner. An hour

and fifteen minutes later, the smoke had fallen to thin
streams, and they reached the flat shoulder of the mountain and rode past a few tents and shacks, one abandoned
mine, and finally into Dead Broke.

Duncan reined in at the smoking ruins of the building.

Footprints in dried mud, and one abandoned bucket,
told how townsfolk had tried to put out the blaze, but
wood burns up fast, even in thin air. Luckily, the building, now just charred ruins and smoking debris, stood
alone in a fair-sized lot. The closest building would
need a new whitewashing from the smoke and mud, but
at least only this one building had been lost.

Drift Carver, pulling the worn-out packhorse, reined
in and spit tobacco juice into the mud.

"Thought you said Dead Broke had a crackerjack fire
department," Duncan said.

Carver spit out the shredded cud of tobacco and wiped
the thick facial hair covering most of his lips. "Did." He
nodded at the shell. "That was the fire station."

Looking closer at the ruins, Duncan could make out
the metal and tin of two wagons, which might have,
could have, been old engines. He shook his head, wondering what he had gotten himself into, when he spotted
a man walking down the street toward them. He let his
left hand hold both reins as his right one pushed away
the tail of his coat and rested on the butt of his revolver.

"He's all right, Mick," Carver said, and called out to
the stranger, "Howdy, Logan."

"Drift," the man said with a nod. He kept his hands
spread away from his body, specifically from the bulge
from a holstered revolver. "Welcome back."

He stopped a few feet from the two riders and pack-horse.

"Logan," Carver said, "this here is Mick MacMickin'. Mick, say howdy to Logan Ladron. He deals an honest game at the Crosscut Saloon."

That got Duncan's attention immediately. He nodded. "Pleasure."

"Same here." Logan nodded.

"Where is the Crosscut?" Duncan asked.

The dealer turned and pointed north and west. "Two blocks up, two blocks west. You're welcome to sit at my table anytime. It'd be an honor."

"I look forward to it." His head tilted toward the burned-out fire station. "What happened here?"

The professional gambler's laugh revealed no mirth but a healthy dosage of sarcasm. "Bryn Bunner's bunch." He shook his head. "That's hard to say. Our firefighters saved the house of one of the last mine owners still brave, or stupid, enough to call this town his home. Bunner's been leading the fight for miners here for twelve or fourteen months."

"Any witnesses?" Duncan asked.

"To the fire?" He grinned. "None, I doubt, that would be willing to incur the wrath of Bryn Bunner." Now he even laughed aloud. "I don't think even one of our vol-unteer firefighters would testify in a court of law or tell a lawman that he saw Bryn Bunner or recognized any of the arsonists."

"Bryn likes to burn things," Carver explained. "Joyful Mine headquarters—boss's home."

"Jansen's bank," the gambler added. "That hat shop, though they just wanted the bank to burn."

"Anything else since I been gone?" Carver asked. "Other than that shooting we heard about."

The tall dealer's head shook. "It was quiet up until this morning." He turned back toward Duncan. "I don't think Bunner knew you were coming. No one knew even if you would take the job they are offering you. I'm assuming . . . you have?"

"Appears that way," Duncan said.

"Glad to hear."

Duncan didn't think the gambler was running a bluff. "I reckon I'll have to talk to Mr. Bunner myself."

"You might want to get sworn in first," Carver whispered.

"An excellent idea." The gambler laughed. "Why don't we do it at the Crosscut Saloon? It and the Lucky Dice are the two best establishments remaining in Dead Broke. But the Crosscut's whiskey won't leave you blind or dead, and the dealers only cheat when they have to." He winked. "Besides, you have a better chance of getting our erstwhile mayor to a saloon than to the council offices above the pawnshop."

"I like that idea." Duncan knew he had spoken too quickly and too fast. He cleared his throat. "So . . . I can get started now. Is there a hotel or bathhouse? I'd like to get the trail dust off me and put on my good suit." He sounded like a schoolkid. "For the swearing in, I mean."

Carver chuckled and shook his head. "You don't wanna be wearin' a good suit, Mick. Not today, anyhow."

"Drift's right," Logan Ladron agreed. "I mean, you'll have to fight Bryn Bunner as soon as you pin on that star."

Swinging out of the saddle, holding the reins, Duncan led his horse away from the remains of the firehouse.

They made it the two blocks up, but found a welcoming committee waiting for the new lawman when they turned the corner.

The biggest of the trio stood in the middle of the street. He looked pale, but not sickly. Pale from practically living in dark tunnels searching for silver, or any other metal folks wanted or needed. Probably had come across the Atlantic from one of those European countries not too many Americans could name, unless they hailed from that part of the world, too. He wore thick boots, tough pants held up by suspenders, a filthy shirt, and a porkpie hat. The chest was thick, the arms bulging tightly against the sleeves, and the nose crooked from more than one fist.

"Law no want in *Ddbrk*." The town's name came out as one word, one syllable, no vowels. Duncan couldn't place the accent.

Two other men stepped from the boardwalks on both sides of the street.

"Go back to Durango, lawdog," said the one coming from Duncan's right. But at least Duncan knew an Irish accent when he heard one. The other miner, bigger than the first behemoth, said nothing, but spit into both palms and began rubbing his whale-fin-sized hands together. He had the look of a German.

A window opened upstairs. Duncan shot a glance upward, but saw only curious faces. No rifles. No shotguns. No six-shooters. Just spectators. More and more people began crowding the boardwalk, but Duncan didn't see Sara Cardiff, or hardly any women except a couple of tired dance-hall girls.

"Want some help?" Sara's card dealer asked.

"Just hold my coat," Duncan said, as he slipped the coat off, folded it neatly, and draped it over Logan Ladron's arms. "And this." He unbuckled his gun rig, which the gambler took with his right hand. Then he removed his hat, but that he gave to Drift Carver.

"Spurs." Carver nodded down at the lawman's boots.

"Might need those," Duncan whispered.

He moved to the nearest boardwalk and pulled out his pocketknife, watch, a pouch holding his coins, and a billfold. "Don't let anyone walk off with those," he said, but discreetly picked up the pouch and let his balled fist cover that in his left hand. With his right, he started loosening his bandanna as he turned and walked to the big galoot standing in the middle of the street. Over the behemoth's right shoulder, he could make out the facade of the Crosscut Saloon.

It's a hard thing to do, untying the knot of a bandanna with one hand. But Duncan MacMicking had mastered that trick years ago. Syd Jones had showed him the proper technique.

"Spurs!" The giant Duncan approached pointed at Duncan's boots, but the lawman kept walking. Then when he had just about reached the massive miner, Duncan jerked the well-worn neckerchief off with his right hand. The miner's eyes followed that hand. Which is why Duncan brought the left hand up, and slammed it, the coins in the leather pouch jingling when the fist caught the miner's cheek just above the jaw.

The man fell to his knees, and Duncan stepped

back, shaking some feeling back into his left hand and throbbing fingers, but not releasing the money pouch. The dazed miner tried to stand, but Duncan got into the right position and kicked him with the foot and heel of his boot—right in the sternum. And that blow sent the miner onto his back.

"Cheat. Cheater!" The miner to Duncan's left charged, and Duncan cocked back his left arm and fired the money pouch right into the man's big nose. Blood spurted, coins jingled, and the miner stumbled and dropped to his knees. By that time Duncan was spinning around, narrowly avoiding the haymaker the other miner had thrown at him. Duncan felt the whoosh, and saw the man spin, lose his balance, and fall to his knees.

Duncan took a quick step forward and kicked. The man caught himself with his arms, not planting his face in the dust until the next kick came. This time, Duncan raised his foot a little so that the rowels of his spur raked across the man's left buttock.

The thick denim protected the miner a bit, but he still yelped and reached with both hands.

Duncan's eye caught the flash. He ducked as his money pouch whistled past one ear and shoulder. Turning, he saw the leather hit the dust and slide toward the street. "Get that for me," Duncan shouted, not caring who grabbed the pouch, as long as it was either Carver or Sara's top dealer.

He ducked the swinging haymaker from the burly man, gave the attacker a short jab into the side ribs, then leaped back. He caught his breath, surveyed the three men, and went after the closest one.

Two swinging rights with a belly punch with the left

in between doubled that one over, and Duncan brought right knee up to catch the man's face. Usually he broke a man's nose that way, but this chap had a very long forehead and his head was as hard as granite. Duncan figured he would be limping for a day or two, but the damage was done. The man sprawled out in the dirt and did little more than breathe and bleed.

One was left, and he unbuckled his belt. What was it Syd Jones had once told him? Never trust a man who doesn't wear suspenders. Grinning a bloody-mouthed smile, the miner started wrapping the black leather around his right fist, stuck two fingers inside the buckle, and flicked up the metal tongue.

He whispered something in a foreign language. The words sounded venomous, but not as strong as the angry eyes. The fist came flying. Duncan blocked it easily with his left hand and let the momentum carry the miner about three yards past him. The big man staggered, slipped and fell to his knees, and tried to push himself back up, but Duncan was too fast. His left boot planted between the miner's shoulder blades and drove him to the ground. Then Duncan jumped on his back, grabbed a handful of hair, jerked the head back, then rammed it into the dirt. He brought the head up once, then slammed it down again. Two more times and then the man's left arm began pounding the dirt.

That was the sign of surrender, and Duncan shoved the head down, releasing his grip, and pushed himself to his knees. He looked at the other two men and saw them slowly coming up, sitting in the dirt, chests heaving, bleeding all over, and looking lost.

Duncan rubbed his own knuckles and got to his feet.

First, he found his coin purse, tightened the drawstring before shoving it into a pocket, then walked over to the leader of the crew.

"You had enough?" he asked.

"*Áno. Áno.* Go us. *Väzenie.*"

He didn't know what the language was, but he knew the fight was over. "Just go home." He turned back toward the other miners. "You two. Go home. Next time, though, you won't get off so easy."

When he reached the gambler and the old scout, he made himself laugh. "Guess that settles that." He gathered his possessions first, buckled on his gun belt, and went to fetch his hat and coat.

Neither Ladron nor Drift Carver looked impressed.

"What's . . . the matter . . . with . . . you two?" he asked, still trying to catch his breath.

"Nothing," the gambler said.

"Good fight," said Carver. "But you still gotta put Bryn Bunner on the dirt and hope the count reaches ten."

CHAPTER 20

"He didn't look all that tough to me." Caleb Holden helped himself to some of Conner Boyle's best brandy.

"You said he put three of those bruising miners on the ground," Boyle said.

"Yeah." The gunfighter gulped down the good stuff and quickly refilled the glass.

Brandy, Boyle seethed, *is for sipping*. He bit his lip, breathed in and out, and reminded himself that Holden was good with a gun, really good, and didn't cost too much, either—unlike some of the gunmen who were coming to Dead Broke.

"He cheated, though." Holden held out the glass of brandy as though making a point. "Had a coin purse in his fist. That put that big cuss down."

Boyle reached up and felt the almost unnoticeable scar on the corner of his left forehead, above the eyebrow. "So . . . he's still using that trick, I see."

"He even used his spurs in the fight." He finished the brandy, but this time set the glass on the table, which made Conner Boyle feel somewhat better.

"Couldn't have licked them three any other way." Holden walked to Boyle's cigar box, and Boyle moved to the decanter to pour a drink of his own. But he would sip his. He shook his head as he stared at the gunfighter, who bit off the end of the cigar he had fetched out of the box and spit it into the trash can.

This is what I get for a hundred dollars a month, he thought. *A ruffian. Who complains about a man using trickery to best three behemoth miners in a street brawl. When Holden would have just shot them down . . . in the back.*

He swirled the brandy he poured, sucked in the aroma, and let the liquor wet his lips and tongue before swallowing a small sip.

"Any word from Ben Usher?" Holden asked.

Boyle shook his head.

"Well, that leaves it up to Mora or Gunderson to gun down that slick dude." The grin stretched across the gunman's face, and he used his free hand to rest it on the butt of his revolver. "Or I can take him, right quick, and real dead."

"Dean Hill showed up right as I was having breakfast," Boyle said.

"He did?" A sly grin creased the young punk's face, and he shook out the match after lighting the cigar, then scratched the palm of his right hand on the hammer of one of his revolvers. "I guess El Paso ain't as excitin' as that border town used to be."

"When does these gunfights start takin' place?" Holden smiled again. "I can't wait to show those dime-novel man-killers just how much better I am."

"The idea," Boyle said, "is to kill our new lawman."

"All you gots to do, boss, is let me have a crack at'm."

Boyle briefly considered that option. It might be

worth it, just to have Mick MacMicking shoot down that punk, who could easily be replaced with the three killers who had already accepted the invitation to Dead Broke and were here earning pay for drinking, gambling, and womanizing. And then there was always that chance that Caleb Holden might take MacMicking after all. Stranger things had happened, and guns weren't always dependable. Cartridges misfired. A thumb could slip off the hammer on a revolver. A man might move left when you expected him to turn right. Old hands and arms got slower. Young toughs sometimes found that extra bit of speed. Besides, even the greatest of all gunfighters could have a bad day every now and then.

"Let's just wait a spell," Boyle finally said. "Besides, MacMicking just got here. He might see what this town is worth these days and light a shuck back down to Durango. That town's not hurting as bad as Dead Broke is."

Perhaps, he thought, *because you don't have to climb halfway to heaven to get to Durango.*

"Suit yourself." Holden finally lighted his—*Boyle's*—cigar.

Then the door suddenly banged open, and Allane "Nugget" Auchinleck stumbled in.

Luckily, he recovered before crashing into the side table that held Boyle's mother's finest set of china.

"Why ain't ya at the Crosscut Saloon?" he roared, then noticed Holden. "Ya's havin' a confab with this gun toter? Didn't ya get my message? No. Course not. I didn't send no messenger. But ever'body in creation that's still in my town already knowed he was here. Figgered you did, too. Well, c'mon. We gots ourselves a new marshal to get swored into his office. And speakin' of offices, who burnt down the fire station?"

"I wouldn't know," Boyle replied honestly, "but I'm sure our new marshal will apprehend the culprits and see they suffer the consequences."

"He cain't do nothin' till he gets hisself swored in. Now, c'mon." He glanced at Holden. "Not you. Well, ya can come iffen you wants to. Jes don't wear that hogleg. That MacMickin', he gots a peculiar notion about lawin'. He ain't gonna let nobody wear no gun on the streets—concealed or in plain view."

"I believe former Sheriff Jones had the same edict." Boyle drained his brandy.

"Well, I'll see if that fella is as good as his reputation." Holden pulled out his revolver, let the hammer reach half-cock, opened the loading gate, and turned the cylinder on his left forearm, checking the loads. "If he wants my guns, he'll—"

"You're not showing your face today." The clicking of the revolver's cylinder stopped. Holden glared.

"You need to find Hill, Gunderson, and Mora." Boyle's tone took any fight out of the tough punk. Holden knew where his money was coming from. "Tell them that our boy has arrived in town, but they are not—and you are not—to do anything till I give the order." Smiling though he was in no good mood, he nodded at the box of expensive cigars. "Take a handful of those fine cee-gars and relax. I want our new marshal to feel welcome. Before he dies."

He watched Holden fill his hands with the good cigars before walking to the door, which the mayor opened for him and closed behind him.

"You comin'?" Nugget asked.

"Of course." Boyle began straightening his tie. He wanted to look his best for Dead Broke's new peace officer.

The Crosscut Saloon was just as Duncan had expected.

Plenty of space. A fine bar. He knew without tasting that a bottle labeled Old Overholt actually held real rye whiskey, that the bourbon came from Kentucky or Pennsylvania, that the brandy came from France, and that the Scotch wouldn't blind a man because the bottle hadn't been filled with homemade poison that would kill most men. The saloon was clean.

He stopped at the piano and tickled the keys. In tune. The F chord sounded perfect. He moved to Logan Ladron's table, where the gambler was opening a new deck, then moved to another one, the one with the best view out of the plate-glass window. His sore right hand touched the felt. He breathed in deeply, hoping to catch a scent of that perfume Sara used to wear.

No luck. The odor he recognized came from stale cigars and cigarettes, from men who sweated all day and came in here for an honest game of chance or some whiskey, beer, or wine to wash down the dust and grime that had been filling their throats and mouths for ten to twelve hours, maybe more.

"Want a drink, Marshal?"

Duncan turned to the gambler and smiled.

"I'm not marshal yet."

Logan Ladron's eyes brightened. "Which is why I asked if you wanted a drink."

"Let me get some trail dust off me."

The gambler pointed. "We got ourselves a washroom right through the door. Indoors and all. We're civilized here in Dead Broke. Or used to be."

"Much obliged."

Duncan entered the room and was impressed. A washroom with all the fixings. Pump and all. Gaslight and an overhead window that allowed sunlight and moonlight in, with wallpapering that was soothing, not obnoxious. This was Sara's business, all right, but Duncan sure didn't like the reflection he found in the mirror. He had entered the saloon carrying his kit and a fresh shirt.

No hot water, but a lawman got used to shaving in cold water, or not shaving at all. He lathered his face and went to work.

He had briefly met the mayor, a cantankerous old coot who probably knew nothing about governing but a lot about mining. Nugget said he knew MacMicking like a book—"On account I read all 'em books writ 'bout ya . . . well, had 'em read to me, anyhow. Yer what we need. Glad to have ya. Hope ya don't get kilt by any of 'em gun-toters."

"Well, my first rule, pending approval by you, Mayor, and the council, will be that only peace officers can carry firearms in the city limits. That's been my policy—and it was Syd Jones's policy—in every town we ever had the honor of serving."

"Darn right." Nugget shook his hand again. "Ya know

what ya's doin', sonny. Gonna be my pleasure to swear you in."

Logan Ladron had suggested they do it, that swearing in, in front of the Crosscut. Nugget had agreed. He had shaken Duncan's hand and started singing a song from the long-ago Civil War before heading back to his mansion to admire his Hope Diamond of Silver.

Somehow, Duncan survived his shave despite chuckling over that mayor—maybe the craziest old fool Duncan had met in all his years.

He wet his comb and went to work on his hair. Then stopped.

Hope ya don't get kilt by any of 'em gun-toters.

He set the comb on a shelf above the sink. Gunter Benson, according to that newspaper article, shot down a man named Fanning in front of Percy Stahl's place in Dead Broke. Gunter Benson. An alias for Ben Gunderson. Then seeing Dean Hill on the train to Denver. But for a killer like Hill, Denver would offer a lot more, these days anyway, than Dead Broke.

What in Sam Hill would bring a man like Gunderson to Dead Broke?

Duncan laughed out loud. What would bring *me* to Dead Broke? But he knew that answer.

The size of the crowd surprised Joey Clarke. He didn't know that many grown-ups still lived in Dead Broke. And while Joey knew that Mick MacMicking was a legend and how much Mayor Nugget loved to hear those stories read about him, Joey didn't think the

new town marshal for Dead Broke ranked up there with
Kit Carson, Wild Bill, Buffalo Bill, and Texas Jack.

He didn't look as tall as the artists showed him on
the covers of those books. Now, Joey would give the
lawman a little bit of a break, because it wasn't cold
enough for Mick MacMicking to be wearing a buffalo
robe, but that gunfighting lawman sure could've done
better. After all, a black coat and a black string tie just
did not look fancy or heroic.

"Not one single fringe hanging from none of his
clothes," Oscar Johansen whispered into Little Joey's
left ear.

"Where's all 'em scalps he taken of red injuns?"
Patsy Muldoon asked.

"Shhhhhhh! He's about to talk," Little Joey whispered.

His friends obeyed.

"Thank you, Mayor." The tall man took a step
forward. "Dead Broke has seen hard times. Like all of
Colorado. And all across the country. But this isn't the
first setback our country has seen, and every single time
we have had a financial panic, depression, whatever
you want to call it, and every time we've been through
a war, a rebellion, we've endured. Western folks—and
we're all Westerners, no matter if we came from
Europe"—he nodded at the miners—"or if we came
from China"—Joey had never heard anyone mention
China in a speech before, but this lawman nodded at
the little gal who ran that little restaurant on Silver
Street—"or if our ancestors called this country theirs
while we were on the other side of the Atlantic or Pacific."

And most certainly, as far back as Joey could recollect,

no one had ever talked about the Utes and Arapaho. Even the schoolteacher seemed scared to mention those two names of Indian tribes, but that teacher was afraid of mice and worms, too.

"So we're in this together," Mick MacMicking said. "All of us. Together. And I understand our erstwhile mayor . . ."

"What's that mean?" Oscar asked.

Patsy told Oscar to "Shhhh!"

Nugget spit out tobacco juice and bowed to the crowd, and the laughter caused Joey to miss the rest of what Marshal MacMicking said.

"It'll be my honor to serve this city," the legend said. "But here's the law of the land."

He pulled back the coat to reveal his sidearm. Joey frowned. That was wrong, too. All the books had Mick MacMicking wearing fancy guns, with shiny handles, gold inlays, and silver or at least nickel plating, and a giant solid buckle with a star in the center. Mac-Micking's revolver was big, but had no gleaming grips of ivory or pearl. And the metal was black, not silver or, like in one or two of those paperback novels, gold.

"Firearms will not be worn in plain view or concealed within the city limits. First offense is seventy-five dollars."

That got everyone's attention.

"Second offense is a hundred dollars. Third offense and your weapon is not returned, but you won't have need of it for the next thirty days, as you'll be spending nights in jail and days at hard labor beautifying our grand city."

"Does 'beautifying' mean something like 'beautiful'?" Oscar asked.

"Yes," Patsy said. "Beautiful . . . like me!" She pulled on her curls.

"I welcome your suggestions," MacMicking was saying. "This is a fine city, with a grand history, and despite the collapse of the market for silver, we have lots to offer. Our great mayor has told me some of his plans to bring people up to our town, to spend money in our city, to see all the beauty we have to offer."

"Has he seen our fire station?" a grown-up standing behind Joey asked.

Little Joey knew better than to *Shhhhhhhhhh* one of his elders.

"There are a few other . . ."

Marshal Mick MacMicking stopped when a woman came through the doors to the saloon. Joey almost didn't recognize her. She was wearing a skirt and jacket bodice. Joey knew that because his mother ran the dress shop in town. In fact, Sara Cardiff had probably had Little Joey's mother make this for her—after all, women who owned saloons and gambling halls were richer than dressmakers and bookkeepers. Richer, his aunt Merna would say, but still doomed to perdition if not someplace hotter because of being such a sinful woman and living such a wicked life.

This outfit was green like a pea—and Joey never liked peas—but it sure looked good on Miss Sara. It was made of a grand brocade trimmed with black lace. Her shoes even matched. That made her even fancier.

He didn't think he had ever seen her wearing anything but blue.

Some of the women began whispering.

Joey could hear them talking, because their whispers weren't as what anyone would call quiet.

Men were whispering something else, then giggling or elbowing one another.

But they weren't interrupting the new marshal because he had turned, and just stared like he was in complete shock. Stared at Miss Sara, who moved to the far column that held up the awning.

She curtseyed and looked at Marshal Mick Mac-Micking, whose mouth remained open. Joey could see his lips moving, but he wasn't speaking. Maybe his lips were trembling.

One of the men behind Joey snorted and then laughed. "That hussy has done flummoxed him."

And another man said, "If he can't handle Miss Sara, I don't reckon he's gonna be our marshal for too long."

"Bryn Bunner will have him whupped in less time than it took MacMicking to whup 'em three toughs when he first rode in," another man said.

A man let out a war cry. "Let's ride him out of town on a rail!"

"Right now!"

People cheered.

"No, let's tar and feather him!"

"He ain't worth wastin' tar and feathers on. Let's get the rail now."

"Nah." That was a woman's voice. "Let Bryn have a go at 'm."

The nearest woman sighed. "I thought he was a good man. But I thought the same of Marshal Syd . . . and look how he turned out."

Joey had had enough. Even Patsy and Oscar were sniggering over the new lawman's bumbling. Springing to his feet, Joey weaved between legs and skirts, found the closest alley, and ran for home.

CHAPTER 21

The last time he had seen Sara Cardiff in that dress . . .

Duncan had sighed. "Green?" he had asked. "Not blue?"

"Green reminds me of you," she had whispered. "Your eyes, you know."

Sara looked lovelier than he had remembered. In fact, she looked younger, and Duncan suddenly felt ancient. Her beauty and smile left him flummoxed. He felt like some school-age kid who didn't know his right boot from his left, and he could hear a rustling in the crowd, and when he finally made himself look away from Sara Cardiff, he saw Mayor Nugget staring harder than his mouth was working his chaw of tobacco.

His eyes returned to Sara, and she gave him that quick nod. Somehow that relaxed him. He tried to return the gesture, and then made himself look away from that beautiful young woman. He saw the crowd, reading the faces of the closest ones as he would during a high-stakes game of five-card stud.

"Yes," he made himself say, followed by the only words that came to him: "You sure have a real pretty town here."

The crowd laughed.

He thought he was finished with his speech. He thought he was ready to slip away and catch up with Sara Cardiff. He even thought he had made a pretty good decision leaving Durango and, instead of wandering, heading up to the highest part of Colorado to a town that was dying right quickly.

Duncan started: "It has been my pleasure . . ."

But to his left, two men stumbled out into the street, one falling face-first, the other sliding on his knees—while the men, and two women, quickly moved out of the way.

The biggest man Duncan had ever seen stepped off the boardwalk and took a few steps forward. The two men he had pushed out of his path saw him, and in a flash they were running down the street, not bothering to look back.

Nugget chuckled. "Look at 'em yeller-bellied fools. They musta thought ol' Bryn Bunner was a-comin' to start a ruction with their sorry hides." The skinny old cuss whirled and grinned through that filthy beard at Duncan. "When he's here to settle things oncet and fer all."

The mayor had pulled out the shiny silver star that he was supposed to pin onto the lapel of Duncan's vest to finish the ceremony, but now he just breathed on it and wiped it on his filthy sleeve, right before he slipped it into a pocket.

"Reckon ya's gonna have to earn this here star first."

Duncan breathed in, then out, and pushed back the tail of his coat, revealing his revolver. His right hand found the walnut handle.

"No, no, no, no," Nugget said with a chuckle. "You ain't official yet. Can't go shootin' down nobody."

"You've already sworn me in," Duncan told him.

"Don't matter. You ain't marshal till you've whupped Bryn Bunner."

And, the way Duncan figured things, there was a lot of truth to that.

When he started working the buckle, he heard Sara whisper a curse or a prayer or maybe some advice, but the crowd was getting eager for what was about to happen. Logan Ladron stepped forward and took the gun rig from Duncan, who waited for some advice, a tip, a whisper of some weakness that behemoth of a miner might have. But the card dealer said nothing, just backed toward the batwing doors to the Crosscut Saloon.

Maybe, Duncan thought, *Ladron knows that there is no weakness to that barrel-chested brute.*

So Duncan removed his hat and gave it to Sara, who sighed and shook her head but, like her best dealer, also offered no tips for defense or a quick, lucky victory. Duncan removed his watch and coin pouch, kneeling to set those on the edge of the boardwalk, then loosened his tie and laid it next to those, and began walking toward that mountain of a miner while unbuttoning his vest.

A woman in the crowd hollered out the only advice Duncan was to receive:

"Don't be an idiot. Run for your life, Marshal!"

He glanced at both sides of the street, not looking for any escape route, but just to make sure no one was aiming a rifle or revolver at him. He wouldn't put an ambush past Conner Boyle, especially since he had not seen that sidewinder anywhere in the crowd. That caused him to look at some of the two-story buildings. A gun poking out of a window? Nothing caught his eye. But most of those second stories were false fronts, and the legitimate buildings didn't have the angle. Besides, he was grasping at straws. Conner Boyle was no fool. He wouldn't risk murdering Duncan when Bryn Bunner might very well solve the cheating gambler's problem in the next few minutes.

He went back to unbuttoning the vest. Bryn Bunner stopped walking and grinned ruthlessly. People began stepping off the boardwalks or moving around in the street, forming a ring for the two men about to go at it.

Gentleman Jim Corbett and Peter "Black Prince" Jackson's sixty-one-round no-decision in 1891 over in San Francisco . . . Corbett knocking out John L. Sullivan last year . . . Sullivan's clash with Charlie Mitchell ten years ago . . . Andy Bowen versus Texas Jack Burke earlier this year in New Orleans. Ah, the greatest boxing matches in history. And now, right here in Dead Broke, there was about to be a brawl that would top them all.

Unless Bunner kills me early.

They stopped. About two feet separated them. The loud banter from the gathering of Dead Broke citizens quickly dropped to hushed whispers, and then to a stillness one might expect from a mountain stream on a winter morning.

The leader of the area miners spoke: "I'm gonna whup you till there ain't enough left of you to spit on."

Duncan worked on the last button on his vest. "Just a minute," he said without looking up. He had seen everything he wanted to see about Bryn Bunner while covering the distance that separated them. And Duncan didn't want the behemoth to say another word. Bunner's breath was as nasty as his looks.

The last button came out of the sliver of a hole, and Duncan looked up, smiling as though he had just won a hundred-dollar pot. "There," he said. "Just let me get this off."

His right arm came through the opening, and the vest dropped down.

That was fine, he thought. Just fine. Most brawlers Duncan had met as a lawman would have been more inclined to have knocked him off his feet while he was busy with the buttons. But Bryn Bunner fought fair. Of course, he had all the advantages of winning this fight anyway, and he probably didn't want the men he worked with—or had worked with—and the people in town that he did business with to think that he was unscrupulous, unfair, a cheater and a low-down dirty dog.

The vest slid down Duncan's left arm, and he caught it with his left hand.

Bunner's eyes remained locked on Duncan.

Smart fellow, Duncan determined.

"Here," Duncan called out to a boy in the crowd. "Will you take this for me, sonny?"

Still, the big miner would not look away from Duncan's face.

Too smart, Duncan decided, for his own good.

The left hand came up fast, the fingers released the garment, and the vest landed perfectly over Bryn Bunner's ugly face.

A gasp escaped the crowd.

Bunner swore and reached with both hands to throw the vest down. The vest, which had cost Duncan $4.25 in Durango, fell on the miner's giant left boot.

Just before Duncan's right fist slammed into the big man's jaw.

Duncan couldn't tell if the gasp came from the crowd or the big brute who staggered to Duncan's left. Or if Duncan had gasped himself. His fist felt like it had been run over by a freight wagon loaded with a ton of gold. But he had to block that out, because Bunner planted one of those miner's boots firmly in the mud and was turning back to face his sneaky assailant.

So Duncan put a hard left right into what little of the lips he could see beneath the beard.

That backed the leviathan up a couple of feet, but the man's teeth weren't knocked loose or down his throat. Instead, Duncan pulled his hand away and began shaking some feeling back into his entire arm and flinging blood and saliva from his knuckles and fingers into the street.

Should have kept that money purse and used the old trick again, he thought.

He faked the right, but Bunner didn't bite, and when he tried a left uppercut, an arm the size of a ponderosa pine trunk deflected that easily.

Deflected? It almost took Duncan's arm off.

The right follow-up punch was also blocked, bouncing off Bunner's left shoulder instead of smashing more lips.

Seeing the left leg swing out toward him, Duncan jumped back, hoping Bunner would lose his footing, but the man had the balance of that act that had come through Dodge City one year, where a fat man rode a small bicycle on a wire about twenty feet above Front Street, from one saloon to the other.

Duncan stopped himself from throwing another punch.

That's what Bunner wanted.

Don't wear yourself out, he told himself. *Save some strength.*

He easily ducked a haymaker from the burly man, and did not try fighting back. It was time to see if Bryn Bunner would start an angry attack and Duncan could wear him down in a hurry.

Blood began to collect in the miner's chin whiskers, but he just smiled, and the smile became a laugh.

They were circling now, mostly lobbing lame feints, both men doing this on purpose until they caught their breaths. Most of the men in the crowd began hurling insults at both fighters, and a few women echoed those criticisms, some using language as salty as some silver miners.

But this, Duncan knew, wasn't a show for some boxing fans filled with bloodlust.

This was a fight with a purse higher than anything those great pugilists of America and abroad had been chasing. This was for control of Dead Broke, Colorado. And respect of the citizens.

"Both of you is the sorriest scoundrels I ever seed in my fifty-nine and three months on this earth!" someone sang out. "My four-year-old niece fights better than you two bums."

Duncan saw the move. Bunner's right foot came up, but Duncan jumped back.

"Kick!" a man shouted. "H-h-h-he t-t-tried to k-k-kick him. That's a ff-ff-ff-ff-foul. Ff-ff-ffoul! Ff-foul! Ffff. . ."

Someone knocked that man into the mud.

"Quit blockin' my view and spittin' on my cousin!"

The two fighters circled each other for a few minutes, then Bunner lunged—lightning fast for a man of his build—but Duncan ducked to his left, letting a massive arm and fist go over his head. Coming up, Duncan tried to plant a right between the man's kidneys, but Bunner pivoted and dropped low, then came up and fired a left that Duncan deflected, although for a few moments afterward, Duncan wasn't sure if his left arm was still part of his body. Then the feeling returned to his arm, and that hurt like blazes.

"You know what?" Bunner whispered with a smile.

Smart enough to save his voice, breath, and strength, Duncan didn't answer or even shake his head.

That made the brute's bloody lips turn upward in a grin.

"I'm gonna beat you to within an inch of your life."

He sprang forward, but Duncan dropped to all fours and braced himself as the miner fell over him and into the filthy street. Before Duncan could get back to his feet and throw a good punch, or kick the man somewhere that would hurt a lot, Bunner was already up, grinning, then swinging and charging.

Duncan couldn't move that fast. He was lucky that the miner's punch simply caught the top of the shoulder, but that was going to leave a bruise for a long, long time. The following jab with the right hand struck Duncan's left wrist as he fought to fend off the blow. That numbed the lower part of Duncan's arm.

But Bunner slipped, dropping to one knee. His head was too inviting a target for Duncan to resist. He kicked.

Too late. Bunner caught Duncan's boot with both hands, somehow stopping the blow, and twisted. That was trouble, but Duncan let himself go, falling, using his forearm to break his fall, then rolling over. Bunner dropped to his back, unable to keep his grip and twist Duncan's ankle till the bones broke or he ripped off the lawman's foot.

Bouncing up, Duncan charged. Bunner pushed himself to his knees, spit, cursed, and dived out of the way of Duncan's right foot. The leg came down. Duncan leaped back, sensing a wild swinging slash from the brute's left arm.

Duncan sucked in a lungful of air, let it out, wiped the sweat, blood, muck, anything off his face with a dirty shirtsleeve. His shirt front was ripped, the mother-of-pearl buttons lost. The undershirt was stained from mud, dirt, blood, and who knew what else. His chest heaved. His heart pounded. He saw nothing—no Sara Cardiff, no men, no women, no town. His focus tightened on Bryn Bunner. Bunner was all there was in the world for this moment, this eternity.

Bunner came up to his knees. He spit out saliva mixed with a good bit of blood. No teeth came with it, as far as Duncan could tell.

No words were spoken. Duncan slipped off the torn

shirt. It would just hinder his punches. It wasn't like an army of seamstresses could do anything for that ruined cloth and thread anyway.

Now the big miner came to his feet. He spit into his palms, which closed again into sledgehammer-sized fists.

Duncan backed up. The left haymaker went over his head when he ducked and leaped to his right. He feinted a blow, kept backing up, sensing the nearness of the crowd, though he didn't have any idea where he was. He couldn't make out the Crosscut Saloon, but not because of sweat or blurred vision. He just could not let Bryn Bunner out of his sight.

The man came quickly. The first punch Duncan knocked aside. The second caught him hard in the shoulder, but Duncan managed to clip the giant's ear. Duncan punched, making contact with something, but Bunner's arms spread out and then sprang shut, like a beaver trap.

Somehow Duncan managed to escape that death hug, leaving Bunner's arms around his own torso. Hugging himself.

Spitting out curses, blood, and saliva, Bunner charged again. Duncan leaped back, but hit something solid. He saw the blur of a punch heading his way, and he spun to his right, inside the onrushing fist. That saved him from a broken nose or the loss of several teeth, but his ankle caught on the boardwalk—he had backed into a wooden column—and down he went on wood, a nice change from mud, dirt, and horse manure.

Wood cracked. Bunner had slammed into the column. The awning dropped about a foot. Duncan came to his knees and saw the miner stepping back, to the side, then roaring like a freight train and charging like an angry bull.

"Noooooooo!" someone shouted.

Duncan couldn't avoid Bunner's shoulder, which caught him in the lower ribs and drove him back. Wood cracked, glass shattered, and they fell inside a building, sliding across the floor till Bunner's head struck something solid, and he rolled over.

Duncan came up on his hands and knees. He smelled something pleasant but powerful. Curses came from behind him, and Duncan reached up, almost blindly, and found a hold. That he used to pull himself to his feet, and he staggered back, hitting a bench, or table, or workplace. His left hand reached blindly behind him. Metal banged against wood.

Bunner was already standing, spitting onto the floor, shaking his head angrily, but Duncan lost his balance and needed both arms to grab hold of a big chair to keep from falling down.

The chair? The chair? What kind of chair . . . ?

Duncan's left hand caught hold of something cold. He gripped it, pulled it before him, couldn't quite make out what he held. Then he saw a flash, realized Bunner was throwing something, and ducked as something hit the mirror behind him, cracking it. Duncan threw whatever it was that he was holding at the miner.

The brute twisted his head and let Duncan's weapon hit the headrest of the barber's chair. He had thrown a comb. Hand-engraved brass, it turned out, but not quite the same as throwing a hatchet or knife. Then again, it might have been a tad more dangerous than the rosewood shaving brush Bunner had flung at him.

They were in a barbershop.

Shaving mugs flew next. The one Duncan threw was solid copper. It would have hurt more than the tin one Bunner fired. But both missed badly.

No straight razors came out. Bunner flung a water bowl, while Duncan could only find a soapy towel that somehow caught the miner squarely in the face.

Seeing a potential advantage and a way to end this fight now, Duncan charged. The towel came off Bunner's face, but not soon enough to stop Duncan's shoulder from slamming into his stomach just above the waistline.

He drove Bunner back into the fancy chair with its towel bar, fancy backrest, and a fancy footrest—obviously, this shop had been built during the boom days of Dead Broke.

The chair's massive base, however, wasn't heavy enough to stop the chair from toppling backward, carrying Bunner and Duncan with it. Bunner somersaulted, which sent Duncan sailing head over heels through what had been the shop's plateglass window. His legs hit the boardwalk, his back, shoulders, and head smacking into the mud next to the water trough.

Which, he figured, was better than breaking his back on a hitch rail or that same water trough.

CHAPTER 22

Duncan felt himself being pulled up and cringed at several stinging pats on his shoulders. Someone started twisting his head one way or the other. A finger went inside his mouth and turned his head left, then right.

"Amazing," a British voice said. "Absolutely amazing."

Duncan started to shake his head once the finger was withdrawn, but before that could happen water smashed across his face.

"Get me a towel!" another voice yelled.

"Never mind." Something rough and hard came to Duncan's face and began wiping away water, sweat, blood, and almost Duncan's eyeballs.

"Is Bryn dead?" another voice roared.

"Nah. But Dexter's place is, sure-nuff. He's gonna be madder'n a hornet."

"That he missed this fight!" That sounded like a woman to Duncan. "Barbershops can be rebuilt, but this fight ain't never gonna be topped."

"Who won?" someone asked.

"It ain't even begun." That had to be Mayor Nugget. "Round one's done, and I reckon it's a draw. Let's start the second round."

"Marquess of Queensbury Rules!" a woman shrieked.

"No. Dead Broke Rules!"

"Which means . . . no rules!"

Yeeeeeeeeeee-hiiiiiiiiiiiiiiiiiiii!!!!

Bryn Bunner grinned. Then he charged Duncan, coming at him like an angry Texas longhorn.

But Duncan had seen longhorns aplenty at all those cattle towns he and Syd Jones had tamed.

He feinted to his left, then sidestepped to his right, twisting and narrowly avoiding one of Bunner's sweeping arms.

Turning—staggering from near-complete exhaustion, actually—Duncan tried to shake his head clear, but his vision still wasn't what any eye doctor would call excellent. Sweat stung his eyes. He squeezed his eyelids shut, then realized too late what a stupid mistake that was.

Before his eyes opened, he was seeing stars, and feeling like a cannonball had slammed into his head. Down he went, in the mud and muck, and that stench and filth revived him. Reviled him. Made him angry at himself, at Bryn Bunner, at Drift Carver for somehow talking him into accepting this job, at Syd Jones for letting him down, and even at Sara Cardiff, because Duncan was fairly sure he would not have left Durango if it hadn't been for the mere mention of her name.

Sensing and hearing, he rolled before Bryn Bunner leaped up and crashed down where Duncan had been. The brute swore and fell to his right, breaking his fall with his forearms, but planting his beard and face in the street.

"Here!"

Duncan turned quickly, expecting one of Bunner's

fellow ruffians to be attacking, but instead he saw a man wearing sleeve garters and an apron tossing him a wet towel. "I got five dollars on you, pardner!" the man yelled, punctuating that with an approving nod, and then hurrying back to the far boardwalk.

The towel felt wonderful on his face, even if Duncan only wiped it for a few moments. His vision cleared enough for him to see that the towel was now filthy. He had hoped to let that coolness rest over his aching forehead, stinging eyes, bleeding nose, and busted lips for a while. Instead he pitched it to the ground.

He could see somewhat clearer now. At least he could see that someone was helping Bryn Bunner. A bucket of water had been dumped over his head, but Bunner had more friends in town than a newcomer—especially a lawman—like Mick MacMicking. The miner got a jug of whiskey, and the man drank it, and if the rough liquor burned all his cuts and scrapes, Bunner did not show it.

After being pulled to his feet, Bunner, who kept one hand on the handle of the jug, nodded at Duncan.

"Here," he said, holding out the stoneware with his left hand. "Take a sip. You'll need it. It's . . . gonna be . . . your last."

He was walking slowly, more like weaving, but his eyes locked onto Duncan.

That was all the warning the lawman needed.

He let Bunner come. The man's bloody, bearded mouth turned into a grin.

"It ain't good whiskey," the miner croaked. "But it's whiskey."

Duncan waited. Once Bunner was just a few feet

from the marshal, the arm with the jug moved fast, swinging. But that's what Duncan expected. He ducked, the bottom of the jug raking through his grotesque hair. The mud packed atop his head probably caused Bryn Bunner to misjudge his aim. Instead of cracking his skull, it barely grazed him. And Bunner swung too hard. He staggered past Duncan, who managed a pathetic attempt at a punch that hit nothing but air and sent Duncan to his knees.

Bunner got the worse of that. He slipped in the mud and fell face-first in it. Worse, the jug shattered against a parked buckboard, and the wretched whiskey that was at least whiskey mingled with urine, rainwater, and whatever else fell on the streets of Dead Broke.

It started raining.

Oblivious to the rain, practically unconscious to everything except Bryn Bunner, Duncan started through the quagmire as the miner pushed himself up and weaved left to right, right to left, then tilted his head back and let the rain wash his face.

He looked to be so close, maybe ten yards, but when Duncan stopped, the miner appeared to be a hundred yards from him, maybe one hundred miles. The rain came down harder now, cold—for all rain is cold at this altitude—but somehow comforting, though some words from the Dead Broke populace reached him.

"Amias, do you want to catch your death? Come back here with me."

"We've called some baseball games because of rain, but does 'em rules apply to pugilism, too?"

"Nah. We's under Dead Broke rules."

"Which means . . . no rules!"

A wild cheer went up and down the streets.

"Ten dollars says the lawman knocks his head off."

"Five—no, fifteen says the lawdog don't even make it to ol' Bryn!"

"Why doesn't someone stop this madness?"

The last voice sounded like Sara Cardiff.

That gave Duncan some hope. He still remembered what Sara sounded like. At least, he thought he did.

Duncan saw mud. His bandanna—well, it might have been someone else's wild rag. He saw channels in the mud made by his boots, and Bryn Bunner's boots. There was a patch of red and black flannel. If his memory was right, that had been the color of the miner's heavy shirt. He saw a tooth. Molar? It was a big one. He ran his tongue over his mouth.

Not mine, he thought. That gave him another lick of hope. All of his teeth were still in place. Except, of course, the last upper big one that Kyle Cunningham had smashed out with the butt of his Springfield in the Crockett Saloon in . . . what town was that?

He stopped, though he didn't remember stopping. He might have stayed there for a week, a month, a millennia. *Millennia.* Sara had taught him that word. He shook his head. Closed his eyes. Felt the rain on his head, running down his back, dripping from the fingers at his side.

Somehow, the lids opened, and he saw Bryn Bunner staring up at him.

"Get up," Duncan whispered hoarsely. "So we can finish this."

The head shook. "Come down here. We'll finish it . . . like . . . hogs."

Duncan shook his head. But the next thing he knew, he was sinking to his knees, and had to reach out with his left hand to grab hold of Bunner's shoulder to keep himself from falling into the mud.

"Give up?" Duncan asked.

"No." Bunner surprised him. He had enough strength to shake his head once. "You're finished."

"Like . . ." But Duncan couldn't finish the thought.

Bunner's head bobbed with what seemed like respect. "You put up a good fight. Too bad you had to lose."

"No. You fought too hard to lose, but . . . who are you?"

The miner's head shook. "I ain't . . . rightly . . . what did . . . you say?"

"You're finished." Duncan hit the man hard right smack in the middle of that cauliflower ear.

The head turned right. Duncan's arm fell to his side.

He saw Bryn raise a right forearm that looked more like a thigh. Duncan's brain told him to use the left arm to fend off the blow. When the arm refused to move, his brain told him to duck, to turn his head, to . . .

His head jerked from the impact of Bryn's iron fist, but his knees remained anchored in the mud, and he didn't topple over, though even if he hadn't lost another tooth by that one, a couple were barely hanging on inside his mouth.

"Say . . . you . . . quit."

Duncan managed to turn his head back to Bryn Bunner.

"I have . . . not . . . yet . . . begun—"

The miner finished the sentence after another punch,

but this one right into the center of Duncan's chest. A rib or two might have cracked.

". . . to . . ."—Bunner spit out blood—"fit."

"Fight," Duncan corrected.

"Fit." The miner's head shook once. "Like I said. Fit."

Duncan hit him in that ugly, fat, knuckle-scarring ear.

"Someone stop this madness!" a man wailed.

Duncan brought his left arm up. His right arm wasn't working too well at this moment.

Thunder rolled.

The wind picked up. The rain started down harder, colder, stinging like hail. Or maybe it was hailing now. That could happen this high up.

Bryn Bunner's left hand lifted, too. No. Duncan shook the rain and the sense back into his head. Right hand. But it was on Duncan's left side. That must have confused him.

They swung. Neither tried to block the other's punch. Both fists slammed into the side of the face each was trying to ruin. Both men fell into the mud, and rolled over, letting the rain wash off the blood, the mud, the sweat.

"Oh," a woman prayed, "the humanity!"

It wasn't raining, Duncan realized. Or hailing. Not now. The shower had stopped, but instead of dark clouds or sun or a Colorado Rockies sky, Duncan saw nothing but faces, though none he could recognize, because some he saw two of, others three, some just blurs.

"Lift him up careful now," someone said.

"Ya sure showed him, Bryn," a voice about as far away as Dodge City praised.

"Easy with him, easy."

"Take him to my office."

"Who won the fight, Mayor? We gots to know. To settle the bets. You was the judge. Who won?"

"I'm covering all of Bryn Bunner's doctor bills. Ya hear that, Doc. You jus' send all them bills to me. Nobody else. Bryn Bunner's my man."

Three cheers rang out.

Duncan felt himself lifted.

"I say it's a draw. Yep. It's a draw. Y'all gots that." That sure sounded like Mayor Nugget.

But then another voice reached Duncan.

"Easy does it. Bring Duncan to the Crosscut. Put him in my office. It's closer than my house."

He was moving. He sensed, but couldn't quite see, Sara Cardiff walking beside him. He felt, or thought he felt, her take one of his raw, scarred, swollen hands into her own. But which hand she held, he just didn't know.

Or care.

"By grab," someone shouted. Maybe it was Drift Carver. "That ain't no draw. Mick MacMickin' is goin' to Miz Sara's room. That means MacMickin' is the unanimous winner!"

It sounded like Fourth of July fireworks going off in Dead Broke, Colorado.

CHAPTER 23

Caleb Holden was giving Conner Boyle bad habits. The wealthy owner of Lucky Dice Gambling Hall—wealthy because of marked cards, rigged roulette wheels, slick faro operators with gaffed boxes, and a handful of women who could relay to Holden's best cheats what the other players were holding—downed the brandy like he was shooting down Taos Lightning.

"Look on the brighter side of things," Holden said with a laugh. "That lawdog will be so stove up, he won't get out of that wench's upstairs room till the crack of doom." The gunman, bold as brass, walked over to Boyle's desk, opened his mahogany box, and pulled out a pricey cigar. Biting off an end and spitting that onto the floor, Holden struck a match and fired up his smoke, then removed the Havana as he laughed. He blew out some smoke from his mouth, and used the cigar as a pointer as his eyes brightened and locked on Boyle.

"Then again, if I was in that room, I doubt if I'd ever leave." The cigar returned to his mouth, and Holden lifted the tumbler he had set down and walked to the window, pulled back a curtain, and looked outside.

"Hmmmmmm," the gunman muttered.

Boyle started to pour another healthy pour of his brandy, but made himself stop. Keep drinking like this and he would wind up worse than Syd Jones.

"Hmmmmmm what?"

The curtain fell back into place, and Holden turned around. "First time in a month of Sundays that I ain't seein' nobody, afoot or with a loaded-down wagon, leavin' this dyin' town." He laughed like a coyote. "You don't reckon folks here is startin' to think that Mick MacMicking is some god, do you? That he can fix all that's wrong with Dead Broke?"

Giving up, Boyle filled his glass with brandy.

"I don't care what people think about that badge-toting piece of filth." He killed the liquor in one swallow. "He won't live long enough to see if the silver market rebounds, because he's gonna be deader than Dead Broke."

The gunfighter flicked ash onto the oriental rug.

"That's what I like to hear." He patted his holstered revolver. "I'll gun that lawdog down as soon as he steps out of the Crosscut. Then I'll pluck that star offen his coat and pin it on myself. That'll show folks who's the king of this mountain."

"No." Boyle walked away from the decanter before he got so drunk he might pass out. "Kill him now, and you'd be lynched."

Which would in its own way be a wonderful thing to see, he thought. *But not till I have what I want. Then maybe I'll shoot that hardcase myself.*

The thought made him laugh aloud. Yes, now Boyle was certain. He had had too much brandy.

"What's so funny?" Holden asked.

"Nothing. Who do we have in the Crosscut that'll tell us what we want to know?"

"Nobody."

"What do you mean, 'nobody'?" Boyle roared.

"I mean nobody." He waved his left hand, trying to calm Boyle down. "Don't work yourself into a stroke, ol' man. That sassy little blonde is in the same predicament you're in. We had a dealer and a bartender workin' for us. Sure we did. You paid 'em both enough. But De Jean give up on this town a week ago, decided to set out for Denver. And Truluck . . . ?" He stopped to finish his drink, then took a puff on the Havana. "He just up and left. He was too fat nohow. Couldn't walk a block without havin' to stop and catch his breath. He's probably down in the Texas Panhandle by now, where it's flat and where a man can breathe without wearin' out his chest muscles."

That monologue left Caleb Holden needing to replenish his lungs.

"Find someone you can trust, someone who wants to earn fifty bucks."

"I'll take that job."

"You can't. Sara Cardiff wouldn't let you inside her place. I need someone who can drink without getting drunk or play cards. I'll stake his hand. Just get into that saloon and listen. Find out when that gunslick is coming out again, so we'll have someone ready to put a bullet in Marshal MacMicking's head when he finally shows himself."

Holden grinned. "I'll do that myself."

"Just get a man who can do this job without botching things."

Boyle reached inside his inside coat pocket, pulled out some bills, and walked to the killer. He handed him four notes, and Holden grinned, shoved the money inside his pants pocket, and killed the last of his drink, then crushed out the cigar in the glass.

Ruffians, Boyle thought. *Why do I always surround myself with ruffians?*

He knew the answer to that, too. Ruffians were cheap. But the gunfighters he was bringing into Dead Broke were pricey. That caused him to think.

"Any word from Telluride Tom?"

Holden's head shook. "He'll show up, though. The jobs for hired killers like T.T. aren't as plentiful as they were a coupla years back."

"And . . ." Boyle paused. "Ben Usher?"

"Nothin'," Holden replied. "But Ben Usher ain't as predictable as most gunhands. I've heard stories that he took on jobs that didn't pay hardly enough to buy hisself any ca'tridges."

Boyle sighed, and walked back to the decanter. Holden found his hat and walked out of the office.

She opened the door and stepped inside, but held the door open.

"Want some coffee?" Sara asked.

Duncan MacMicking wondered if he could answer without screaming. Or feeling some of his teeth come out with his words.

"I suppose." Well, that didn't hurt as much as he had thought it would.

"Would you prefer bourbon?" she asked. He thought he saw that twinkle in her eyes, but he wasn't sure his vision was one hundred percent yet. He wasn't even sure if it was fifty percent. Was that really Sara Cardiff standing there, holding the door open?

Duncan's head shook. "No. Coffee will do." Whiskey, as raw as his mouth felt, would burn like the devil.

"How about some breakfast?"

His head didn't shake as hard this time. Duncan wasn't always smart, but he had always been a quick learner. And shaking his head too hard hurt.

Sara turned to whoever was waiting in the hall. "I'll take the coffeepot, Sandra." She disappeared, leaving the door open, but came back in a moment, holding a silver pot with an oven mitt. Sara then told whoever Sandra was:

"Ask Ignacio to fry—no, scramble—four eggs. If those biscuits are done when you're downstairs—done, but not burned—put a couple of those on the plate." She paused, glanced at Duncan, then looked back at this apparition called Sandra. "Loads of gravy on the biscuits." She nodded, as though confirming her choices. "There's bits of sausage in the gravy, right?"

"Yes, ma'am," Sandra must have answered.

"Good. I think he can handle sausage in gravy. I'm not sure he's ready for bacon. Certainly not steak. And ask Ignacio if he can make a good soup for dinner and supper."

She closed the door with her left foot and walked toward the large sofa that had been turned into a bed.

Her dress, as always, was blue. But it seemed to be the same dress she had been wearing . . . wearing when?

As she poured coffee into a cup on the side table, Duncan asked, "How long have I been here?"

"The brawl on the street was yesterday," she said, spooning sugar into the coffee, then stirring it with a tiny spoon.

"What happened last night?"

She laughed. "You slept. Like a dead man."

Now she sat on the sofa beside him, holding the cup, which smelled . . . No, he was smelling her perfume. His smile hurt, but not for long.

"Where'd you sleep?" he asked.

"None of your business. Can you sit up?"

She had to set the cup down to help him.

"Do you need me to help you drink, or can you do that yourself?"

"I can . . ." But when he raised his right hand, he realized that he couldn't.

The first sip of coffee left him grimacing, but the warmth of the chicory as it traveled to his stomach made him forget about the rawness of his mouth and just how much his entire body hurt. Or maybe that warmth came from having Sara Cardiff sitting close to him.

"I don't . . ." Duncan had to stop for a second. Speaking hurt as much as swallowing.

". . . remember too much."

"No surprise." She made him take another sip. "Two grown men beating each other senseless. I don't know which I detest more. Seeing a pounding like that, or watching men shoot each other."

The next taste of coffee didn't hurt or burn as much.

"I never saw much sense in either, myself."

He waited for more coffee, then looked up into those mesmerizing blue eyes when none came. She had a curious—no, *doubtful*—look about her.

Duncan smiled, and grimaced immediately afterward.

"It's . . . true," he managed before he was forced to drink coffee again.

"You've done it enough."

He sighed. "My curse," he whispered.

Again, when no coffee came to him, he had to look at Sara again.

This time his smile did not hurt.

"I just happen to be good at my job," he said, and let out a long sigh.

She did not make him drink any more coffee. The next time when he looked at her, she leaned down and kissed him on his forehead.

His vision blurred, then focused. "Is that a . . . green dress?" he thought he asked.

"I said I wasn't hungry," Duncan told Sara when Sandra returned with a plate of food.

"You'll—" Sara started, but Sandra finished the statement for her.

"Eat." The platter slid onto the table next to the coffeepot. "If you want to get to marshalin', you will eat. Yes, sir, you will eat indeed."

He wasn't sure he wanted to get out of Sara's office. And he didn't.

Duncan MacMicking slept the rest of that day.

Sara frowned at him the following morning when she brought in the tray of breakfast.

"What are you doing up?" she demanded.

He was sitting on the edge of the sofa, staring down at his boots. But he was still in his longhandles. He was surprised he had made it this far.

"I'm not," he said, pausing because Sara's footsteps as she crossed the room made him ache. "Up. Exactly."

"Lie down. It's time for breakfast."

When she checked on him at eleven fifteen the next morning, he was standing by the window.

"You are stubborn," she said.

He let the curtain fall and slowly, stiffly, turned around and smiled at her. "You've known that for a while."

"I tried to forget," she said.

"I didn't." Their eyes locked. "Not a minute."

Her head shook, and she walked to him, put her arm around his shoulder, and guided him back to bed.

"What's going on outside?" he asked as she pulled the covers up to his chest.

"Quiet," she told him. "For once."

"Your place busy?" he asked.

"Logan and I spend most of our days playing solitaire."

"Together?" He waited for her to look at him.

"Don't be silly," she said. *"Solitaire."*

He shrugged.

"Drift Carver's theory is that everybody is still talking about that barbaric act of violence you and Bunner displayed." She sighed. "Maybe that takes their minds off things. I don't know."

He shook his head. "You know, I can't bring the good old days back to Dead Broke. No one can. The only reason I took this job—"

"I know," she whispered, and brought two fingers to his mangled lips. "Shhhhhhhhhh."

He liked that touch. She didn't hurt him when she touched him. He didn't hurt at all. Even if she was wearing blue today, and not that green dress.

"Our mayor," she said, "and what we have for a council have all sorts of plans to bring people to Dead Broke."

"I've heard rumors," he started.

Her laugh had that same musical quality that he remembered.

"Percy Stahl's idea." She stopped. "Percy's on the town council. He runs a small saloon. No gambling. Mostly beer. Did pretty good business—but everybody did back when silver was king. Anyway. He's bringing in mail-order brides and—"

"Mail-order brides or . . . ?" Duncan interrupted.

"Don't have a filthy mind, Duncan MacMicking," she admonished. "Mail-order brides. He thinks that will help repopulate Dead Broke."

This time, the laughter did not hurt Duncan at all. "That'll take some time."

"Hush," she said. "Women could bring stability to this town. Keep some men out of places like mine. Keep some men where they ought to be."

His head nodded in agreement and understanding.

"One original idea," she said, "came from a painter, Laurent Dubois. He painted my place. Interior and exterior."

Duncan looked at the paint job. It did have a professional touch, but he would have expected no less from Sara Cardiff.

"Laurent aims for . . . I don't know . . . families and . . . well, it would be for visitors, coming up from the overcrowded cesspool that Denver has become. He's going to create ice sculptures. Make a whole city of ice. Animals. People. That might bring people here, to spend money in our hotels and dining establishments. I don't think places like Percy's and mine will get many families in here—but it sounds like a beautiful idea."

"It does." Duncan nodded, but he still had a hard time picturing exactly what Sara was talking about and why a painter would want to chisel out a town and bears or eagles and men and women made of ice.

They looked at each other for a long while. Then Duncan said, "What was your contribution for ways of saving Dead Broke?"

Her eyes hardened. "I said something like maybe we should keep people from killing each other."

His nod was solemn. "So that's why I came here."

"No."

He looked up at her again.

"I wanted Syd Jones back."

He watched her rise and walk to the door. She didn't look back. He said nothing. The door opened, closed, and Duncan felt alone. His knuckles hurt again. So did his mouth. Every part of his body felt raw, tender, and . . .

Hopeless. Like Dead Broke, Colorado.

CHAPTER 24

"He's moving around," Caleb Holden told Boyle.

His boss looked up. "Who?"

They were playing draw poker—but not betting. Just killing time on another dead day in Dead Broke.

"Who do you think? Our new town marshal."

Boyle dropped his cards on the table and stared hard at his hired gunhand.

"How do you know?"

Holden showed off his hand. Three tens with a king kicker, and a worthless two of hearts.

"I see him at the window upstairs." He laughed. "That's that little hussy's room, you know."

Boyle felt himself grinding his teeth.

"I don't know why folks think they gotta live or have rooms above where they work. You don't. But you're richer than anyone in town. 'Ceptin' that crazy ol' loon of a mayor we got. And he ain't as rich as he once was. That seventeen-hundred-pound diamond of silver ain't worth as much as it used to be."

"It's still valuable," Boyle said. Even with the drop of silver's value, that giant monstrosity would be worth a good price to some of those crazy collectors back East or in San Francisco or Chicago.

Boyle sipped coffee. "And some people live where they work. Especially when Dead Broke was booming. It was the only way to protect your place of business."

"You didn't."

"No. But that's because I had paid gunmen here. And . . ." He chuckled, and shook his head. He was like everybody else in Dead Broke. Remembering the good old days. Telling stories about the good times, the rich times, everyone had back a year or so ago—an eternity, now. "This joint never closed back then. Twenty-four hours a day, seven days a week, every month, every year."

Boyle gathered the discards and shuffled. He was dealing when Holden said: "It'd be real easy to kill him."

Three cards were down in front of the killer's hands. Boyle dealt himself a third card and stopped. He said nothing, just waited for Holden to finish his thought.

"Man with a rifle. Good man. Just waiting. MacMicking looks out of the window. Then—bang." He snapped his fingers. "No more lawman. I'd be made town marshal."

"Shooting uphill isn't that easy." Holden finished dealing the hand.

"Don't have to be uphill," the hired killer said. "Found some places across the street that would do just fine."

"No." Boyle picked up his cards. He started to wish he was cheating in this deal and that they were betting money, real money, not just killing another dull day in a dying town.

"Boom," Holden said softly, and tapped his forehead, right above the nose. "One shot. One dead lawman."

"Cards?" Boyle asked.

"Two." He tossed down two cards.

Boyle dealt, then set the deck down. "I'm pat."

After picking up the two cards, Holden shrugged. "Pat hand or not, I wish we was playin' for real money." He smiled, and laid down a queen-high straight.

"So do I," Boyle said. He leaned forward, and dropped his voice into a whisper. "You keep forgetting that we have another plan. On top of killing Mick Mac-Micking, we're getting out of here with as much money as we can, and that big statue that Nugget has in his palace. We leave Dead Broke for the undertakers, the losers who have nothing else to do but dream about ice palaces and ugly women who can't find a husband except through some catalog or newspaper advertisement."

Holden seemed to get the message. He shrugged. "All right, boss man. But I don't see how some gunfightin' contest and nothin' else is gonna help. And, like I said . . ." He looked down at his hand. "I wish we was playin' for money."

"So do I," Boyle said, and showed Holden an ace-high diamond flush.

The pounding of someone running up the stairs made Duncan lower the curtain, and he turned quickly, stepped away from the window, and saw his gun belt hung over the bedpost.

Knowing he would never reach it in time, he picked up the coffeepot Sara had left an hour or so ago, and got ready to heave it. The door swung open, and a kid stumbled in, followed by . . .

"Nugget!" Duncan lowered the coffeepot and shook his head. "What the devil are you doing?"

Dead Broke's mayor started explaining, but Duncan wasn't paying any attention to the man or the boy. He stared at the coffeepot. He turned his hand over and closed his fingers. No pain at all. He looked again at the silver pot. His left hand came to his right shoulder. That didn't hurt, either. He rubbed the top of the shoulder, then began moving both arms.

"What?" He looked up, remembering the uninvited guests. "Huh? Ummmmmm."

"Ya's famouser than ya ever been, Marshal." Nugget held out a newspaper in each hand. "Drift Carver brung these in. He was down in Denver fetchin' some stuff for Miss Sara. Brung these here newspapers for me to read."

"I read them!" the boy shouted. "You can't read. Remember?"

"Hush now." Nugget crossed the room in his bow-legged gait. The boy seemed to pout.

"Lookee here!" The mayor raised both arms and practically shoved the newspapers into Duncan's shoulders.

"They's all 'bout yer brawl with big Bunner," the mayor explained. "Don't mind that story on the bottom of the *Telegram.*"

"*Telegraph,*" the boy corrected.

"'Em few words is just to trick ya. When ya turns to the fourth page, it practically takes up the whole thing. 'Ceptin' fer 'em advertisements on one side."

The pages rattled. Duncan looked at the *Telegraph* and the *Denver City Reporter*, then back at Nugget, and then at the kid.

"Little Joey says as soon as some real writer—not one of 'em newspaper boys—sees these pieces, there'll be another book writ up 'bout ya. Ain't that right, Joey?"

Duncan looked at the boy, whose face tightened, then paled. His head went up and down, but he stepped back as though afraid.

Relax, Duncan told himself. He tried to smile.

The boy seemed familiar. Something from that brutal tussle with Bryn Bunner.

"I tol' Little Joey," Nugget was saying, "that ya'd tell him all 'bout the fights ya's been in. Since I's mayor and you're just the marshal—a marshal that ain't done a licka work in four or five days now, I might point out."

More steps sounded down the hallway, but Duncan recognized those. Sara Cardiff appeared in the doorway. It took her a moment to find her voice.

"Mayor." She shook her head. "Joey. What are you doing up here? Dun— Marshal MacMicking needs his rest."

"It's all right," Duncan said. He shook his head. "I've had enough rest. Four days?" He stared at Nugget, then looked at Sara for confirmation.

"*Five* days," she said.

"Five days," Nugget said, nowhere near as soft and lovely as Sara had. "Five days in bed. Five days in bed when—what salary was it that we's supposed to be payin' ya? All 'em days of sleepin' and a . . ."

He shut up, and slowly turned toward Sara. His Adam's

apple bobbed. He swallowed, and turned toward the young boy.

"Sleepin' and a . . . a . . . a playin' cards. But not for money or nothin'." His head went up and down more times than Duncan could count. "Yep. Restin'. Recoverin'. Gettin' all doctored and . . ." He tried to smile at Sara. "And nursed up."

Duncan felt the need to sit down, and he headed for Sara's rocking chair.

"Town's been quiet," Nugget said. "Well, I been patrollin' my town and all. Makin' sure no one got out of line, broke the laws nor nothin'."

Duncan sat down. Breathed in, exhaled, and looked at Sara.

"Joey wants to hear ya tell all 'bout that fight." Nugget slapped both sides of his pants. "Even though he seed most of it with his own eyes."

Duncan smiled. He turned from Sara and studied the boy again.

"Joey?" Duncan said.

"Yes, sir," the kid squeaked. He tried again. "Yes, sir, Marshal M-m-Mac-Mac-M-M-Mi—"

"MacMickin'!" Nugget finished for him.

"Call me Mick," Duncan told him.

"Nosirree," Nugget shot back. "Nosirree. Not in my town, nosirree. In Dead Broke—in my town— our young'uns treat their elders with respect. That's Marshal MacMickin' to ya, young Joseph. You best mind yer manners."

Sara shook her head, let out a sigh, and said, "I'll see about some lemonade."

* * *

Sara sat on the sofa. Duncan leaned forward in the rocking chair, focusing on young Joey Clarke. The boy and the mayor sat on the floor, legs crossed, eyes staring up, rarely blinking, at Dead Broke's marshal. They seemed to lock in on every word.

Duncan, of course, hardly remembered the fight—the brutal pounding, the senseless contest to determine who was in charge of Dead Broke. But if his listeners caught any error, they did not bother to correct the story-teller.

"I bet you had to take a bath after that fight," Joey said. "Didn't you?"

Duncan's eyelids came down, but not completely. He remembered being clean when he finally woke up, and he almost looked at Sara, but stopped himself, and just nodded. Then he smiled.

"Did you?"

Joey made a face. "Yeah," he said with disgust.

"I didn't take no bath," Nugget whispered.

That, Duncan thought, was obvious.

"Were you scared?" Joey asked. "I mean . . . not real scared . . . but . . . maybe . . . ummmmm . . . worried . . . I mean . . . you know . . . Bryn Bunner . . . he's like . . . Goliath. And you didn't have a slingshot. He's just so big. Wasn't you . . . scared . . . or . . . maybe . . . just worried?"

Duncan tried not to smile but figured he had failed. He rubbed his jaw, which didn't hurt, although his lips were still a bit on the raw side, and he wasn't sure how much longer he could keep talking.

"Concerned," Duncan finally answered Little Joey's question. His nod punctuated the statement. "Let's just say I was concerned."

"But you beat him. You won."

"Yeah. I figured I had to." Though he wasn't so sure he actually won that slugfest. That anyone won. Leaning forward, he reached out and tousled the boy's thick head of hair. "Remember, Joey, I really don't like to fight." That statement made him laugh, and that hurt his ribs.

So, he thought, *I'm not completely healed*.

But he was getting there. And talking to this young boy, and even the crazy old coot Dead Broke had for a mayor, was helping him get there. So was having Sara Cardiff in the room with him.

So, he realized, was having Sara back in his life.

How did I get a bath?

He shook away that thought. It would, he knew, be more than enough to drive him crazy.

"Was that the toughest fight—fistfight, I mean?" The boy was talking as fast as a locomotive running solo across the Kansas Plains. "I've read lots and lots about your gun battles against bad guys and I know a fistfight ain't nothin' like a shootout."

Duncan had a hard time keeping up with the boy.

"But was it . . . was it the toughest fistfight you ever got into?"

He started to laugh, but then a memory came to him, and he sat back in the rocker, thinking about what felt like a thousand years ago.

"It was one of them," he said, but didn't know he had spoken.

"Was there another one? One better or more brutal than what we all saw here?"

For a moment, Duncan didn't answer. The sound of Nugget spitting chewing tobacco into one of Sara's china cups brought him out of his memories and back to Dead Broke.

"There was one," he said in almost a whisper.

"Golly," Nugget said.

The boy whistled in disbelief.

"Who'd you beat?" Joey asked.

Duncan laughed softly. He shook his head.

"No, Joey. I lost that one."

The silence lasted at least a full minute, perhaps longer.

Nugget broke it with the splash of tobacco juice in the cup, which Sara echoed with a soft groan.

"Who coulda beaten you?" Joey said in a whisper.

Duncan answered immediately. "Syd Jones," he said. "Marshal Syd Jones."

"Our marshal?" The disbelief was apparent in the boy's voice and face. "Ex-marshal, I mean."

Nodding, Duncan leaned forward, resting his forearms on his thighs.

"But he's an old man!" Joey exclaimed. "Real old."

That brought out another laugh, which again hurt those ribs, but the memory that started filling Duncan's thoughts seemed to feel healing.

"He wasn't so old back then," Duncan said, nodding firmly. "But that didn't matter. He would have beaten me to a pulp if he had to. And he would have beaten me today, yesterday, tomorrow, or a month of Sundays from now. Old as he is. Even if I were younger and stronger and faster and wilier than I am now. He would have bested me."

"How could ol' Marshal Syd do that?" Joey said, his voice pleading. "When you whupped up Bryn Bunner like he was nothin' but a punk?"

"Because," Duncan said, "I was a punk back then."

He chuckled. "Not as big as Bryn Bunner. I'll give you that. Not bigger than I am now. Maybe a touch faster." His head shook and his laugh was firm, steady. "A whole lot dumber. But Marshal Jones would have won. In fact, if I was trying the same fool stunt I was trying back then today, Syd would have knocked me out and dragged me to jail just as easy as he did it all those years ago."

"How come?" Joey asked.

"Yeah." Nugget lurched forward so fast he spilled brown, thick juice out of the cup and onto the hardwood floor. "How come?"

Sara gasped and jumped up, grabbing a towel and stopping the juice from reaching the closest rug.

Nugget did not seem to notice. Joey, at least, started over to try to help, but Sara shook her head. "I've got it," she said, though her face showed her disgust at scrubbing up Nugget's stinking juice.

"Because I was in the wrong," Duncan said. "And Syd Jones was in the right."

"Does that really matter?" the boy asked.

"It ought to." Duncan nodded hard. "I think it did. I think I knew it did back then. I was just wild and young and stupid and trying to show off for my pals. That's something for you to remember, Joey. When you're young, you don't have to prove yourself by showing off. Showing off gets you in trouble more than it reaps any glory or wins any bets. There are many temptations you'll run into as you get older. There are many forks in the trail, too. You just have to avoid the temptations. And you have to study each path, and figure out which is the right road for you. Sometimes, that path might not look like much—might look impossible to get through. But that might be the path you have to take. So take it."

"How do I know if it's the way I need to go?" the youngster asked.

"Yeah," Nugget said. "How?"

Duncan grinned. "Well, the thing there is, is that . . . you don't know. Not for sure, anyway. Maybe you go by what your gut tells you to do. Maybe you pick the wrong trail. But you'll learn by your mistake, and you won't make that mistake again. Harder trails are some-times the ones you have to follow."

Joey sat back, trying to comprehend that. Duncan was wondering if anything he had said made sense. He turned to Sara, but she was still glaring at Nugget with a look that the mayor was trying to avoid.

"Is that why you come all the way up here?" Joey asked. "I mean, my ma and pa says that's the hardest road they ever took—coming up here two years ago."

Duncan reached up and ran his fingers through the boy's hair. "It sure was a mighty hard climb. But so is life."

"Well, that there sure was a fine story." Nugget sat up and held out his hand toward Joey. "But I've gots mayorin' to do, and our marshal here, he needs to get some rest, so that he can get out of this room and back to the job I'm a-payin' him to do."

He pulled the boy up, released his grip, and hurried to the door, which he pulled open, then turned around and pointed at the newspapers on the floor.

"Fetch 'em papers, Joey. I might wants you to read 'em tales to me later today."

When the door closed behind them, Duncan laughed at himself, and turned to Sara.

"Was that true?" she asked. "Did Syd Jones really beat you up in a fistfight?"

Duncan's head tilted, and he tested his jaw. "Wasn't much of a fight, to be truthful. I woke up in his jail cell, though."

"He should have kept you there," she told him.

CHAPTER 25

"What are you doing?"

Standing in the doorway, Sara put both hands on her hips. Her beautiful blue eyes looked hypnotic, but not in the way of alluring. It was, Duncan figured, more like the look of a timber rattlesnake's eyes—right before it struck. She wasn't wearing that green dress today, either.

"I started thinking—"

"That was your first mistake!"

Yep, she was mad all right.

He didn't let up. "— about what our mayor said yesterday. About me doing my job. Earning my pay. I am Dead Broke's marshal, you might remember."

"Don't be sarcastic."

"I'm not." He thought about telling her that if she didn't want him to leave, she shouldn't have brought his valise—the one with some clean duds in it, and his favorite pair of brass knuckles—to her room. But he wasn't that stupid. And he sure could have used those brass knuckles during that brawl with Bryn Bunner.

She sighed. He pulled on his vest and walked over to her, put his arms on her shoulders, and guided her inside. She managed to kick the door shut, and he pulled her into a hug. She resisted at first, whispering, "You're hurt. Your ribs."

"You've nursed me back to my old self," he said softly into her ear. Then kissed that ear.

"Where will you stay?" she whispered.

"Nugget says I can have my pick of the empty homes."

"There are some nice ones available these days."

"I'll probably find a bunk in a cell." He realized he hadn't seen the city marshal's office yet. For all he knew, it had been burned down like the fire station.

"You haven't changed a bit," she said.

He kissed the top of her head, then put three fingers under her chin and lifted her face. Their eyes met. So did their lips, which stayed there for a long while.

"You haven't, either," he told her after the kiss.

After a sad sigh, she placed her head against his chest. "Sometimes I wish you hadn't taken this job, you know."

"I don't," he said. "Well, I do. But only for Syd's sake."

"I know." She pulled away from him. He saw the tears that she somehow managed to keep from spilling down her cheeks.

She forced a smile onto her beautiful face, cocked her head back, and asked, "Is there anything I can do for you, Marshal?"

He nodded. "There is," he said. "Where is the marshal's office?"

The city marshal's office of Dead Broke, Colorado, reminded Duncan of home. And he whispered his thanks to Drift Carver. His gear lay on the floor across from the stove. Everything he had brought from Durango, except the stuff that had somehow wound up in Sara's room. He hadn't thought about how that valise had gotten there until now—but then that burly miner had given Duncan's head and body quite the pounding. He figured it was a miracle he could think of anything, even now. No saddle, which was likely with his horses. He'd search them out later. First, he wanted to make himself more than familiar with his office and, most likely, his home.

It must have been one of the original buildings in the town, since it was a log cabin set between a frame building and a stone one, both vacant. The jail, on the other hand, had been added on, and it was granite with walls four feet thick and a rock floor that would be impossible to tunnel through. Even if a prisoner could have dug through the floor, it wouldn't have mattered. The ground underneath it was solid bedrock.

Four small cells were on the south side, and a larger one on the north, with a wide passageway separating the two sections. That bespoke of Syd Jones. A jailer, or a trustee, or any deputy, lawyer, or judge could walk through and not get close enough for an irate prisoner to grab and jerk them to the iron bars.

He pulled on the door to the cell closest to the main office and stepped inside. This one had a bunk, complete with a stuffed mattress and clean sheets and a comfortable blanket. Duncan would claim this for his own. The three other cells had small cots, but he could imagine four silver miners locked in one of those cells and fighting for who got the bed. And those beds were permanently placed, the legs locked into the rock flooring. Duncan had tried them all, and no prisoner would be busting up those to make himself a club to swing. Even Bryn Bunner on his best day couldn't budge those.

The large cell had no bunks. Knowing Syd Jones the way Duncan did, he figured men would be given a blanket, and likely allowed to keep their hats to use as pillows and to find the cleanest, most comfortable bit of granite—as if gray granite was ever restful—to sleep on.

It had been a jail like this one where Duncan had awakened many years ago in a Kansas town after getting pounded into oblivion by Syd Jones.

He left the jail, closed the door, slid the two-by-ten blank back into the slots, and went to the coffeepot on the potbellied stove. Liquid sloshed around, but Duncan wasn't going to drink that. He hadn't forgotten Syd Jones's coffee, either.

First, though, he wanted some light in this dark, cold place. He pulled open the heavy shutters and saw where some bullets had plowed into one of them. Into, he noticed, but not through. He tapped the wood. No, a .50-caliber slug from a Sharps buffalo rifle would not have made it through five inches of this hardwood.

Duncan welcomed the sunshine. Just having light inside, revealing lots of motes of dust, warmed him somewhat. Three windows. Two on the sides, the largest one in the front. Iron bars would stop any prisoner from making it out this way, unless he was a midget, and keep anyone from coming in.

But what about getting out, if someone set the cabin

on fire? Syd would have allowed for something. Even Duncan recalled that time in Texasburg, the short-lived town on the Great Western Trail, when Mickey Maelstrom tried to burn Syd and Duncan inside their combination jail and marshal's office.

A search of the office found nothing, though. Through the roof? He checked with his fingers and palms. Nothing there. There couldn't be a tunnel. Not with that bedrock. He removed the bar and went back to the jail cells, knowing the only possibility was in the first cell that had been Syd Jones's bedchamber. Ten minutes later, he gave up. Nothing.

Maybe old Syd had thought he could have waited out anything in the jail room. No. He stared at the ceiling and remembered the roof. All wood. If someone set the log cabin ablaze, that would spread to the roof covering the jail. With all that stone flooring, a man—or men—might cook to death, or maybe die from all the smoke.

So he went back to the office. There had to be something.

"You dumb oaf," he told himself, and started pounding his left boot on the floor. Bedrock. What was bedrock to a silver miner? Hadn't Nugget used nitro-glycerin to found this town and claim his diamond of silver? But the sounds all told him he was on solid ground.

Until he moved Syd Jones's heavy desk.

He looked around, grabbed the ring of keys on a peg, let those rattle as he found a good-sized key of iron and stuck it through a sliver in the wood, then pulled up. The wood rose, and Duncan grabbed it and set it aside.

Well, Bryn Bunner never would get through that hole, but Duncan could. Certainly it was big enough for Syd Jones. He wasn't going to explore it, though. He just wanted to make sure he knew how to get out of this place if it ever came to that.

The key ring went back to the peg, and Duncan was sweating by the time he pushed the desk back into place. He wouldn't need a fire right now, he decided, and mopped his forehead with his bandanna.

Then he went back to work.

The woodbox was full, as was the large bucket of kindling. This high up in the Rockies, the nights got cold—sometimes the days stayed cold—and the stove was cold to the touch. The office could use a fire—not now, not after all that work to find his escape route, but certainly before the sun went down—and Duncan felt like he needed some coffee. Real coffee, the way those cooks had made it on the cattle trails. Nothing against Sara or whoever was cooking for her at the Crosscut, but he had acquired a taste for his own coffee.

He kept the shutters to all three windows open and looked at the mail that was stacked on the desktop. Wanted dodgers, a few letters from peddlers of handy items a lawman might want, old issues of the *National Police Gazette*, which he could use to light that fire whenever he got around to it.

Thirsty all of a sudden, he rose from the desk and found the coffeepot and a tin mug that looked clean enough. Sara Cardiff would scold him like that schoolmaster Duncan had when he was a boy. But the coffee went down and settled his stomach.

When he sat back down, he realized that he wasn't

hurting. All that work with the desk, moving around, hauling his grip and arsenal to the office from Sara's room over her gambling parlor, it could wear out a man. But Duncan felt just a bit stiff. The pounding he had taken from Bryn Bunner was becoming a memory that he would like to completely forget.

Finding his watch, he checked the time. Duncan shook his head. He had been at this for better than two hours. And he was hungry. Rising from the desk, feeling just a bit of stiffness in his legs and back, he pulled on his hat and had headed for the door when it slammed open. A big man in a red plaid shirt and striped trousers stepped inside.

"Marshal!" he yelled. "Either you do somethin' 'bout 'em cheatin' thieves or I will—the Scotsman's way." The brogue seemed like a mix of Scots Gaelic and Deep South.

"Hold on, partner," Duncan said, and he stepped back, pulling off his hat and gesturing at the rickety chair in front of the desk.

"Nae, I dunnah sit till suppertime. Are ye gonna give me justice or must I take it into me own 'ands?"

"Give me a minute," he said, and moved behind the desk, pulled open the drawer that he remembered held notepads, and withdrew the top one and a sharpened pencil. Sitting in the chair, he studied the point of the pencil, figured it was good enough, and said, "All right, sir, what's your name?"

"Ye shan't arrest me! Archie Baird has done no wrong."

He wrote the name down. "I'm not arresting you, Mr. Baird. I'm just putting the complaint in writing."

"Words. Writing. I dunna wan' words or writin'. If

those were what I wanted I'd be teachin' at Miss Mary's schoolhouse instead of searchin' for zinc."

Duncan looked up. "Zinc?"

"Aye, lad, zinc. But zinc has nae to do with the cheaters at that Lucky Dice, where there is no such thing as luck—just thievery."

The pencil had stopped after the words "Lucky Dice."

Duncan was standing, finding his hat, and pulling it back atop his head.

"The Lucky Dice," he said.

"Aye. Ye know the place, even if ye've yet to set foot anywhere except the muddy streets an' Miss Sara's establishment."

Duncan smiled. "I'd say it's about time I did visit Mr. Boyle's establishment. But first, sir, I need to hear everything you have noticed that would bring you to believe that they are cheating at the Lucky Dice."

The man's face reddened. Duncan, even though he felt like he was practically healed now from the Bunner bout, wasn't sure he could last half a round against this angry miner.

"If I were to tell ye all that I've seen—and me eyes be used to dark mines, so I see ever'thin' and I sees it all quite well—but that would take two days or more, and that pencil won't last that long, nor will that notebook ye have there before ye." He shook his head, and spit onto the floor. "I heard that ye was a man of action. Not some scrivener. Now I am beginnin' to think that those stories I heard of ye bestin' Bryn Bunner was somethin' I'd expect to hear from Drift Carver or Moses Malone. If that be the new law you bring to Dead Broke, I'll have nae to do with it, sir. I'll find justice on me own terms."

He stopped at the door when Duncan called out, "Mr. Baird."

The man turned slowly, frowning. "Mr. Baird be my fadder's name. I am jes Archie."

"Archie." He rose from the desk and walked to the gun case, found a shotgun, opened the breech, saw that it was loaded. Syd Jones was always ready. Snapping the weapon back to where it was ready to fire, he crossed the room and held the door open for the big miner.

"Lead the way to the Lucky Dice, sir," he said.

The big man now smiled. "It'll be me pleasure, Mr. Sheriff."

"Marshal," Duncan corrected, but Archie Baird was ten yards ahead of him by then, and Duncan had to run to catch up with him.

CHAPTER 26

"You wait here," Duncan told the miner before he could kick open the closed doors to the Lucky Dice.

The burly man turned around, glaring, and Duncan hoped he wouldn't have to fight that big man, too. Cowboys were typically pretty easy to lick. They were young, puny, and worn out from driving longhorn cattle four hundred to eight hundred miles. But miners were big, strong, and used to hard work, plus if they were inside mines and not panning for gold, they had really good vision in the dark. Lumberjacks—well, Duncan couldn't say. He had never tangled with a lumberjack, though he had clubbed a drunken carpenter once with a two-by-four.

"Just give me a couple of minutes." Duncan lowered his voice. "I need to do some investigating, and you sought me out. You must believe in law and order."

He frowned. "Me wife . . . she made me go to ye."

Duncan smiled. "You have a good wife, sir. If I need you, I'll holler." He waited, and, with great reluctance, Archie Baird stepped to the side.

Duncan pushed his coattail back and tugged his revolver, which came up easy. Satisfied, he let the weapon drop back into the slick leather and, keeping his right hand over the butt, tried the doorknob with his left hand.

It clicked easily, and he glanced at Baird one more time. "Do you have a weapon, Mr. Baird? On your person?"

"Archibald Baird need nae gun nor knife to pound cheating scoundrels into the dirt," he said. But then he pulled back his coat far enough so that the shoulder holster could be seen. "But jus' in case, Archibald Baird is nae fool." The coat fell back. "And I keep a dagger in me left boot top."

"You'll do fine, sir. But only if shooting commences."

"I'll be here, Marshal, if ye be needin' me assistance."

Duncan entered the saloon, closing the door behind him.

A man with a red mustache stood behind the bar, wiping out shot glasses. "We're clo—" Seeing the badge and recognizing Duncan, he closed his mouth, set the towel and glass on the bar, and started to reach below.

Duncan drew his revolver slowly and smiled.

"Looks like you've got plenty of glassware to clean, buster," he said evenly. "So just keep right on doing just that. And only that."

The man looked upstairs. His Adam's apple moved up and down as he debated his next move.

Duncan helped him make up his mind.

"A bullet between your eyes will get your boss and his hired killer down here as quick as a shout, friend. Make up your mind."

He made the smarter choice, grabbed the cloth, and

turned around to go to work on the other glasses. Duncan left his hand on his gun and moved easily to the roulette wheel. The bartender remained busy. Duncan looked underneath the table, but kept his eye on the bar and the top of the stairs. Outside, he heard a bull-whacker cussing his oxen as a wagon rumbled down the street, and the usual sounds of a town on a weekday morning—even a dying town like Dead Broke.

Rising from the floor, he made sure the bartender was still cleaning, and then he walked to the faro layouts. Unlike checking the roulette outfit, Duncan could examine the card boxes and keep an eye on the bartender and the upstairs at the same time.

There were four faro layouts, all together, and the boxes were on the tables. At the poker tables, he randomly pocketed some decks. Those he could check later for markings, but there were other ways a sharper could cheat at poker. The most common method was to have a saloon girl pretending to be getting cozy to a player while letting the dealer know what he was holding.

At the craps table he picked up a pair of dice and hefted them, then let them roll across the felt. Those were clean. So was the next pair. That figured, too. Sharpers would bring in their own loaded dice and swap them out when it was necessary.

A door opened upstairs, so Duncan straightened. The bartender laid down the towel and looked up, then he turned to show off his ugly smile.

Conner Boyle saw him first, catching Duncan through the corner of the eye, but the gambler must have thought he was one of his employees, because he took four more steps before stopping, recognition striking him like a thunderbolt, and he whirled. The gunman with him stopped, too, and reached for his revolver.

"No." Boyle held out his left hand to stop the man from making a serious error of judgment. But the gunfighter kept his hand on the butt of his revolver.

"Best listen to your boss, sonny," Duncan said with a smile.

That did it.

The punk swore, stepped aside, and started to draw.

"No!" Boyle screamed, and fell to his knees, covering his head.

The kid stopped his draw before the pistol got out of the holster. Duncan could see those eyes widen and the Adam's apple bob.

Without looking away from the two men upstairs, Duncan said to the bartender, "You just go right on cleaning your glassware, buster. And when you've gotten those all spotless, wipe the spit off the bar. Then maybe you can empty the spittoons."

Duncan waved the Schofield's barrel up and down.

"Help your boss up, kid. He's not as limber as he used to be."

The hate-filled glare from the gunman was one Duncan had seen many times.

"My .45's still out, kid," he said, "and it's cocked. And while some people have problems shooting uphill, I've done it enough to have confidence in my ability to hit one of you." He shrugged slightly. "But I might hit your boss where it counts instead of you." He steadied the barrel. "Or I might get the both of you."

The gambling den remained quiet until Duncan spoke again.

"I probably can get the bartender, too. Ask your boss. He's seen me at work before."

"Help me up, Holden," Conner Boyle grumbled.

"Follow your orders, kid," Duncan said. "But be careful you just help him up. You'll be closer together. My aim won't have to be perfect to hit both of you."

"Just . . . help . . . me . . . up." The cardsharper who wanted to be a big high-rolling moneymaker had to space out his words. His blood must have been boiling.

Holden—that would be Caleb Holden, Duncan figured—pulled the heavier, older, balder, and slower Conner Boyle to his feet. He had to grip the balustrade and glare down at Duncan, who kept his pistol ready.

"What are you doing here, MacMicking?" His face was redder than a turnip.

Duncan smiled. "I'm closing you down."

"You're . . . *what*?"

"You heard me." Without looking away, he shrugged toward the roulette wheel. "A miner filed a complaint that you were not running honest games here, so I had to follow up on it. And, my, what would I discover in just a few minutes? Well, you have wires rigged up to your roulette wheel." His chin then tilted to the faro layouts. "And your faro boxes are gaffed."

Boyle's face got even redder.

The door opened, and everyone looked that way, though Duncan managed to position himself so he could see the upstairs men—the most dangerous ones—as a man with a bowler hat, a vest of yellow brocade, and matching sleeve garters stepped inside with his both hands raised. Behind him came Archie Baird, holding a relic of a .44 in his right hand.

"Says 'e works 'ere, Marshal," the miner said. "Dice roller, 'e is."

"You dirty little Scottish pig," Boyle said.

"Well, now, this might add to the charges I'll have." Keeping his revolver trained upstairs, he told Baird to bring the dice roller over, and when the trembling, fancy-dressed man stopped shaking, Duncan held out his left hand.

"Let me see your dice."

He nodded. "They're on . . . the . . . the . . . table."

Duncan's head shook. "The ones in your pocket."

The man's left hand reached inside his coat. Duncan stopped him with a grunt.

"The vest pocket," he instructed.

The left hand began shaking.

"Now," Duncan said, and the friendliness had vanished from his voice and face.

The dice came out, and the gambler dropped them into Duncan's waiting palm. He tossed them up, caught them, and put them inside his coat pocket. "Now, I don't think those are proper tools for an honest gambler."

He shot Baird a quick look. "You saw him hand those to me. You'll testify that to a judge or in a trial, right?"

"Aye. An' I be an honest man."

"I know that." Stepping back, Duncan looked upstairs again. "And I know who isn't honest."

"I'll have your hide for this, MacMicking," Boyle said.

"We'll see. I'm not arresting you, but don't leave town. And you are officially shut down until a hearing can be held."

"You can't shut me down, MacMicking. Not without a court order."

"Well, if the judge overrules me, so be it. But if I catch one card dealt, one roulette wheel spun, or just one die in somebody's hand, I'll run you out of town—just like the old days. Remember?"

He nodded at the gunfighter beside the cheating gambler. "Unbuckle that holster, kid, and let it—with that hogleg still in the leather—drop to the floor. Then both of you boys keep put, your hands over your heads, fingers locked, and don't move, don't sneeze, and hardly breathe—till we're out the door."

The gun turned toward the bartender. "And you put that towel in one hand and a glass in the other and busy yourself till we're gone, too. Savvy?"

He complied right quickly.

Duncan faced the trembling gambler. "You're coming with me."

"Wh-what f-f-for?"

"Well, you were the one I found with loaded dice. You're under arrest." Duncan grinned. "My first arrest. You'll be my honored guest. First one I get to put in that cold, uncomfortable, snake-ridden, rat-infested, stinking ol' cell. Hope you're not used to sleeping in a comfortable bed."

He put the barrel of the pistol closer.

"Move." He looked over the gambler's shoulder at Baird. "Stop as soon as you're out the door," he whispered.

"What's your name?" he asked the dice man.

When the man looked again upstairs, Duncan told him: "You can use an alias if you want. I just need to know for now."

"Winston DeMint."

"Well, Mr. DeMint, I want you to go over yonder."
He nodded at the roulette wheel. "Crawl under there,
and pull out those trip wires and such. Then I want you
to go to the faro layouts and grab two of the boxes. It
doesn't matter which table. They're all gaffed. Keep
those in your hands. I want your hands filled. And don't
drop anything. I get nervous when I hear noises like
that. And my Schofield will be aimed at you when
we're leaving. Savvy?"

It took DeMint a while to figure out the rigged
wiring, but once he had the wiring and even the mech-
anism out, he shoved those into his pockets, pulled
himself to his feet, and grabbed the first two faro boxes
he saw.

"Thank you, Mr. DeMint," Duncan said. "I'll mention your cooperation to the judge when it's time for
your sentencing."

"You'll be the one facing a judge!" Boyle roared.
"You, dirty, stupid, miserable son of—"

Duncan aimed his revolver, ending that curse before
it ever escaped the cheater's mouth.

After a nod from Duncan, the miner led the way,
with DeMint following quickly.

Duncan told the bartender to move down the bar, all
the way from the door, and keep busy cleaning glasses.
Then he backed up, able to see the barman but, most
importantly, keep his revolver aimed at the gunfighter
and the angry gambler.

"I'm going to post a notice on your front door later
today," he said. "It had better stay on that door, Boyle,
and that door had better remain locked. Seven days a
week, twenty-four hours a day."

"Dead Broke's local judge might say something about that."

Now Duncan had him. "He might. If he hadn't taken his lawbooks with him yesterday and lit out for Cheyenne, Wyoming." The look on Boyle's face was a wonderful sight to behold. "We'll have to wait for the circuit judge to get here."

"I'll have my lawyer—"

"Wait until the circuit judge is here. Whenever he gets up this way." Duncan nodded. "Till then . . . I am the law. And, like I said, you remember how that goes, don't you, Conner?"

"All . . . too . . . well."

Once his boots hit the boardwalk, Duncan pulled the door tight with his left hand. Baird started up the boardwalk with the still-shaking Winston DeMint, but Duncan whispered for him to stop.

"Too many windows on that side," he whispered, and tilted his head down the boardwalk. "We'll take the back way. Step off the boardwalk. The ground'll make less noise."

Baird nodded, and the gambler turned around; both men moved off the wood and into the dirt. A few people on the other side of the street stared, but Duncan gave them a smile, showed them his badge, and then brought a finger to his lips.

"Let's go," Duncan said, and he followed the miner and the gambler.

"You ever thought about being a deputy marshal?" Duncan asked when they turned down an alley.

"Nae," the man said, "and it won' be 'appenin' today, neither."

"Too bad," Duncan said. "I'm about to need one handy."

"Aye. But it shan't be me, laddie. I'd admire to live a while longer."

Duncan smiled. It was nice to find a smart man now and then.

Conner Boyle stormed back into the office, found the brandy, and shot two down the way Caleb Holden did. Then he flung the glass, which shattered against the wall.

The hired gunman chuckled, and found his own glass.

"What's so funny?" Boyle growled. "I didn't see you doing anything out there except sweating and standing mighty still and quiet."

The smirk didn't leave Holden's face. "Well, I offered to kill him a while back. You didn't want to. Change your mind?"

The brandy had steadied Boyle's nerves.

"I can kill him for you, boss," Holden said, like a child begging for a birthday present. "Kill him dead, and you can take back what's left of this town."

"The only thing left in this town is our mayor's big nugget of silver. But right now, the only thing I want is Mick MacMicking dead."

"I can take him. Fast as he is, I can—"

"No." Boyle suddenly smiled, and he found another snifter, filling it with brandy and nodding at Holden.

"Go find Ben Gunderson," he ordered. "He'll be in Maudie's brothel. Bring him back. Tell him he's going to earn his pay. Gunderson is going to kill Dead Broke's new lawman. Shoot him down dead."

"Gunderson!" Holden shook his head. "Why, he ain't nothin' but a back-shooter."

This time, Boyle sipped his liquor. "That's why I brought him to Dead Broke."

CHAPTER 27

THE CARRYING OF FIREARMS
BY ANY MAN,
TOWN CITIZEN, OR VISITOR
WITHIN THE CITY LIMITS
OF DEAD BROKE
— CONCEALED OR IN OPEN VIEW —
WITHOUT A PERMIT
IS STRICTLY PROHIBITED
FINE: $75
AND CONFISCATION OF WEAPON

Seventy-five dollars for a misdemeanor. That's one way to get Dead Broke on the path back to riches. Duncan thought.

Duncan nailed the first placard on the board of wanted posters outside the city marshal's office. Today being a Saturday, however, Duncan hired Little Joey

Clarke to take the rest of the signs and put them up all over the city.

For that, he made Joey a special deputy for one day, and handed him a badge.

"But you can keep that," Duncan said. "I might need you again sometime."

The kid took the posters, but when he reached for another poster, face down, that Duncan had left on the bench underneath the board of posters and notices, Duncan said, "Not that one. I'll take care of that one myself."

He pinned the badge on the boy's shirt, told him to hold up his right hand. "And say, 'I do.'"

"I do!"

Duncan shook his hand. "You're a deputy. Get to work. But"—his tone turned serious—"don't go anywhere close to the Lucky Dice. Understand?"

"Yes, sir."

Smiling, Duncan watched the boy rush off with the posters tucked under his left arm and a hammer in his right hand. Then he took the remaining poster and went inside his office, where he picked up another parchment on his desk that he had filled out earlier. Holding both in his left hand, he left his office and headed for Conner Boyle's Lucky Dice.

The firearms ordinance he nailed up first, using the handle of his revolver as a hammer. He made sure to make as much noise as he could driving in the nails he had fished out of his vest pocket. It looked good, he thought with admiration. Then he went to work on the other door, making the same amount of noise. When he stopped, he stepped back, one extra nail in his mouth, and shifted the Schofield in his hand when he heard the lock clicking and the door opening in a rush.

"What the—" Conner Boyle stopped his rant, and Duncan smiled as the gambler's face flushed to a deep crimson color.

"Careful," Duncan said easily. "You'll drop dead before the hangman can fit a noose around your neck."

Boyle's teeth rattled, and he stepped outside and read the gun ban ordinance, spit on the boardwalk, and looked at the other sign.

> **TILL FURTHER NOTICE**
> **THE LUCKY DICE**
> **IS CLOSED BY ORDER**
> **OF THE TOWN MARSHAL**
> **ON CHARGES OF CHEATING**
> **VIOLATORS OF THIS ORDINANCE**
> **FACE POSSIBILE JAIL SENTENCES**
> **AND FINES OF UP TO $50**

Possibile? Duncan frowned at his spelling error. But Conner Boyle probably didn't even notice that. Duncan almost grinned at the thought that the cheating louse was likely too blind with fury to read sloppy printing.

Boyle reached for the sign, but stopped at the clicking of the hammer of Duncan's .45.

The man froze, then said in a wheezing voice, "You . . . wouldn't . . . shoot me." He coughed. "Not . . . in the . . . back."

"Not in the back. But back of the knee? One of your elbows? Shoot off an ear? Those are inviting targets."

The gambler slowly turned around, leaving the signs untouched.

"The fine for littering is five dollars," Duncan said easily. "The fine for removing city property is thirty-five. And remember this: Your gamblers can't be raking in lots of wages till a judge says otherwise. So those fines will prove costly. I'd better see these signs hanging right where they are."

"I can't help if the wind takes one or both down." Conner spaced out the words. "I can't . . . Some drunk might rip them off. Or a man who thought he could find a friendly game inside and lost his temper."

With a shrug, Duncan lowered the Schofield's hammer and slowly let the revolver slip into the holster. "Well, shucks, Boyle. Have one of your faro dealers, your roulette spinner, or a dice artist, another cardsharper—or even that gunslick pal of yours—just drag a poker chair out here and keep an eye on things. Weather is turning colder, but winter's a long ways off. And those gamblers you hire sure look like they could use some good clean air and some nice Rocky Mountain sun. They're all as pale as death."

He pulled the brim of his hat down and stook a few steps toward Boyle.

"Point is: If one of those signs goes missing, I'm holding you responsible."

"This isn't legal. I'll telegraph Denver!"

"You could, but the wires are down . . . again."

Duncan nodded. "Remember what I said. I'm holding you responsible. Don't forget."

"Don't worry." Boyle started back inside. "I won't."

He stopped at the cheapest café he had found in town and ordered some grub for his prisoner and a bowl of soup and cup of coffee for himself, hardly tasting his food or the bitter brew, but leaving a nice tip and taking the hash browns, bacon, and eggs on a plate with him to his office and jail.

Winston DeMint was happy to have the food, and Duncan focused on sorting through the mail that had been delivered.

"You didn't lock the door."

Duncan slid a new wanted poster across the desk, then twisted in his chair and stared at the prisoner.

"Your cell was locked," he said.

"Yeah. That's how your mail got here. But someone could have just walked right in." He nodded at the ring of keys hanging on the peg. "Got me out of here without any trouble."

Duncan shrugged. "And then what?"

"What?" The gambler was astounded. "I could just walk out of here."

Duncan nodded. "Then what?"

"Then what?" DeMint shook his head. "I'd . . . I could . . . I'd . . . well . . . I could have gotten my horse and valise and ridden right down off this tall mountain."

"Yep. You sure could have." He turned around and quickly went through the rest of the mail.

Ten or so minutes later, the door opened and Little Joey Clarke ran inside, still carrying about four or five posters with him and the hammer.

"Shouldn't run with a hammer, sonny," Duncan told him, and then waited for the kid to catch his breath.

"It's . . . the . . . the . . . Nug- . . . Nug- . . . Nugget!" The boy's chest kept heaving, and he was sweating.

Standing, Duncan moved to the water bucket, grabbed the ladle and filled it, then brought it to the boy.

"Drink some of this, son. But not too fast." Then he motioned toward the visitor's chair. "And grab a seat." He took the hammer and posters, put those atop his mail, and sat on the edge of the desk, waiting for Joey to drink and catch his breath.

Finally, the boy said, "Nug- . . . The mayor. Mayor Nugget. He wants . . . he wants to . . . see you."

"Oh." He smiled. "How many signs did you get to hang up?"

"Most of 'em." He nodded toward the leftovers. "All but . . . them."

"You want to hang those?"

The boy nodded. "Am I still . . . your deputy?"

"Of course." He slipped off the desktop. "You brought me a message from the mayor. That's what deputies do. Now have yourself another drink of water, and get those other signs posted. Then go back home and study and do all your homework."

The expression of the lad's face soured.

"Something wrong?"

"I still gotta study . . . even when I'm . . . your deputy."

Duncan nodded soberly. "All deputies have to study

and never stop learning. That's how deputies get to be marshals or sheriffs. Or lawyers and judges."

"Yessir." That didn't come out with any enthusiasm, but the boy drank more water, hung the ladle where it was supposed to be, grabbed his hammer and the posters, and walked to the door.

"Is Mayor Nugget in his office or at his home?"

"He was at Percy Stahl's place. Mr. Stahl had to read that notice to Nug—... to the mayor. He was still there when I left."

"Probably still there now, I reckon. Thanks, Deputy."

The boy's eyes brightened, and he nodded, turned around, and left the office.

Duncan helped himself to the water, wiped his face with a handkerchief, and then found the ring of keys. Winston DeMint was standing in the far corner of the cell—probably because the stone floor was too cold and hard to sit on for longer than a couple of minutes at a time—and stared at the marshal in silence as Duncan twisted the heavy key until he heard a loud clang as the lock disengaged. Then he walked back to the peg, hung the keys, and withdrew his revolver, checking the loads by spinning the cylinder as he spoke.

"Guess I'll go see what the mayor wants." He holstered the .45, then walked to the long arms and found a sawed-off shotgun. "That'll probably take a good spell. Then probably patrol the streets for a while. And I guess I should check Joey's work. No telling if he got those posters put up to my liking. I don't reckon I'll be back here till the middle of the afternoon." He went to the door and opened it. "You know, sometimes a man of your profession needs a change of scenery. I mean, shucks, I don't see why any gambler would spend much time in a town like Dead Broke. A skilled gambler. Honest or not. Denver. Fort Collins. Colorado Springs. Trinidad. Or out of the state. Cheyenne or Laramie. Ogallala or Guthrie. Albuquerque. Heck, even Durango, my old stomping ground. Lots of places a gambler can make a decent living." He shook his head. "And, gosh, I've never heard of a bounty hunter going after a cardsharper for breaking out of jail. Not much of a bounty on a fine of under a hundred bucks. Don't think most lawmen would even send word that a cardsharper escaped jail. Most lawmen would just be glad he didn't have to feed a prisoner. Be seein' you. I'll try to give you a better supper—if I see you."

He closed the door behind him, and headed for Percy Stahl's saloon.

Nugget must have gotten Percy to open his grog shop early today, Duncan thought as he peered through the doorway. The owner and the mayor were the only ones inside.

Nugget turned at the slapping sound of the batwing doors when Duncan entered, and the old codger set his empty shot glass on the bar and grabbed the notice that Little Joey must have hammered onto the wall outside.

"What's the meanin' of this?" the major exclaimed.

"Well, it means you'll have to fine yourself five dollars, Mayor, for taking down, without authorization, an official decree."

It took a long while for Nugget's intoxicated brain to consume and digest and understand what Duncan had just said.

"But I'm the mayor," he finally muttered.

"No one is outside the law." Duncan smiled and shifted the shotgun from his right hand to his left. Well, he was certainly pushing the law's boundaries. But that's what a town like Dead Broke needed—just the same as all those wild, crazy towns he had helped tame. He and Syd Jones and other men with similar renown and guts.

Percy Stahl shook his head and poured himself a shot of whatever he kept underneath the bar—the good stuff.

Nugget blinked. "What's the fine?"

Duncan smiled. "Well, as it says on the posting, seventy-five dollars for carrying a firearm in the city limits. Unless you have a permit."

"'Permit'? What's that?"

"A note that says the bearer is allowed to carry a weapon."

"Bearer? Like a griz?"

"The holder of the permit."

"How's I . . . how's a feller to get that permit?"

"That's your department, Mayor. I just uphold the laws. Fines. That's what you'll have to say—till we get a regular local judge." He nodded. "Yeah. And I figure since I just enforce the town laws, it would be the mayor's office." He turned and nodded at Stahl. "Or the city council. They'd be in charge of collecting the fee for getting a permit to carry a firearm in Dead Broke."

Percy Stahl got that quickly. He was moving back toward the bottle but stopped and set the empty glass atop the rough pine.

"Fees?" Stahl asked.

"Taxes, fines, and fees, gents. That's how cities don't go broke."

"So . . . ?" Nugget started.

"So." Duncan smiled. "A man like you, Mayor. With that nugget of yours in your home. That needs protecting. And you're the head of this city—the founder. A man like you would probably need some protection. You don't want to be held up on the streets. So you'd apply for a permit to carry a weapon. Like the one you're carrying now. Then, should someone . . . well . . . let's say I came up to you and told you that you were breaking the law with that pistol. Then you'd say, 'Marshal, I have a permit.' You'd reach into your pocket—very, very slowly and very carefully—and show me the signed notice that says you are allowed to carry a pistol for personal protection."

He nodded at Stahl. "Same would likely apply to Percy there. I imagine he takes his nightly cash to the bank and—"

"No." Stahl shook his head fiercely. "No banks for me. No, sir. Three banks I had money in closed. I keep my money now in . . ." He cleared his throat. "Ummm. No banks for me."

Nugget tugged on his beard and slowly turned toward the saloonkeeper. A moment later, he looked back at Duncan. "How much would 'em licenses cost?"

Duncan answered with a shrug. "That depends on what the city council decides. The fine is seventy-five bucks for violation. First offense, anyway. What do you think? Ten dollars. No, twenty. You don't want to make it affordable for everyone. Then you have too many people still carrying pistols. What I've learned is that when folks don't carry shooting irons, not as many folks get killed."

Nugget again looked silently at Stahl.

"What'd you want to see me about, Mayor?" Duncan asked.

Facing the marshal again, the mayor said, "Huh?"

"Joey Clarke—Little Joey—said you wanted to see me."

"Joey. Oh. Yeah. But . . . no . . . ummmm . . . Percy an' me figgered it all out."

Duncan nodded. "All right. I'll get back to my office. And you . . ." His face went stern and cold. "Make sure those posters go back where Little Joey put them. Wouldn't look good for the mayor and a councilman to be jailed for breaking a city ordinance."

"Jailed? Fer—"

"Well, yeah. Until a magistrate or judge brought you up to hear the case."

He started back toward the office, but slowed his gait, remembering he wanted to give Winston DeMint time enough to get out of Dead Broke, so he stopped at the Crosscut Saloon. The two notices were hanging on the wall there, too, and he entered, only to find it empty. He chatted with one of Sara's other dealers and then walked around town, commenting on the weather with some of the women shopping, and got an earful from Laurent Dubois about his ice castle and complete city of ice he was creating for all the visitors who would flock to Dead Broke. The man was so excited, he wanted to show it to Duncan, and since Duncan had time to kill, he let him.

Three wagons were parked on the city park, with giant cubes of ice sheltered by canvas tarps propped up with two-by-fours or poles from small trees.

The artist all but dragged Duncan to one of the canvas workplaces.

"My goodness." Duncan almost dropped the scatter-gun. Straightening, he stared at a woman of ice. "Is that . . . ?"

"Miss Sara Cardiff," Dubois answered. "A fine lady. The finest in Dead Broke."

Duncan shook his head. "It looks . . . just like . . . her." Well, not exactly—he wasn't sure how Sara would take it if he told her that a cold block of ice looked just like her. But he had to resist the urge to reach up and put his palm on the statue's glistening face. He might have done it, had he not been carrying that shotgun.

He wanted to touch her face . . . *its* face . . . but feared it might melt the cheeks, the nose, those wonderful eyes.

"I have horses and cattle and even the mayor's Hope Diamond Nugget of Silver started. And the city hall. And boys playing baseball. And the first cabin that was built in town. And animals. All the wild animals that we have here. And even the mountain on which we live."

"Amazing," Duncan whispered.

"It will bring thousands of visitors. Millions."

Duncan had his doubts about that, but he was certain of one thing. "You, sir, should be in Europe. You are a visionary."

The man bowed.

After checking his watch, Duncan left the park. He stopped at a bakery and ate a stale doughnut, and then decided he had spent enough time out of the office, so he walked back to his office, opened the door, stepped inside . . .

. . . and saw a man sitting at his desk, holding a Winchester rifle.

The man, he realized, was Winston DeMint—who had not escaped jail and fled Dead Broke after all.

CHAPTER 28

Duncan's hand started to jerk up the shotgun, but stopped almost as soon as the motion started. The cheating dice roller was oiling the brass receiver with a rag, and a long pole with another rag, much smaller and dark with grease and grime, lay on the desk. The lever was pulled down. The man was *cleaning* the rifle.

Once Duncan had shifted the shotgun to his left hand and closed the door with his right, DeMint wiped the barrel again before laying the rag on a burlap sack.

The gambler even had manners, letting the sack, instead of papers or furniture, soak up the oil and grease.

"I don't know when any of these weapons of yours were last cleaned," the gambler said.

The breech of the shotgun opened, and Duncan pulled out both shells. "Those aren't mine," he said, and took the sawed-off twelve gauge to the gun case.

"You're the town law," DeMint reminded him.

Syd Jones kept his guns clean all the time. He preached that to Duncan in Kansas. Yeah, the Syd Jones who had fled Dead Broke wasn't the Syd Jones Duncan had known.

Duncan's prisoner cleared his throat.

Turning, Duncan studied the man. "I'm surprised to find you here." He paused for a second, then added, "Winston."

DeMint went back to wiping the .44-40 with a cleaner rag. "To be completely honest with you, Marshal, I'm surprised to be here myself."

Duncan moved to the stove, grabbing two cups on his way and filling them both. He sipped one and walked back to the desk, extending his left hand, which held the other tin cup.

For a moment, the gambler stared at the cup. Then, with a heavy sigh, he wiped his hands on his pantlegs and accepted the coffee.

"It's awful," Duncan told him.

The gambler sipped, grimaced, and then smiled. "Just the way I like it."

Duncan set his cup on the desk and picked up the Winchester, jacking the lever and looking closely at the cleaning job. With a nod, he finished cocking the empty rifle, put his thumb on the hammer and gently pressed on the trigger, then let the hammer fall into place as he walked to the case and set the rifle in its place. Wiping his hands on his pants, Duncan walked back to his coffee.

"Want your seat?" DeMint asked.

Shaking his head, Duncan picked up his cup.

They drank in silence for a few minutes before Duncan asked: "Why didn't you light out?"

"I don't know." DeMint took another sip of coffee. "I guess . . ." His head shook again. "I dunno. I just . . . Well, maybe I got a look at how I've been living my life and didn't like the looks of where I was going."

"Turning over a new leaf?"

The gambler shrugged. "Just seeing . . . maybe . . . what it's like to be on the other side for a change."

That caused Duncan to chuckle. He drank more coffee, then wiped his mouth with his shirtsleeve and said, "Well, the money isn't as good. The hours aren't any better. You don't get to sleep in till afternoon. Oftentimes, you don't even get any sleep. Everybody wants something from you, but nobody really likes you." He tugged on his badge. "This shiny chunk of metal makes a good target for someone who wants to do you harm. Lots of people are scared of you, and quite a few want you dead."

DeMint emptied the last of the coffee down his throat. "Well," he said with a sigh as he set his cup on a rag. "I reckon I ain't as smart as you. I wouldn't blame you for throwing me back inside that cell, and keeping the door locked this time, and I wouldn't blame you for running me out of town on a rail, or tarred and feathered. I don't know much about the law—about all I know is how to swindle a sucker in a gambling hall—but I got a feeling you need more than a little boy as your deputy." He nodded at the door that led to the cells. "Or at least someone to mind the prisoners. You ain't got none now, unless I'm still one of them, but I don't reckon that'll be the case pretty soon."

Studying the tinhorn's face, Duncan kept sipping coffee in silence. The gambler looked away, toward the door, then back at the open door to the cells. Finally, he sighed and raised his head, his eyes meeting Duncan's.

"I don't blame you, Marshal." He started to rise. "I'll

head back to the jail. Wait for the judge to sentence me whenever he gets here."

He was standing now, still looking at Duncan.

The lawman nodded at the front door.

"You can still ride out of Dead Broke."

"I've lost count of all the towns I've been run out of, Marshal." He held out his right hand. "Though this was the friendliest offer I got to leave a town. Usually it was on a rail. A time or two I spent weeks before I got all the tar off of me. Sometimes I was on a horse at a fast lope with bullets and buckshot whizzing past me. Reckon I'll take my comeuppance. Then maybe start living an honest man's life."

Ignoring the extended hand, Duncan sighed and nodded at the desk.

"Top drawer," he said. "There's a deputy's badge. Pin it on and say, 'I do.' But you best get this through your head. Conner Boyle and that gunslick of his won't look fondly on you, even if all you do is mind the jail. They'll be likely looking for the first chance to put a bullet in your back."

The drawer opened, and DeMint brought up a badge. He unfastened the clasp, ran the pin through his lapel, and secured the badge. "I do," he said, and held out his hand again.

This time, Duncan accepted it. The man's hands were soft—like most gamblers'—but he had a firm grip.

"Guess you think I'm stupid," DeMint said.

Duncan shook his head. "You're smarter than I was. Syd Jones had to beat the tar out of me before I got to believing that being on the right side of the law, and not disrespecting or ignoring it, was the best trail to follow."

The door swung open, and Little Joey Clarke leaped inside. "Marshal MacMicking! Marshal MacMicking! There's a terrible fight a-goin' on at the livery on Fourth Street."

Duncan went to fetch his shotgun.

"How many men are fighting?" he asked.

"Just two."

"Best get a cell ready, Deputy DeMint." He found the shotgun, opened the breech, and shoved in two shells, then pocketed two more just to be safe.

"And why aren't you home?" he asked Joey.

"'Cause it's Saturday. And Billy, Patsy, Clyde, and me was watching the fight," the kid answered.

"And you left to find me?"

The boy frowned, and then touched the badge on his shirt. "Patsy reminded me that I was a deputy." He sighed. "But I didn't think I could stop those two men. They're huge."

Hearing that, Duncan turned and walked back to the gun case, where he picked up a shortened baseball bat that would come in handy against two "huge" men.

Two days later, Winston DeMint had five prisoners to feed breakfast and supper, empty their slop buckets, and throw buckets full of water on when they got too vocal in the cells. But some semblance of peace was returning to Dead Broke.

Only one person had torn down one of the posters banning the carrying of firearms in the city limits, and he wasn't complaining about anything now since his busted jaw was wrapped up and he was sitting in one of the cells with the two brawlers from Fourth Street.

Duncan was on his way to the Crosscut Saloon when he saw Conner Boyle's top gunman, Caleb Holden, walking on the other side of the street, his coat open and a buckle around his waist. The bulge of a revolver on the right hip was apparent, and Duncan smiled. It would be a pleasure to lock that killer up until Boyle had to pay his fine.

He turned and stepped into the street, pushing his coat back to make his Colt easier to reach.

"Holden!" he bellowed, and put his right hand on the Schofield.

The killer stopped, turned, and smiled.

Still walking, still feeling the coldness of his weapon, he ordered: "With both hands, I want you to slowly pull back your coat so I can see what's on your right hip."

The few other people on both sides of the street stopped to watch, all except one woman with a bag of groceries in her hand. She ducked inside the first building with an open door, and Duncan didn't think she planned on getting a shave or haircut—especially since that barber had left two days ago for Ogden, Utah.

Holden smiled when Duncan stepped onto the boardwalk.

"Somethin' wrong, lawdog?"

Duncan nodded at the nickel-plated revolver in the tooled black holster. His left hand pointed at the poster on Clarkson & Bros. Company Mercantile's wall.

"I know you've seen those, buster. With your left hand, unbuckle that rig and let it drop to the boardwalk."

The lips turned upward into a sinister smile. Holden's head shook.

Duncan thought about how much he would enjoy ramming the barrel of his Colt against the punk's forehead.

"What's going on here?"

Duncan stiffened at that voice. Conner Boyle was coming up behind him, but there was no way Duncan would take his eyes off a punk gunfighter like Caleb Holden.

"Our marshal's makin' himself a big mistake," Holden said with a smirk. "See, lawdog . . ." With his left hand he slowly reached into a shirt pocket and pulled out a slip of yellow paper.

By then, Conner Boyle had walked past Duncan and stepped onto the boardwalk. He took the paper from Holden, pretended to read it, and turned to grin like a man who knew he was holding the winning hand. And for men like Conner Boyle and Caleb Holden, that was because they were cheating.

"Why, Marshal MacMicking," Boyle said loud enough for anyone on this side of Dead Broke to hear. "This citizen has a permit to carry weapons."

He held out the wrinkled paper, and Duncan took it before the wind did.

Caleb Holden

That name was about the only thing legible, printed in a firm hand that Duncan figured was the gunman's own. But the rest was a hard scribble that was recognizable enough as the cursive of the artist, painter, and sculptor of ice, Mr. Dubois.

*Is Allowed to Carry Firearms
in Dead Broke with This Permit
Until It Is Revoked*

The signature Duncan recognized, too.

X

Allane Auchinleck. Old Nugget himself.

"You ain't gonna try to revoke my license," Holden said with an evil grin. "Is ya?"

Duncan held out the paper, which Holden took and slipped back into the pocket.

"Man has a right to protect himself." The killer turned and walked away, whistling as loud as he could.

Duncan turned and glared at Holden's boss, who, likewise smiling, pulled back his coat and pointed at the derringer in a vest pocket.

"Would you like to see my permit, too, Marshal?"

It would have been so easy for Duncan to rip that smirk off the man's ugly face, but the wind started to pick up and Duncan nodded.

"I reckon I'd better. Just to make sure you're all legal."

Frowning, the gambler reached inside the coat pocket. This paper was on the back of a telegram slip, but that was the same wording and the same mark of Dead Broke's mayor.

Duncan nodded, and held the slip out for Boyle, but let the wind take the telegram from his fingers just before the louse could grab it. Duncan turned, watched the slip float down the street, started after it, but stopped as the paper lifted higher than some of the false fronts.

Turning back, he saw Boyle's reddening face.

"That's a shame, isn't it? How much did our mayor charge you for that permit?"

The gambler's teeth chattered. He looked like he might explode.

"You best go back to the mayor, see if he'll give you a replacement. I'd hate to have to arrest you for violating the town ordinance."

"You just—"

"I'm just following the law. Which says you have to have a permit on your possession." He was adding the "possession" part, but figured the law would be on his side to arrest a person. If Boyle's gunfighter brought over a permit later, he could be released. That made sense. But now, he just wanted to get away from that gloating Boyle. He turned and walked down the street. "And my memory isn't as good as it used to be."

CHAPTER 29

The pawnshop was closed, and Duncan didn't really expect to find Dead Broke's mayor in the office above Dante Lupino's business, but that was on the way to Percy Stahl's saloon. Those doors were locked, too, but Stahl didn't open till dusk, unless he was in there drinking himself or with Nugget.

Moving to the large window, he was peering inside when a voice called out.

"Percy rode out of town a coupla hours ago."

Duncan turned to find big Bryn Bunner a few feet from him.

"Took a wagon to Denver," Bunner explained. "Two wagons. Jim Bob Swafford was driving the other one."

Duncan didn't recall meeting any Jim Bob Swafford.

"To fetch those mail-order brides." The miner grinned.

"Oh." Duncan nodded. "Thanks."

"Yer welcome."

Just looking at Bunner made Duncan ache all over. That had been one brawl they had had, but the big man didn't seem to be in any hurry to ask for a rematch. Which was good news. Duncan wouldn't bet on him winning a second fight against that man. He still wasn't sure how he had survived that one brawl.

But he noticed something else.

Bunner must have seen where Duncan was looking, because he also looked at the self-cocking H&R revolver in his waistband.

"Oh." Bunner pulled open his mackinaw to give the lawman a closer look. "I got a permit from Nugget." His right hand moved and dug into the rear pocket of his trousers. "Here." He held out a certificate from Jansen's bank—which had folded before Duncan had even gotten here. All Duncan had to see was Nugget's big but sloppy diamond drawing with an X in the middle.

"I'm not the most popular man in Dead Broke, Marshal," the big man explained. "There are strong sentiments against any man who says 'union' or 'fair pay.'" Duncan thought he was about to hear a speech, but Bunner kept it short. "I have a right to protect myself, don't I?"

"You'll get no argument from me." Duncan thought, then added, "Bryn."

That brought out a smile on the man's face.

"I appreciate that, Marshal."

"Call me Mick," Duncan said, and held out his hand. "Most folks do."

The shake was firm but brief. The miner didn't try to crush every bone in Duncan's hand.

"I don't know who taught you how to fight . . . Mick . . . but—"

"I got lucky. And Syd Jones was my first teacher."

"Good man, Syd. Till he took too much to drink."

"Yeah."

Sliding the permit back into his pocket, the man nodded again. "Guess I'll be seein' ya."

But Duncan had one more question. "How much did Nugget charge you for that permit?"

"Fifty bucks," Bunner spat out. "Talk about robbery. But I'd hate to get shot dead because of my miserly ways."

"Just watch yourself. And if you need any help, come see me."

They shook again, and Duncan made a beeline for Mayor Nugget's mansion. If that man wasn't in Stahl's saloon or the city council office, he would most likely be admiring his Hope Diamond Nugget of Silver.

But before he got there, in front of Sara's Crosscut Saloon, he saw another armed man. This one was a stranger, and he wasn't even wearing a coat to conceal the two Schofield .45s holstered on both hips.

"Hold it there, mister," Duncan called out to the man's back, drawing his own revolver and cocking the hammer slowly so the man would know not to do anything. "I'm the city marshal and you're breaking the law."

The man spread his arms away from his pistols and smiled.

"What's the problem, Marshal?" the man said with a grin.

The barrel of Duncan's .45 pointed to the wall.

"Those posters are all over town."

The man's ugly face turned and saw the notice. Nodding, he looked back, smiling. "Yeah, I read right good. Ma taught school before she married my pa.

Learned my sisters and me and my kid brother to read pretty good."

His left hand pulled back, allowing Duncan to also see the hideaway gun in a shoulder holster. The stranger's head tilted toward the pocket. "My permit—signed by yer mayor—is in here. All right if I pull it out, let you read it fer yerself?"

Duncan nodded. "Just move slow, stranger."

"I always move slow, Marshal. Unless I be pullin' leather. And I ain't pullin' leather on you—least, not today."

The slip came out, and this one appeared to be from a newspaper, but when Duncan took it and read, he saw Nugget's mark and the words explaining that John Smith was allowed to carry firearms with this permit for the duration of his stay in Dead Broke.

"And you are . . . John Smith?" Duncan extended the newspaper/permit back to the stranger.

"I am . . . for the time bein', anyhows." Smiling, he took his permit and returned it to his pocket.

Duncan saw the silver buckle on the holster with the raised engraving of two letters. Then he smiled.

"Well, John Smith, I hope you enjoy your stay in Dead Broke. Any idea how long you'll be here?"

"Oh, not long, I'd be guessin'. Got a job to do. But I reckon I can do that one right quick."

The man turned and had taken five or six steps when Duncan called to his back, "Mitchum."

The stranger stopped, then slowly turned back, his eyes beaming. "Like my permit says, the name's Smith. John Smith."

"Like the permit says." Duncan nodded. He let the

hammer down on his Colt and slid it into the holster. "We could settle this right now, Mitchum. If you'd like."

The doors to the Crosscut opened behind him, but Duncan did not dare turn around. He wasn't about to turn his back on a cold-blooded outlaw like Killin' Ben Mitchum.

"You got me mistook for somebody else, Marshal. I'm John Smith. Down Tucson way. And, well . . ." He chuckled. "That lady behind you looks like she'd put a bullet in my belly if I even looked at you crossways." He nodded, tipped his hat, turned around, and walked down the street.

Turning, Duncan stared hard at Sara Cardiff.

"What are you doing with that derringer?" he snapped.

She slid the hideaway four-shot back into the purse she held in her left hand.

"What derringer?" she asked.

He wasn't amused. "I could fine you seventy-five bucks, lady."

Her head shook, and she pointed at the poster.

"Nope. You couldn't. That says 'By Any Man,' sugar. And in case you haven't noticed—I'm not a man."

She turned and started back inside her place, but stopped and looked at him.

"Want a drink, sugar?" she said. "First one's on the house."

"No . . . I . . ." He hadn't seen her in a while. And Nugget could wait. "On second thought . . ."

She was smiling as she went inside. Duncan wasn't smiling. But he sure could use a drink.

* * *

"Killin' Ben Mitchum?" Sara's best dealer set down his snifter of brandy. "You sure?"

"A big 'BM' on his big silver belt buckle. Never met him. But the description sure fits." Duncan picked up his beer and drank down half of it, then wiped the foam off his face with a cloth napkin.

That, he figured, would impress Sara. He wasn't as rough and uncouth as he had been a few years back.

"How many gunmen does that make?" Sara asked.

Duncan shrugged. "Well, Mitchum's the only one I've seen. Think I've seen anyhow. I'll have to look at a dodger—if there's one in the office—when I get back."

"D.B. Mora—if it was D.B. Mora," Logan Ladron said. "Ben Gunderson."

"Dean Hill." Duncan finished the brandy. He felt the temptation to ask for another—he would even pay for it—but he knew better than that. One drink was enough when several of the West's top guns were heading to town.

"Conner Boyle must really want you dead," Sara whispered.

"No." Duncan's head shook. "Yes," he added suddenly. "He wants me dead, of course, but he wouldn't pay for all those gunmen when he has one already on his payroll who could send me to my Maker by back-shooting me."

"Don't talk like that," Sara admonished.

"There has to be another reason," Duncan said.

"How about some coffee?" she asked.

"That sounds fine."

"I'll get it." The dealer rose, and Duncan caught the

wink he gave Sara before he turned and walked toward another door, leaving Sara and Duncan alone.

"Never thought I'd see a place you ran this deserted," Duncan said softly.

"It's not empty now." She smiled.

He looked at her, then at his empty snifter, then through the big window, and finally sighed. "Listen, I don't know if you got that letter I wrote. After . . . After . . ."

"I got it." Her voice was a whisper. "I should have sent you a note, thanking you for . . ." The words trailed off.

"Wasn't much of a letter," he said. "But . . . well . . . I was sorry . . ."

"It was nice of you."

"You didn't keep his name," he said.

She shrugged and let a sad smile briefly show. "Didn't seem like we were married long enough for me to hold on to his name. Three weeks. Wheel came off a stagecoach." Her head shook. "Driver, guard, ten passengers, six mules. And the only one to die was . . ."

He reached over and took her hand into his. She gave him that smile of hers, then sighed when the door opened and Logan Ladron reappeared carrying a tray with a pot of coffee, a bowl of sugar, a tin of milk, and three cups.

But before he reached the table, the saloon doors slammed open and in ran Little Joey Clarke.

"Marshal! Marshal! Marshal!" he screamed, racing—practically staggering—to the table.

Duncan stood. The gambler stopped. Sara twisted around in her chair.

"Joey," she said.

"Marshal!" The boy slid to a halt. "I found this,

Marshal. I found it. I was gonna pick it up anyhow." He reached into his schoolbag. "Honest. Because it was trash. And Mama says we don't want trash in Dead Broke. She says we gots enough trash already. 'Trash of the two-legged kind.'" He shot Sara and Duncan a quick look and wet his lips. "Ummmmm."

Then he remembered. "Oh." His right hand reached into the deep pocket of his trousers and he withdrew a crumpled telegram.

Duncan took it and saw the scribbling of Nugget's handwriting. It was the permit he had issued Conner Boyle.

"Yeah," he said, and nodded at the kid. "Well, thanks, Joey. I was checking someone who had a gun and . . . the wind took—"

The boy's head shook violently. "No, no, no, Marshal. It's the telegram that you gots to read, sir."

Duncan frowned. Then he turned the paper over and stared in disbelief.

THE WESTERN UNION TELEGRAPH
COMPANY INCORPORATED
21,000 OFFICES IN AMERICA.
CABLE SERVICE TO ALL THE WORLD

RECEIVED AT Dead Broke, Co. May 8, 1893

TO: C. Boyle, Lucky Dice Gambling Hall
I would be pleased to accept your invitation to join your company in Dead Broke with the chance to reacquaint myself with your new lawman, Mick MacMicking.
                    Ben Usher

Duncan shook his head. "I guess the telegraph line got fixed."

"Ben Usher," Winston DeMint whispered, then whistled.

"I've read those dime novels to Mayor Nugget." Little Joey's voice squeaked, not with excitement, but fear.

Smiling, Duncan reached out and raked Joey's hair with his fingers. "I've read two or three of those myself," he said. "Don't worry, son. I'll be pleased to reacquaint myself with Ben Usher, too."

"But he's . . . he's . . . he's . . ." Joey started and DeMint finished.

"Your archenemy!"

Both the lawman and the boy turned to the reformed gambler and stared at him in disbelief.

DeMint shrugged. "I've read a dime novel or two myself. And some newspaper accounts. And I've seen Usher before. In person. He put on a shooting display in Deadwood some while back. He was so fast, you couldn't really see him draw. One moment the gun was in his holster, and before you knew it, he was shooting six bottles to pieces. Did that five or six times. And never missed a one. And never even slowed down. Fact is, the more he shot, the faster he seemed to get."

Duncan nodded. "He's a top gun."

"But you're faster, right?" Joey asked hopefully. "And you're always on the side of the law. And . . . and . . . and . . . the good guys, they . . . they always win, don't they?"

Duncan smiled again. "They seem to in those storybooks." He stuck the telegram in his vest pocket. "Don't worry—either of you." He shot a glance at his new jailer. "Ben Usher isn't in Dead Broke yet. We'll have to see if he comes here at all. Meanwhile"—he started for the door—"I need to find Nugget."

"Oh," Joey said. "He's at Mr. Gustafsson's pool hall."

"What were you doing in a pool hall, son?" DeMint asked.

"I wasn't inside. I was throwing a ball with Sissy Duncan on the street. I just saw him go in there. That's when I saw that telegram blowing down the street."

He found the Swede's Pool Room just as Nugget was stumbling out with two men Duncan recognized. He palmed his Schofield, cocked before it was halfway out the holster, and bellowed, "Hold it. Don't move. That includes you, Mayor!"

Dean Hill smiled. Caleb Holden did not.

Not lowering the .45, Duncan covered the twenty yards fast.

"There are notices posted all over town, Dean, about carrying firearms in Dead Broke," Duncan said when he stopped a few feet in front of the three men.

The gunfighter nodded. "Still up to your old tricks, I see, MacMicking." He slowly pulled open his coat, reached inside, and pulled out a piece of paper—most likely, Hill being known primarily as a bounty hunter, a wanted dodger—and held it out for the lawman.

"But I have a permit," he said with a smile.

"And you know I've got one," Boyle's hired gunman said easily.

Duncan saw the mayor's scribbling and nodded.

"All right if I go about my business, MacMicking?" Hill asked.

"Go right ahead."

The two gunfighters crossed the street, and when Nugget started after them, Duncan grabbed his shoulder and turned him around.

"A minute of your time, Mayor?"

Nugget frowned, looked at the two men, and then shrugged. "Well, I got lots to do today, bein' mayor an' all, but . . . what ken I do fer ya, Sheriff?"

"Marshal," Duncan corrected.

"Oh, yeah."

"Mayor," Duncan said, sounding more like a schoolteacher than a lawman. "The idea of issuing a firearms ordinance is to keep guns off the streets. If you start giving them to every man who comes into town—"

"I'll be richer even without no silver fortune!" Nugget bellowed with joy.

This would be harder than Duncan thought. "The money for those permits to carry a gun should go into the city's coffers—not your pocketbook."

"Coughers? We ain't got no consumptives here. Not many, nohow. Too high up for folks with bad lungs."

Duncan sighed. Nugget opened his coat to pull out his chewing tobacco, and that's when Duncan saw the revolver.

"What's that?"

Nugget was tearing off a chaw. "What's what?"

Duncan pointed. "That . . . pistol."

Working the tobacco with his teeth, Nugget looked at the ancient Colt.

"That's Bertha."

"Forty-four?"

He shook his head. "Thirty-six. Was cap-and-ball, but I got it converted."

"Where's your permit?"

Nugget stopped working his jaw. "My what?"

"Your permit to carry a gun in the city limits."

Nugget froze. "I be mayor. I be—"

"Not above the law."

Flecks of tobacco flew out of the old miner's mouth. "But—"

"You're coming with me, Mayor," Duncan said. "You're under arrest. The fine, you know, is seventy-five dollars."

"But I ain't got no seventy-five . . ."

"Then I reckon the city of Dead Broke will be putting you to work till I think you've paid off the fine."

CHAPTER 30

"Hmmmmmmmm," Winston DeMint whispered when Duncan brought the mayor into the marshal's office and was told to lock him up.

"But he's the mayor," Duncan said. "Give him that big cell. He can have it all to himself."

"You aren't joking?" the jailer asked.

Nugget turned to Duncan with a hopeful, practically pleading, look on his face, but the stern shake of the head left the mayor sighing and the jailer shaking his head.

"Things sure are changing in this town," DeMint said as he walked to get the ring of keys to the cells. "Where do you reckon you and I are going to sleep?"

Finding the coffeepot, Duncan filled a cup. "We'll share that one cell—for the time being." He tested the brew, then looked back at the jailer.

"Did you make this?"

DeMint gave a tentative nod.

Duncan cocked his head. "You're a man with many talents. Lock up the mayor."

When the former cardsharper started toward Nugget, the mayor backed up and turned quickly and clasped his hands as he faced Duncan. "Ya can'ts does this. I'm mayor. I made this town. I don't . . ." He started sobbing. "I don'ts deserves none of this." By then DeMint was standing next to him.

"Does I?" Nugget begged.

"It's a seventy-five-dollar fine, Mayor," Duncan told him. "Remember? I suggested fifty. But you thought seventy-five would be better. It would reduce the number of men willing to carry a gun and it would help Dead Broke's coffers."

None of that was true, but Nugget was too upset to realize that.

"I gots seventy-five bucks. I gots a nugget made of solid silver. I gots whiskey and chawin' baccer and I gots lots of friends. I even gots an account in the bank."

Duncan checked his pocket watch, and looked at the clock on the wall to make sure. "Bank's closed. You can pay the fine in the morning, Mayor, if you can get that seventy-five dollars."

"The money . . . it goes to me," Nugget tried again. "So since it'd be paid to me, it don't make sense . . . I mean . . . it would just . . ."

"The money," DeMint corrected, "goes to the city. Not to you."

"But—"

He wailed like a cat whose tail had been stepped on as DeMint led him to the jail cells.

"I hope you know what you're doing," DeMint said after closing the door and shaking his head. "He's angrier than a polecat—and scared out of his britches."

"One night on that hard floor and maybe he'll get the idea and stop issuing permits to every man in town,"

Duncan said. He held up the coffee cup in a salute. "Who taught you how to make coffee?"

"My mother."

"Bless her heart." He finished the cup, wiped his mouth with his shirtsleeve, and asked, "How many gunfighters have you seen in Boyle's gambling hall lately?"

"Other than Caleb Holden, I couldn't say. The boss—Mr. Boyle—he paid me to win some money for the house. He didn't talk about other deals he had going. I didn't ask."

"So Boyle didn't tell you to let some strangers in town win a few hands?"

"Nope. There were some strangers about. They wore guns, and they wore guns the way men who know guns and who use guns quite frequently wear them. Who they were? What brought them to town? That I can't say. None came to try their luck against me."

"Well, I didn't hire you to rat out your boss. Forget I asked."

"I'd rat out that scoundrel if I could." DeMint took the cup to the wash basin, rinsed it out, and set in on a table near the stove. "I just don't have any answers for you."

Duncan shrugged.

"Why not ask the mayor?" DeWitt hooked a thumb toward the closed door to the cells.

"I will," Duncan said. "In the morning. After one night trying to sleep on that cold, hard floor."

"Boyle will be posting his bond first thing in the morning," the gambler said. "You might not get a chance to question him—and he's crazy as a two-legged goat, but Nugget was in these mountains when only a handful of white men dared come this high. He's seen more country than you and I have—and the two of us have traveled some miles. But we weren't living off pine nuts after seven feet of snow got dumped on us. And we weren't sleeping in the skin of a bear that we killed before that bear killed us. Dealing and trading with Indians who'd more than likely want to cut a white man's throat and lift that dead man's hair. And deep down, even if he'd cheat a preacher's widow for a half-dime novel, he's a likable cuss."

Duncan smiled. "I won't argue with any of that. Hungry?"

The answer was a shrug.

"I'll make my final rounds, then bring us back some stew. How many prisoners do we have?"

"You ought to know. You're the only one arresting anybody." He straightened. "Hey, can I arrest anybody?"

Duncan laughed. "I'd rather have you just make the prisoners mind their manners and stay locked up."

"You need another deputy." DeMint grunted. "And I don't mean that little boy."

Duncan laughed again. "I probably need two or three. But right now, I need some supper."

Two wagons were creeping into town four days later when Duncan stepped out of the café, followed by a thin waitress and the son of the owner of the place. He tipped them two bits to take the food to the jail for his jailer and the prisoners.

Then he moved between two businessmen and stepped onto the street for a better look at the wagons.

"You should have done what Percy's doin', Bryn." The speaker's laugh got a few other watchers to echo the cackle.

"Mail-order brides won't save this town." Duncan turned to watch Bryn Bunner. "Me and some pards have been looking for gold."

The merchant—Duncan thought he ran a grocery on Second Street, but he wasn't sure—chuckled. "Fat chance of finding any metal."

"There's lead. There might be zinc," Bunner said.

"Might be nothing," someone else said.

"I say—" Bunner tried, but someone shouted him down.

"I say . . . Percy . . . how many wimmin did ya fetch us?"

Yes, Percy Stahl was driving the lead wagon, and he stood in the box, holding the leather lines to the oxen, and shouted out an answer.

"Six?" A man in sleeve garters shook his head. "Six." He spit into the water trough.

"Where's Swafford?" another voice bellowed. "How many brides is he bringin'?"

"None," Stahl called out. "He found one for himself and rode off for Raton Pass."

"Six women," a businessman said. "Six new women."

Someone let out a war cry, then screamed, "We'll auction 'em off inside my place."

Some men cheered, but Duncan stepped onto the street. "Hold on," he said. "You're not auctioning off women like they're—"

He heard the gunshot behind him, dropped his bowl of stew in the dirt, and spun around, jerking the Colt out of the holster. A lone figure stood beside an abandoned business. Duncan could see the white smoke rising from the barrel of the revolver he held. He was aiming up, though, and now came more screams from the wagon, as three women jumped out of Stahl's wagon and another poked her head through the flap of dingy canvas and pointed up.

"Look! Look at that feller! Oh—" She gasped, then screamed.

Turning, Duncan saw a man on the rooftop of the false-fronted building. A rifle slipped from his hands and toppled first, hit the awning, flipped over, and landed in the street. Then the man fell. He hit the awning, too, and crashed right through it.

One of Stahl's brides-to-be-for-the-right-price took a few steps. "I saw him. I saw him. He was gonna shoot—" She searched, and then pointed at Duncan. "He was drawin' a bead on you." She must have seen the city marshal's badge. "Oh, my Lord, he was gonna shoot down this lawman. Shoot him in the back."

"Don't go anywhere, miss," Duncan ordered, and he rushed to the body on the boardwalk.

The body was spread-eagled, boots and legs in the dirt, the upper part on the warped, and now mostly busted, wooden planks.

"Well, I'll be a one-eyed polecat," said the closest miner. He looked up at Duncan. "Marshal, ain't that Ben Gunderson?"

There was no mistaking that murdering mad dog of a killer.

"Reckon he won't be shooting nobody else in the back," Bryn Bunner said.

"Did you see him?" Duncan asked.

Bunner shook his head. "No. I was on this side of the street. I just heard the shot." He looked at the man still standing in the middle of the street. "Why . . . I'll be . . ."

Duncan turned around. "Percy," he said. "I need you, your driver, and those six women to follow me to my office."

"But—"

"Now!" He looked across the street. "Any of you. Did any of you see what happened?"

The Methodist minister raised his hand and stepped away from the apothecary's store.

"Anybody else?" He drew in a deep breath, and let it out. "The man's dead. He can't harm you. All I need is statements of what you saw. Honest statements. If you didn't see anything, you're free to go."

To Duncan's surprise, one woman and three men stepped off the boardwalk and headed toward him.

"My brides didn't—"

"Shut up, Percy. You're bringing them to the office now. And if they didn't see anything, they'll say they didn't see anything. But one has said what she saw, and if I find anyone lying to me, I'll file perjury charges. Bunner." He whirled around. "I'm deputizing you for one hour. Get these people to the office."

He found the telegraph operator, but couldn't recall his name. "You. You're going to be the stenographer. All you have to do is take down what they say. You'll be paid for your time."

He walked to the man who still held the smoking Remington .44, but stopped when he spotted two men standing in the corner.

"Boyle," he said. "Holden. Your man-killer made a bad mistake."

Conner Boyle stiffened. "I don't know—"

"I do know. You two boys better get off the streets and stay inside your Lucky Dice till morning. If I see you before then, I'll be shooting first."

"Now, that's—"

But they disappeared after one shot kicked up dirt between them.

That gunshot pretty much sent everyone else indoors. But not everyone. Bryn Bunner was doing his job, taking the witnesses to the marshal's office. Percy Stahl turned his wagon around, and so did the other driver, and the wagons hauled six women past the white-haired man still holding the Remington.

"Duncan!"

He watched Sara Cardiff run to him, holding up the hem of her blue dress. Then she stopped, face pale, lips trembling. She blinked. Blinked again. Then she looked at Duncan, and back at the man who had saved his life. Slowly she walked past Duncan and stopped in front of the tall, frail old man.

Duncan ejected the spent cartridge from his Schofield and thumbed in a live round. He checked the other rooftops, the windows, the alleyways, everything—but of all the killers he thought Conner Boyle had hired, Ben Gunderson was the only back-shooter. So far.

He didn't holster the .45, though. Not even when he faced the man who had saved his life.

"Syd." He shook his head and chuckled.

Syd Jones nodded, then looked at Sara and whispered her name.

Sara moved closer, and took the old man's left arm. Duncan held out his left hand, and Syd looked at the .44, which was still warm. His wrist worked like a younger man's, and he reversed the gun, the long barrel now against the inside of his forearm, the index finger coming out of the trigger guard and the hand holding the silver-plated weapon butt forward.

Taking the Remington in his left hand, Duncan finally holstered his .45 and held out his right hand.

"It's good to see you, Syd," he told his mentor and friend.

"Yeah." The old man suddenly looked old and drunk and scared. "You arrestin' me?"

"I'm just getting your statement."

"Come on, Syd," Sara said, and led him down the street.

It was past nine that night by the time all of the statements had been approved, signed, and notarized and most of the men and women had gone home.

Syd Jones sat at Duncan's desk, and Sara Cardiff was making her kind of coffee. DeMint kept shaking his head and repeating in soft whispers, "I've never heard anything like this before. I've never heard anything like this before."

"What brought you back to Dead Broke?" Duncan finally asked.

The old man was shaking a bit now, and Sara found a blanket, which she draped over his shoulders. "Can you add some wood to that stove?" She directed that question at no one in particular, but DeMint went to the woodbox.

"I . . ." Syd Jones shrugged and sighed. "I thought I'd dreamed it all. Dreamed hearing about gunfighters going to Dead Broke. Didn't make no sense to me." He found the cup of coffee Sara put in his hands. His head shook.

"Don't remember how I even got here. Don't remember much of nothin' . . . till I . . . saw that hombre on the rooftop."

"I'm glad you did," Duncan said.

"So am I," Sara whispered.

"Well." Syd sipped some coffee. "Someone woulda seen him."

"Yeah. After I was deader than dirt," Duncan said.

"Who was it I killed?"

"Ben Gunderson," Duncan told Syd.

"Hmmmm."

"Can I take him to my place?" Sara asked. "He's cold and . . ."

"Scared." The old lawman chuckled. "Dang right I'm scared."

"We're all scared," DeMint said. "Now."

"That we are," Duncan said. He turned to Sara. "I don't think having Syd at the Crosscut is a good idea."

"But—"

"He's right, miss." Now Syd sounded like the Syd Jones that Duncan remembered. Strong and sure and right. "The hombre that hired that back-shooter isn't gonna take kindly to me ruinin' his plans. Don't want you to get hurt on my account."

"Or mine," Duncan said.

The old man finished the coffee and his eyes locked on Duncan. Syd Jones smiled first, but it was the new jailer who spoke first.

"I think you got yourself another deputy, Marshal MacMicking."

A wry smile appeared on the face of Syd Jones.

Duncan turned to his jailer: "You aren't quitting, are you? I need a deputy and someone to keep a lid on these prisoners."

DeMint shrugged. "Well, I've been a gambler for too many years. It gets in your blood. And I think I'd like to see how this hand plays out."

CHAPTER 31

The warm spell started two days later. By then, Conner Boyle had paid Nugget's fine, and Duncan figured more permits would be issued. Maybe he should have cut himself in for part of the booty he thought. But, no, honesty had always been part of his being—after Syd Jones had beat some sense into him, anyway.

Even without gunfighters flocking to Dead Broke, Duncan, Jones, and the jailer had enough work to keep them busy.

Percy Stahl's mail-order brides created havoc. Apparently, they had not realized that Dead Broke had been a silver town. Three of them weren't even aware how that market had collapsed, and one of those thought that the "Panic of '93" was a show with lots of singing and dancing.

Duncan had to pull a petite blonde off Germaine, the town's only undertaker since Jenkins retired to Lake City. Sara Cardiff took her to the Crosscut Saloon, where she gave her a job in the kitchen—at least long enough till she earned enough money for a stagecoach ride back to Denver. Duncan helped Germaine to the doctor's office, where that ugly scratch on his cheek got stitched up and the broken nose was put back together where the undertaker could breathe almost as good as he had been before his briefly betrothed found out what he did for a living.

"My trade gets no respect," he moaned.

"But there's always a corpse, or if there isn't, there will be one before too long," the doc said, then added: "The three of us . . . well . . . our jobs aren't affected by panics and depressions and the like. Are they?"

By the end of the week, Percy Stahl was hauling four of the girls back to Denver—including Sara's kitchen helper. The oldest one married Dylan Pugh, the one-time mine foreman and councilman. And the redhead with a glass eye accepted a proposal from Newman Kinerk, one of Boyle's dealers, who left town that same day to head up to Laramie, where a friend had offered him a job at a faro layout.

"Kind of sudden," Duncan said when he was sipping a beer at Sara's table at the Crosscut Saloon.

Sara rolled her eyes. "Mail-order brides usually get their courtship done by post," she said. "And she must have liked Pugh's business plan."

"What plan?" Laurent Dubois asked after sipping some whiskey. "He hasn't worked since the Keyes Mine closed."

Sara shrugged, and that told Duncan enough. He finished his beer, paid for the round, and walked outside. He was headed toward the mining district when a man called out from the other side of the street: "A moment of your time, Marshal?"

The stranger wore a striped blue suit and a bowler,

with a thick mustache and spectacles. Duncan hadn't met or even seen everyone in Dead Broke yet, but he was certain this man wasn't local. He crossed the street, stepped onto the boardwalk, and took the man's hand when he introduced himself as, "Paul Paxton. Of the *Cheyenne Citizen*."

He gave Duncan a card, which he tucked inside his vest pocket.

"You're a long way from home, Mr. Paxton," Duncan said.

"Unique stories bring reporters to many places, so here I am." He withdrew a notepad and pencil from his coat pocket. "May I ask you a few questions?"

"I reckon so, if I can ask you one first?"

The man smiled. "Well, if you ask just one. After all, I am the reporter."

"And I'm the town marshal. What's so unique here to bring you two hundred miles from Cheyenne?"

"Nearer two-fifty, through Laramie and Virginia Dale."

"And there are enough silver towns in the state of Wyoming to get your own 'Panic' stories."

"Ahhhh. But Dead Broke is more than a dying silver town, sir. May we talk about your duel with Ben Gunderson?"

Duncan sighed. "Are you writing for your newspaper . . . or one of those publishers of dime novels?"

"I am a journalist, sir."

Which didn't exactly answer the question, but Duncan let it go. "Well, you're talking to the wrong person. There was no duel between Gunderson and me. He was trying to shoot me in the back, but the Almighty was looking after me. Someone saw Gunderson, took aim, and fired. I didn't even see Gunderson till I turned around and watched him fall."

"Ah." The man scribbled enough for three pages, smiling all the while he wrote. "So it has begun."

"What has begun, Mr. Paxton?"

The reporter didn't have a chance to answer, because a woman's voice bellowed Paxton's name, with some adjectives that most—all—ladies would not use, especially shouting them on a public street.

She was a fat redhead with more rouge on her face than four prostitutes combined. And her breath stank of cigarette smoke.

"Harriet Coogan, Marshal, of the *Denver Trumpet*. If you want your name to be remembered in history, you'll talk to me, and not this rabid wolf. When's the next gunfight taking place, Marshal? Are you going to be in it, or do you have to wait to see who wins the next shootout?"

Duncan ran those sentences through his head again.

"Ma'am . . . I have no idea what you're talking about."

"See, Harlot-a-lot Cookey," the Cheyenne journalist barked back. "You don't start off an interview like that. That's why they'll never give you a byline. You're stupid. Now why don't you just shut up and listen to me interview this brave man! Or better yet, why don't you go back to collecting wedding engagements and obituaries!"

"I might be writing an obituary about you, you tinhorn who'd never have a job anywhere if all those tramp printers stopped correcting your mistakes before running ink over the lead."

His hat was black, and a brown patch covered the left eye on a scarred face covered with graying beard stubble and a long-handle mustache.

"Excuse me," Duncan told the feuding newspaper reporters, though he needn't have bothered. They didn't hear him or even notice as he walked toward the rider. He was planning on pointing out the notices.

Then the rider looked up with his good eye and pulled the dun to a halt. His right hand did not move any farther from the Smith & Wesson. By then, Duncan recognized him.

"Mr. John Smith." Duncan nodded.

"MacMickin'." The rough man smiled.

"It has been a spell," Duncan said.

"Three-to-five ain't what I'd call a spell. Not that cold dungeon in Cañon City."

"But you must have gotten out early."

"Good behavior."

Duncan cocked his head and let his eyes gleam.

"Good behavior comes right easy, MacMickin', when two years, nine months, and twenty-seven days comes in solitary." He turned in the saddle and looked up and down the street.

"I read in a Denver newspaper," he said as he turned around, "that your ol' boss come back up here and become your deppity."

Duncan just nodded. He heard the voices behind him before he noticed their footsteps. Killin' Ben Mitchum didn't even bother looking at the two newspaper scribes.

"That's Killin' Ben Mitchum," the woman said. "I

covered his trial, gosh, four years ago or something like that."

"Mr. Mitchum," the Cheyenne reporter said, "would you be so kind as to grant an interview with me, sir? I'll be happy to supply you with—"

"Shut up. Both of ya."

The killer looked at Duncan with that cold, deadly eye.

"There's an ordinance in Dead Broke, Ben," Duncan told him. "Without a permit, you can't go around town armed. That applies to concealed guns, too. The fine is seventy-five dollars. For the first offense. With confiscation of any and all weapons on your person."

The man smiled. "Gonna arres' me now, pardner?"

Duncan shook his head. "No. I'm just pointing out the law of Dead Broke, Colorado. Find yourself a hotel. There are vacancies all over. But when you go out of that hotel, make sure you leave your hardware in the room or the hotel vault."

"I'll keep that in mind, pardner." He started to kick the horse, but then leaned forward. "I hear ya deppity kilt ol' Ben Gunderson."

Duncan nodded.

"Well, he shouldn'ta done that. Ben was a pard of mine."

Duncan shook his head. "No, he wasn't. Gunderson didn't have a friend or partner in this world."

"Friends ain't worth havin'. But I'll be seein' ya. And ya deppity."

Now he kicked the horse, and Duncan watched him turn at the next street.

Duncan lost interest in the two reporters until their banter moved away from insults.

"Marshal," the woman said, "how many of the West's top gunfighters are coming to this town?"

"And when does the first shooting begin?" the Cheyenne man followed up.

"It's already started, you dern idiot," the woman said. "Ben Gunderson. Remember?" She turned quickly to Duncan. "Have there been other gunfights, Marshal? Who all is coming? Cole Younger?"

"Cole Younger's in prison for life in Minnesota, you dumb petticoat," the Cheyenne man said. "I've heard a lot of talk about this man at the Lucky Dice—Caleb Holden. Is he representing Dead Broke as the best gun in town? Or do you still claim that honor?"

"What are the rules of this contest, Marshal?" the woman said. "Is it anything like billiards? Or is it baseball?"

Duncan didn't answer. He just walked away, moving to the corner at a fast clip.

A gunfighting contest. That would explain all those hired killers coming to town. Duncan had taken part in shooting matches, even seen some barkers hold fast-draw contests. But pitting mankiller against mankiller? Winner wins, loser dies, or, if lucky, is just crippled by a bullet or two. That sounded more like something from one of those cheap, stupid novels.

It had to be a ruse. The contest, that is. Those gunfighters were all too real.

He started trying to figure out what Conner Boyle was really up to.

But then Little Joey ran up to him. "Marshal! Marshal! It's Nugget, Marshal! He's in trouble!"

Duncan turned. Yeah, Nugget was in a passel of trouble. He held his tongue.

"They're robbing him, Marshal. They're robbing him!"

Duncan stopped. "Who's . . . What?"

"Five miners are robbing Nugget. They're stealin' his silver diamond nugget."

First, Duncan thought it was a trap. That some of those gunmen Boyle had hired were trying to lure Duncan into their gunsights. But the boy was running, yelling at Duncan to hurry up, that they might kill the mayor. Duncan sighed, then ran after the boy.

Two blocks later, Syd Jones saw them, and he ran after them. The boy was starting to outdistance Duncan, who had never been much at running, but now he let his long legs work. He wasn't all that young, but he sure couldn't let a boy outrun him. He caught up and grabbed the boy's shoulder, then coaxed him into a stop. They were just about a block from the road to Chasm Park.

Duncan's lungs burned from the altitude and the sprint.

"All . . . right . . . Joey. Now . . ."

He waited until the wheezing Syd Jones slowed down.

"What's . . . this . . . about a . . . robbery?"

Tears started to stream down the kid's cheeks.

Duncan breathed in deeply.

"Wagon tracks." Syd Jones pointed.

Now Duncan looked at the path to the mayor's

house. It wasn't what you'd call a road, but much of Dead Broke was the same.

"Two horses with them," Duncan said. He looked at Joey.

"Three men? Or more?"

"More. Five. Three came in on the wagon."

Syd asked: "Did they see you, son?"

The boy's head shook. "I had to go . . . you know . . . potty. I heard them pull up, and then I heard Nugget come out and ask if they was here . . . were here . . . to see his Diamond Nugget of Silver. He said that he didn't recognize those fellers but they was welcome. He always liked to show folks this crown somethin' another. Then I heard one of 'em say that they was here for that very thing. And he told them how much it would cost them to see it, and then, just before I was about to open the door to the privy, one of 'em said that'd be taking the tour for free and takin' the nugget with 'em. And then I heard Nugget cry out in pain."

He bawled for a moment, then shook his head and stamped his feet, as though the tears shamed him.

"It's all right, Joey." Syd Jones put his right hand on the boy's shoulder.

"They hurt him!" the boy said. "I looked through the star on the outhouse door. A man with a red beard had pistol-whipped Nugget, and another fella was jerking him to his feet."

"They didn't see you?" Syd Jones asked.

"No, sir. I thought it'd be best to wait till they got him inside. I was afraid one of them . . . you know . . .

might have to go, but they all went into the house, and closed the door."

"Doesn't Nugget have guards?" Duncan asked.

The boy shook his head. "No. They quit him. Nugget said he couldn't pay them no more and they quit him. Oh, we've got to do something. Don't we?"

Duncan started to say something when a mule brayed.

"They're coming," Syd Jones said as he drew his Remington .44.

CHAPTER 32

Duncan spoke softly as he pulled the Colt from his holster. "Joey, you're still my deputy, right?"

"Me?" He straightened and made himself as all as he could be. "Yes, sir!"

"All, right, and deputies follow orders."

"I do!" the boy shouted.

"Close enough." Thumbing open the loading gate, he pulled the hammer to full cock and adjusted the cylinder, then filled the empty chamber with a .45 cartridge. "Deputy, run as fast as you can to the Crosscut Saloon and tell Mr. Ladron to come here. You know him, the card dealer, don't you?"

"I know who he is. My folks say I'm not supposed to know folks like that."

"Well, mind your folks. But just tell Mr. Ladron to get here in a hurry. You can deputize him since I've just deputized you."

"All right." The kid didn't sound happy to be leaving, though.

"Don't tell Miss Sara," Duncan told him. "Think you can do that? Fetch Mr. Ladron?"

"Yeah, but . . . awww, I thought I'd get to shoot somebody."

"Maybe next time. Then run to my office and ask Mr. DeMint if he would kindly hurry up here, too. Tell him to bring a half dozen pairs of handcuffs and the guns of his choice."

He pulled the hammer to full cock.

"Best hurry, Deputy. That's an order."

The kid took off at a sprint.

When Joey was out of sight, Duncan let out a long sigh of relief. Keeping the .45 cocked, he lowered the revolver and stepped even with Syd Jones, then, without saying a word, both men sidestepped about four feet from each other, still standing on the trail.

"Warm day," Jones said easily.

"That it is."

Jones ran his left hand over his face. "Eighty-nine. That was a warm year up here. But we also had a number of forest fires that year."

A mule brayed. A whip cracked. A wheel squeaked.

"Remember that year in Kansas when half the town burned to the ground?" Duncan asked.

"Criminy, boy, it ain't that warm."

"I know that. I was just thinking—"

"Oh, yeah. When the Bickerstaff boys tried to make off with the Dickinson and Company vault."

Duncan nodded. The squeaking wheel got closer.

"Donkey cart, wasn't it?" Jones asked.

"Yep. Three of the boys managed to haul the vault to the cart, but—"

Jones laughed as he finished Duncan's sentence. "The vault fell right through the bottom."

"The two jackasses took off," Duncan said with a smile. "Pulled Wilbur Bickerstaff right off the seat and into the mud."

Shaking his head, Jones said, "Those Bickerstaffs weren't smart at all, was they?"

"I dunno. Probably smarter than these boys coming into view."

"Yeah." Jones nodded. "Hauling a seventeen-hunnerd-pound chunk of silver don't make for no fast getaway."

Duncan said: "Unless you got something going on that'll grab most folks' attention."

Jones started to turn toward Duncan, but the cart was coming into view now, being led by two rough-looking men on slow horses.

"That fire had burned out by then," Jones reminded the marshal. "There wasn't nothin' goin' on—except for me and you capturin' those fool Bickerstaffs. Criminy, that boy Joey coulda taken them fools in by hisself."

"I wasn't thinking about the Bickerstaffs or Kansas," Duncan said, and he brought up the Schofield and aimed at the rider on his left.

"You boys going somewhere?" he asked as Syd Jones pointed his Remington at the other horseback rider.

The wagon and the two horses stopped.

"Tell him," the wagon driver told Nugget, who was pale, bruised, and trembling.

"Ummmmmm," Nugget started. "We's a-goin' to . . ."

"Leadville," another big man on the wagon whispered.

"Leadville," Nugget repeated.

"What for?" Duncan asked.

"'Cause . . . ummm . . . I'm showin' off my Hope . . . Diamond Nugget . . . of . . . Silver."

"I thought you were gonna do that at the park here. For Mr. Dubois's exhibit."

"I is," Nugget said, and he was sweating. It wasn't that hot. It never got that hot at this elevation. Warm. Above freezing. But never really hot. "But Leadvillians ain't gotten a look-see at my nugget."

"Yeah. Well, Mayor, tell me one thing."

"What?"

"Do these five men have permits to carry weapons in Dead Broke?"

He paled, wet his lips, then said, "Why, course they do. They paid me seventy-five dollars for 'em."

"Fair enough." He nodded, but kept his Schofield level. "Let's see them, boys."

"Sure," said the driver.

The man sitting atop the heavily wrapped silver nugget stood up quickly with a shotgun, but he kept the barrel pointed at the back of Nugget's head.

"Easy does it, lawdogs," the miner said. "Or you'll be pickin' up pieces of your mayor's brains till Judgment Day."

Nugget almost swallowed his tobacco.

"What do you think?" Duncan asked Syd Jones.

"I dunno. You reckon I could replace him as mayor?"

"Heck, yeah. Nobody would run against a man with your reputation."

"And I wouldn't get shot at."

Duncan shrugged. "Not as much, anyhow."

The shotgun man raised his eyes, and his mouth opened. "Ya don't—"

The barrel moved just enough. Duncan shifted his hand and pulled the trigger.

The shotgunner cried out and fell, pulling one of the double-barrel's triggers, but part of that blast hit the rump of the horse on his right. The shotgun dropped against the canvas, bounced up, fell to the ground as the man went backward, then rolled off on the opposite side.

All that time the horse bucked and screamed, sending its rider crashing against one of the donkeys. That caused the team to lurch. By then, Nugget was leaping forward, landing between the two-wheelers.

The driver was coming up with a handgun, but Syd Jones put a bullet in his leg, and before that man could even scream, a second slug hit the man who had been sitting next to Nugget in the belt buckle. He fell back into the seat, clutching his waist and begging the Lord to save him from a horrible gutshot wound.

The last rider was trying to draw a rifle out of the scabbard. Why he hadn't been carrying it at least was a wonder, Duncan would later say, but criminals—especially miners who turn to crime because they're out of work—never had much brains. After all, the James-Younger Gang and the Daltons at least knew better than to ride skittish horses to a gunfight.

That horse was bucking from the get-go, and the rider crashed against the rear wheel.

The donkeys started moving quickly now, and Nugget screamed that he'd be stomped to death, but the wagon maybe went six feet forward before Syd Jones moved toward the leader on his side and stopped the potential runaway.

Not that the donkeys would have run very far. Not carrying seventeen hundred pounds in the back of a cart.

"You all right?" Duncan called out to Nugget as he cocked his revolver and aimed at one of the wounded men who kept clawing at the pistol still in his holster.

"I . . . think . . . so . . ." Nugget whined.

"Too bad." Duncan kicked the miner in his boot. Then pushed the .45's barrel closer to the idiot. "You sure you want to pull that hogleg, mister?" he said. "Because it'll be the last mistake you make on this earth."

Winston DeMint and Logan Ladron arrived just ahead of Little Joey Clarke. The newspaper reporters from Denver and Cheyenne weren't far behind. Several townspeople gathered, and once Nugget managed to crawl between two donkeys and somehow not get stepped on or kicked, he started for the closest wounded would-be silver thief.

"No you don't, Mayor." Duncan stopped him.

"They tried to steal my silver diamond!" he bellowed. "We'll hang 'em."

"We'll lock them in jail and give them a fair trial."

When Nugget started to kick one, Duncan jerked him around. "Hey, old man," he barked. "You're the one who started giving anyone who could afford it a permit to carry a gun around."

"I—"

"You put a boy—this boy—in harm's way, Nugget. If he had poked his head out of that privy, one of these fool miners might have blowed his head off. Did you ever think about that?"

The mayor's face paled.

Syd Jones picked up the conversation by shoving the Remington's barrel into the wounded miner nearest him.

"Tell me something, mister? Do you have a permit to carry that carbine in this town?"

The man squeaked out a noise that might have been a "Yes" and nodded rapidly.

"When did you get it?"

"Y-y-yes-ter-dee."

"How much did it cost you?"

His head shook. "Nothin'. Nugget owed me from a mumblety-peg game."

Jones lowered the hammer and put away his revolver. "Mumblety-peg game," he whispered, shaking his head.

Logan Ladron went with the wounded men so Doc Cartier could patch them up before they were hauled to the Dead Broke jail. Nugget went with Joey, Duncan and DeMint with the prisoners with superficial injuries to the jail. Syd Jones climbed aboard the wagon and parked it in front of the marshal's office, figuring that was about as safe a place as any in Dead Broke.

Inside the jail, the miner who had thought he had been gutshot but only had a really bad bruise begged to be let go, screaming that he wouldn't have been part of that scheme if not for Dylan Pugh.

Duncan turned his head at that, and walked to the big cell.

"What about Dylan Pugh?"

That's when Duncan learned all about the councilman's plans to salt mines to lure in investors.

So Duncan arrested Dylan Pugh.

"Jail's getting crowded," Winston DeMint complained. "And hot spell sure ain't making those prisoners happy."

It wasn't a hot spell, Duncan knew, but it sure was warm. Still, things were falling into place, or, at the least, settling down.

Two days had passed since the attempted theft of the mayor's diamond-shaped silver nugget, and Duncan had talked Nugget into rescinding the firearms permit policy without hearing any argument. That morning, the newspaper's tramp printer brought over a bundle of papers to the office.

Little Joey was in school, but Nugget agreed to help post the notices all over town. Since things were turning quiet everywhere except inside the jail, Syd Jones said he could take half of that bundle. Duncan MacMicking took only one.

He was hammering it up next to the previous notice at the Lucky Dice when the door opened and Caleb Holden stepped outside, cursing.

Stepping aside, Duncan gestured toward the fresh new poster. Then he smiled and held out his left hand. "I'll take that pistol, Holden."

"I gots a permit," he said.

Duncan shook his head as Conner Boyle stepped out of his gambling hall.

"Permits aren't good anymore," Duncan said casually, still holding out his left hand, palm up. "So I won't fine you this time, but I'm impounding your pistol."

"You can't—" The Schofield that Duncan had used as

a hammer flashed out, the barrel slamming into the side of the killer's head and driving him off the boardwalk and into the dirt.

Holden rolled over, dazed but deadly, as he reached for his holstered pistol. The bullet slammed into that holster, ringing loudly as it ricocheted into the water trough, and Holden jerked back his stinging hand. By then Duncan's .45 was cocked again and pointing, this time, a few inches from Conner Boyle's nose.

"I'm done playing games, Boyle," he said. "Get your gunfighters and go play somewhere else."

"You can't run me out of town. This is—"

Stepping forward, Duncan now placed the warm barrel closer to the cheater's nose.

"My town." He didn't have to look back at the gunfighter lying in the dirt. "Holden, if you move one more inch, your boss is going to be dead before I am. And I bet I'll have enough meanness in me to take you with me."

"Don't be a fool, Holden!" Boyle screeched.

"Even if I don't kill you, your life won't be worth spitting on. Because all those gunfighters you boys have brought to town will be mad at you because you'll have ended their days getting paid for sitting around and doing nothing."

Holden's sigh told Duncan there was nothing to worry about from that punk, so he smiled at Boyle.

"You remember the old days, don't you, Boyle?" Duncan said. "The white affidavits we passed out? Notices to unwelcomed folks to get out of town. Well, we're going back to those days—"

"That was different. Different times. And you can't get away with this in eighteen and ninety-three. You—"

"Do you think the politicians and lawmen in Denver give a plug nickel what's going on nigh twelve thousand feet in these Rockies? I don't. You have two days, Boyle, to get out of town. If you're not gone by then, you'll never leave Dead Broke. Unless your next of kin comes along to dig you up and take you back to the family plot."

He lowered the revolver, but kept it cocked for the time being.

"And I don't think none of your kin wants to remember that you are related to them."

Stepping away, he nodded at the new poster.

"That stays up. If it doesn't, you'll be put down." He stepped over the cringing Holden.

The newspaperwoman from Denver and the newspaperman from Cheyenne stood gawking in the middle of the street.

"Put that down in your papers," Duncan told them, and walked away.

Conner Boyle did not bother pouring brandy into a snifter. He took a long pull from the bottle, which he slammed down onto the table. Caleb Holden was explaining to the gathering of gunfighters what had happened.

"Criminy," said Faro Scott. "And I jus' got here coupla hours ago. Now ya sayin' I gots to leave?"

"I'm not paying you for jokes, gunman," Boyle told him.

Scott laughed. "Ya thinks Mick MacMickin' is good enough to take all of us?" He waved his hand around.

Boyle looked at the gunmen he had brought to town. All of them . . . even Caleb Holden. He had lost just one, Ben Gunderson, and that had been poor timing. If that drunken fool of a lawdog Syd Jones hadn't sobered up and shown up when he did, this town would be all his by now.

Someone tapped on the door, and Boyle nodded at Holden, who crushed out his cigarette in an ashtray and walked to the door.

"If you're ending your need for my services, Boyle," D.B. Mora said softly, "I'll be taking my pay— right now."

"Pity," Faro Scott said. "And that big ol' chunk of silver still in that wagon parked right in front of the marshal's office. How much does that thing weigh?"

"Seventeen hundred and seventy-six pounds." Boyle didn't even realize he had answered.

"What's that worth now?" someone asked. Boyle wasn't paying much attention now.

"Not as much as it was before the Panic."

"But I read in a Chicago newspaper that the uniqueness of that chunk, and its history, would still fetch a good deal of cash—to the right buyer."

"It sure don't belong to no miner who ain't got a lick of sense."

The door closed, and Holden walked across the room with a telegram. He handed the folded slip of paper to Boyle, whispering, "I tol' the clerk to keep his mouth shut. Paid 'm with a ten-doller piece."

Unfolding the telegram, Boyle smiled.

"I think," he said as he looked up, "our worries are over. Ben Usher will be here tomorrow morn."

Holden grinned. "I bet he'd kill that lawdog for nothin' but pers'nal satisfaction."

CHAPTER 33

Stepping outside the next morning, Duncan looked at the wagon holding Nugget's massive chunk of silver in that flimsy wagon. The "diamond" was still wrapped in canvas, tied up with heavy ropes. The team of donkeys had been unhitched and led to one of the livery stables that was still in business.

He studied the sloping road to the west. The day was still warm—by Dead Broke standards—but the skies were darkening. Even a little spring rain would cool things off.

"Good morning." That was a voice he would always recognize. Smiling, he turned and stared into the mesmerizing blue eyes of Sara Cardiff.

"That it is," he agreed with a nod. "And good morning to you."

"Think it'll rain?"

He shrugged. "I've never been much of a rainmaker. Ran three out of town, though. During my Kansas years."

She fanned herself.

"It sure is warm."

Duncan nodded. "Yeah . . . it sure—*oh, no!*"

Turning, Sara stared at Duncan, who stepped off

the boardwalk, staring down the street. Then he yelled, "Quick, Sara. We have to hurry." He reached out, took her hand, and pulled her down. Then he started running, and she had to lift the hem of her dress with her free hand.

"Where—"

That was all she got to say for about a block.

He slowed down, but that was probably because of the altitude, or the fact that he heard Sara screaming when she saw the mud.

"My dress! My dress! This dress is new, Duncan!"

He stopped, looked at her, then guided her onto the boardwalk.

"What's the—"

"Your sculpture," he said, and hurried down the board-walk, still clutching her hand, nodding at the ladies, begging their pardons, saying, "Make way, sir," when he had to pass a salesman or someone who wasn't moving fast enough.

He stepped off the boardwalk at Dead Broke's city park, and into about two inches of mud. Stopping, he turned around and extended his arms.

"Have you lost your mind?" Sara asked.

"Come on," he said. "I'll carry you."

She gave him a mischievous grin, and then let herself settle into his arms.

That got a round of applause from a few people on the other side of the street as Duncan slogged through the mud. It wasn't that deep. Didn't even cover the feet of his boots. Then he reached the grass, most of it green, all of it wet, and moved to the canvas tents.

"You can let me down now," she said.

He stopped, and gently lowered Sara to the ground.

Feeling the wet grass, she lifted her dress slightly and followed Duncan to Laurent Dubois, who sat in a chair in front of a canvas tent, sobbing like a baby.

"What's the matter, Mr. Dubois?" Sara asked tentatively.

Somberly, Duncan pulled back the piece of canvas and looked at what had been an ice sculpture of Sara Cardiff. Most of what he had seen earlier that week was now soaking the tops of his boots.

Nature. Nature can be just plain vicious at times. He shook his head, and was about to pull the canvas tarp back into place, like covering a corpse with a shroud, when Sara stepped beside him and peered inside.

"Oh." She looked up into Duncan's eyes. "One of his sculptures?"

He smiled sadly. "One of them."

She turned away and went back to the painter—the artist—and, no longer caring about her dress, knelt in the wet grass, grabbed one of his trembling hands in her own, and patted it like a kind mother.

"Mr. Dubois," she whispered, "it's all right."

"I'm ruined," he said.

"No you're not."

His head shook. "I am a fool. A failure."

"You, sir," she said, "are an artist."

"She's right," Duncan said, and made his soaking feet move away from the shroud. "This was just practice, Lamont."

"Laurent," he and Sara whispered at the same time.

"I'll get that right one of these days. But Sar— Miss Cardiff . . . she's dead-on. Practice. That's all this was. You've seen what you can do. I've seen it." He turned and stared at the other covered statues of ice, all melting rapidly. "We'll do this again, maybe early winter."

"Folks won't come up here in the winter. Many of our citizens leave in the winter!"

"They'll come," Sara told him. "People will travel a long and hard trail to see beauty. And I know—even though I haven't seen your ice carvings . . . I know they are beautiful. Because you are the one person in Dead Broke who has vision. Who has nothing in his heart but beauty. Even your paintings . . . just the paintings of walls and ceilings. You do that with so much integrity, with so much care, it's amazing. We'll even pay for the hauling of ice blocks out of the mountain lakes." She looked at Duncan. "Won't we?"

His nod was tentative. He wasn't sure how much men charged to haul giant blocks of ice from mountain lakes. Maybe they could store ice in the caves like most folks did. Bring those big blocks in before winter took firm hold. But, yeah, paying men to bring in ice sure sounded better than hauling ice in when it was ten below zero.

"Sure we will. We'll get some newspapermen from New York City. Chicago. San Francisco. We'll make Dead Broke the busiest city in Colorado in January."

"No-vem-ber," Laurent Dubois said between sniffles. "Maybe. I do not . . . wish to . . . be here in . . . January or . . . February."

The man riding the zebra dun into Dead Broke that afternoon had the look of a man who had traveled far. Dust and old mud stains covered the linen duster he wore, and there was a rip across the outer upper half of his right arm, a rip with edges marked by gunpowder. Like many a Westerner, he held the reins in one hand, his right. His left rested at the side—never moving far, though, no matter the zebra dun's gait, from an ivory-handled Colt Thunderer.

His face was bronzed, the eyes a cold, dark brown, almost black, the hair dirty from days of travel, somewhere between brown and blond. The mustache and goatee were darker, and a tiny scar could be spotted on the right side of his head—not hideous, but impossible not to notice as it cut about an inch into his hair about even with the top of his ear.

He wore black boots with a maroon star inlaid into the uppers, with old U.S. Army spurs over the heels, striped gray britches, a blue shirt, black vest, yellow-and-black-checked bandanna, and a short-crowned black hat with a wide brim curled up along the edges.

No one on the streets recognized him, but not many were on the streets. Most of the people who came to Dead Broke these days rode straight to the marshal's office to look at the wagon that held the Hope Diamond of Silver, even if nobody could see through the dark canvas tarps that covered the blessed thing. This man rode straight to the Lucky Dice. He swung from the saddle, slapped dust off his pants with his hat, then resettled that atop his head, and stopped when he saw the posters. He read about the gun ordinance and the one that said the ordinance had been revoked.

That gave him a chuckle, and he looked up and down the boardwalk, shook his head, still smiling, and went into the gambling hall.

The stairs were to his right, so he took them, and stopped only when the bored bartender yelled at him, "Hey. Where do you think—"

He never finished, for the stranger stopped and turned. He said nothing. Made no threat. No move to pull the double-action pistol. He just stopped, turned, and stared.

The bartender paled, cleared his throat, and began to work furiously on a shot glass that was handy.

"Beg your pardon, sir. Thought you were somebody else."

The man turned without a word, and reached the second story. The newcomer did not look back at the bartender, and when those footsteps had stopped and the barman heard a tapping at his boss's door, the barkeep, still trembling, breathed out a sigh of relief and poured himself a double rye.

Conner Boyle smiled when D.B. Mora opened the door and Ben Usher walked inside. The gunman stopped briefly, stepping aside as Mora closed the door.

"Keep your hand on that doorknob, D.B.," Usher said. "Until I tell you to open it or let go. If a hinge squeaks, I'm gonna have to assume you're trying to shoot me in the back. So you'll be the second to die."

He stopped after two more paces and nodded at Boyle.

"Your boss will be the first."

His eyes took in the others in the office.

Usher smiled. "After that, we'll just have to see how many more I kill."

"You're not going to have to kill anyone here, Mr. Usher," Boyle said. "But you'll have the pleasure of killing someone else in this town. And then I'm gonna make you—and these other gunmen—rich." He shrugged, and reached slowly for a bottle of brandy. "And me . . . a bit richer."

Ben Usher stood with his back to the wall, away from the window, and kept his eye on D.B. Mora, who still kept holding the door closed.

He didn't know the punk who worked for Boyle, but he recognized the name from a paragraph or two in the newspapers he read. Caleb Holden was the young kid's name. Faro Scott and Killin' Ben Mitchum he knew from notices put up on them over the years, though the charges were usually dropped—after witnesses wound up dead. Telluride Tom was a lucky hombre Usher had tracked three times, but that man could turn into a mountain goat or a salamander and just disappear. Dean Hill once put a ball from a derringer into the watch pocket of Usher's pants. Which could have hurt a lot, but wound up just killing his watch. The bullet that took off the ring and pinky fingers on Hill's left hand probably hurt that gunfighter more than Usher's nasty bruise and the need for a new watch and britches.

"What do you think?" asked Conner Boyle, who seemed sure of himself after explaining his plan. At least, part of the plan.

"You brought all of us up here to steal the Hope Diamond of Silver?" he asked, then shook his head and chuckled.

"Seventeen hundred and seventy-six pounds of silver. You're stealing that? Then hauling that down this mountain?" He shook his head again but without the laughter. "How you plan on getting anywhere with that load?"

"I'm not getting anywhere. We'll be getting just as far as the railroad tracks. All except two of us— Mitchum and Mora. They'll stay behind to keep pursuit back just long enough for us to reach the tracks." He looked at those two gunman. "You will be paid before the rest of us leave. And fresh horses will be waiting for you at the sharp bend in the road. You'll escape with your money."

Both men seemed to like that idea.

Boyle continued: "An express train will be waiting for us. We get aboard. Nugget's treasured silver diamond gets on board. And, trust me, no one will stop that train."

Dean Hill must have figured he needed to talk. "Why won't nobody try to stop that train?"

Usher chuckled. "Because a man who owns a railroad, even during this Panic, can influence a lot of governments—and the law." It pleased him to have robbed that blowhard of a cardsharper of explaining things to everyone. Usher kept going: "Let's see, silver's down from more than a dollar to . . . hmmmmm . . . sixty-something cents an ounce. With just rough math, dealing in regular ounces, that'd bring, oh, eighteen thousand dollars to be divided . . ."

"Twenty-five hundred apiece for each of you," Boyle said. "The rest to me."

Three men whistled. The young punk of Boyle's said, "That's mighty generous of you."

"Not really," Usher said, and winked at Boyle, whose face began to redden. "The silver market's shot for the time being, but a man who owns a railroad and is willing to pay for a stolen chunk of silver, he isn't buying this for riches, hoping the silver market recovers. He just wants something different, something original, something to call his own. I guess a man might think of Nugget's fortune as a miracle like the *Mona Lisa* or *George Washington Crossing the Delaware.*"

"The what?" Killin' Ben Mitchum asked.

Still holding the door handle, D.B. Mora called out: "Usher's got a point. What makes you sure that railroad boss, well, he might want to kill you and us rather than pay for that monster nugget?"

"There is honor among thieves," Boyle said.

Usher laughed aloud and walked to Boyle's personal bar. Now he poured himself a drink, but still managed to keep everyone in his sight. "That's a load of hog-wash." He sipped bourbon.

"So you reach out to several of . . . well . . . the West's most wanted gunmen, or at least some notorious ones who work for hire." He nodded at Boyle. "But let it slip out to some newspaper folks that this is going to be a championship gunfight. Target shooting, sort of, but the targets being other top guns."

"No one would be suspicious," Boyle said. He didn't look like he was used to being challenged by someone he paid to come visit him and hear his plan. "There would be excitement. No one would think anything was going to happen until the determined day of the gunfight."

Usher nodded at the explanation.

"That's one way of seeing it," he told the planner and his hired guns. "But it sure would bring a lot of attention to a town that's losing money each day and is seeing its population shrink to nothing. If you'd just reached out to one or two of us, on the sly, you could have gotten the guns you needed without any attention."

Boyle flung his glass, which shattered against a wooden stove.

"I don't want Mick MacMicking's death not to get any attention!" he roared. "I want the whole world to know that he died . . . and that he died in Dead Broke, Colorado."

Usher's head nodded as though he had known that answer all the time.

"So I'm here to kill your lawman," he said, and sipped more bourbon.

"Yes."

"Does that twenty-five hundred dollars include me helping you get that treasure on the train and killing a top gun like MacMicking . . . or do I get more than these other . . ." Grinning, he shrugged. "These other professionals?"

"I'll pay you one thousand dollars more."

Usher nodded, but noticed that the other gunfighters did not care much for his bonus payment.

"When do you want him dead?"

"Now." Boyle looked around for another glass, found one, and filled it with a shaking hand.

"Now?" His head tilted and his eyes twinkled. "Don't

you think that would bring more newspaper scribes up this mountain?"

"By the time they learn about MacMicking's death, we'll be on that train or riding out of Colorado with twenty-five hundred dollars each—in gold . . . not silver."

Standing near the window, Killin' Ben Mitchum let a curtain fall and cleared his throat. "Well, now's as good a time as any." He tilted his massive head toward the window. "The marshal's walkin' down the street with that sassy gal from that other, better, gambling place and some fool man sobbin' like a newborn kitten."

Ben Usher turned his back on those killers and moved to the window as Mitchum stepped back. The gunman looked for no more than two or three seconds, grinned, and walked toward the door.

"You boys want to see a show, gather 'round that window." He stopped and stared at Boyle.

"Twenty-five hundred for the Hope Diamond of Silver. A thousand dollars for killing Dun— . . . Mick MacMicking. That's the agreement."

Boyle nodded.

"Say it."

"If you help us get Nugget's diamond—and it's right outside the marshal's office. All we have to do is hitch a team and hightail it down this mountain."

"I don't need to hear your plan, sonny. I just want you to say the deal."

"Get the diamond out of Dead Broke and twenty-five hundred dollars is yours. Kill the marshal, and I'll pay you a thousand more. You can ride the train—all of you—as far as you want us to take you."

Faro Scott asked: "Is that eastbound or westbound, sir?"

Usher laughed. "I think the direction is up or down, gents. Excuse me. Gather 'round the window. It's gonna be better than *A Trip to Chinatown*."

CHAPTER 34

"I never knew you appreciated art," Sara told Duncan when they were back on the boardwalk, heading away from the park and all that melting ice.

He gave a slight shrug. "Guess it depends on the art."

"You were very nice to Laurent."

"I'm not always mean and stubborn."

"No." She giggled. "Not always."

Yet his green eyes kept darting, always looking for something that didn't seem right. Intentionally, he took the long way back to the Crosscut Saloon, partly because it meant more time he would get to spend walking with Sara, but also to see what the Lucky Dice looked like. He didn't think those hired gunmen would take off. Paid guns couldn't do that kind of thing—not if they wanted to keep getting paid.

"Those clouds don't look pleasant," Sara said.

He had observed that, too, but now he concentrated on Conner Boyle's gambling hall. The posters remained up, the front door closed. He could see someone looking at him through the upper-story window, and a zebra dun at the hitch rail. That horse was one he hadn't seen before. Not that a new horse in town—or an old horse that he just hadn't noticed—was something to worry about, but anything in front of Boyle's business put him on alert.

Should have taken Sara to the Crosscut first.

Well, he never thought all that clearly when he was near her.

He saw the Chinese restaurant a few abandoned businesses before the next intersection. Just to be safe, he thought, and cleared his throat before pointing at the sign ahead.

"Want to do me a favor?" he asked.

"Depends." She was in a giddy mood.

Reaching into his pocket, he pulled out a gold piece. "Can you stop and get some food for the boys at the office and jail?"

She cocked her head and gave him that questioning look.

He offered an explanation. "I've ordered my deputies to stay inside, and I ought to start making my rounds."

"A bit early," she said, "for rounds . . . and supper . . . isn't it?"

Nodding, he tried another lie. "Those clouds. Could drop rain on us or hail. I'd rather not have to send anyone out and get them soaked or pounded."

"Those clouds," she said flatly, "are still a long ways off."

His face hardened, but he knew he would win in the end. "All right. I'll do it myself."

"Ohhhhhhhh." She even stamped a foot on a loose pine plank. "Give me that gold piece. I'll do it. Run along and make your rounds. Do I need to get supper for the prisoners?"

He shook his head. "No. We loaded up on spuds and

rice. Got enough coffee. I'd just rather feed my deputies something better."

"Uh-huh." She took the coin and walked past him toward the restaurant. "Since when have you ever considered Chinese food good?"

But she went inside, and Duncan tugged on the holstered .45 and stepped onto the street, walking down the middle, head straight, moving toward the Lucky Dice, eyes darting left and right, but mostly forward, taking in every window and the big doors of Conner Boyle's place.

I'm probably just jumpy, he thought.

But when he made it to the intersection, the door to the Lucky Dice opened, and a man in dark clothes and hat stepped outside, the tail of his trail-worn black coat swept behind a holster on a gun belt.

Duncan stopped, stared, let his hand touch his holster, and walked toward the man.

They stopped at the same time, thirty feet separating them, the Lucky Dice right behind the armed man. At least Duncan could keep an eye on Boyle's business and the gunman in front of him.

"Been a long time," Ben Usher said.

Nodding, Duncan suddenly tensed. Little Joey Clarke had stepped off the corner and froze.

Duncan wanted to tell the kid to get out of here, for he stood several yards away from the Lucky Dice but still too close to those doors and the big windows. If Boyle's hired men started coming out of there, they'd likely be shooting at anything that moved.

"I said . . ." Ben Usher raised his voice. "Been a long time."

"Two years at least," Duncan said.

"Two years and three weeks if I recall correctly."

"Sounds right."

Usher's eyes flashed, and then his head shook.

"You hiring women as your deputies these days, Mick?"

Duncan's teeth started grinding—he could taste enamel on his tongue. "Sara," he said without turning around. "What the devil do you think you're doing?"

She didn't answer, but Ben Usher chuckled. "Don't worry. It isn't pointed at me."

Duncan laughed. "I didn't think it would be. Most likely, it's aimed at me."

Duncan took a step forward. So did Ben Usher.

"I think I owe you a sound whuppin'," Usher said. "Making me out to be some ruffian and loser."

"If the boot fits . . ."

They were twenty feet apart.

"I wouldn't mind so much, but the writers you hire to pen those penny dreadfuls are . . . well . . . dreadful."

"I don't hire them. I don't even get to see them, and when I see them, I don't read them. I burn them."

They stopped, six feet from one another.

"What brings you to Dead Broke?" Duncan asked.

With his left hand, Usher hooked the thumb behind him. The right hand stayed right above the double-action Colt in the holster. "Man in that gambling joint wants me to kill you."

"Is the pay good?"

Usher shrugged. "Not bad. Made more money. But I don't think you're worth a thousand dollars."

"You'd have to be pretty fast to earn that money."

He nodded, then smiled. "Yeah, but the thing is . . .

I've always been faster than you. Fact is, the only person
I know who's faster than me is—"

"Syd Jones," Duncan said.

Usher grinned.

"He's here."

"So I heard."

"Agreed to be my deputy."

Usher's head shook. "Should be the other way around,
shouldn't it?"

Duncan sighed. "Well, times change."

"Ain't that the truth. Kinda a shame, ain't it?"

"We all get older."

"Yeah."

They looked at each other long and hard.

"You gonna try to earn that money?" Duncan asked.

They resumed walking.

"Well, I figured that would be . . . too . . . easy. . . .
It'd be like . . . I was stealing."

They stood inches apart, then Usher laughed and
wrapped his arms around Duncan, pulling him into an
embrace, and Duncan pounded his best friend's back,
cursing as Dead Broke's marshal called Usher a few im-
polite words. Quickly, the embrace ended, and they
both spun around, palming their pistols and aiming at
the upper window of the Lucky Dice.

"You hired the wrong man, Boyle!" Usher called out.
"I reckon I'm like most fellows. I have a price. But I
don't think a thousand dollars, even with an extra twenty-
five hundred, is worth gunning down my old pardner,
saddle pal, and best friend."

"Besides," Duncan called out, "he couldn't take me
on his best day."

"Keep that up, pard," Usher said, "and I might just change sides."

"Sure."

They waited, but nothing happened.

"What do you think?" Usher whispered.

"How many men are with Boyle?"

Usher answered softly.

"Sara," Duncan said without turning away from the Lucky Dice. "That scatter-gun is worthless from where you are. Just get that supper for Syd and DeMint and get out of here."

He frowned when he heard the footsteps on the muddy street.

Usher laughed again. "She listens to you about as much as I do, pardner."

Then she stood on Duncan's left.

"I told you—"

She cut him off. "You told me the shotgun wasn't good from where I was. So I got closer."

"It's still not—"

"Shut up!" she barked.

"Who's that?" Usher started to swing his Thunderer.

"Don't shoot Logan," Sara said. "He's my best dealer. And that's Bryn Bunner coming up behind him." She put her left hand next to her mouth and called out to both men:

"Keep your guns on the back door to Boyle's place! If anyone comes out of that door, blow them back inside!"

When the two men moved as ordered, Duncan spit in the mud.

"Why don't you—"

But Duncan knew there was nothing he could do. And for the moment, they had Boyle and all of his gunmen trapped.

"Boyle!" he said. "I'm going to give you a present. You have five minutes to come out through the front door, hands over your heads. And all of those gunmen in there with you right behind you. One at a time. Then line up side by side. If I see one gun—one knife—if I see something that I don't like—we start shooting."

He waited.

A muffled voice came out. "And if we don't come out?"

Duncan's head shook. "The businesses next door to you are empty, and . . ." He started to praise Dead Broke's fire department, then remembered that the station and engine had burned down when he arrived. "And . . . since the wind's not blowing—those would be the only ones that would likely be damaged after my deputies finish tossing coal oil on the wall. Got some volunteers already tossing water on the other buildings."

The window faced the front. Duncan was guessing that no one would call his bluff. On the other hand, if Boyle did, Duncan might torch that place anyway. He didn't like policing a town with far too many gunmen hanging their hats here.

"You got no proof—"

"I have a witness who says you hired him to kill me. But I'll tell you what. All I want is you and every one of your gunmen out of town. I'll have some volunteers bring your horses from the liveries, and then once they're here, you can come out, hands up, mount your horses—take anything you can carry in your saddlebags or grips or wrapped in your bedrolls—then ride out of town. And don't come back."

"Generous terms," Ben Usher whispered.

"Just trying to avoid an all-out gun battle with that crew," Duncan said quietly. "Keep some innocent people from getting hurt."

"Would you really set the Lucky Dice on fire?" Sara asked.

"Buildings," he said, "can be rebuilt. . . . Lives, that's something different."

He cleared his throat and called out: "I'm giving you one minute, Boyle. Once that fire starts, we're shooting everyone who comes out that door."

"I'll take this to the governor and the attorney general. I'll take this to Washington."

"Go right ahead. But the only way you're getting to the state capital or Washington is if you come out now. Otherwise, the farthest you'll get is Boot Hill."

He waited, then smiled.

"Get our horses!" Boyle bellowed, and the men started naming the liveries.

"Wait!" Duncan yelled. "Boyle, write down those liveries and the names those hired killers used." He waited before asking, "Do you have a bartender or someone working inside?"

"My cook," came the answer.

Well, it wasn't like bartenders and gamblers had any reason to come to work these days.

"All right. Have him bring out that list of liveries. When all the horses are saddled, I'll let you know. You can come out then. But again . . . hands clear, guns in holsters, and you ride out of town pronto. And none of you sets foot in Dead Broke again."

CHAPTER 35

It looked as though everyone who still called Dead Broke home came out to watch Conner Boyle and his gunfighters ride out of town. Some brought their children with them. The reporters from Denver and Cheyenne called out questions to the gunmen, but none responded. They all rode with their eyes looking at the road ahead, between the ears of their horses.

Duncan and Ben Usher came up from the jail, standing away from the crowd—though some might say "crowd" would have been an overstatement anywhere except in Dead Broke, Colorado.

Bryn Bunner came over when the last rider, D.B. Mora, fell out of view and the crowd began breaking up, talking loudly about what they had seen, some waving at the lawmen, a few calling out their thanks. Duncan nodded and waved back, while Ben Usher kept looking at the now-empty road.

"Just wanted to thank you, Marshal," Bunner said. "We don't need gunfighters here." His mouth opened, then closed, and he looked sheepishly at Usher, who just grinned.

"I'm just a man with a gun," Usher said. "Never considered myself a gunfighter."

"Well . . ." The big man swallowed and looked back at Duncan. "Half the miners were worried those killers might have been to town after them."

Duncan just nodded, shook the big man's hand, and watched him walk up the street. The wind started picking up.

"Feels like some rain's coming," Usher said.

"Yeah." Duncan was hoping for a clear night.

Hoofbeats sounded and both men turned to see Syd Jones riding a palomino and cradling a sawed-off shotgun in his arms. He reined up at the corner.

"Follow them to the big cut," Duncan said. "You can watch them from there till they turn into the narrows."

Usher added: "And make sure they can see you when you ride back here."

Sara shook her head before an understanding came to her. "They're coming back," she said.

"They have to," Syd Jones told her, and kicked his horse into an easy walk.

"Why?" she asked. "Pride?"

Duncan shrugged. "That's part of it."

"Men," she whispered.

"That's part of it, too," Usher said, and pulled a cigar from his inside coat pocket.

"Revenge?" she asked.

"Money." Duncan nodded at the wagon still parked in the muddy street.

"But that's not worth—"

"What it once was," Duncan said. "But seventeen hundred pounds of silver will mean a good payday.

And as you pointed out, there's revenge to figure into this, too."

Sara looked at the two men as though they were ridiculous fools.

Usher lit his cigar and pulled it from his mouth. "If it were just Boyle, that would be one thing. He's a gambler. And gamblers win and gamblers lose. But hired guns . . ." He shook his head. "They have to win. They have to prove they're the best."

Nugget rounded the corner. "There you be!" he said. "What the Sam Hill is you two lawdogs thinkin'? You's here, leavin' my Diamond Nugget of Silver unprotected in front of yer office. Evildoers could steal that and I'd be left with nothin' but misery and my rheumeytism."

"The whole town was right here," Sara pointed out. "And the badmen just rode out of town."

The old miner snorted. "The whole town wasn't right here, missy, cuz I wasn't here, and my boys wasn't here, neither. They was right by that wagon, protectin' it. But if this is the protection—"

He stopped. "What badmen just rid outta my town?"

"Conner Boyle. Caleb Holden. Every other hired gun that Boyle brought to town." Duncan put his hands on his hips and glared. "You want to tell me about how all these gunmen came into Dead Broke for some shooting contest?"

"They's all . . ." Nugget turned and spit out tobacco juice. ". . . They left? Ever' one of 'em?"

Duncan nodded. "Every one."

The old man grinned. "Well, call me a suck-egg hen." He slapped his pantlegs with both hands. "That's a weight off my nerves, that's fer certain. Marshal, iffen it's all right with ya, I'll be takin' my nugget back home and puttin' it where it belongs. Now that 'em evildoers has left Dead Broke, I reckon it's safe. I'll get my reg'lar guards back an' all."

"You sure you want to do that, Mayor?" Sara asked.

"Yes'm. I don'ts sleep as good when that nugget ain't with me, missy. But y'all can come anytime and see it—fer free. Cuz y'all done good to me and all. Y'all and Little Joey. That's all." He spit again, and looked at Ben Usher. "But not Ben. Ya wasn't here to stop 'em thievin' varmints. And I's read 'bout ya and all 'em evil things ya's tried to do to our town marshal."

Usher smiled and let his right hand fall and his fingers tap the Thunderer's grips.

"But I'll give ya a good discount. Half off. Iffen that's fine with ya."

Shaking his head, Duncan's friend chuckled. "I appreciate your generosity, Mayor."

Once Nugget walked away, Sara shook her head again. "Do you think that's a good idea? Letting Nugget take that big rock back to his home, I mean."

"It's his big rock," Duncan pointed out.

"Yeah, but if Boyle and those men are going to try to steal it . . ."

"It'll be good bait," Duncan said.

She stared at him, then at Usher, and shook her head.

"I don't understand. Are those men coming back—if they are coming back—to steal that silver or to kill you?"

"If it were me," Usher said after removing the cigar and blowing smoke toward the darkening skies, "it'd be both. If I weren't so despicably honest. But there's one thing a gunfighter likes more than revenge—and that's—"

Sara understood. "Money."

"How do we want to play this hand?" Usher asked.

"You know, Ben, this is really not your problem."

"Then you best deputize me, pardner," he said, "so it is my problem."

The rain had been falling for maybe twenty minutes when someone pounded on the door to the marshal's office.

Duncan set down the cup of coffee he had been sipping and walked to the door, opening it without a question and letting a soaking Syd Jones step inside.

"No password?" Ben Usher's tone was facetious.

"Recognized the knock." Duncan closed the door.

"Where's Nugget's wagon?" Syd Jones said as he pulled off his waterlogged hat, banging it against his left leg before hanging it on a peg, and then removed the yellow slicker off and hung it, dripping water, on another peg.

Duncan explained what had happened and handed his old mentor his cup of water, saying, "It's warm."

"Thanks."

The old man took the cup and headed to the stove. Rain pounded on the roof.

"I followed them just like you said," the old lawman said. "Let them see me. They were in no particular hurry. Didn't look back. Once they disappeared into the narrows, I rode back here. Gave them a good view of my back."

"You wasn't scared of getting back-shot by them vermin?" Winston DeMint asked.

Jones coughed out a laugh. "Not them boys. They are right good with short guns, but not long guns. Besides, it was raining, they'd have to shoot uphill, and I was well out of rifle range."

"How do we play this hand?" Usher asked.

Turning to the jailkeeper, Duncan said: "Kick all the prisoners out. Tell them to go home and stay there—and they'll be summoned when the judge comes to town."

"They can't burn us out," DeMint argued. "Not in this frog strangler."

"Just let them out," Duncan said, and the former gambler and cheat sighed, grabbed the ring of heavy keys, and walked to the heavy door, pulling it open and stepping inside, then shutting the door behind him.

"How many of those prisoners want you dead?" Usher asked.

"They're not killers. Crooks. Drunks. Fools. Tinhorns. But not professional gunmen. And there's no telling what Conner Boyle will do."

Shaking his head but still smiling, Usher crushed out his cigar in a tin plate and found the coffeepot.

"Maybe I picked the wrong side to be on this time," he said.

Duncan grinned. "Wouldn't be the first time."

Usher laughed. "The same, pardner, can be said for you."

The door to the cells opened, and the prisoners came out slowly. None made eye contact with Duncan, Jones, or Usher. They just walked to the door. The first man removed the bar, leaned it against the wall, opened the door, and stepped into the steady rain. The others just walked into the deepening darkness. Lightning flashed, and thunder followed a few seconds later. Winston DeMint followed the line of prisoners, and when the last one was outside, he closed the door and put the bar back up.

"You might as well go home, too, Winston," Duncan said.

But DeMint shook his head. "I've got buckets to empty, and I might as well throw those blankets outside. Let the rain wash away the stink and filth."

Duncan started: "Those cells—"

But DeMint cut him off. "Are my job. Yours is filling them. And tonight—emptying them. But keeping them clean and taking care of the prisoners—and the prisoners that'll be coming in after tonight. That's my job, Marshal. And I'll do it my way."

He marched to the door, opened it, and slammed it behind him.

"Well," Usher said. "I see some things haven't changed."

Duncan didn't respond. He looked at Syd Jones.

"Ben and I will go find a good place to keep an eye on Nugget's place."

"I might as well go," the old man said. "I'm already soaked."

Duncan shook his head. "You get warm. My guess is Boyle will leave a man or two near here. When the shooting starts, don't open the door."

"Don't intend to." He pointed at the heavy shutters. "I can shoot fine through those slits."

"You can't see a thing out there."

"My eyes ain't that bad, sonny. I can see a muzzle flash."

Duncan wasn't going to win this argument, so he started filling his pockets with .45 cartridges, then found a dark poncho. Usher did the same.

Ready, the two men walked to the door, and Jones walked ahead of them, removed the bar, and stepped back.

Duncan pulled on the handle slightly and peered into blackness and wetness and a cold wind.

He gave a quick nod and said, "Good luck," then stepped into the night. Usher held out his hand.

"Good to see you, Mr. Jones."

"Same here."

Usher slipped out easily, and Jones whispered to both of the gunmen: "Keep your powder dry."

Then he closed the door and set the bar back into place.

He moved to the gun case as Winston DeMint came out of the room of cells.

Jones looked up, then went back to work.

"Help me load these," he said.

"Which one?"

"All of 'em." He fed a shell of buckshot into a twelve-gauge. "Like as not, we'll have need of ever' last gun we got."

CHAPTER 36

"This town looks a whole lot bigger in the dark and rain," Usher said as he pulled down the front brim of his hat.

"It is big." The raindrops stung like hail, and the wind howled. "Big and empty."

"Not that empty," Usher said, and palmed his Thunderer. Duncan spun around and spotted a shadowy figure coming toward the jail.

"Hold it!" Duncan barked, and palmed his .45.

The figure stopped, sniffled, and said, "It's me, Marshal."

"Me who?" Duncan snapped.

"Dylan Pugh." And the man slowly came forward till he was close enough for Duncan to see the man's face.

"Pugh." Duncan was already wet and cold. His nerves were raw, and he couldn't get Sara off his mind. "I just kicked you out of jail. Salting a mine is a felony, buster. And judges and juries frown upon that. You're already facing time in Cañon City. You want me to add this to the charges when your trial comes up before the circuit judge?"

374 William W. Johnstone and J.A. Johnstone

He could tell his lecture wasn't getting anywhere with the big man.

"Are you in a hurry to go back in that miserable cell?"

Pugh shrugged, and Usher quickly moved, shoving Duncan aside, pulling his .41-caliber pistol, and aiming it at the bridge of the miner and councilman's nose. "What do you have under that coat, buster?"

Duncan hadn't noticed. That kind of mistake could get a fellow killed right quick—especially on a night like this.

"A shotgun," Pugh answered. "Double-barrel. Twelve gauge."

"What in blazes are you doing with a shotgun?" Duncan barked. "Permits aren't any good anymore, buster. I ought to throw you in the calaboose and drop the key into the town well."

"This is my town, Marshal. I've lived here a lot longer than you have." He frowned at Usher. "And I ain't never seen you here, Mr. Usher, till today."

Duncan was trying to comprehend that when the big man continued. "I was told to come help your jailer. And that's where I'm going."

"Jailer. Who told you to come here, Pugh? You get home. You take you and your twelve-gauge home and you stay there."

"No, sir, buster. You ain't got the right. You haven't lived here long enough to tell me what to do, star on your vest or not. Now you two boys get out of my way. You got your jobs to do. And I got mine."

He shoved past both of them, and they turned and watched him as he reached the door to the marshal's office and started pounding on the door with the butt of that big scatter-gun.

"Syd!" he cried out. "It's me, Dylan. Open up. I got a shotgun and Clara Mae gave me some sandwiches to feed you and Mr. DeMint."

The door opened, Dylan Pugh disappeared, and Duncan gave Usher a quick look, then shook his head, turned around, and hurried down the street before Usher said something that really got into Duncan's craw.

Two blocks later, lightning flashed, and Duncan caught a glimpse of something inside the old Silver Queen Hotel, which, he had been told, for the past three months had been a home for squatters, but those had left town. When he went inside the wreck and stink of the old place, it appeared that even hobos and squatters had found better places to sleep. And even on a night like this, there were plenty of better empty buildings to spend the night.

"Who's up there?" he shouted.

When no reply came, he bellowed. "Show yourself now, buster, or we're coming up there, and when we get upstairs, we'll be shooting."

Usher chuckled. "There isn't enough light out for us to figure out how to get up there, pardner."

"Be quiet." He thumbed back his hammer, let the thunder stop rolling, and fired a shot that hit the shutter near the window where Duncan was sure he had seen someone.

A voice cried out, "Do not shoot, Marshal. Do not shoot." He recognized the voice. A candle came up, shaking, then went dark.

"Forgive me!" the voice said. "The wind. The rain. It blew out my light."

It was too dark to see much of anything. The man might be standing. He sounded like he was shivering.

"Lamont?" Duncan called out. "Lamont Dubois? Is that you?"

"Laurent," came the reply. "Laurent. Not Lamont. Laurent Dubois. Yes. It is I."

Duncan shook rain off the brim of his hat. "What the devil are you doing up there?"

"I . . . I . . . I am painting."

"Dubois. I don't know what the Sam Hill is going on, but get downstairs and get back to your home. The rain is likely to wash what's left of that hotel all the way down to Chasm Park. Do you hear me?"

"Yes. I hear. I go. I go home. Please do not tell . . ."

"Tell who what?"

"Never mind."

Duncan drew in a deep breath and opened his mouth, trying to think of what to say, but Ben Usher cleared his throat.

"Let it go, pard. We need to find us a place near your pal Nugget's place." Usher was already walking down the boardwalk. "Conner Boyle and those others aren't gonna wait too much longer. The way this storm's coming, they'll have to hurry things up or nobody's gonna get to any railroad anytime soon."

Usher was right.

Duncan hurried to catch up with his old saddle pard.

Rainwater flowed like a mountain creek down the road as they neared Chasm Park. Duncan felt a bit of relief. He hadn't seen or heard any town resident since

Lamont—*Laurent*—Dubois. He almost said something about that to Ben Usher, but then he saw the yellow tint rising to about knee-high and moving left to right, right to left.

"Duncan?" a voice called out.

"Yeah." He was just about ready to quit.

"Got a place for us. Come ahead." The lantern was lifted to about shoulder high. Duncan swore softly and walked toward it.

Logan Ladron nodded when the marshal and gunman came into view. Then Sara Cardiff's top dealer turned and led the two men into the woods, where a canvas tent had been erected by poles. It was a good spot, Duncan had to concede, with a clear view of the trail that led to Nugget's house and his treasured Hope Diamond of Silver. If Conner Boyle and those gunmen came into town, they'd have to take a wagon down that hill—just as the last fools who tried to steal the mayor's treasure had—and back uphill. That would be a tough challenge in this weather, but he had no reason to doubt that Boyle, desperate for glory, money, and revenge, would have to try it.

He had too many hired gunmen who would want to be paid at least their healthy traveling expenses.

He swore softly when he ducked and started inside the lean-to.

"What the devil are you doing here?" he barked at Sara Cardiff.

"This is my town, too," she said, adding, "Marshal."

Then she went back to loading a Marlin repeater. Five other rifles—though two were single shots—two shotguns—one a sawed-off—and a half-dozen revolvers were on a small camp table.

Other people emerged from the trees, all of them wearing Indian rubber ponchos or slickers. He recognized Doctor Aimé Cartier and the undertaker, Germaine. Then Drift Carver stepped inside, two pistols in his belt and a Sharps rifle in his hand.

"Where the devil have you been?" Duncan asked.

"Sleepin' off a drunk. But I'm ready to defend my town. And our claim to fame, Nugget's diamond!"

Duncan shivered, but not just because of the cold and dampness.

"Listen," he said. "Conner Boyle will be coming here with gunmen. Professional killers. This isn't your fight. That's why I get paid. That's—"

"Duncan," Sara said. "You're mistaken. This isn't *your* fight. It's *our* fight. Because Dead Broke is our town. Maybe one of these days, it'll be your town, too. But that's something that you'll have to earn."

She turned and smiled at Ben Usher.

"And you, sir, you haven't even been here as long as our marshal. Now, if you'd like to get out of the rain and cold, that's fine with us. Or you can lend us a hand."

Usher removed his hat, shook the rain off the crown and brim, then settled it back on his head and squatted beside Sara. "Hand me that Yellow Boy, if you'd be so kind," he said. "And," he added, nodding at the stacks of cartridge boxes, "that box of .44 rimfire."

* * *

"Where's Joey?" Duncan asked when he saw the boy's father step into the lean-to.

"In Miss Cardiff's place," he said with a sheepish grin. "All the kids in town are whooping it up. Lights are on. And some of our older citizens."

"The plan," Sara said as she set a fully loaded Winchester on the blanket next to her, "is that when Boyle brings his thieves and killers into town, he'll think most of the citizens are there celebrating his departure."

"And," Aimé Cartier said, "that'll explain why our mayor isn't home."

"They'll just load the Hope Diamond of Silver into their wagon and try to get out of town as fast as they can."

"If they can get that wagon up this hill in this gully washer," the undertaker said, then opened the breech of his shotgun for the tenth time just to make sure the twelve-gauge was loaded.

"And Nugget went along with that plan?" Duncan asked.

Logan Ladron chuckled. "Well, he went to the Crosscut because Joey said he'd read him some dime novels."

"And let his guards come with him?" That didn't sound like Nugget to Duncan.

"Not exactly," Sara said. "Two of them took a place in the old mine. Just in case some of those gunmen take off that way when they realize they're in an ambush. The other two I sent to help Mr. Dubois."

"Help Mr. Dubois do what?" Duncan asked.

She gave him a slight smile. "You'll see."

* * *

The rain had not slackened an hour later when Duncan heard the traces of a wagon.

"Snuff the candles," Sara said, and tapped the closest one to her. "And no talking. Not even a whisper."

Blackness came quickly. Duncan heard nothing but the pounding rain and his own breathing. The chill worsened.

He realized the biggest problem with Sara's plan. No moon. No stars. Just blackness and pouring rain. They wouldn't be able to see a thing, and even hearing the bandits in this weather would be difficult.

He peered into the dark, hoping for a flash of lightning—anything—so he could make sure that was indeed Conner Boyle in that wagon headed toward Nugget's treasure. But all he saw was rainfall and a wet darkness.

The sound of the wagon faded as it went down the slick, wet path, more river now than trail. He tried to count the minutes. One . . . Two . . . Five . . . Ten . . . Eleven . . . Fifteen . . . Twenty.

"What do you think?" came Sara's whisper.

Duncan shrugged, then realized Sara couldn't see him any better than he could see her.

"It'll take them longer," he heard Ben Usher tell her. "Seventeen hundred pounds isn't easy to load. And in this weather, it might take them an hour. Maybe more."

Usher, it turned out, was a pretty good prognosticator.

An eternity later, Drift Carver slogged into the lean-to, rainwater pouring through the canvas like a waterfall. Duncan couldn't see Carver, but he recognized the rough whisper.

"They're on the way up."

"All right," Sara said. "Let's start the ball."

But someone else started it first.

Gunshots rang out. Duncan made out the noise of ricochets. Curses followed. Then more gunfire, followed by echoes and the crashing of thunder. Lightning struck something in the woods.

"Yer chirpin' off pieces of my silver nugget!" Nugget bellowed. "Aim better or I'll start a-shootin' you all!"

"I thought . . ." someone started near the lean-to.

The undertaker sighed. "Nugget."

Joey's dad said, "I guess even Joey's reading couldn't keep Nugget in that saloon forever."

"They's gettin' away with my baby diamond!"

"Let's give them what my pa gave 'em Johnny Rebs at Bull Run!" someone screamed outside the lean-to.

"Come on." Ben Usher said calmly as he passed Duncan. "I know where these fellas have tethered the horses."

"It needs to be centered!" Conner Boyle yelled as he turned in the driver's box of the wagon. Beside him, Caleb Holden whipped at the big Percherons pulling the wagon.

"It's a steep, tight road down."

Lightning flashed, revealing a big miner standing in the middle of the path that led out of Chasm Park. Water flowing down the trail came up to his ankles. Lightning flashed again. The miner's shotgun blasted, but he must have shot high.

"You center it!" called out Killin' Ben Mitchum. "I've had enough."

He started to leap off the wagon, but a bullet caught him in the side of the head, and he crashed onto the giant piece of silver and slid down into the wagon bed.

"Throw that body off—" Boyle began, then stopped. Blackness returned.

A bullet nicked Boyle's left ear. He grabbed it, felt the hot blood mingling with the rain.

He had brought all of the hired killers with him. Well, they had insisted on coming along. Honor among thieves was a myth, Boyle knew. Gunfighters, gamblers, and thieves had no honor. They trusted no one. But now, on this horrid night, they all needed each other.

"You said this would be easy!" Dean Hill yelled.

"I didn't expect this storm!" Boyle saw something, snapped a shot, then swore.

"Don't shoot till you see what you're shooting at!"

He couldn't tell who said that.

"Don't slow down." That was Telluride Tom, kneeling now in the bed of the wagon, the barrel of a Winchester between Boyle and Holden. "Horses see better than we do in this foul mess. Just run 'em. All we gots to do is get to the main street. Then we'll be home free."

"A posse can catch us."

"No, it can't," Telluride Tom said. "This place is gonna flood. We just have to get past that crick before it turns into Niagara Falls."

That, Boyle thought, made sense.

The miners and citizens were game, but inexperienced. They shot without looking as the wagon came past. No one could see a thing, but Duncan thought he heard the hooves and one squeaking wheel ahead, then moving down the street.

Later, when daylight came and the rains stopped, they found the body of Faro Scott in the mud. Fifteen men and one widow claimed to have put that ball in his forehead.

But now, Duncan and Usher raced up the path, slipping in the mud. Three men passed them. Sara Cardiff stopped to help Usher to his feet.

"We'll never be able to see them," Duncan seethed. "Or catch them. Not in this dar—"

And then, the windows of every building on both sides of the street exploded in light. Lantern light. That lit up the quagmire that was Tenth Street in Dead Broke, Colorado.

And from every window came a fusillade of gunfire.

Duncan wasn't certain as to what he saw next. Those giant Percherons must have pulled the tongue off the wagon.

The front wheels turned sharply left. Then the wagon was rolling over and over until it wasn't much more than splinters.

Duncan stopped running. His lungs burned. Everything else about him was freezing.

"Oh, my." Sara raced ahead, and that's when Duncan saw Little Joey, standing at the edge of the jail, looking at the carnage in the street. The boy's parents ran forward.

Dylan Pugh stepped out from the marshal's office front door, holding a smoking rifle. Syd Jones came out, too, and pushed up the brim of his hat.

Other men—Bryn Bunner among them—began taking charge. Doc Cartier was working on a miner who had taken a flesh wound to the arm in the doorway of the old Silver Nugget Hotel.

Nugget charged toward the wreckage. Then he was yelling for help. Two women and three men came to their mayor's assistance.

"There's nothing you can do for Boyle," a woman told Nugget. "He's crushed flatter than a pancake."

"I don'ts gives ten hoots 'bout that turkey," Nugget said. "I don't want this rain to erode my Hope Diamond Nugget of Silver!"

"Hey," someone said. "That's Caleb Holden. Deader than dirt."

The people of Dead Broke, oblivious to the torrent of rain, filled the streets.

Duncan was shaking his head when Ben Usher put an arm around his shoulder.

"Marshal," Usher said, nodding his head in approval, "your plan worked plum perfectly."

Behind him, Logan Ladron laughed.

CHAPTER 37

Morning came, the sun rose, and the water began to recede.

Most of the townsmen had been filling sacks with dirt and piling them up to keep the lower parts of Dead Broke, which included Tenth Street and the marshal's office and jail—not to mention Chasm Park—from being covered with floodwater.

"That's a beautiful sight," Nugget said.

Duncan walked up to him and looked down at the Hope Diamond of Silver. Boyle and his men had not bothered trying to cover the giant chunk of metal, and now it glistened in the morning light.

"What's so pretty about it?" Little Joey asked.

Nugget spit out tobacco juice, wiped his mouth, and turned to the boy.

"I've had that nugget in my house for so long, I never noticed how perty it is, catchin' the sunlight this way." Nugget shook his head. "I oughta . . . I oughta . . . maybe I can make it a statue. On the town square. So ever'body can come see it. That might save my town after all!"

It did sound better than gunfighting contests, mail-order brides, and ice sculptures, Duncan thought, but he said nothing.

Doc Cartier walked over and shook Duncan's hand. So did Laurent Dubois.

"Good job, Marshal," they said.

"I bet when that Denver gal and that newspaperman from Cheyenne get their stories published, folks'll be flocking to come visit Dead Broke," said Percy Stahl. Duncan tried to recall when Stahl had gotten back from Denver, but it didn't matter.

Then Bryn Bunner walked over and whispered, "Marshal, can I have a word with you . . . in private?" He swallowed, paled, and said, "Err . . . you, too, Mr. Usher."

They slogged through the mud and stepped onto the boardwalk. Bunner's right foot went through a rotted plank, but he pretended not to notice.

"Marshal, Will Ketchum and Clint McMann . . . well . . . they found a good bit of lead."

"There's a good bit of lead all over town after last night," Duncan said.

"No, sir. I mean, yes, sir. But that's not the lead I mean. I mean . . . real lead."

"A mine," Ben Usher said.

Bunner nodded.

Duncan sighed. "If that's some of Dylan Pugh's salting . . ."

"No, sir. This mine wasn't salted."

Duncan straightened. "I thought you and others were looking for zinc."

"We were. And there's some zinc, too. It looks like a good mine. And where there's one mine, there's bound to be others."

"Lead," Duncan whispered. "And zinc."

It didn't quite have the ring of silver and gold.

Sara Cardiff must have sneaked up behind Duncan. She stepped between Duncan and Usher.

"What's the assay?" she asked.

Bunner shrugged. "I can't say. But it's a good claim. Lead was bringing in a bit over twenty-one dollars per thousand." His voice lowered. "And there's some zinc, too. That's thirty a ton. Or was. Might have gone up."

Duncan looked at everyone gathering around Nugget's—and Dead Broke's—prized possession.

"I've never heard of zinc or lead wars," Ben Usher said.

"I haven't, either." Duncan smiled. "You know, I've always wanted to be marshal in a quiet, little, friendly town."

Sara was staring at him. She was smiling, too.

"Hey," he said. "That dress ain't blue."

Her head shook. "No. It's green. Like your eyes."

**TURN THE PAGE
FOR A DOWN AND DIRTY PREVIEW!**

In this action-packed new series,
a rascally pair of prospectors run for their lives
from a gun-toting posse—and discover
a million ways to die in San Francisco's
criminal underworld . . .

HARD MEN TO KILL

Charlie Dawson and his partner Clem
don't consider themselves bad guys.
But they definitely made a bad error in judgment
on a gold mine deal—turns out there was no gold—
and ended up in a shootout with some very angry
claim jumpers. Now a man is dead and a posse
is in hot pursuit of Charlie and Clem.
The unlucky pair hightail it to San Francisco,
where they try to blend into the notorious
red-light district known as Barbary Coast.
Another bad decision on their part . . .

San Francisco is one wild place.
Horses get stolen, folks get shanghaied,
and Charlie and Clem get offers from some very shady
characters with money to burn, so the boys can't refuse.
A big boss banker wants to hire them to find
a crate that was lost in a train derailment.
Inside is a priceless golden spike created for the
opening ceremony of a new rail line.
Sounds like easy money to Charlie and Clem.
Problem is, they're not the only ones looking for it.
A vicious gang of outlaws, a cold-blooded gunman—
and a scheming femme fatale—are on a direct
collision course with the hard-to-kill duo . . .

And they're all heading for one very dead end.

National Bestselling Authors
William W. Johnstone
and J.A. Johnstone

HARD MEN TO KILL

First in a New Western Series!

On sale now, wherever Pinnacle Books are sold.

JOHNSTONE COUNTRY.
WHERE DYING IS EASY AND LIVING IS HARD.

Live Free. Read Hard.
williamjohnstone.net
Visit us at kensingtonbooks.com

CHAPTER 1

"Give us the money." Clement leaned forward, square jaw jutting out belligerently. His gnarled hands curled into fists the size of ham hocks. The muscles in his forearms tensed, threatening to rip his soiled denim shirt. He gritted his teeth and then tossed his head like a fiery stallion getting ready to buck. Long blond hair flew back.

His hard gray eyes bored into the banker's rheumy blue ones, but the portly man refused to flinch. He leaned forward and braced himself on his desk.

"You do not deserve a dime, Mister Clement. Not a single, solitary penny. As long as I am president, you shall not get it from this bank."

"I can take it." Clem's voice rasped with menace.

"We have guards. In the lobby. They are watching you right now. Make a move to harm me and, I swear, they will fill you so full of holes there won't be five pounds of your bellicose manner left to bury." He cleared his throat. "I might add that your grave will be in the potter's field, since you can't afford even a simple burial."

"He's an Elk," Charlie Dawson said uneasily. He had listened to the men insult each other and now they moved on to outright threats of bodily harm. "The order will see that he gets a decent burial."

"You, too, Mister Dawson? Will they bury you, as well?" The banker settled back and tented his fingers atop his bulging belly. "Leave. Both of you. My patience has worn out."

"You can't take what my partner says too seriously, Mister Norton. It's just that Clem here's all excited. We found the biggest, best vein of gold in the whole of California, and it's just waiting to be dug out. We need supplies so we can get it pulled out of the Betty Sue. There's enough blasting powder, but we can use supplies. To eat."

"Food," growled Clem, not budging an inch from his crouch of looming halfway across the banker's desk.

"You should have left him buried in the mine," Norton said. "You're reasonable. Him," he said, sniffing pompously as he looked down his bulbous nose at the two miners, "he needs to be taught manners."

"Clem, go on and wait outside. I can handle this," Charlie said. He felt a tad uneasy now. The banker had pushed too hard. Clem had neared the end of his fuse and was about ready to explode like a keg of Giant Powder.

Clem reared up to his almost six-foot height and glared. He spun about, growled like an angry wolf, and stalked out. The two guards in the lobby watched him with some trepidation, hands resting on their holstered six-shooters. They breathed a sigh of relief when the troubled Clem promised left, slamming the door behind him.

"Now, Mister Norton, how about—?"

"You owe money all over town. The general store. Jones won't give you another loan. Sam, over at the Blue Spruce Saloon, won't even stand you a round of drinks. Not a drop of that panther piss he calls beer. No, Mister Dawson, you have drained this entire lake we so fondly call Potluck of money. There is not a drop to be had. None." Norton pointed a stubby finger at the door. "Get out. Now."

Charlie Dawson reared back and looked over his shoulder. Both guards looked more comfortable with the idea of throwing him out than they had his partner. He was solid enough and his hands were powerful from swinging a pick all day. He was four inches shorter than Clem, but his shoulders were broader and his chest thicker. And they had no idea how fast he was with the Colt Army tucked into his waistband.

He pushed his flat-brimmed hat back on his forehead enough to let a lock of brown hair pop out. If ever a man looked ready for a fight, it was him.

Charlie stood and glared at the banker.

"You're making a big mistake. The Betty Sue Mine's going to produce the most gold California's seen since the Rush of '49. That's twenty years, Mister Norton, twenty years. It's time for the next big strike, and we're it. The Betty Sue's going to produce more gold than you will ever be able to lift with those fancy manicured hands of yours. This bank could have been part of it. Your stockholders will look back on this day and wonder what kind of banker you were to pass up this golden opportunity. I'll say it again—golden!"

"Leave. Now." Norton jabbed his finger several times in the direction of the door.

Charlie left, giving the two guards a baleful look. He stepped out into the northern California sun. His partner leaned against the brick building, smoking a cheroot. The puffs of smoke rose and disappeared in the gentle breeze blowing off the mountains where their mine stood waiting silently for them to become millionaires.

"No luck?"

"You know he turned us down," Charlie said glumly. "We're going to need a new pick. I broke our old one. And some food . . ."

"I can hunt. I'm a better shot 'n you."

"We'll need ammunition. All I've got is in the cylinder." He touched the Colt in his waistband.

"Not much better," Clem said. He drew the Walker Colt he carried at his right hip. "Maybe two more cylinders. No more."

"Twenty rounds or so between us. You'll have to make every shot count, and there won't be any chance of bringing down a deer for some venison stew, not with a pistol shot. The Winchester's out of ammo."

Charlie hitched up his britches.

"All this means is that we've got a lot of work ahead of us, and our bellies are going to rumble a mite." Charlie wanted to say more but had nothing to add to detailing their problems.

"Mine already thinks my throat's been slit." Clem finished his smoke and went to his swayback nag. He stepped up and waited silently for his partner.

"We'll show everyone in Potluck. We'll show Norton and Jonesy and Sam and every last one of them when we strike it big. We'll buy the saloon and the general store and . . . and . . . the bank!"

Clem shrugged and turned his horse's face toward the road leading from town. Charlie dug his heels into his scrawny horse's flanks, wondering how horse stew tasted.

"Ready to blast," Clem bellowed.

"Go on, then. I'm already halfway out of the mine." Charlie Dawson stopped and waited. There was something Clem was holding back. "You need a lucifer? Use the flame on the candle."

"Ran out of matches a couple days back."

"So what is it? Spit it out."

"This is the last of our blasting powder. We might try blasting somewhere else. This don't look like we're blasting into the mother lode. Looks like quartz, but I'm not even seeing fool's gold."

"The rock's fine," Charlie protested. "All we need to do is clear it out to get to the mother lode." He fell silent for a moment. "You're saying there isn't any gold?"

"Ain't seen a single flake. This isn't blue dirt. We're wasting our powder." He looked around. "Betty Sue's sucking the life from us."

"The mine's got plenty of gold. I feel it."

"The assay doesn't say it."

"You know the assayer wouldn't give us the report. I feel it in my bones that the report was a good one."

"He wouldn't give us the report because we couldn't pay for it."

"Then you don't know what it said. I'm beginning to think you're turning into a chicken, Clem. We've been

398 William W. Johnstone and J.A. Johnstone

together going on two years and this is the first time I've seen you so negative."

Clem ran his calloused finger around in the bore hole tamped with blasting powder. He pulled it out and looked at the black grains clinging to his skin.

"It'll be a waste. There's no gold here."

"Betty Sue'd never lie to us. You said so yourself!"

"That was six months ago."

"Look. Look at this spot! It's gleaming with quartz. There's gold behind this patch and—"

The clatter of horses' hooves caused Charlie to fall silent. Clem moved beside him and whispered, "You got your gun?"

"It's in the cabin."

"Mine, too." Clem picked up a pry bar and started for the mouth of the mine. Charlie followed close behind, carrying their single good pickax.

The day's fading sunlight blinded him. Charlie squinted as he made out four riders. Three remained mounted. Their leader strutted over and stopped a few paces away, his hand resting on his holstered six-gun.

"Good," he said. "You gents are already leaving."

"What do you want, Jimmy Norton? Did your pa get tired of you stinking up the bank so he sent you into the countryside to air out?"

"You talk big, Dawson. Do your jawing somewhere else. I got papers." He held his coat open. A sheaf of folded documents caused an inner pocket to bulge.

"What are they?" Clem tapped the pry bar against his left palm. Two of the mounted men flinched at the noise. The third went for his six-shooter.

"Whoa there, Fredricks," Norton said, holding up his hand. "There's no call to cut down these two. They're just leaving. And shooting them'd be a waste of lead."

"Get your mangy carcass off our land," Charlie said. He stepped closer, readying the pick.

"You stay where you are. I got papers. This here mine's changed hands. You got foreclosed on for not paying taxes. When I heard that, I put up the money outta my own pocket to buy the Betty Sue." Norton spat. "That's a lousy name. I'm calling this here claim the Gold King Mine."

"Taxes?" Clem pushed past his partner. "We don't have to pay taxes for another eight months."

"It was an early assessment, and you missed the deadline. Not that you deadbeats coulda paid, even in a thousand years." Norton drew his six-shooter when Clem took another menacing step forward. "You back off or I swear, I'll gun you down."

"You have to give us a notice," Charlie said. "Nobody told us squat."

"Consider yourselves served," Norton said, yanking the sheaf of papers from his pocket. He thrust them at Charlie.

"We'll get a lawyer to fight this," Charlie said, glancing over the top page. A few sheets fluttered down. Clem picked them up and looked at them.

"You don't have money to patch a leaky bucket. Get off the land right now." He snatched the papers from Charlie. "Get off *my* land, you deadbeats."

The metallic click as pistols cocked caused Charlie to reach out to restrain his partner. Clem had a way of flying off the handle. He never said much, but his fists often did. Matching up against four armed and angry men was a sure way to get ventilated.

"Let us get our bedrolls from the cabin."

"Go on," Jimmy Norton said.

The solitary mounted man called out a warning, but it was too late. Both Clem and Charlie used their weapons to whack at Norton and the other two. Their horses reared and fought them. The mounted man tried to shoot, but his horse bucked.

The two miners raced for their cabin. Clem kicked in the door, not bothering to push it open. He dived for their pistols, hanging on a peg by the door. Charlie fielded his and swung around, blazing away.

His first shot caught Jimmy Norton in the gut. The man staggered away, clutching his belly.

Huge chunks of wooden wall began filling the air. The other three fired wildly. The flying splinters made Charlie and Clem duck low. They pressed against an overturned table that gave hardly more protection than the thin cabin walls.

"We're in a world of trouble now," Charlie said.

Clem held up the papers Norton had dropped and started to pass them to his partner. A new fusillade tore through, causing him to stuff the papers into his waistband. He spun and fired through the door. His lead caused some consternation. Another of their attackers yelped in pain.

"We don't have much ammunition. I'm about out. What about you?"

Clem shook his head.

Then their troubles multiplied. A piece of roof fell in. Charlie looked up and saw flames spreading around the hole.

"They're burning us out!"

The entire cabin exploded in a fireball.

CHAPTER 2

"This way!" Clem rolled away from the table and kicked like a mule. A section of the back wall blasted outward, already on fire.

Charlie wasn't going to argue. The roof was collapsing overhead, showering burning fragments all around. He rolled and rolled again, colliding with his partner. For a moment they lay in a pile, gasping. Smoke billowed out, filling their lungs. Both coughed. Eyes watering, they made their way from the cabin.

Charlie began swatting out embers that threatened to set fire to his clothes. Beside him Clem rolled over and over in the dirt to accomplish the same end. They sat upright when bullets began kicking up tiny dust devils around them. The fire hadn't ended the assault. Norton and his cronies had come around the cabin and spotted them.

Clem steadied his Walker Colt against his upraised knee and fired.

A loud screech rewarded his marksmanship.

"He shot me!" Jimmy Norton cried. "Help me. Help me!"

Charlie couldn't see Norton through the smoke

gusting from the cabin, but he homed in on the voice. He emptied his Colt in that direction. New cries of anguish greeted him.

"Not Norton," Clem said.

"At least one of his henchmen. Maybe two." Charlie clicked the trigger a couple more times. "I'm out of bullets."

"Me, too."

The two got to their feet and staggered as their cabin roof collapsed fully, sending out more waves of flame and heat and smoke. Using this as a cover, they got to the shed used as a stable. They saddled their horses, tucked whatever lay around into their saddlebags, and mounted.

Just outside the shed they saw two of Norton's gang tending the other two. From where they sat astride their horses, they couldn't make out who was shot or how badly.

"Let's ride," Charlie said. "There's nothing we can do here."

Clem led the way from the now-smoldering ruins of the cabin. In minutes the trail curled around the mountain and led down to a small river flowing along the floor of the valley that led to Potluck. They rode in silence until they reached the outskirts of town. It took the better part of three hours to reach their destination. For all the gunplay and arson at the Betty Sue Mine, the town stretched out all quiet, even peaceful.

"What do you think we ought to do?" Charlie asked. "Go to Marshal Thompson?"

"He's banker Norton's brother-in-law."

"I don't even know who the sheriff is, much less where he hangs his hat."

"Whoever he is, he's out serving process. That's the only way he gets paid." Clem shrugged. "It don't matter. He wouldn't cross the local marshal, no matter what."

"We can't let Jimmy Norton steal our mine."

"He dropped this. Norton did." Clem held out the two sheets he had picked up when Norton declared himself to be owner of the Betty Sue.

"There's something wrong here, Clem. This is our assay report."

"The one we couldn't pay to see."

"Norton got it and it doesn't make a lick of sense. It says the gold content of the ore we turned in for assay is . . ."

"Danged near zero," Clem finished.

Charlie scowled. "So why'd Norton want to run us off if the mine's not worth the powder it'd take to blow it up?" He read down the first page. "There's nothing in the rock. Not a speck of gold."

"Not worth throwing the assay sample through Jones's Mercantile's plate glass window," Clem said. He looked at the merchant's store. The owner stood in the doorway, glaring at the two miners.

"There's more on the second page." Charlie had started to read when a loud shout caused him to look up. The page got away from him, but Clem snatched it in midair. He tucked the pages away in his vest pocket. With his partner, he twisted around to face Marshal Thompson.

The lawman bustled down the street, his bowed legs working as fast as he could without falling over.

"You two. Climb on down from them horses. I got a bone to pick with you."

Clem and Charlie exchanged a glance. Without a word, they wheeled their horses around and galloped away. The lawdog shouted after them. Then came an errant bullet that missed by a country mile. When they reached the town limits, they slowed to give their horses a breather.

"It doesn't look as if we're welcomed with open arms in Potluck."

"Not any longer," Clem said.

"What are we going to do? We owe 'bout everyone, and the marshal isn't inclined to listen to us. Not if he takes a potshot at us just for coming to town."

"Ride." Clem sucked on his teeth for a minute, then said, "A long ways away."

"Sacramento?"

"Too close," Clem decided.

"San Francisco? We haven't been there in a spell. It's big enough a town to get lost in."

"We need to get lost fast." Clem jerked his thumb over his shoulder.

"A posse! Marshal Thompson's got a posse coming after us!"

"There's no chance to outrun them, not on these nags." Clem patted his horse's neck. The mare turned a large brown eye in his direction, as if taking offense at being called a plug.

"I've got an idea. Follow me."

"Why not? You can't get us into worse trouble than we're in."

Charlie Dawson grumbled at that as he guided his horse off the road and down a steep incline to the river that ran past Potluck. The horses splashed in the fetlock-deep water. He headed back up the stream rather than away. He hoped the posse would think he and Clem wanted to escape by going north away from town. The deep stream curled back and ran past Potluck, just a few yards from buildings in a few places.

They splashed along until they passed the town and the stream turned into steeper going. He kept up the diversion until his horse began to stumble from the effort of fighting both the increasing elevation and the rapidly flowing water. Charlie cut away from the stream and worked his way into a stand of pines. Weaving about to confuse the trail, he rode deeper into the woods until he knew his horse had reached the end of its strength. He dropped to the ground and waited for his partner to catch up.

Clem had taken a different route to keep from creating a noticeable trail where they left the stream. He finally rode up from higher on the hillside. A quick kick to get his leg over the saddle and he jumped to the ground. His swayback horse was in better condition than Charlie's, but not by much.

"We can't hide out here forever," Charlie said, "but we can rest and let the posse chase its tail around. Knowing the kind of men Marshal Thompson recruited, they'll get real thirsty fast and head on back to a saloon to brag on how they chased down two desperadoes and run us plumb out of the county."

Clem snorted in contempt.

"Why'd you think the marshal came after us so quick?"

"We rode in. Jimmy Norton didn't. That'd mean we done the slimy snake in," Clem said.

Charlie sank down, back to a sap-sticky tree trunk. He was too tired to care.

"What'll we do in San Francisco? If you remember the last time we were there, it's a gol-darned expensive town. We don't have a dime between us."

"Not so. I've got two nickels." Clem pulled them out of the watch pocket on his jeans and held them in the palm of his hand.

"So we can buy a beer apiece. I could use a brew right now."

"You weren't just flapping your gums. Things cost a lot more in San Francisco. Maybe we could split one."

"I know you. You'd drink the mug danged near dry before you gave me a turn."

"My money."

"Our money. We're partners." Before Charlie went on with his notion of how partners shared everything, the sound of riders approaching through the forest brought him up short. Clem had already heard and reached for his gun. He relaxed when he remembered his six-gun was as empty as a banker's promise.

Darkness hid them as two riders passed by not ten yards away.

"Ain't got no reason to think they came this way. We'll never get a share of the reward."

"We won't get shot at, neither," replied his companion. "Those are dangerous owlhoots."

"They only shot up Jimmy Norton. He's gonna live, the doc said."

"He's too cussed to die. Him and his old man. They'd steal pennies off a dead man's eyes."

"And you wouldn't?"

"It'd be more money 'n we're likely to make from wanderin' around blindly in this danged forest."

The two riders drew rein. Cloaked in shadow, they were hidden. If Charlie and Clem hadn't heard their approach, they wouldn't have known the posse members were anywhere near.

Clem nudged his partner. He went to his horse and pulled off the lariat. He played it out into a loop and spun it expertly. With silent steps he went to where the two deputized townsmen sat on their horses. Charlie grabbed his rope and followed. He wished they'd had a chance to discuss this. Clem had an impulsive streak that got them into trouble.

Ahead, a lucifer flared. For a few seconds he saw the eerie visage of the man lighting his cigarette. Then only the glowing coal showed in the twilight.

"We need to claim part of the reward when the marshal runs them two down. Do you know them?"

The other rider puffed on his cigarette. The pungent smoke drifted through the still forest.

"I think so. They have a mine up on the mountain above town. Never talked with either of them varmints. I think—"

He never finished his thought. Clem's rope sailed through the air and neatly dropped around his target's shoulders. A quick yank on the lariat sent the man flying through the air. He landed on the pine-needle forest carpet with a dull thud. Charlie threw his loop. The rope missed and fell in front of the other rider.

The rope hadn't secured his target, but it did spook the horse. It reared and threw the rider to the ground. He landed flat on his back. Charlie heard the air gust from the man's lungs. He pulled in his rope and threw a quick hitch around the gasping man's boots. When the man sat up, Charlie finished the job, making a double loop around the shoulders and then finishing with the man's hands.

He plucked a Smith & Wesson from the man's holster, cocked the six-gun, and pointed it at his captive.

"I'll shoot you if you make even a tiny peep."

"Do that and you'll have the rest of the posse on your neck!"

"Won't matter to you. You'll be dead."

Charlie's logic convinced his prisoner to stay quiet. Behind him Clem spun another couple loops around the other downed posse member.

He held up the man's pistol for his partner to see.

"We've got guns again," he said.

"What do we do with them? I don't want to waste ammo shooting them. We can string 'em up, I suppose."

"Yup."

"Wait, you can't do that. We don't even know you. We can tell the marshal we never caught a glimpse of you. Right, Flaco? Right?"

The man Clem had tied up grunted in agreement. Clem had taken the man's bandanna and gagged him with it.

"It would be a waste of rope, too," Charlie said, enjoying being in charge for a moment. He whipped off his captive's bandanna and quickly gagged him with it. He dragged his prisoner to where Clem was securing the other man to a tree. The two were bound and gagged side by side.

They bucked and strained, but the ropes were tied too well.

Charlie stepped back and looked at their handiwork. "Where'd you learn to throw a lariat like that?"

"Worked as a cowboy," Clem said.

"You never said anything about that." There wasn't very much he knew of his partner's life before they teamed up. "Around here?"

"Texas. He was easier to rope than a longhorn." Clem prodded his captive with the toe of his boot.

"We've got two more horses, guns, and from the look of their saddlebags, enough to keep us on the trail for a week."

He and Clem stared at each other. A slow smile came to Clem's lips.

"It'll be enough to let us ride to . . . San Francisco."

"Yeah," Charlie agreed, seeing what his partner did. "It'll get us to San Francisco. Do they have any money we can spend by the Golden Gate?"

He and Clem rifled the men's pockets. They left watches but found almost two dollars in small change. They split it between them.

"It hardly seems fair," Charlie said. "You've got ten cents more 'n me now."

Clem fumbled in his jean's watch pocket and pulled out a nickel. He silently handed it over. Charlie hesitated, then took it.

"Partners," he said.

"Partners." Clem turned and mounted the nearest horse in their new remuda. With two horses each they could make better time, riding until their mount tired, then switching to their own horses. It'd have to do to keep them ahead of the posse.

Charlie fetched their mounts, took his seat on the new horse, and said loudly, "Let's head for San Francisco!"

They rode off. Toward San Francisco. They had given the two the idea that they mentioned the city to throw the posse off their trail. What better place to go than where Marshal Thompson was least likely to track them?

Visit our website at
KensingtonBooks.com
to sign up for our newsletters, read
more from your favorite authors, see
books by series, view reading group
guides, and more!

Become a Part of Our
Between the Chapters Book Club
Community and Join the Conversation

Betweenthechapters.net